NO LONGER PROPERTY OF
SEATTLE PUBLIC LIBRARY

FIRE ON THE ISLAND

Also by Timothy Jay Smith

Cooper's Promise
A Vision of Angels
The Fourth Courier

FIRE ON THE ISLAND

A Romantic Thriller

TIMOTHY JAY SMITH

An Arcade / CrimeWise Book • New York

Arcade Publishing books may be purchased in bulk at special discounts for sales promotion, corporate gifts, fund-raising, or educational purposes. Special editions can also be created to specifications. For details, contact the Special Sales Department, Skyhorse Publishing, 307 West 36th Street, 11th Floor, New York, NY 10018 or info@skyhorsepublishing.com.

Visit our website at www.arcadepub.com.

10 9 8 7 6 5 4 3 2 1

Library of Congress Cataloging-in-Publication Data is available on file.

Cover design by Erin Seaward-Hiatt
Cover photo credit by Michael Honegger

Print ISBN: 978-1-950691-60-9
Ebook ISBN: 978-1-950691-64-7

Printed in the United States of America

Everything is for Michael.

This book is especially dedicated to the

Giannakou family of Molyvos, Lesvos
Krallis family of Molyvos, Lesvos
Damigos family of Vourvoulos, Santorini

and

my many Greek friends who inspired me.

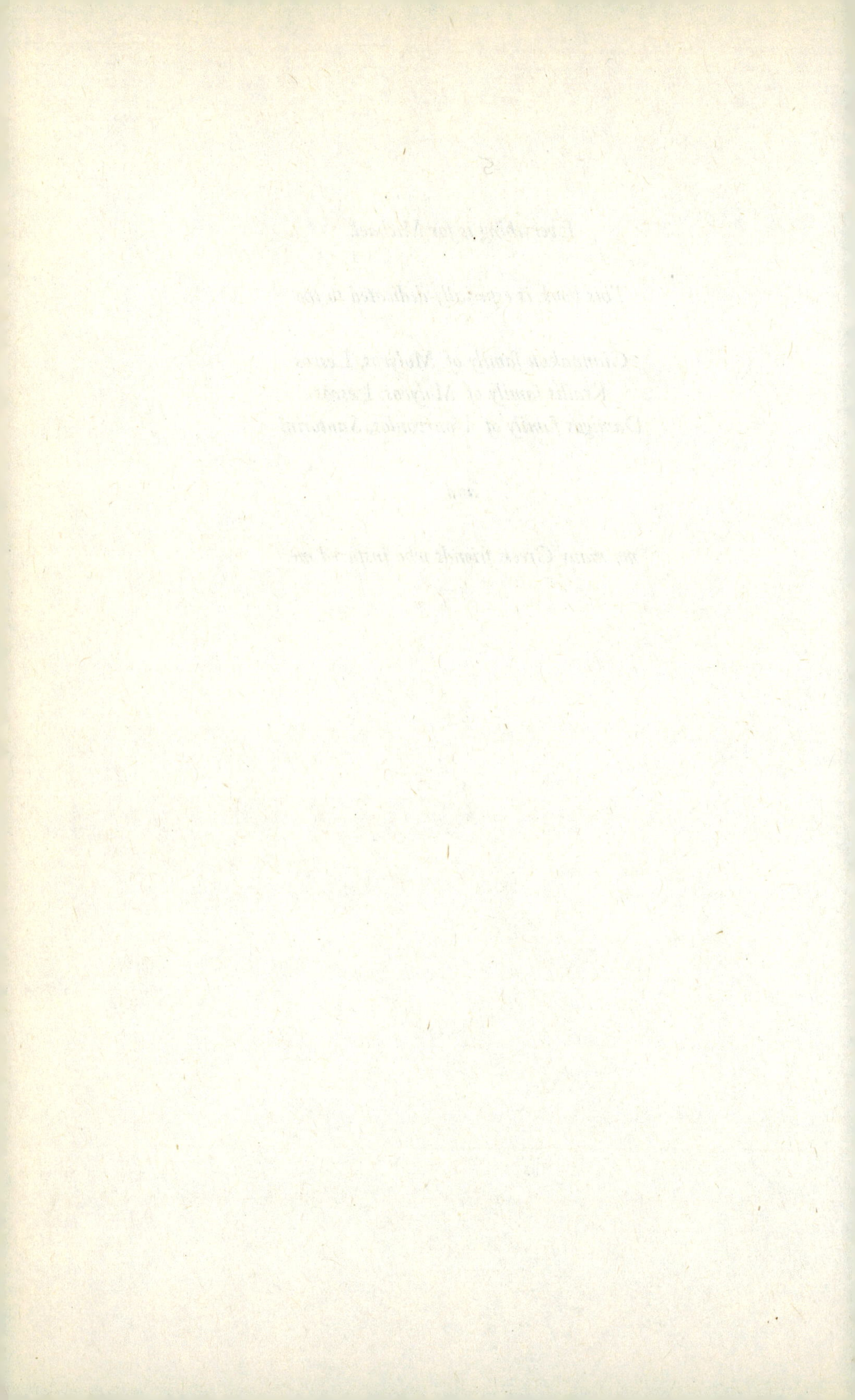

FIRE ON THE ISLAND

CHAPTER ONE

NOTHING HAD PREPARED NICK FOR the sheer beauty of the village perched above the purpling sea. Atop the steep hill, the last rays of sunset licked Vourvoulos's lofty castle walls while necklaces of red-tiled roofs clung to the cliffs below. He pulled the small car off the road and grabbed his binoculars.

His socks collected burrs as he trudged through the dried weeds to stand as close to the cliff's edge as he dared in the gusting wind. Through the binoculars, Nick slowly panned the houses spilling down to the water. From a mile away, he couldn't make out much detail, but after too many hours flying economy class, he was just glad to know that somewhere in that tangle of stone buildings was a bed with his name on it.

He heard the putt-putt-putt of a motor and spotted a fishing boat aiming for the village's small port. Shifting the binoculars, he searched beyond Vourvoulos's headland for the black speck of an approaching raft silhouetted against Turkey's distant shore. Nick didn't expect to see one. The refugees usually arrived at dawn not sunset, and with winter approaching, their numbers had started to drop; though the traffickers would ensure that they didn't stop altogether. Misery drove their business, and a few refugees drowned in the narrow channel wouldn't change that.

Nick was still looking for rafts when he smelled the smoke. The wind carried it to him. He panned the village again, looking for its source and saw nothing. Then he scanned the cove-dotted shoreline. At first he mistook the flames for the sunset's reflection off a limestone outcropping, but with a second look, he saw the wind pushing the fire quickly uphill in the dry brush. A gust sent sparks into the tops of the tall trees overhanging a lone house.

In its yard, a dog, barking frantically, strained at its leash.

Nick sprinted back to his car.

• • •

SHIRLEY TOOTLED ALONG THE COASTAL road with her back seat filled with nine dead cats. They weren't exactly dead, only dead-to-the-world under anesthesia from being fixed, as if removing sensitive body parts could be considered a fix. Shirley didn't think so. A cat meowed weakly and she sped up, wanting her daughter, who came up with the idea of fixing them, to have the pleasure of uncaging the maligned animals when they came to. A second cat meowed, and Shirley accelerated, her tires complaining as she took a curve too fast.

In the same instant, Nick shot back onto the road and, slamming on his brakes, barely managed to avoid a collision.

"Look where you're going, you bloody fool!" Shirley shouted in English, seeing him screech to a halt in her rearview mirror.

Moments later, he was on her tail, trying to pass on curves with no shoulders and a long drop to the sea. When they reached a short stretch of straight road, Shirley edged over. It was also where she habitually caught the first glimpse of her house, and that evening, she couldn't see it for the billowing smoke. Forgetting Nick, who was already alongside her, she stomped on the accelerator, leaving him in the wrong lane approaching another curve. He hit the brakes hard, and swerved back behind her.

He was still swearing at the stupid woman when she bounced off the road to park alongside a pickup truck with a swirling blue light fixed to its roof. Nick skidded to a stop behind her.

Shirley scrambled from her small car as fast as her generous body would allow. "Apostolis!" she cried. "Dingo is up there!"

The fire chief was busy directing villagers who'd shown up to fight the fire, some carrying shovels, others hauling water in the backs of pickups. "Are you sure only Dingo is there?" Apostolis shouted back.

Nick sprinted past them, unbuttoning his shirt while clutching a water bottle. "Is Ringo the dog?"

"Dingo!" Shirley shouted after him. "His name is Dingo!"

Nick disappeared in the smoke.

Airborne sparks had set the tops of the tall trees ablaze, but the weedy fire on the ground wasn't especially hot. He moved too quickly for the flames to do more than singe his cuffs. "Dingo!" he shouted. "Dingo! Dingo!"

The dog stirred.

"Dingo!"

He struggled to stand, shaking feebly.

"Dingo!"

He barked once and collapsed.

Nick found the unconscious dog and slung him around his neck. He gripped its bony legs while using his foot to slide open the patio door. "Hello! Hello! Is anyone here?" he shouted, and moved quickly through the house, checking all the rooms. He kicked in a locked door. "*Einai kanena etho?*" The house was remarkably smoke-free, and the dog, bouncing on Nick's shoulders, soon recovered, but he didn't let go of him for fear he'd bolt back into danger.

When certain no one was trapped inside, he ran back out. Dingo, unhappy to be in the smoke again, bucked hard as Nick jogged downhill through the burning brush. A glowing ember landed on his forehead, but he couldn't risk letting go of the dog to brush it off. Once back on the road, he gladly rolled the unhappy animal off his shoulders.

"Dingo!" Shirley cried as he leapt up to kiss her.

Nick, between coughs, told the fire chief, "*Kopsete ta megala dendra na pesoun pros to meros mas.*" Cut the big trees to fall toward us.

"Not Lukas's beauties!" Shirley exclaimed.

"If they fall this way," he continued, "they will suffocate the fire on the ground. Then your men can get above the house and shoot water down on the flames. But you can't wait."

Apostolis made a split-second assessment of the situation and agreed. He shouted an order, and trucks carrying water took the scrubby hill on both sides of the endangered house.

Two cars pulled up.

Lydia jumped out of the first one. "Mum! Are you all right?"

"Of course I'm all right," Shirley replied. "It's your father I'm worried about."

That was Lukas, who got out of the second car. The flames played on the old fisherman's face, bronzed by years at sea. He asked the fire chief, "Can you save the house?"

"Only if we cut your trees."

Lukas's beauties. The four red eucalyptus trees he had planted, one for each of their daughters, cutting notches in them as the girls inched up, until they stopped growing taller though the trees never did. Eventually even their tallest notches towered over the house. Lukas clenched his jaw, tears welling in his eyes; and that was all the time he had to grieve for his beauties, or he'd be grieving for his home, too. "Do you have a spare chainsaw?"

"In the back of my truck," Apostolis told him.

Lukas grabbed it and trudged up the hill.

CHAPTER TWO

NICK WOKE UP IN A big brass bed in a white room and at first didn't know where he was. A full-length mirror in the corner confirmed he was the only familiar thing in it. He lingered under the covers, recalling his last twenty-four hours: his grandfather's funeral, a hasty departure for the airport to catch his flight to Greece, the long wait in Athens for his connection to the island, and the fire and the dog. When he'd finally found his room—and the bed with his name on it—he had sipped wine on the terrace watching moonlight spill across the sea to the dark shadow of Turkey. Slowly the village had gone to bed, and eventually he did, too, crawling between sheets that smelled a lot fresher than he did.

Outside his window, the cawing birds that woke him could have been Baltimore crows. He got out of bed to open the shutters overlooking the small port with its restaurant umbrellas and brightly colored fishing boats. Only the black fuel tank looming behind the buildings marred the otherwise idyllic scene. What sounded like crows were hundreds of noisy seagulls flocking around a fishing boat coming into the harbor. Nick moved quickly, wanting to get down the hill to see them. He had forgotten the burn on his forehead until he glanced in the mirror, and decided he should tend to it. That led to a shower, ointment, and a bandage.

By the time he made it down the steep cobbled road, the birds had flown off. A man heaved a crate of sardines onto the dock, shouting "*Sardeles! Sardeles! Sardeles!*," but his entreaties to buy the fish were unnecessary. Village women, attuned to the fisherman's routine, were already appearing along the wharf, adjusting a strap here or blouse there, and walking with a spryness that sometimes belied their advanced years.

Having eaten nothing except bad airline food for as long as his stomach could remember, Nick hungrily checked out the restaurants pressed in a single line along the wharf. The only options for breakfast appeared to be bread and honey or yogurt and honey, until Nick spotted *English Breakfast* on a sandwich board outside Vassoula's Bar. As a bonus, the place had a lush arbor of lavender roses that were especially fragrant in the warming sun. He sat at a waterside table where he could watch the fisherman untangle sardines from his nets.

"What do you want, bread or yogurt?" he heard, and turned to Vassoula. Her eyes, as black as the thick hair falling down her back, were hardened by too much makeup, making it hard to guess her years; thirty, maybe thirty-five, Nick wondered. Despite a thin sweater buttoned against the morning chill, her cleavage wasn't shy. "Honey comes with both," she said, and flicked her cigarette into the water.

"I'll take the English breakfast, please."

"We don't have an English breakfast. That's the restaurant next door."

Nick realized his mistake when he glanced over and saw a waiter shaking out blue tablecloths beneath a sign for Lydia's Kitchen. His table had a yellow one. "You only have bread and yogurt?" he asked.

"Stavros!" Vassoula called to the fisherman. "Save some sardines for me."

"I always save some for you."

She said to Nick, "You want fresh sardines?"

"Sardines? For breakfast?" Fresh or not, Nick could not imagine eating them first thing in the morning. "I was hoping for something unhealthy, like sausage and runny beans. Sorry," he said, and slipped from Vassoula's yellow zone to Lydia's blue one.

"She's not really English," Vassoula warned him.

"That's okay. Neither am I."

• • •

Lydia had hardly slept all night. Every time she closed her eyes she saw fire, or smelled smoke, or imagined the scratch of a match by someone creeping up to the Coast Guard's fuel tank not fifty meters from their front door. She finally left her husband, Lefteris, alone in bed and brewed a pot of tea.

She carried a cup out to a small balcony. The sun had barely peeked over the horizon. She felt like a zombie seeing that side of dawn, though growing up she'd certainly seen it enough times. If a fisherman's daughter didn't know the sunrise, she'd have to be blind. She watched the night fishermen chug into port, and the day fishermen head out, and her father wasn't among them. She would have been surprised to see Lukas set out that morning after losing his beauties, but then, the solace of the sea might be exactly what he needed. They all needed solace. They had all lost their beauties.

A cloud of squawking seagulls announced Stavros rounding the end of the dock. No other fisherman attracted so many of the birds. They flocked around him competing for a chance to dive at his glistening sardines. He tied up and heaved a tub of them onto the wharf's wooden planks. A few lucky fish spilled out and flipped themselves back into the water. He hooted and playfully grabbed for them, not caring if he caught them; they'd be back in his nets tomorrow. Lydia felt a pang of desire for him. At some point most of the village women had. Stavros was a man to share, and none would complain that he shared himself too generously, including Lydia—who'd had all she'd wanted of him, though not necessarily all she desired.

Ping! she heard from the living room.

"Damn it!" Lydia muttered and went inside to find the phone. Her daughter had a habit of tossing her stuff anywhere on the way to bed, and that morning she found the girl's bag scrunched on top of the microwave. She was rummaging through it when Athina came into the room.

The girl's green eyes filled with accusation. "That's an invasion of privacy," she said.

"It's an invasion of your father's sleep is what it is," Lydia said as quietly as possible while still conveying her annoyance. She handed her daughter the phone. "You better turn it off before he kills you. I'm too tired to clean up the blood."

Ping!

From the bedroom: "I'm going to kill that girl!"

"See what I mean?"

"All right. Okay." Athina made a point of turning it off. "You woke me up making tea, but I guess that doesn't matter."

"I couldn't sleep. Your grandparents' house almost burned down last night."

"But it didn't. I heard."

"Maybe you could try to be more sensitive to other people?"

"What's that supposed to mean?" Athina said, unable to keep her voice down.

"*Shh.* Some people have good reasons why they don't want to be woken up by someone sending you a heart message."

"You read my message?"

"I didn't *read* your message. I *saw* your message. There's a throbbing heart on your screen. So who is sending you his heart this early in the morning?"

"How should I know?"

"You could look."

Exasperated, the girl checked her phone. "I can't tell. It's a blocked number."

"Who do you think it is?"

"How am I supposed to know?"

"Let me see your phone."

"You don't trust me?"

"We don't have secrets in this house."

"We don't have any fun either!" Athina said, throwing off all pretenses of whispering.

She pocketed her phone and stomped off.

From the bedroom: "I'm going to kill her!"

Lydia considered aiding her husband. Their daughter's terrible twos had continued unabated to the present, only days shy of her eighteenth birthday. She replenished her tea, picked up her map of the fires, and returned to the balcony, mulling over the land mines that could hijack her day. Was her daughter's secret admirer one of them? If secret, he wouldn't be for long. The competition for the girl was too fierce for the hapless boy not to declare himself. No, Lydia's land mine was not a message with a beating heart, but the fires. They weren't going to stop until the arsonist was caught or achieved his goal.

She unfolded her map, wrote #11 where her parents' house was located, and circled it. She shuddered when she thought of how different last night's fire could have turned out. The danger was no longer theoretical but real. Initially, the fires had been attributed to refugees, careless with their cigarettes or cooking fires while hiking through the hills to reach the island's capital. Lydia never took the notion seriously; for one thing, all the fires had been in a craggy and steep valley that the refugees mostly avoided, preferring instead to hoof it across the island on the flatter, albeit longer, main road. Blaming the refugees was entirely debunked when a detonator was found after the fifth fire, and more thorough searches discovered that similar devices had started the previous four fires.

The fires' isolation had conveyed a sense of randomness, but once the detonators were discovered, Lydia felt something more sinister was afoot. After the ninth fire, she decided to map them, hoping to reveal some clue that would identify the arsonist. It took her time to find some sites, so she didn't map them in their actual chronological order, which is why initially she overlooked how they relentlessly approached the village of Vourvoulos. They jumped between the two sides of the valley, which further obscured their steady march. It was not until she numbered the fires that their pattern—and threat—revealed itself. Lydia was convinced that burning down the village was the arsonist's goal, and what better way to do it than blowing up the Coast Guard's fuel tank?

As the sun pulled itself high enough to promise another blistering day, she leaned against the balcony's rail and watched the last women walk off with their sardines. Stavros saw her, and did a little jig imitating the slippery fish before lifting a tub and offering it to her. "Do you want some?" he shouted.

Did she want some? Yes, she wanted some of his fish and some of him, too. Lydia was perfectly content with her husband snoring away in bed; it didn't mean that she couldn't remember the fire the fisherman had once lit in her. She noticed that he wasn't holding the tub as high as he used to—time had a way of showing itself at unexpected moments. But his smile was as bright as ever and she did want some. Raising an open hand, she shouted, "Five kilos!"

From the bedroom: "I'm going to kill them both!"

• • •

RIDI SHOOK OUT BLUE TABLECLOTHS while eavesdropping on the argument that had resumed between Lydia and her daughter in their upstairs apartment. Ridi, an Albanian youth barely in his twenties, had arrived in the country six months earlier determined to learn Greek. He wanted a real shot at making a new life, unwilling to settle, like many of his compatriots, for getting by on a few easy phrases. Now he had a second language goal—to be able to woo Athina—and challenged himself to learn five new words a day. Topping his list that morning was the word for heart. *Kardia.* He had looked it up before sending her a flashing one. He never expected her mother to see it, though he heard *kardia* enough times to assume that's what they were arguing about, and worried Lydia might step onto the balcony and fire him on the spot.

"*Ena kafédaki?*" Nick tried to get his attention by asking for coffee in Greek.

"Five minutes!" Ridi answered, straining to understand an especially quick exchange upstairs.

"Five minutes?"

Denied coffee long enough, Nick looked for another option. Among the half dozen establishments scattered along the wharf, Vassoula's was still the only one open. She had perched herself on a high stool at her front door, smoking a cigarette, and smirked when she saw him looking around for another place for coffee. He decided to wait the doubtful five minutes and stayed put.

Besides, it gave him a chance to reconnoiter the port. From the photographs he'd seen in guidebooks, he hadn't realized that the harbor was largely man-made. The line of restaurants, some touching each other, followed the natural curve of the land to a point where a long dock paralleled back along the shore to create a protected port. A drive separated Lydia's Kitchen from the next building, which had a sign over its door reading *Elliniki Aktofilaki.* Greek Coast Guard. Nick looked for the fuel tank that he expected to be there, and it was:

black, looming behind the restaurants, more menacing than pictured in the guidebooks.

In the overhead apartment, the mother and daughter stopped arguing and a door slammed.

Ridi stared at the corner of the building, waiting for one of them to appear. When he saw Athina, he grinned like the love-smitten kid he was, but she wasn't smiling when she marched up to him.

"Now you got me in real trouble!" she hissed, and stomped up some short steps to disappear in the kitchen.

"Coffee?" Nick ventured again this time in English.

"She sets up now," Ridi told him.

That morning Athina's setting up the kitchen sounded more like a teardown as she clanged pots, ripped open drawers, and slammed cupboards. In Ridi's estimation, no one pouted more endearingly, which was a good thing since Athina pouted frequently. When she flung a spoon into the sink, he stopped shaking out a tablecloth to admire her.

"Those tables won't set themselves," Lydia said, coming up behind him, "and there's a man over there who needs breakfast." She went up the steps, but paused on the porch that ran the width of the building, wide enough only for two small tables. She checked her purse for something and went inside. Mother and daughter started arguing almost immediately, passing between English and Greek, and since Nick spoke both, he understood it had something to do with the fire the night before.

Ridi interrupted his eavesdropping by asking, "You want breakfast?"

"I'll take the English breakfast," Nick ordered.

"No Greek?"

"No, English."

"No English?"

"Yes, the *English* breakfast, and no sardines. With coffee."

"What coffee you like?"

"Caffeinated."

Scratching his head, the young waiter went into the kitchen.

• • •

A MINUTE LATER, ATHINA FOLLOWED her mother onto the porch. "You make it sound like I started Grandma's fire!"

"Don't be ridiculous," Lydia replied, exasperated. "I'm just asking you to telephone her and tell her you're sorry it happened. It'll make her feel better."

"All right, I'll call her! I still can't do the whole shift."

"Why not?"

"What about my costume?"

"What about your costume?"

"It's not finished."

"Is that my problem?" Lydia glanced over at Nick. "Why hasn't that man been served?"

"His order confused Ridi and I haven't had a chance to straighten it out because I had to talk to you."

"What did you order?" Lydia called to him.

"English breakfast with coffee," he called back.

"English breakfast with coffee," she repeated to her daughter. "How complicated is that?"

"He asked for 'kafeneion' coffee and we don't know what kafeneion coffee is."

"*Caffeinated* coffee," Nick corrected her. "Even one bean will do."

Lydia said, "I think the man wants his coffee."

The girl went back inside in a huff.

Lydia went down the short steps and approached his table. "You're the man who saved my mother's dog last night, aren't you?" she asked.

"If his name is Dingo and he's a heavy smoker, I am."

"People are calling you Superman, the way you just showed up, rescued him, and then disappeared before anyone could thank you. I'm Lydia, and I thank you."

"I'm Nick. Nick Damigos."

They shook hands.

"Damigos? Are you Greek?"

"Greek American. Are *you* Greek?"

"I know, I don't look it." Lydia didn't. She had carrot hair and freckles, certainly not a Greek's typical olive skin and black hair. "Around here it's usually best to blame that on Alexander the Great. But in my case, I'm half English. My mother married a Greek. You seem to know something about fires."

"It's bad luck having one, that's for sure. Is Dingo okay?"

"Mum says he won't eat anything."

"That happens with dogs and fires."

"So, are you visiting for a few days?"

"I'm working on a novel," Nick lied. He had used the cover before, giving him an excuse for asking questions, and as the FBI agent posted to Athens, he asked a lot of them.

"A novel set here?" Lydia asked.

"It might be. I'm still looking for my story."

"Not very far along, are you?"

"You sound skeptical."

"We get a lot of writers."

"Anyone famous?"

"William Golding."

"You're too young to have met him."

"My mother met him."

"He wrote *Lord of the Flies* here?"

"That came later. Like you, he was still looking for his story."

Nick laughed. "Okay, you got me. Who knows? Maybe I'll win a Nobel Prize, too!"

"Write about the fires," Lydia suggested.

"The fires? There's been more than one?"

"There've been eleven of them. I'll show you." She unfolded her map and pointed to a line of numbered circles dotting both sides of a narrow canyon. "Eleven fires in eleven months. The first one was here, and last night's here at my parents' house. Each fire has come closer to the village."

"I can see that."

"I'm glad you can because not everybody does. They'd rather blame the fires on the refugees who sometimes cross through the hills to get to the main town."

"That doesn't make sense for a lot of reasons."

"Try telling that to people who want to believe anything bad about other people. The only sense I can make of it is that someone is threatening to burn down the village, and if that's true, then that's probably his target." Lydia pointed to the fuel tank behind the Coast Guard station.

"A water tower?" Nick asked, playing dumb.

"It's for petrol—"

A gray patrol boat interrupted her with its horn as it rounded the dock to enter the small harbor. Crammed on its deck were dozens of refugees in orange life jackets.

"—for that boat," Lydia continued. "Shit. A raft must have capsized. Athina!"

Nick knew she was right. The Coast Guard only picked up refugees already in the water or at serious risk of capsizing. He'd witnessed other rescues, and the group on the patrol boat's deck looked the norm: soaking wet, huddled together for comfort, and totally silenced by the enormity of what they were experiencing.

Athina stepped onto the restaurant's small porch. Ridi followed her. They watched as the boat edged up to the dock. A guardsman jumped from its bow to tie it up. He secured a second line at the stern. The two guardsmen still on board stopped the refugees from standing up all at once, then pointed to people when it was their turn to disembark. Infants were passed over heads to hands reaching back for them. Slowly they formed a line along the dock. The only sound was a baby's plaintive cry that carried over the water.

"I'll make sandwiches," Athina said.

"I'll help," offered Ridi.

"We'll all help," Lydia said, and called next door to Vassoula, "Is your brother awake yet?"

"I'm awake," Takis said, and appeared in the doorway running his fingers through his thick black curls. "I heard the horn. How many?"

"Fifty or sixty. Looks like a lot of kids."

"Good thing I restocked yesterday." He ducked back inside, but not before exchanging a glance with Nick, who noticed his eyes were bluer than the sea.

Nick volunteered to help and joined the others inside Lydia's Kitchen, which he discovered was only a kitchen with no inside tables. He'd grown up in a Greek restaurant, and pondered the extra challenge of having only outdoor seating while slicing tomatoes for their assembly-line sandwiches: slices of white bread slapped together with a square of yellow cheese, a round of unidentifiable processed meat, and a piece of tomato until he ran out. As they worked, they watched the guardsmen go down the line of refugees, checking their IDs and writing down their names.

"Are there more tomatoes?" Nick asked.

Lydia shook her head. "I bought all the grocery had. So only women and children get sandwiches with tomatoes. But you can take that box of apples outside."

He did, and saw that Takis had readied bottled water, small cartons of juice, sesame bars, and a stack of blue plastic bags. Lydia came out with a tray of sandwiches.

"Everybody gets a sandwich and an apple," Lydia instructed Nick. "Anyone pregnant gets two of each."

Athina and Ridi brought out two more trays.

"And everybody gets a bottle of water from Takis," Athina said. "*Yeia sou*, Takis!"

"*Yeia sou*, Athina!"

"They're coming," Lydia told them.

Everybody glanced around to watch the boat's commander lead the refugees off the dock. His white uniform was a sharp contrast to their drab clothes; and he was taller than all of them, who, burdened with kids and belongings, struggled to keep up with him. At the bottom of the dock's narrow steps, another guardsman instructed them to toss their life jackets into a garbage bin. The captain brought them to where they waited behind tables with the trays of sandwiches.

"Good morning, Captain Tsounis," Lydia greeted him.

"Good morning, Lydia," he said. "Fifty-three adults plus ten kids."

"Anyone injured?"

"No injuries, and no drownings either, but we fished a few out of the water. The captain shook his head in disbelief. "Putting sixty-three people on a raft made for thirty. How can someone do that?"

The captain's chestnut brown eyes filled with sadness at the injustice of the refugees' plight before he turned back to enter the Coast Guard station. Then the miserable lot, encouraged by guardsmen, shuffled forward—soaked, somber, and suspicious when offered the sandwiches. One man rubbed his thumb and forefinger together to ask how much. "Nothing. You pay nothing," Lydia made them understand. "Free. No money." Their initial suspicion over, the refugees had a second one: what was in the sandwiches? They peeled back the spongy bread and looked unhappily at the unidentifiable meat. Lydia was ready for that question, and held up two photos: a picture of a pig with a big X through it and a picture of a chicken inside a green circle, which prompted her to cluck and flap her elbows like chicken wings. Some of the children laughed, which was why Lydia always did it, and the word spread: free food, chicken, no pork. Then everyone started shoving to get to it. "Make a line! A line!" Lydia motioned them into one. "There's plenty for everyone!"

Some gobbled down their sandwiches on the spot, while others saved them. Mostly Syrians, the women were predictably wary and shy, but the men touched their hearts and thanked them profusely. The four of them working together dispatched the refugees quickly, but they backed up at Takis's table where he handed out water and sesame bars while also helping put all the things they were trying to juggle into the plastic bags. Again people started to get pushy, and Nick said, "I'll help him."

In a few steps he was next to Takis and grabbed one of the bags. "My first job was bagging groceries."

"Everybody gets a sesame bar and water. Kids get the juice."

"How many children do you have?" Nick asked a woman.

"Three," her husband answered for her.

Nick put three cartons of juice in the bag.

"Please, one for my husband," she asked. "He is so very sick."

The man did look ill: gaunt, pale, and drooping with exhaustion.

"It's okay, give him one," Takis said. "Give one to anybody who asks. They aren't used to asking for anything, so if they want juice, they really need it. I have more inside."

They worked with a sense of urgency. The refugees were hungry and traumatized. Later, Nick would think of them as a tsunami that swept in and washed as quickly back out. In ten minutes, they had come and gone, carrying away something to eat and water to wash it down. Most thanked them profusely, as if they had been given a feast. "How often does that happen?" he asked.

"Almost every day," Lydia said. "We feed them here in the port when they arrive. If they spend the night, there's a volunteer committee that makes more sandwiches for dinner."

"A lot more land on the beaches and walk to town," Takis added. "There are lots of them, really, but they're not really here. They're almost not around. It's weird."

"So where are they going?" Nick asked, referring to the refugees the guardsmen were leading away.

"To a field up behind an old police station. There are some blankets and a couple of plastic tarps they can crawl under if it rains."

"Sounds pretty basic."

"For this village, it's pretty good," Takis replied.

"It's more than pretty good," Lydia retorted. "A lot of people would prefer they drown than be rescued. Well, I'm off to see the mayor. Ridi, make sure Superman gets his breakfast and he's not to pay for it."

"That's not necessary."

"Of course it's not, but that's how we're going to do it. Wish me luck finally convincing him to relocate the tank."

"Good luck, and thanks for the idea for a story. About the fires."

"You better write it fast. Unless that tank is moved by the end of next month, we might not be here."

"Why next month?"

"We've had eleven fires in eleven months. To some people, twelve months sounds like a round number, or an anniversary, or simply a compelling date. Enjoy your breakfast."

She walked off, and Takis said, "Thanks for helping."

"No problem." Nick stuck out his hand. "We didn't really meet. I'm Nick Damigos."

"Takis Vatis."

They shook hands.

"This is your sister's bar?"

"I live in Melbourne. I'm helping her for a while."

"That's a long ways to commute."

"Her husband died. I promised her a year."

"I'm sorry for the bad joke."

"That's okay. What about you?"

"I'm here a few days working on a book. I'm a writer."

"Are you famous?"

"Not yet."

"Come by later and tell me anyway," Takis suggested. "We open for sunset. The first drink is on the house."

"Every night, or just the first night?"

"I could make it happen every night."

Nick grinned.

Athina appeared with his breakfast.

"I guess I'm finally eating," Nick said, and took a seat at one of Lydia's blue tables. "So it *is* a proper English breakfast."

The girl scowled at Vassoula, who had returned to her stool by her bar's door once the refugees had passed. "I suppose she said my mom's not really English, too. She's always saying stupid things like that. Just because my grandma grew up in Australia doesn't mean we're not English if my grandma was English to start with. My mom is so ready to kill her!"

"Then maybe you shouldn't tell her. I don't want my breakfast to be implicated in a murder."

"Are you Superman? I bet Ridi that you are, so I hope you are."

"What did you bet him?"

"A kiss."

"A kiss?"

"We each bet a kiss."

"So who loses?"

"No one!"

"I like your odds."

"You're funny, Superman. I bet you have to work at it."

"Why?"

"Because you look so serious when you're thinking."

"If you call me Superman again, you'll learn just how serious I can be. So she doesn't help with the refugees?" he asked.

"Vassoula? Sometimes she sits there and watches. They're both a little weird."

"So you don't like him, either?"

Athina shrugged. "Most of the time he's okay. I don't know. People say weird things about him. What happened to your face?"

"Did something happen to my face?"

"You have a plaster on your forehead."

"Oh, that. I burned myself shaving."

"You *burned* yourself *shaving*? On your *forehead*?"

Nick shrugged. "I was careless."

"Are you burned here, too?" Athina reached to touch a pinkish spot on Nick's jaw that his beard only partially concealed.

He grabbed her hand to stop her. "That's from another fire."

"Okay, I'll stop bothering you. I hope you enjoy your kafeneion coffee and non-English English breakfast." The girl went back inside.

Nick set about eating his quivery eggs, runny beans, and mealy sausage. He watched as Takis came out to retrieve the plastic wrapping for the bottles of water. Balling it up, he headed for a trash bin between the two buildings. On his way, he smiled at Nick before disappearing out of sight. He returned to his eggs and runny beans. He couldn't guess all the weird things that might be said about Takis, but he was pretty sure about one thing: he was gay, too.

• • •

Not many years earlier, when money seemed to arrive in buckets flown in on northern Europe's national airlines, the villa that served as City Hall had been restored and painted the frivolous colors of a Venetian palace: lavender walls with orange trim and teal balconies. That morning, as Mayor Dimos Elefteros clutched an iron rail overlooking a turquoise sea, his thoughts weren't on the beauty of the building's colors but their costs. The shipping charges alone for the imported paint could have paid to repair the lengthening crack on the church's bell tower, from which, at that moment, Father Alexis was ringing the hour, each toll an insistent reminder of the thousands of euros the priest expected the bankrupt village to ante up for exactly that purpose.

Mayor Elefteros believed the priest should repair his own damn tower. The Church had enough money, even if the local parish did not. Unfortunately, as Father Alexis had painstakingly documented, the freestanding tower was situated on municipal property adjacent to the church. Around the country, it was not an uncommon situation for churches to have encroached on bits of land around them. How else to expand a cemetery, for instance? What had changed were new European Union rules governing public safety which had convinced the priest he could demand the village repair the bell tower, though he still gladly rang the bell at civic liability.

There was a knock on the office door and Apostolis let himself in. The mayor came off the balcony to shake the part-time fireman, part-time policeman, part-time waiter's hand. A little plump, a little bald, and blinded in one eye from an accident, Apostolis embodied civic spirit, volunteering for everything. He set a blob of charred Styrofoam on the mayor's desk. A half dozen cigarette butts were stuck in it; others had fallen over and become encased in the milky white plastic.

Mayor Elefteros didn't need to ask what it was. All the fires had been started with a similar crude detonator made from Styrofoam soaked in gasoline to make it soft. Lit cigarettes were stuck in it and slowly burned down before igniting the fuel-soaked plastic—giving the arsonist time to get away before the flames were spotted. There were never fewer than a dozen cigarettes used. Whoever was setting the fires wanted to ensure the gasoline would catch. That was about the only thing anyone could say with certainty going on a year since the first fire—except that they were getting dangerously close to the village.

"We had to cut down Lukas's trees to save his house," Apostolis reported.

"I don't suppose he was happy about that."

"He used my chainsaw to help."

The mayor nodded, not surprised; he wouldn't have expected otherwise. He and Lukas were of the same white-haired generation for whom honor and tragedy were synonymous. But he was surprised when the volunteer fire chief added, “A stranger saved their dog. He got there first.”

“A stranger?”

At that moment, Lydia burst in. “Dimos!”

Immediately Apostolis’s neck sunk into his round shoulders. “I’ll let you two talk.”

“You stay, Apostolis. This concerns you.”

“Good morning, Lydia,” the mayor said.

“Don’t you ‘good morning’ me, Dimos!”

“I know you’re upset.”

“Of course I’m upset! Tonight the whole village could burn down”—she picked up the Styrofoam detonator on his desk—“because of a fire started by one of these!”

“There is no point exaggerating the situation.”

“As long as that fuel tank is where it is, am I exaggerating the situation, Apostolis?”

“I am not officially trained to say.”

“Well, I don’t need official training to know that I am not exaggerating. What is it going to take to convince you to move that fuel tank, Dimos?”

“I’m waiting for a reply—”

“From Athens. You’re always waiting for a reply from Athens.”

“We don’t have enough money—”

“Of course we do. Only you’re thinking of giving it to the Church, which God knows doesn’t need it.”

“If the bell tower falls down, someone could be killed.”

“If the fuel tank explodes, a lot more people than some *one* will be killed.”

“People can see the crack in the tower, Lydia. They can’t see an anonymous threat.”

“How anonymous is this?” She unfolded her map, and tapped her finger on it saying, “The first fire was here. The next here and here and here until last night’s fire here that almost burned down my parents’ house. How could the pattern be any clearer? The village is next. Isn’t it clear to you, Apostolis?”

"I can see the pattern."

"I can see the pattern, too," the mayor added, "but you forget, relocating the fuel tank will disrupt the Coast Guard's operation at a sensitive time. It's a decision for the Ministry of Defense. I don't have the authority to act unilaterally even if we had the funds."

"By the time you finally decide that you have the authority to protect this village, there won't be anything left to protect! That's the pattern I see."

Lydia stormed out, leaving her map opened on the mayor's desk.

• • •

FATHER ALEXIS, PULLING THE ROPE hanging down the side of the bell tower, tolled the hours especially vigorously that morning, wanting the heavy bronze bell to resonate through every conversation in the village, the subject of each surely being the fire the night before. He didn't want some paranoid suspicion about an arsonist to sway public opinion in favor of relocating the fuel tank over repairing the bell tower.

In reality the priest couldn't give a fig for the ugly tower, hastily rebuilt with concrete blocks after an earthquake toppled an ancient handsome one. In fact, he rather wished it would fall down, but his status—indeed, his future in the Church—was at stake in preserving it. Historically the island had been a communist hotbed, and the youthful priest had taken on the challenge of bringing Vourvoulos's renegade congregation into the fold. Convincing the village to pay for the bell tower's repair would be proof that he had succeeded. In exchange, he had been promised a post in a respectable city, not another hovelish village on the priestly circuit. With that promotion would come a salary enabling him to move his mother to another apartment, out of her dead husband's house, the oily stench of whose murder laced every sea breeze; a stench that Father Alexis—back then a seventeen-year-old called Manolis—had caused with a flick of a cigarette; consciously or unconsciously, he forgot, if he ever knew.

Indeed Vourvoulos *was* a hovel where people ate sardines for breakfast. The thought nauseated the young priest, as did the villagers' insistent fish breath, which was especially virulent at noon prayers when their ichthyological halitosis disagreeably peaked. His good looks and calculated charm were his own undoing, by attracting unsatisfied housewives to every service. He retaliated by strategically placing bowls of mints around the church, which several people had mistaken for incense and had tried to light the pale green lozenges. The locals soon caught on, but not always the occasional strangers who wandered in. The priest had taken to sneaking up on them, plucking the singed mint from their fingers and popping it into his mouth. "It's a mint!" he would cry. "Try one! You'll like it!" Unfortunately on one occasion, it *had* been incense, ignited by an Indian family who somehow found their way into Vourvoulos's church with their own pale green tablets. Christians from Goa, they later explained; as if Father Alexis, suffering with a blistered tongue, gave a hoot for their primitive origins.

His energetic ringing of the bell caused bits of stucco to fall from a crack running down from the corner of a window bearing the bell's headstock. He watched as flecks sprinkled the choked grass, and let go the rope to gather them in a plastic bag. It felt lighter than air. Certainly they were not substantial enough to convince the skeptical mayor that the bell tower's imminent collapse was a greater threat than a catastrophic fire.

Father Alexis glanced around. Seeing no one, he picked up a stone and knocked a couple of chips off the tower's corner. Deciding they gave him sufficient evidence to keep his cause alive, he rubbed dirt onto the chipped spots to conceal them and, clutching his cassock, hurried out the churchyard gate.

• • •

KOUFOS LEFT HIS HIDING PLACE behind the ossuary and imitated the priest hurrying out the gate. The deaf boy had been caught one hungry afternoon stuffing his pockets with mints, and ever since, Father Alexis ran him off whenever he saw him. Being run off was something Koufos was used to, but he couldn't stop himself from going to the church when certain natural urges overcame him. Though unable to hear a word, he could "hear" the bell's tolling—or rather, he felt its sound—and its resonance, buzzing through his body, aroused him. On Sunday mornings, when the priest freely rang it, sometimes Koufos stood behind the ossuary and came without touching himself. That morning, though, hunger, not hormones, had driven him to the church. The mints made for an unsatisfactory meal but stopped his empty stomach from growling. He darted inside and made a quick circuit grabbing handfuls of them.

It wasn't easy living off the few coins he begged in the restaurants or the scraps that diners left behind, which had recently grown more meager, as had the mysterious packages of food he would occasionally find wrapped in aluminum foil. He had no way of knowing about the country's economic crisis; he only knew he was hungrier. He couldn't read or speak, and didn't have a proper name. He had been abandoned in the port like dogs sometimes were at the end of summer by yachtsmen bored with that season's man's best friend. No one could remember precisely when Koufos showed up, but the villagers collectively blamed the Gypsies for exchanging the boy for a few stolen chickens. He never spoke a word so they christened him Koufos. Deaf. He'd already been in the village three years though his actual age was a matter of guesswork. The prior year he'd started sprouting dark hair where none had been before. He was turning into a man and all that meant.

He crawled into a cubbyhole under the bank of wooden seats attached to the wall. He wouldn't be seen if someone entered, and the boy sensed that what he wanted to do was a private matter because he never saw anyone else doing it. Only the woman in a painting high on the wall could see him; and he believed she did see him because her eyes roved, following him from mint bowl to mint bowl, and finally into his hiding place. If he expelled his breath in a certain way, he felt the same erotic flutter as when he sensed the satisfying resonance of the church bell. He did it then, and took care of himself, with Mary watching from her spot above the altar.

Then like guys are inclined to do afterward, he dozed off.

• • •

LYDIA FRETTED HER WAY DOWN the stony footpath, catching glimpses of the port between the angled red-tiled roofs. Still fuming over

Apostolis's "I'm not officially trained to say," she came to a spot where the village lay revealed before her: the small harbor, the arc of cafés and restaurants that lined it, the narrow dock jutting out like an angled exclamation point, and looming over it all, the Coast Guard's fuel tank—a malevolency that in a spark could destroy everything else. Lydia scowled at it around every corner; and around the next one, she ran into Father Alexis.

"Good morning, Lydia," he greeted her.

"Good morning, Father."

"I certainly hope that frown is not for me."

"Of course not, Father. I have a special frown for priests."

The priest was never quite sure what to make of her, but nevertheless held out his hand. "I may have a cold," he cautioned, "but if you want to kiss my ring—"

"I don't want to kiss your ring," she assured him.

"You'd be surprised how many people do, even after I warn them."

"I have a restaurant to run. I have to be careful about catching a disease."

Disease! The very word offended the priest. In fact, he didn't have a cold; he had lied to dissuade her from the unhygienic practice. The older Vourvouliani women especially had taken to kissing his ring hungrily while tickling the back of his hand with their rogue whiskers. "I am obliged by canon to offer my ring to be kissed," he reminded Lydia. "But here I am worrying about giving you a cold, when your parents almost had a tragedy last night."

"My parents did have a tragedy last night. Lukas had to cut down his beauties to save the house."

"Trees grow back but not lost lives."

"Not my father's trees. Not in his lifetime. He planted the first one the day I was born. That's forty-three years ago. He won't see another tree grow for forty-three years."

"He will if he has faith."

"Well, if you are talking about watching trees grow from heaven, that's not the perspective he wants. He likes to look up at them from down here on earth."

"I understand."

"Do you, Father? Because if you did, I don't think you would worry more about your bell tower than protecting all of this." Lydia opened her arms to embrace the whole village.

"It's not the tower that I worry about, but public safety." Father Alexis showed her the chips in his plastic bag. "More than this falls off each time I ring the bell."

Lydia shook her head incredulously. "You're worried about those flakes?"

"It adds up. Think about it."

"I am thinking about it, and the solution is remarkably simple. Stop ringing the bell."

"It's my job to ring the bell. People expect it. God expects it. It's how He hears our communal prayers."

"He might be glad to hear less communal bellyaching. Anyway, the mayor doesn't have any more money to fix your tower this week than he had last week, if that's where you are headed with your bag of flakes."

"Because of these flakes, as you call them, the bell tower becomes more dangerous every day, to the point that it's become dire!"

"Dire my derriere! Which I would ask you to kiss, except I don't want to catch your cold!"

• • •

Father Alexis emptied his bag of stucco chips onto a sheet of paper on Mayor Elefteros's desk. "This is less than half of what falls off each time I ring the bell, so you can see how the situation is becoming more dangerous every day."

"No matter how dangerous it's becoming," replied Mayor Elefteros, "the town has no money to repair your bell tower."

"Of course there is money, only you've chosen to use it for another purpose."

"I must be prepared to move the fuel tank if I am instructed to do so by Athens."

"Then Athens should pay for it."

"Athens has no more money than we do. I'll need whatever money I can find, and with the tax base shrinking because of the bad economy, it's going to be very difficult.

"My 'tax base' is shrinking, too. Attendance at services is way down."

"Really? I heard you were very popular," the mayor replied.

"You are always welcome to come to a service to find out for yourself."

Father Alexis smiled insincerely. They both knew that attendance had shot up ever since the striking, stubbly bearded priest had taken up his post in the village. The women jockeyed to glimpse him through clouds of incense during the overcrowded services, not one complaining about her tired feet, and each finding coins she didn't have to spare to drop into the collection box.

The mayor reached for the sheet of paper holding the bits of stucco. "Have you weighed these?"

The priest had not, but added confidently, "They are not as insignificant as they look."

The mayor placed a postage scale on his desk. "We shall measure exactly how significant or insignificant they are, so as not to be accused of making wild claims."

Father Alexis bristled. "With all the evidence I have provided you, I don't think I can be accused of making a wild claim."

"We shall see how wild or not. Ultimately it's a matter of numbers."

"Numbers?"

"Mathematics. By profession, I was a structural engineer."

The priest paled hearing that, and worried even more as he watched the older man weigh an empty sheet of paper and then the one holding the flakes. After some quick calculations, he muttered, "Hmm."

"Hmm what?"

"Let me double-check my numbers before I say more."

It was hardly a question of saying more when the mayor had said nothing at all, but Father Alexis kept his complaint to himself while watching the old man recalculate everything. His whole future was balanced on that scale.

"So you estimate this is about half of what falls off when you ring the bell?"

"Or less. It's hard to find all the pieces in the grass."

"So what if we call it a third?"

"That would be more precise."

"You ring the bell how many times daily?"

"Twice for services, and then for every hour."

"Yes, but you ring it one time for one o'clock, and twelve times for noon, and miss most hours during the night." Or sometimes you ring it thirteen times for midnight after finishing off the communion wine, the mayor wanted to add.

"It is true, of course, that noon is more wear and tear on the tower than one o'clock," agreed the priest, "but don't forget, I also ring it for early services on Sunday."

"Who could forget? Shall we say you ring the bell three times a day?"

"Five would be more accurate."

"Four," the mayor conceded, and again made some quick calculations. "Well, now we have that."

"Now we have what?"

"The loss of mass."

"The loss of mass? What exactly does that mean?"

"Let's exactly find out." The mayor searched through his piles of teetering files. "Here it is," he said, and blew dust off a folder.

"Here is *what*?" Father Alexis asked, his jaw clenched, growing impatient with the cryptic old man.

"Your application for money to repair the tower. I recall your measurements were very precise."

"To the millimeter where I could."

"That should make my job easier." The mayor flipped through the file until he found the drawing of the bell, and took a moment to study the priest's notes. "Does the bell really weigh so much?"

Father Alexis proudly clasped his hands on his chest. "That is why its resonance is so deep and satisfying."

"At the time you reported the crack to be eighty centimeters long. Has it worsened?"

"It must be at least ten centimeters longer."

"To be on the safe side, shall we call it one meter?"

The priest smiled unctuously. "Of course we should error on the side of public safety."

"Then we agree on that." The mayor finished his calculations and leaned back in his chair. "We can also agree that you are not making a wild claim. In fact, given the evidence you have presented, it's a mathematical certainty that the tower will collapse."

Father Alexis wanted to leap for joy. He had won his case! Instead, he reigned in his enthusiasm and simply said, "I knew we would eventually agree."

"In fact," the mayor continued, "it is an engineering miracle that it has not collapsed already. I have no choice but to order you to stop ringing the bell until the tower is repaired."

"What?"

"By ringing it, you are endangering the public."

"You have no authority over Church property!"

"That's right, but as you have so ably documented, by a fluke the bell tower is on municipal land. It is my legal duty to ensure public safety, so I am ordering you to stop ringing the bell. If you do not, I will have no choice but to arrest you."

Father Alexis was dumbfounded. "You would arrest me for ringing the church bell?"

Mayor Elefteros grinned. "It would be a pleasure."

• • •

THE FRIVOLOUSLY PAINTED CITY HALL was easy to spot between the stone houses. Nick swung open its gate and stepped into a garden of statuesque rose bushes, pruned and contorted over the centuries to grow as tall as small trees. A gardener, hidden from view on a ladder, clipped off the dying blossoms, blanketing the ground with their withered petals of exotic colors—eggplant, tangerine, aqua.

"*Kalimera sas*," Nick said, bidding him a good morning.

The man peered around the tree to see him. He had a beakish nose and thick silvery hair, and was surprisingly old to be a gardener. "*Kalimera*," he said back.

"Is this City Hall?"

"It is."

"Is Mayor Elefteros here?"

"Do you have an appointment?"

"No. Do I need one?"

"Not today. Come with me."

The old man led them onto the veranda. He brushed dirt from his hands and swung open the villa's door. A puff of cool air escaped. "Please," he said, and motioned Nick inside.

Passing under a chandelier, they entered a formal reception room with dark, heavy furniture pushed against whitewashed walls. Displayed on them was a museum's cache of old black-and-white photographs. A spiral staircase in a corner descended to the basement. Another door led into an office streaming with sunlight, and filled with stacks of books and file folders on every flat surface.

The old man removed a suit coat from a hook and slipped it on. "Welcome," he said, extending his hand to Nick.

"*You* are the mayor?"

"We have no budget for a gardener, but the roses do not stop growing. So why have you come to Vourvoulos at this time of year? Most tourists have already left."

Nick reached into his daypack and passed him an envelope. "Did you write this letter?"

The mayor, fingering it, smiled conspiratorially. "I wasn't sure if I sent it to the right place."

"You did," he assured him, and flashed his badge. "Nick Damigos, FBI."

"You came all the way from the FBI to help us?"

"Actually, I'm posted to Athens. We have agents in every country that plays a strategic role in terrorism, human trafficking, or refugees, and Greece has a problem with all three."

"That's not a very honorable distinction."

"It's a function of your geography, and it's America's policy to help Greece however we can."

"America helped our island in the past," the mayor told him. "After the second world war, during Greece's civil war, we were a communist island, and still Americans gave us food. It saved many lives, including my father's, and I was not conceived yet so I have always been especially grateful."

"Saving lives is why America wants to help again. Unfortunately Turkey is threatening to open the refugee floodgates. There could be a thousand refugees arriving here every day. Your Coast Guard station is too strategically located to be put out of commission for even one day."

"Greece would be a happier country if it were in a less strategic place."

"Then you wouldn't have had Homer. Or the Trojan War, which brings up the other reason why the ambassador wants the FBI to help. Do you know what ISIS is?"

"Yes. Islamic State."

"It's threatened to mix jihadists in with the refugees. Maybe not in a Trojan horse but on a Trojan raft. If there's any evidence that's happened, the Coast Guard is going to play a much bigger role in intercepting and processing refugees before they're allowed into the country. If the station is destroyed, it's almost guaranteed that ISIS will flood this route with jihadists."

"So let me understand correctly," the mayor said. "You want to keep the Coast Guard in operation, so you oppose moving the fuel tank?"

"I want to stop the arsonist." Nick picked up the blob of Styrofoam from the desk, gingerly so as not to dislodge the cigarettes still stuck in it. "Did this start last night's fire?"

"Something like that started every fire." The mayor opened two file drawers to reveal his collection of them. Though sealed in plastic bags, the room immediately reeked like an ashtray.

"Petrol bombs," Nick gave a name to them.

"You've seen them before?"

"The design is on the internet. Every kid in Afghanistan knows how to make them. We dumped our trash in their desert, and they collected the Styrofoam, melted it in gasoline, set it on fire, and catapulted it into our camps. The ones from your fires relied on cigarettes to burn down and ignite the Styrofoam, which gave the arsonist time to get away before flames were noticed. Did you date them?"

"Yes."

"Good. I'd like to examine the first one, the fifth or sixth one, and last night's. In your letter, you said you have proof that the arsonist plans to burn down the village. What proof?"

"Perhaps proof is too strong a word."

Mayor Elefteros lifted a metal box out of another file drawer. Opening it, he showed Nick a pile of colorful worry beads spilling out of envelopes. They were the cheap plastic kind found in every tourist shop. "One of these has arrived after each fire."

Nick draped a string of orange beads around his thumb and deftly snapped it back and forth. "We call them worry beads in English, but I didn't think that was their name in Greek. In fact, I make fun of my dad, calling them his non-worry beads. He always said he used them to relax, not worry."

"You're right, they do not exactly represent our worries," the mayor replied. "But our Greek beads—our *komboloi*—come originally from the Turkish *tesbih*, which are used for prayers, and most people pray because of their worries. So symbolically, I think it is no mistake that the arsonist sent these to me."

"I agree. There's no reason to send them except to underscore a threat. No messages came with them?"

The mayor shook his head. "Nothing."

Nick rifled through the envelopes to check their postmarks. "Were they all sent from Australia with no return addresses?"

"Yes, and in fact they all came from Melbourne."

"Who has a connection to Melbourne?"

"Almost every Greek has a connection to Melbourne. And we have a lot of tourists from there."

"Enough to ensure a letter with worry beads gets mailed back anonymously every month? Who else?"

"Shirley's from there. You saved her dog last night, didn't you?" the mayor realized.

"That would be me."

"She has friends visiting from Melbourne all the time. There's also the boy Takis. His sister owns the bar in the harbor next to Shirley's daughter's restaurant. He went to Melbourne for a couple of years and came back a year ago."

"Before or after the fires started?"

"If I recall, a month before. Then you might as well include the priest, too. He arrived two months before the first fire."

"Do you suspect him?"

"Isn't it enough to know that he's a priest?"

"So, we are already up to three suspects."

"I don't think you can include Shirley."

"You'd be surprised who turns out to be guilty in arson cases. Why didn't you mention the beads in your letter to the embassy?"

"I thought it was better not to write everything."

"When the next envelope comes, don't open it. Who else knows about them?"

"No one."

"And your letter?"

"Also no one."

"Not even Lydia?"

"Sometimes it is useful to have one secret that no one else knows."

"You should be working for us. And that's two secrets. Let's keep them that way. As far as you know, I'm doing research for a novel. That gives me an excuse to ask questions."

Suddenly the church bell started ringing clamorously. The mayor stepped to his window and looked up the hill. He could see the massive bronze bell swinging in the damaged tower. "God damn that priest!" he swore.

CHAPTER THREE

LYDIA FUMED ALL THE WAY up the steep hill. A wildly ringing church bell unnerved people. It made them fear a war or other catastrophe, and every Greek village had known enough of both. Entering the churchyard, she aimed straight for the bell tower to confront the priest, only to discover that it was Koufos riding the rope up and down with a rapturous look on his face. She whirled around and headed for the church's wide-open double doors.

Father Alexis saw her advancing. When she broke stride to take a mint from the bowl at the entrance, he misread her mood to be non-hostile. Then their eyes met. Lydia rolled the mint in her mouth, so exaggeratedly she could have been doing yoga stretches with her jaw, before opening it to show the priest the gooey green glob on her tongue. He barely had time to register his disgust before she plucked it out of her mouth and plunged it back into the bowl. The priest's sense of horror quickly turned to revulsion when the women following Lydia into the church blithely popped mints into their mouths. He hurried to the entrance, pushing his way through the milling crowd; there were no seats except for the boxy stalls along the walls that the old women always claimed for themselves. At the entrance he plunged his hand into the mints, and was fishing around for the offensive candy when Mayor Elefteros arrived. He furrowed his brow at the priest's submerged hand.

"*Kali spera, o Kyrios,*" Father Alexis unctuously greeted him, and held out his hand, hoping for a public display of the mayor kissing his ring. If he didn't, the priest was already thinking how to use the snub against the old man.

It never came to that. The gooey mint was stuck to the priest's ring like a melted emerald. Horrified, he flicked his wrist to dislodge it but the glob was firmly attached. He reached into his pocket for a tissue to use to pull it off, and had to fight back nausea at the sight of its sticky green tendrils. He looked around. There was nowhere to dispose of it, and though tempted, he couldn't just chuck it into the churchyard. He had no choice but to stuff the pestilent wad deep into his pocket.

"Why are you ringing the bell?" Mayor Elefteros's voice, naturally distinguished, rose above the hubbub. The villagers instantly hushed; the only sound was the bell's insistent tolling.

"We have an emergency," the priest announced.

"An emergency?" the mayor scoffed. "What emergency?"

"What *emergency*?" Father Alexis opened his arms to embrace the villagers and pleaded, "Is it not an emergency when we are forbidden to ring the church bell?"

"Forbidden to ring the bell!" a woman cried in disbelief.

"It's not possible!" another exclaimed.

"Is it not an emergency when we are forbidden to bid God to hear our prayers?"

"How do you expect God to hear your prayers, when I can hardly hear *you*?" the mayor demanded. "I order you to stop ringing that infernal bell!"

"*Infernal* bell?" By his tone, the priest might as well have called the mayor the Devil incarnate. "You have no authority inside this church."

"As we all know, because you never tire of pointing it out, your bell is in a tower on *public* property. Until Athens relieves me of my duty, I am responsible for public safety, and based on the evidence that you gave me—and very precise evidence, I might add—that tower should have collapsed already. I order you to stop ringing the bell, or I will close your damn church!"

The villagers took a collective intake of breath.

"Did Dimos really say that?" someone asked.

Another answered, "Of course he did! Everyone knows he was a communist."

"The church *is* on Church property," Father Alexis reminded him.

"Which I can close for posing a threat to public safety until the gods in Athens fight it out and order me to reopen it!"

The two potentates glared at each other as the bell continued clanging, seeming to grow louder as the moment grew tenser. The priest had overplayed his hand on the loss of mass; he knew the mayor could close the church as he threatened. Flummoxed by the situation, he momentarily forgot the boy was deaf when he shouted toward the bell tower, "Koufos! Stop ringing the bell!"

The boy didn't stop. Someone snickered; it became contagious as people stifled giggles.

Aggravated, Father Alexis shouted even louder, "*KOUFOS STOP! STOP RINGING THE BELL!*"

"*Einai koufos!*" someone yelled. He's deaf!

There was an explosion of laughter.

Stavros the fisherman bolted out the door, exclaiming, "And soon *I* will be deaf, too!"

Moments later, the bell stopped. When its last echo died in the stone church, the people looked expectantly at the priest who, confounded by how things were developing, experienced an unusual loss of words. "Let us pray!" he finally said, falling back on his most reliable line, and made his way to the altar.

Lydia was having nothing to do with that. "I didn't come here to pray when I have a restaurant to open. Unless, of course, God is about to shower us with manna from heaven. So if there is a reason for this emergency meeting, let's start with that. Those who have the time can stay and pray later."

Father Alexis whirled around to face her. "Under the circumstances I thought we should pray for our safety."

"Our *safety*?" exclaimed a toothless widow. "Have the Germans invaded again?"

"Nothing as serious as German soldiers, Granny," Lydia assured her.

"What about German bankers?" Petros, a smart-alecky kid, shouted.

Lydia, ignoring him, told the old woman, "You're safe, Granny. It's only that Father Alexis is worried about his cracked bell."

"Cracked tower," he corrected her.

"*He* is what is cracked," Stavros muttered, coming back inside.

Everyone was laughing when Nick slipped in after him.

"Despite whatever—or whoever—is cracked," Father Alexis said, and smiled to convey his ability to laugh at himself, "until the tower is repaired, the mayor has forbidden us to ring the church bell."

"Because you convinced me it is close to collapsing."

"I might have exaggerated a little."

"Exaggeration or not, shouldn't we fix it before it does?" a man asked.

"That's a question for Mayor Elefteros," the priest said.

"It's a question for all of us," the mayor responded. "We are a democratic community with limited funds. We have requested help from Athens for two projects: relocating the fuel tank and repairing the bell tower. On our own, we can only afford to do one."

"Athens is as bankrupt as we are," Vassoula interrupted him. "Why do you think there is a new tax every day?"

"So let's do one project and shut up half the bellyachers," Stavros suggested.

"We still have to decide which problem to solve first," Mayor Elefteros pointed out.

Immediately the women's shrill voices went into overdrive as did the men's worry beads. Of course the question had been asked before, but it had been posed rhetorically, not in a state of near emergency. The close call Shirley and Lukas had the night before, and its reminder that the arsonist was creeping ever closer, juxtaposed with the mayor's acknowledgment that the bell tower was in imminent danger of collapsing, added urgency to the villagers' dilemma.

"It's a sacrilege not to ring the bell!" one woman declared.

"Or a blessing," her husband piped up.

"How do we know that there *is* an arsonist?" someone wanted to know. "Maybe it's just a practical joker trying to scare us."

"Precisely!" said Father Alexis said. "The fire is guesswork, but the crack is a visible fact!"

"Then sell more of your fake icons and fix it yourself!" Petros suggested.

"I can't paint them as fast as the tower is crumbling!" the priest shot back.

Lydia asked, "Did you bring my map, Dimos?"

The mayor handed it to her.

"I'll show you how we know there's an arsonist." She unfolded it while reminding everyone that there had been eleven fires, if they included the one last night at her parents' house, and it had to be the same arsonist because the same type of detonator had been used.

She held the map over her head so people could see the line she had drawn on it. "The fires crisscrossed the valley, and that's why they seemed random. It wasn't until I mapped the first nine fires that I saw the pattern, and it's the same for the two since then: each one is a step closer to Vourvoulos."

"Anybody can draw a line between random dots and make them look like something," Vassoula scoffed.

"I connected them in chronological order, not randomly. I'd say it's rather ambitious for a practical joker to situate his fires so precisely. No, it's a message. Someone has drawn an arrow that points straight at Vourvoulos."

A worried grumble passed through the crowd, though sentiment remained divided. For every *Oh my God! What if she is right?* there was a *Have you seen the crack in the tower? It's bigger every day, and every day people walk under it!*

"Wouldn't it be hard to blow up a tank like that?" Takis asked. "Does anyone know?"

Everybody looked expectantly at Lydia, who admitted, "I don't know."

A man said, "It would take more than a match, that's for sure!"

"Or dropping a cigarette while taking a piss behind it, because we'd all be dead by now!" another man added.

"You're right, it wouldn't be easy to ignite it," Nick spoke up.

"Who is that?"

"Superman?"

"He speaks Greek!"

"I know something about tanks and blowing them up. Yours looks like it dates back to World War II. Is that right?" Nick asked.

"Actually, the tank was constructed in 1923," Captain Tsounis answered. "It was built to refuel boats crossing between here and Turkey during the Exchange."

Nick knew the captain referred to the two million Greeks and Turks, long-settled in each other's country, that had been forced to return to ancestral homelands most never knew. "Then that fuel tank is heavy gauge steel, it's what they used back then," he replied. "It would take more than a rabbit rifle to ignite it."

"What about dynamite?" Stavros asked. "That's easy enough to get."

"It wouldn't take much dynamite," Nick admitted.

"We can't move the tank," Captain Tsounis spoke up. "As you all know, we are in a worsening refugee crisis. The numbers are increasing despite the end of summer. If we move the tank, we will have to curtail our operations for several days or weeks, and potentially thousands of people could drown."

Immediately the villagers were in an uproar.

"My God, thousands! How many does he think are coming?"

"We're ruined!"

"We'll lose everything!"

"Let them drown!"

"Quiet everyone! Let Captain Tsounis speak," Mayor Elefteros said to no avail. "QUIET!"

When the crowd finally quieted, Captain Tsounis said, "When it turned colder, we expected the number of refugees to drop. In fact, they are increasing. About three hundred people land every day along the coast. We pick another hundred out of the water every couple of days."

"That's only the number who make it," Stavros reminded them, and everyone recalled the recent morning when he had returned to port with two young men tangled in his nets. Word spread quickly of his catch that day. Before an ambulance had arrived from the island's capital to haul away the bodies, the village had turned out to watch the fisherman uncurl their fingers from the yellow nylon mesh and lift them onto the wharf—a visceral reminder of the deadly toll taken by the treacherous narrow channel separating them from Turkey. Desperate refugees, fleeing wars as far away as Afghanistan, sometimes tried crossing with little more than balloons tied at their waists to keep them afloat.

"When is it going to stop?" asked a local restaurant owner. "No one wants to come inside my restaurant when people are sleeping on the sidewalk out front."

"I don't have an answer, Petrina, except not soon," the Coast Guard captain replied. He looked around, his expression solemn, before he added, "The reality is, there are three million refugees in Turkey who want to come here."

The number stunned them. They gasped as if receiving a collective blow. Across their frightened faces sailed the armada of rafts they imagined bearing down on them. "Three million?" Petrina barely managed to ask.

"Shoot them before they ever get to shore!" an older woman cried. "When they do, they have more rights than we do! SHOOT THEM!"

The murderous outburst from a village matriarch hushed the crowd. People glanced at each other. Who else harbored such dark thoughts? How much did they personally agree?

"No, we can't let them drown and we can't shoot them," Lydia said. "Tourism is already bad enough. Mass murders and dead bodies washing ashore won't help any of our businesses."

"You just want to keep selling your sandwiches!" Petros sniped.

"You know that's a lie," Lydia shot back.

"I can vouch for her," Takis said. "We're ten meters apart when we're handing out stuff and she doesn't sell anything."

"You are both traitors!" the matriarch shouted.

"Hush, Myra, you're embarrassing yourself," a friend told her.

"I won't be quiet! People in this village go to bed hungry every night, but who's giving them free sandwiches and sesame bars? Who helps us when the tourists stop coming and our businesses are ruined? No one! We have to help ourselves. But first, we have to stop them. STOP THEM!"

For a long moment, no one spoke in an uneasy silence. "It's a stressful time for everyone," Mayor Elefteros finally remarked. "If anyone is truly going to bed hungry, I will find a way to help. Captain Tsounis, did you want to add anything?"

"In fact, I do. In my opinion, the fuel tank is a threat, arsonist or not, and I have shared my reasons with the mayor."

"Which I put into my request to Athens," Mayor Elefteros confirmed.

"The tank has developed hairline fractures with some seepage which increases the risk that it could catch fire. Also, its base is showing signs of exhaustion that someone with dynamite could easily exploit. I'm very skeptical that the tank can survive a move. We need a new tank first before we dismantle the old one, if you want to make sure the Coast Guard stays operational here."

"In which case, we will absolutely need financial help from Athens," the mayor added.

"Which you won't get," Vassoula said.

"Then why not repair the bell tower?" the toothless widow asked.

"Precisely!" exclaimed Father Alexis. "Let us pray!"

• • •

SEATED AT HER KITCHEN TABLE, Shirley put a second drop of precious truffle oil on a cloth and offered it to Dingo. Again the dog turned his ungrateful snout away. He usually drooled at its funky odor—to Shirley, it reeked of something half-decomposed—but dogs liked odd scents, the stinkier the better. That day, though, Dingo wasn't interested in sniffing anything. Obviously he was put off by the pervasive smell of smoke. She hoped not for long. They had made a small investment of both money and hope in training the dog to sniff out truffles; specifically rare white ones, and their growing season would peak in a couple of weeks. They didn't need much to replace what little money Lukas made from fishing, which he should have stopped doing years ago, but kept on as long as he could. Like everyone, they'd been punished by the chronic economic crisis, but at seventy, his knees could barely keep him upright through rough seas. For what people were prepared to pay for a nauseating white fungus, Dingo only needed to find a half dozen of the truffles a year to offset Lukas's fishing income—itself dwindling in the overfished Mediterranean.

Shirley's sense of smell was disoriented, too. She felt plunged into an ashtray. Cutting a lemon in half, she inhaled its bitter freshness, and pressed it to the dog's nose. He would have nothing to do with that either. "Oh, Dingo," she fretted.

The dog hadn't left her side all night, even though Lukas didn't like him sleeping in their bedroom. He claimed Dingo's solemn eyes looked disdainfully at his every lovemaking move, but that night Lukas had relented. Sure enough, he awoke feeling amorous, surprising Shirley, because she hadn't spiked his usual nightcap of ouzo with Viagra, something she'd started doing some months earlier, with results they both enjoyed. That morning he had managed entirely on his own with Dingo as a witness. Their sex had been good at every age, but that morning Lukas's lovemaking was especially desperate; driven, she knew, by the loss of his beauties. She gripped him tighter to encourage his pleasure, wanting him to forgive himself for the sawed-off trees in the yard. When they finished, he didn't roll away but held onto her, and she nuzzled his broad hairy chest, enjoying their extra intimacy despite his stale breath. Only when the dog rested his chin on the bed, groaning pitifully for attention, did they stir themselves to face the reality of that first day after the fire.

They glanced out the windows to confirm that the nightmare had been real, not imagined, and tried not to look again. They had seen enough by moonlight to know the extent of the heartbreak. They went about their routine as if nothing were different—using the toilet, brushing their teeth, making coffee—but it was all different because of their lack of annoyance at getting in each other's way or hogging the bathroom. They remarked how much worse the fire could have been: the house had been saved, the smell of smoke wasn't too bad, luckily a stranger had rescued Dingo.

Lukas left to have his usual coffee with "the boys," the old men who gathered every morning in the port to rant about the news in general and the government in particular, all the while puffing on cigarettes that stained their bristly moustaches yellow. Village life didn't offer much stimulation—Stavros accidentally shooting himself in the foot while hunting rabbits was about the most exciting story of the year—so the boys would exaggerate anything, turning their small sardines into Moby Dicks; but that morning the only story told would be last night's fire, and that needed no embellishment. Out the window, Shirley watched her husband pause on the porch judging his Pyrrhic victory. He had saved his home by sacrificing what he loved the most about it. Lukas would get no pleasure exaggerating that story.

He walked slump-shouldered to his car, and that's when Shirley finally broke down and cried. Dingo pressed against her leg to comfort her. His snout sought her hand and licked it, and that made her weep more. "Oh Dingo! Dingo! Our beauties!" But they weren't their real beauties, Shirley reminded herself—though sometimes the three of their four daughters who had left for jobs in Germany felt as lost to her as the fallen trees outside. She sighed, pulling herself together. "What's done is done," she murmured.

She fluffed a couple of wispy scarves around her neck, hoisted her shoulder bag, and braced herself for her first foray into the charcoaled landscape. Her car was still parked on the road and she had to wade through ashes piled ankle deep by the breeze. Dingo, heels, nose to the ground, sniffing the singed earth behind her. Fretful that his sense of smell was permanently doomed, she hoped to rouse the dog's enthusiasm by flinging open the car's back door and exclaiming, "Let's go truffling!"

Apparently the dog's sense of smell *was* seriously compromised. Not noticing the cats, he jumped into the back seat and provoked an explosive hiss as the animals attacked their cages intent on shredding him. If Dingo had wings, he couldn't have flown any faster out of the car.

• • •

Every time her daughter convinced Shirley to drive the stray cats to the veterinarian's to get them fixed, she swore that she would never do it again. There was always an upsetting event, and that morning was the last straw. The miserable animals, forgotten overnight, had horribly messed themselves; and now, moaning like witches in heat, clawed at their cages until their paws bled. The car reeked despite having the windows open and the air conditioning at full blast. To no avail, Shirley pressed a lemon to her nose. Dingo, upright in the passenger seat, trembled each time the cats' tortured chorus swelled.

Shirley pitched into the harbor's tiny parking lot. "Oh, thank God!" she heaved when she saw a free space. She fled the car, gulping fresh air. "What a horror! A dreadful horror!"

Dingo bounded out after her. The cats howled in unison, and Shirley slammed the door on them. "Oh shut up!" she yelled, though in fact she felt sorry for the animals. If she had lost what they had lost, she'd be howling too; and a moment later she *was* howling *"Lydia!"* all the way down the wharf, her scarves trailing behind her.

Her daughter glanced up from taking an order. "Oh crikey, what now?"

Shirley collapsed into a chair. "I am never never *never* taking your cats to the vet's again. My car is ruined!" She pressed the lemon to her nose and tossed it into the harbor. "Even my lemon smells like cat piss!"

"Ridi!" Lydia shouted.

He peered from the kitchen.

"Bring Mum a fresh lemon!"

"Bring Mum her wine!" Shirley bellowed. "And remember my ice!"

"Isn't it a little early for wine?"

She scowled at her daughter. "It's too early for cat piss, too!"

A minute later, Ridi appeared with the iced wine. Lydia told him to get the cats out of Shirley's car and clean up their mess, and he went back inside for a bucket and rags.

Athina, fuming, said to her mother, "They're *your* cats and *Grandma's* car. Why does Ridi have to do it?"

"They are not my cats. They are feral cats, and Ridi works for me."

"He's a waiter. He's not your slave."

"Whose job should it be? Your grandmother's?"

"Why do all the worst jobs have to be Ridi's? Because he's Albanian?"

"It's not because he's Albanian."

"Then why?"

Her daughter's question brought Lydia up short. She didn't want the girl to have an affair with the boy, or worse, marry him. She admitted she felt that way because he was an Albanian, but she didn't like to think that she singled him out for the worst jobs, either.

Ridi came back sloshing sudsy water out of a bucket. "Is the car open?"

"Open? Can't you smell it from here?" Shirley asked. "And you'll need more water than that."

"Maybe you're right," Lydia said to Athina.

"I'm right?" The girl was immediately suspicious. Her mother rarely ever conceded anything, and nothing so easily.

"I need Ridi at the restaurant." She took the bucket and handed it to her daughter. "I want you to clean your grandmother's car."

Athina looked incredulously at the bucket she suddenly found herself holding. "You're kidding, right?"

"No, she cannot," Ridi protested. "It is a job too dirty."

"We all have to do dirty jobs occasionally."

"But the cages are too heavy for her to carry."

"Well, she manages to carry trays of food when it suits her mood, so I think she can manage a cat. Only be careful of their claws when you let them out. As soon as you're done, we'll rehearse for the procession."

"I hate you," Athina said, and stomped off.

As Lydia watched her go, she saw her hips in her daughter's, and recognized her own strong will as well. She was determined that they would be friends—someday.

• • •

When Father Alexis started ringing the bell, the mayor had correctly assumed it was to call a meeting to assail his injunction against doing that very thing. He explained to Nick how the bell tower's repair had become inextricably entwined with the village's response—or lack thereof—to the threat posed by the arsonist. Nick had agreed that he should attend the village meeting, but let the mayor go ahead of him, thinking it better if they weren't seen together. When he'd entered the churchyard five minutes later, he'd discovered a boy joyriding the bell's rope. Stavros, whom he recognized from the port, ran outside to stop him. He hadn't shouted, instead waving his arms to get the boy's attention. Evidently the kid was deaf. Nick had trailed the fisherman back inside.

In all likelihood, the arsonist was a local someone with a grievance, he or she had probably been in the crowd. Nick had observed the villagers as they argued, looking for an expression that seemed more eager than concerned about the prospects of a calamitous fire, or maybe smugly satisfied for managing to create an atmosphere of fear. But he'd noticed no untoward expression; no especially smug or pleased look among their genuinely worried faces.

Takis and Vassoula had stood together. Shoulder-to-shoulder, they seemed a team, yet other than both having black hair, the brother and sister bore little resemblance. Hers was a haunting beauty, the kind that launched ships and broke souls, whereas Takis, with lively blue eyes and bushy curls, was robust by comparison, and youthful. Nick guessed him to be in his early twenties, which made him at least ten years younger, which marred his passing fantasy of seducing the youth who would probably regard him as an old man. In a way, it was a relief. When Nick was twelve, he'd been burned in a fire that left his back badly scarred. He'd grown up shy about his body, never confident of his rugged handsomeness, frequently relieved a sexual encounter he fantasized never transpired. Takis was so beautiful, he was intimidating.

Takis had been checking him out, too, and a couple of times their eyes met. When the meeting ended, and everyone jostled to leave the church, he was suddenly at Nick's side. "You haven't forgotten about your free drink, have you?"

"I never forget a free drink, but what about last call? I might prefer to coordinate with that."

"Come twice."

Nick grinned. "I can do that."

"Good."

They parted and Nick continued down the village path. Coming around a bend, he had a view of the morning's refugees hunkered down in a field, tucked against a rocky outcropping that gave little protection from the midday sun. In the church, he'd heard people commenting that the bus to take them to the detention center in the island's main town had broken down, so they were destined to spend the night there.

Back in his room, Nick removed the three plastic bags with the detonators from his daypack. Nothing about what remained of the smooth egg-shaped blobs, peppered with cigarette butts, was recognizable as the puckered Styrofoam they had once been. He pulled on rubber gloves, and with a scalpel from his forensic kit exhumed the cigarettes into three small piles and used tweezers to look through them. Some still had traces of lipstick; a couple, gold paper filters; the number of Greek versus foreign brands was roughly equal; and among foreign cigarettes, Marlboro was most prominent, which was true for the whole country. There was no discernible trend in brands or nationality over the eleven months, and nothing to suggest where the butts had originated, except for the obvious: one of the island's many restaurants and bars frequented by tourists. He put the detonators bag into their plastic bags and slipped them into the dresser's bottom drawer.

He felt coated by cigarette breath and smelled his hands. They disgusted him. In the distance, the sun sparkled on the sea. He wanted to be in it. Grabbing his trunks, a change of clothes, and a towel, he went out the door. From guidebooks, he'd scoped out the best swimming spots. He looked at his map before driving out of the village to cross the headland.

As he crested a hill, he saw the first refugees coming over it. They straggled up both sides of the road. He slowed, glancing at them, never immune to their fretful dark eyes. They had survived the channel, but what next? How far now to their final destination? Where would it even be?

He wound down the other side of the hill. Discarded life jackets peppered the way. He reached a secluded cove and pulled over. Standing next to the car, he stripped and tossed his clothes into the back seat. He put on his trunks, and then slipped on his shoes leaving them untied. He walked clumsily over the pebble beach to the water, where he took them off and lined them up. He looked around to make sure no one was watching and buried the car key between them. In case someone stole the shoes, he arrayed stones in a way that would mark the key without being obvious. Seconds later, he was in the water, pulling himself deeper, seeking the chilly currents streaming south from the Black Sea through the narrow and deep channel. He stayed down as long as he could before kicking to the surface. Breaking into a steady crawl, he headed straight for Turkey's shore.

With every stroke, he felt the rancid smell of his childhood washing away. He'd grown up in a cloud of cigarette smoke. Around the house, his mother had scattered lumpish glass ashtrays big enough to hold a mountain of butts, and usually did before anyone thought to empty them. Sometimes his parents' heads disappeared in smoke when they stood up in the living room. Chain-smoking killed his mother, though not from the usual cancer. When a burner wouldn't light on their restaurant's stove, she set aside her cigarette to check the problem. Nick, a year shy of being a teenager, walked into the kitchen carrying his new puppy, when a ball of flames whooshed up. His mother screamed *Get out! Get out!* and he turned to run. In that instant, the propane tank exploded, blowing apart the stove and launching the deep fryer across the room, hitting Nick squarely on the shoulders and dousing him with scalding oil that trickled down his back. That happened more than twenty years ago, and he still hadn't forgiven his mother's smoking. Not for his scars, but because he had loved her so much that he still missed her. He wanted an adult friendship with her that he would always be denied. Cigarettes had stolen that from him.

Those were the thoughts beleaguering Nick as he pulled himself through the water, his strokes strong and steady, stopping only when he felt the currents streaming from the north grow colder and stronger, signaling an approaching storm. Ahead of him, Turkey didn't seem that distant. A good strong swimmer could make it across the channel in decent weather. He imagined many lesser swimmers had drowned trying. From the Turkish side, the narrow channel made Europe so close, too tempting for any desperate person who could swim not to try. A channel so narrow that whole populations had been exchanged across it, yet wide enough to nurture enduring enmities. Glancing back, Nick wasn't out as far as he thought. The channel was wider than it seemed. He wouldn't necessarily count himself among those who could swim the distance, but out of desperation he would have tried. Fortunately he never had to. Life had not put him on that far shore looking west.

He turned around and swam back.

• • •

BACK IN HIS ROOM, NICK showered, splashed himself with talc, and decided that the burn on his forehead wasn't worth another bandage. He dressed and carried a glass of wine to the terrace to catch the last of the sunset. The muggy breeze carried laughter and snippets of conversations up to him. He'd finished his wine and left to find dinner.

The cobbled road pitched steeply downhill. Then, with a quick turn of a corner, he found himself on the wharf with its string of restaurants and tables pushed close to the water's edge. Fishermen, balancing on their rocking boats, untangled nets and deftly repaired holes caused by the day's catch. Restaurant owners tried to tempt Nick with *I saved you a table by the water* and *Nobody has fresher fish!* but he aimed for the dock, wanting to walk out it for the view back across the harbor of the whole village.

Outside Vassoula's Bar, Takis was serving ouzo to a trio of old guys flicking their worry beads. "*Yeia sas*," he greeted them.

"*Yeia sas.*"

"If you're looking for happy hour, you found it," Takis said.

"I thought I'd take a walk. I need some exercise."

"You look like you get plenty."

"*Aftos einai Superman?*" asked one of the old men. Is he Superman?

The old guys chuckled, showing damaged teeth behind their nicotine-stained moustaches.

"*Eimai*," Nick confirmed. I am.

Surprised he spoke some Greek, they insisted that he join them for an ouzo. "I guess you'll have to take that walk later," Takis said, and went to fetch another glass.

Immediately Nick was bombarded with what had become a familiar litany of questions. Was he a Greek American? was always the first one, and they nodded knowingly when he said his father owned a restaurant in Baltimore. What good Greek American in Baltimore didn't own a restaurant?

"*Eixei akoma lepta styn Ameriki?*" one of them asked. Is there still money in America?

"Not as much as before," Nick told them. Though no one still believed that America's streets were paved with gold, at least they weren't paved with worthless money; and in those old guys' lifetimes, they had seen the streets paved with two types of money—drachmas and euros—and only the second had ever sparkled as bright as gold for a fleeting moment.

Takis returned with glasses, a bottle of ouzo, and a heaping plate of fried anchovies that he slid onto the table. "These are from my sister. The ouzo is on me." He filled two glasses and handed one to Nick. "I thought I would join you for a shot before the hordes arrive."

"Hordes?" Nick asked skeptically. Inside the bar was empty.

"It gets busy enough. *Styn eyeia mas!*" Takis lifted his glass.

To our health! they all repeated and drank.

Vassoula appeared in the doorway, and they toasted her health as well—though there appeared to be nothing unhealthy about her. The old guys couldn't ogle her enough, their wives having grown as square as boxes, while there was definitely nothing square about Vassoula's curves. She paid no attention to them, instead fixing her raven eyes on Nick. "I thought Superman might need some nourishment," she said, meaning the anchovies.

Nick, wishing his new nickname would disappear as easily as it had been bestowed, tipped his glass in her direction. "*Efharisto*," he thanked her.

"*Tipota*." Vassoula slipped onto her stool by the door and lit a cigarette. Sometime during the day, she had put on fishnet stockings, and crossed her long legs in a move that went unremarked but not unnoticed.

Night fell fast, and when it did, customers started showing up. Takis went inside to help, and left the ouzo bottle behind, which Nick and the old guys managed to polish off while downing two more platefuls of the small fish. When the conversation lagged, Nick signaled Takis for the bill. The men refused to let him pay for anything, going so far as to clutch his arm to stop him from reaching for his money while shoving bills in Takis's direction.

He refused their money. "It's all on the house tonight."

The old guys, happy they had offered but didn't have to pay, drifted off.

The bar had filled up, and Nick commented, "You were right about the hordes."

"Yeah, I'll be busy for a while."

"I think I'll take that walk now."

"How about a nightcap on your way back?"

"I've reached my limit for one night."

"You look more fun than that."

"Than a half bottle of ouzo?"

"I'll be here if you change your mind. I'm here every night, unless someone gives me a good excuse to be somewhere else."

Vassoula, working the bar, watched him walk off. She knew her brother was attracted to Nick, spending money he didn't have on a bottle of ouzo to impress him. How crudely had he propositioned him? she wondered. What did men say to each other when it was all about sex to start with? Would Nick be interested? She didn't think so. He reminded her too much of Omar, his tan skin as brown, his hair as sandy, his beard as trim. He walked like him, too. A man's walk. She only had to watch him move to know Takis had guessed wrong. She could tell, too, how a man made love by how he moved, and especially how he danced. She definitely wanted to dance with Nick.

He pulled up his collar and zipped up his jacket. The weather had deteriorated quickly. Lydia had already closed her restaurant for the night. He glanced up the drive between it and the Coast Guard station, wide enough for small trucks, which was the only access to the fuel tank. He could see it looming in the night, but only gave it a passing glance, not wanting to appear too interested in it. He didn't want to give himself away to whoever's eyes might be watching along the shadowy wharf.

He climbed the narrow steps to the long dock. A roughening sea crashed into it, but along its protected side, boats were tied up, mostly excursion crafts and rowboats, and a few yachts seeking refuge in the stormy night. Midway along, a sleek black yacht had docked. *Birch Runner* was painted on its stern and its gangplank had been raised.

Some light escaped from inside, as did the voices of two men arguing. Nick noted its flag indicating a Monaco registration before continuing to the dock's end where a commercial trawler had tied up. In the light cast by its swinging bare bulbs, swarthy men in stained undershirts culled the day's catch. More than one caught his eye, but none friendly, and Nick retraced his steps. By the time he passed the sleek yacht again, its lights had been extinguished.

A full amber moon appeared balanced on the castle's tallest turret. Along the wharf, everything had closed except Vassoula's Bar, which had grown rowdier. Her smoky laughter reached him over the water. At the drive between the Coast Guard station and Lydia's place, he saw no one around, and decided to take a closer look at the fuel tank. He darted behind the buildings.

The tank was even more imposing in the moonlight than during the day. A platform, roughly at eye level, and constructed with massive crossbeams, held a black metal drum looming some twenty feet high. Attached to its front, a long hose, wound around a reel, was secured with a heavy padlock. It was sturdy; not a structure easily set aflame by a few cigarettes stuck in Styrofoam, and Nick wondered how the arsonist planned to deal with that challenge. He smelled petrol, strong enough to suggest a leak, and stepped behind it to investigate.

While there, he decided to answer nature's call, and was in midstream pissing when the back door to Vassoula's Bar opened. The noise of the crowd momentarily burst outside. He heard steps approaching and zipped up. Whoever it was passed close to the fuel tank and knocked lightly on Captain Tsounis's window. Curious who had a secret rendezvous with the handsome captain, Nick took a step to peek out, accidentally crunching a stone.

Vassoula, eyes flashing in the moonlight, whirled around looking for a spy.

The door opened to flickering candlelight. With a last searching glance, she slipped inside.

The captain, bare chested, closed the door behind her.

CHAPTER FOUR

THE BUZZING OUTSIDE THE HOUSE steered Shirley's dreams to Zanzibar, where she had spent some shameless weeks in her decadent youth traveling like young Aussies did back then: for so many months that they ran into years. It was too far and too expensive to go anywhere for a shorter period of time. At least that was her excuse for staying away, when the truth was she simply wanted to travel. With that era of traveling coinciding with free love, Shirley slept her way from Melbourne to Vourvoulos along a zigzag route that dipped to the Spice Island—where blue plastic bags, snagged in trees, buzzed in the steady wind outside her beach shack. She associated the sound with afternoon trysts; and that morning, hearing buzzing, she was dreaming of a lover's touch before the sound grew menacing and woke her with a start.

Chainsaws.

Outside, men were cutting up the beauties.

She reached for Lukas. He was gone. Of course he was gone. No doubt he held one of the chainsaws. He was that kind of man. He would take on the hardest tasks without a whimper, yet tear up over some sentimental commercial on the telly.

Dingo, on the floor, groaned, dropped his chin onto his legs, and shivered for good measure. "Oh Dingo! Don't be so dramatic!"

"Mum!" Lydia appeared in the doorway. "I came when I heard the chainsaws."

"Good morning, precious."

"You must be really upset if you are calling me precious."

"I was dreaming about Zanzibar."

"Of course you were. You only have dirty dreams."

"You make them sound dirty because you've never experienced so much passion."

"So much or so many?"

"Have you ever made love in a bed filled with blue plastic bags?"

"No, Mum, I haven't. I didn't know that you had."

"Well, you don't know real passion until you've done that."

"Do they have to be blue?"

"Oh, you know what I mean, and that's all I'm going to say about it!" Shirley tossed aside her covers and went into the WC. Dingo tried to follow, and she pushed him out by his snout.

"Come here, Dingo," Lydia said, but the anxious dog stayed put, pressing his nose to the closed door.

From the window, she watched the cloud of sawdust grow over the men. They'd been at it since daybreak, trimming off the limbs, slicing the beauties into rounds, and then halving those so people could manage to carry them away. Word had been spread that Lukas would be giving away the wood, and already a half dozen guys were loading pickups.

The toilet flushed and Shirley emerged.

Lydia said, "Dad must be so upset."

"He hasn't said a word."

"That's when he's most upset."

"After forty-five years, I know how to interpret your father, and yes, he is upset. If you talk about it, I'll start crying, too."

"Oh, Mum."

"Don't 'oh, Mum' me or I really will cry. Now what shall I wear today?" Shirley searched her closet, sliding hangers back and forth and rummaging through untidy piles of clothes, finally whirling around to display a green satin blouse paired with even shinier leopard pants. "What do you think?"

"It's a little over the top for daytime, don't you think?"

"Good. Over the top is the only way I can bear today."

"That won't surprise anybody."

"I am also going to ignore anything unpleasant that you say."

"Well, I do have some bad news."

"Can it wait until I'm dressed? I'll be all prickly without my shower."

"Of course it can wait. I wouldn't want you to be all prickly."

Shirley inched her nightgown over her head, revealing a sagging belly and defeated breasts, and the stretch marks from being a mother four times over. On the spot Lydia redoubled her commitment to exercise, though she knew she couldn't ward off gravity's pull. She sought to see beauty in her mother's aging body, but instead begrudged its window onto her own future.

"It smells like your dad made coffee," Shirley said, and closed the bathroom door. A moment later the shower was running.

Lydia went into the kitchen. Sipping coffee, she watched more men arrive to start their saws and cart away a stash of wood. It was only wood, she had to remind herself, and not the real beauties, though the whole scene was unfolding with the drama of a mass murder.

Vassoula pulled up and got out of a truck. She waited for the saws to fall quiet, which they did, one by one, before she said to Lukas, "I hear you're giving away wood. I could use some. It's already turning into a cold winter."

"I'll give you *my* wood!" jeered one of the guys.

"And your syphilis!" she spat back.

"And I always blamed that on you."

"You gave it to yourself. *Malaka!*"

The other men laughed.

Masturbator! she had called him, the most bandied-about word in Greek, used as a joke or a slur; and in that instance, Vassoula meant it as both. She knew all the guys. When they were younger and smelled better, she'd kissed a few and sometimes did a little more. They never forgave her for not marrying one of them; or for continuing to deny herself the pleasure of them when she no longer had her virginity or fidelity to protect.

"A couple of you guys want to load her up?" Lukas asked.

More than a couple of them competed for the task, heaving thick branches and splits into the back of her truck. "I'll cut those into logs for you when they dry out some," one guy offered.

"Takis can do that for me."

"I didn't know he could do anything for a woman."

The men snickered, until Vassoula stared them into silence. "My brother came back to help me when none of the 'men' in this village would. Thank you for the wood, Lukas. I know you didn't want to cut down your trees. At least your house was spared."

She got into her truck and drove off.

Every man standing there fantasized about the one shot he'd like to have with her. Then someone fired up his angry chainsaw. A second one started, and a third. Soon a cloud of sawdust was rising over their heads again.

"So, am I over the top?" Shirley asked.

Lydia spun around to her mother, hip askew in the doorway, and wearing the leopard pants. They shimmered in the bright morning light, as did a gold braid looping through her hair. "The Mount Everest of over the top," she replied.

"I knew you wouldn't like it."

"At least get rid of that hair thing."

"Yes, I know, it doesn't always work." Shirley pulled it out.

"Sometimes, listen to your own doubts. Who wants to kill you?"

"*Kill* me?"

"Yes. You, or Dad, or both of you. Who pops into your mind?"

"You!"

"Be serious. I'm trying something."

"Well, I don't know what you're trying, but I'll be ready to kill somebody if there is no coffee left." Shirley took a mug from the cupboard and filled it.

"You don't seem very concerned that the arsonist might have been trying to kill one of you."

"Kill one of us? Nonsense! Some fool threw a cigarette out the car window. Anyone knows, it's been dry enough for a fire."

"Someone set it, Mum. They found a detonator."

"A detonator?"

"One of those lumpy Styrofoam things."

"They've been finding them everywhere."

"It wasn't found *everywhere*, it was found here, down the hill from your house when the winds were blowing in this direction."

"That could have been coincidence."

"The winds? They've been blowing in the same direction this time of year since anyone thought to mention the weather."

"Who would want to kill us?"

"That's my question."

Shirley sipped her coffee. "No one. So if that's your bad news, I don't believe anyone wants to kill us. They just put that thing where they could."

"Maybe. But that's not my bad news."

"I could have guessed as much. Go ahead, try again to ruin my day."

"I'm closing the restaurant."

"I know. You told me. In two weeks."

"I mean permanently."

"Permanently?"

"I've barely managed to survive for the last two years, and this year is even worse. The shitty economy was hard enough to deal with, and now the refugees."

"You've also managed to feed your family and give Athina a job."

"That's called robbing Peter to pay Paul, and Peter is officially broke."

"Oh honey, I'm sorry. I know how hard you've worked. Do you need to make the decision now? They're predicting the economy will improve next year."

"They're also predicting more refugees, so they can predict what they want but I pay the rent. I don't want to pay it all winter if there's a chance that I won't reopen."

Shirley poured herself more coffee. "I can't think of a time when there wasn't a restaurant in the family."

"Neither can I, and that's part of the problem. It's all Athina knows. I want her to have a chance to do something else."

"Does she want to do something else?"

"How can she know until she gets some experience? I'm going to encourage her to use it as an opportunity to spend a year with her cousins in Australia. It would also solve another problem before it becomes a bigger one."

"Oh dear, more bad news?" Shirley asked.

"Athina thinks that she's in love with Ridi. She's not said or done anything, which makes me think it's serious. Usually she's all gaga by now and can't stop talking about a new boyfriend. This time she's being secretive."

Lydia sighed, recalling the girl's many admirers, and how much trouble they had always been. Every testosterone-driven male had gawked at her—almond-eyed, tawny, and tall—and a few had tried to do more than that. Lydia knew the day was coming when one of them would succeed. She hoped it would be someone special and not an Albanian kid in heat.

"Isn't he a nice boy?" asked Shirley.

"I didn't say he wasn't a nice boy."

"And hardworking? And handsome?"

"He's got bad teeth."

"Bad teeth? Have you looked at some of the boys in this village? What if she truly loves him?"

"I don't care if she truly loves him. We're finished with restaurants in this family. We don't need an Albanian waiter."

"You are trying to arrange your daughter's life, and she won't like it."

"I'm trying to encourage her to do better, not arrange her life. It's just all happening serendipitously, that's all."

"Serendipitously?" Shirley asked. "What, that she loses her job, loses her boyfriend, and is sent into exile all at the same time?"

• • •

NICK BOUNCED UP THE ROUGH track and pulled into the square of an abandoned village. Weeds grew in the cracked and tumbled down walls of the buildings that once surrounded it. On the tallest surviving wall, a red hammer and sickle had been freshly painted. According to Lydia's map, the arsonist's first fire had been there—or at least the first fire attributed to the arsonist. There was always the possibility that fires had gone unnoticed, too remote or burning themselves out too fast, and briefly Nick wondered if those other fires would change the pattern on Lydia's map enough to suggest a different target. He decided not. The arsonist had sent the worry beads to make sure the threat to Vourvoulos was not underestimated.

Walking around the ruined square, he imagined the shops and houses that had been there, easily identifying the common well by its basin and the bakery for its clay oven, and finding a couple of broken chairs in what he guessed had been the *kafeneio*. The largest building had partially caved in, but half its dome ceiling remained, and where the flooring was missing, an elaborate drainage system was revealed. It had been a hammam, Nick guessed, so the village had been Turkish before the Exchange.

He poked around the ruins looking for traces of the fire, and finding none, followed a rough path into the fields where he came to a cemetery enclosed by a low wall. He pushed through its drooping gate and walked alongside the graves, each demarcated by a long slab of marble flush with the ground. Solemn photos of the deceased looked out from behind squares of cloudy glass mounted on simple headstones. Examining them, Nick realized many had been young men who died in the civil war that followed on the heels of World War II. That would explain the hammer and sickle in the square: it had been a communist village, and probably evacuated by the government when it was defeated. The villagers would have been exiled, and apparently none had returned. Or had someone? Who painted the hammer and sickle?

Nick came to another low wall. On the other side, he spotted a partially burnt tree amidst a second section of graves with elaborate headstones. He found the gate into it. The flat groundstones were chiseled from local rock, not marble, and the headstones were tall, skinny, and capped with carved fezzes. Nick realized it must have been the Turkish cemetery before the Exchange, and looked as if it hadn't been tended since then. All the headstones tipped at odd angles, caused by tree roots, or were toppled by earthquakes, and were overgrown with wild lavender roses. He saw where some bushes had burned and scorched the tree over them, but the fire hadn't spread, probably because it had been set in December when everything would have been green. But why had the arsonist chosen to start a fire at that particular spot when there were many off-the-beaten-path spots easier to reach? Why an abandoned cemetery? Did that spot in the cemetery have a special significance?

Nick took pictures of the headstones immediately surrounding the burned shrubbery with close-ups of the calligraphy he guessed to be the deceased persons' names. He rolled over a couple of headstones that had fallen over, and when he overturned a third, hundreds of black widow spiders scrambled in every direction, some springing onto his shoes and pants. Frantically he hopped around brushing them off his legs. Stumbling backward into the Greek section of the cemetery, he pulled off his pants and turned them inside out to make sure no spiders lingered there. Confident there were none, he dressed, and returned to his car to find the second fire.

• • •

"I KNOW IT'S ALL SECRET and everything, but who is she going to be?" Shirley asked, plopping into one of Lydia's easy chairs, careful not to spill her wine. "If we don't know who she's supposed to be, how can we criticize her costume?"

"I think she's asking us for helpful hints, Mum, not criticism."

"You know what I mean."

"Yes, but will Athina know what you mean?" Lydia sighed and sank into a chair beside her mother, so the two women appeared to be waiting for a movie to start. "Cheers, Mum," she said, and sipped her own glass of wine.

"Isn't it at least two hours until your approved cocktail hour?" her mother pointed out.

"I need this," Lydia said, and she did. The lunch crowd had gone almost before it arrived. No latecomers, no lingerers over an extra bottle, no last-minute change of mind to ditch the diet while on vacation and order dessert. Her few midday customers had been as lean as the whole mean season. "Besides, isn't it all right that I take after you?"

"Oh darling, of course it's all right! But did you have to marry a fisherman, too?"

"What's that supposed to mean?"

"There are never enough fish."

Lydia set down her glass. "Half the time I don't know what you mean."

From the hallway, Athina called, "Are you ready?"

"We're waiting!" her mother answered.

The girl stepped into the room draped in a white sheet, looking adoringly at her teddy bear pressed to her breast as if nursing. Her hands were wrapped in gauzy white bandages.

"She's so pretty, isn't she?" Lydia whispered.

"Yes, but I don't know who she's supposed to be. Not everyone knows all that hocus-pocus well enough to recognize Saint Hoozits at her spinning wheel, or Saint Peter turning himself into a fish, or maybe it was a fish into wine—or whatever they all supposedly did."

"Try to be helpful," Lydia urged.

"I could be more helpful if I knew which saint had a teddy bear."

"I'm sure it's only symbolic."

"That's my point. Symbolic of what?"

Athina stopped and cast her eyes heavenward, feigning a pious look.

"What's she doing?"

"Be patient, Mum."

Suddenly, the girl's expression turned ferocious and she flung the teddy bear against a wall. She clenched her fists at her chest as an Amazon warrior might, and then flung open the sheet to reveal a second costume.

The two older women gasped.

The girl wore a black miniskirt that started and ended in the six inches above patterned stockings that disappeared into red tennis shoes. A shoulder harness held a pillow against her stomach making her look very pregnant. "I still need to make something to cover the pillow. I didn't have time to work on it because I had to clean Grandma's car. These—" she held up her bandaged hands—"are because of the cats."

"I told you to be careful."

"Thanks, Mom. Can you guess who I am?"

"You're the Panayia!" Shirley exclaimed, using the popular name for the Virgin Mary.

"Grandma! How did you know?"

"It's obvious. Mary is the only saint who got pregnant."

"It's not the Miss *Saint* Contest, Grandma. It's the Miss *Icon* Contest."

"Saint or icon, it doesn't matter," Lydia interjected. "You are not dressing like that. I'll not have you embarrass this family."

"I'm part of this family, too."

"It will embarrass your father."

"Why will he care? He's not religious."

"In villages, people care about these things."

"That's because they're old-fashioned. I'm portraying Mary as a modern woman."

"Don't you 'Mary' me when you look like a knocked-up whore."

"That's my point exactly," Athina defended herself. "Mary, a virgin? How real is that? She was too embarrassed to admit she got pregnant by Joseph and blamed it on God? How repressed is that? I want to show both sides of Mary, because women have two sides: the side society allows us to show, which means what *men* allow us to show, and our other side. Our natural side."

"It's rather wonderful," her grandmother said. "Like one of those Shakespeare plays set in modern times that's meant to be symbolic that nothing has changed for people."

"You stay out of this, Mum. You're only here to criticize."

"At least one of you gets it, but will everybody? Will they think 'Mary' or just see a 'knocked-up whore' like you do? Maybe I should hold my teddy bear like she always holds Jesus, you know, feeding him?"

"You will not make a mockery of things people respect."

"I'm not mocking anything. I'm trying to make a point about men, and especially about men taking responsibility."

"You're too young to know about men."

"Are you kidding me? I'm eighteen."

"Not until next week. If you participate in the procession dressed like that, Father Alexis will use it to convince everyone that we are heretics. We will never get the fuel tank moved."

"Is everything in life about the fuel tank?"

"If it explodes and kills us, yes, it is."

"And you call me dramatic!"

"You need a crown like Mary has in the church," Shirley suggested. "Whores don't wear crowns. That way everyone will get it instantly that you are a Mary for our times. I'm sure you will win the contest on creativity alone!"

"Do you see, Mom, how that's a helpful suggestion, and not criticism?"

• • •

Nick entered the City Hall's gate and found himself staring at Mayor Elefteros's generous rump. The old man was bent over touching up the tangerine-colored paint on the steps.

"*Kali mera*," he greeted Nick.

"Good morning."

"Have you solved the mystery of our fires?"

"You might be able to help me." Nick explained that he wanted to examine the land records to see if there might be a clue why the arsonist had chosen the specific sites for the fires. Was there some link, something they shared, beyond being secluded? Secluded, that is, until the Dingo Fire.

"We don't have exact maps," Mayor Elefteros warned him. "Only the church has always used surveyors. Everything else is speculative."

"Speculative?"

"You will see."

The mayor closed the lid on the can of paint. "Walk on this side," he cautioned, and led Nick into the building.

A minute later, they descended the narrow spiral staircase into a spacious underground room. In the middle stood a sturdy table and chair, and around them, a circle of filing cabinets. "Our land documents are in drawers on this side of the room," the mayor said.

"And in the others?"

"Our memories."

"Your memories?"

"You will see."

The mayor left, and Nick, curious about the memory drawers, started with them. Several were crammed with photographs dating back decades, a visual record of how much—or little—the village had changed. A couple of shots from the port up the hill suggested it hadn't expanded much, in terms of size or structures, but the port itself had been transformed. For decades, only the Coast Guard station, an ice house for fishermen, and a couple of shabby restaurants had shared the wharf. A photograph dated 1923 showed the fuel tank being erected during another refugee crisis. Decades later, the ice house had been converted into what became Lydia's Kitchen. Eventually, the euro prosperity that had rippled through Greece reached tiny Vourvoulos as well, filling every waterfront space with restaurants, cafés, and free-spending tourists—until the economic crisis.

Other drawers contained Bibles and diaries, letters and notes—some bound by ribbons, most in a jumble. A pile of ornate worry beads filled another. Obviously old, they were made of polished stones or ceramic beads, and the silver caps for their tassels were hand-worked. What he initially mistook for designs he realized were Turkish letters. He picked up a set, and flicking it back and forth, thought how he would like to hear the stories the beads had witnessed.

He crossed the room to the files containing the land documents. Their disorganization was apparent from the crumpled papers crammed into voluminous folders covered with scribbling. The more important documents were relatively better sorted, and he soon found the cadastral maps for Vourvoulos and the area around it; though, as the mayor had predicted, they were far from exact. An effort had been made to create proper maps by assigning GPS coordinates to specific geographic features—a rock outcropping, bend in a stream, or turn in a fence—then extrapolating property boundaries from there. It was a nice, neat exercise in good governance, the outcome of which met with fierce hostility. Rolled together with each map was another copy for public comment. On them, people had redrawn property lines, crossing out names and adding their own, repeatedly writing *diko mou!*—mine!—and signing the changes, defiantly staking their claims to plots of meager land.

Nick opened his phone to retrieve the GPS coordinates he recorded that morning for the half dozen fires he'd located, some not far off the road, others that took trampling through rough fields to discover. They had all been close to small abandoned settlements or a lone house—but always a building. None had turned into a major fire, which Nick attributed to planning and more than a little luck. The island's long dry summer could turn almost any spark into an inferno, so especially in those months, the arsonist must have selected windless nights to set them. He'd also chosen isolated clumps of bushes and trees, lessening the chance of the flames spreading. No, the arsonist hadn't failed in setting a bigger fire. He was playing a game. Toying with the village. Waiting for it to catch on to what was really happening. He wanted to torture it with fear before destroying it. Somehow the village must have tortured him.

He set about the task of pinpointing the fires' GPS positions on the cadastral map, which proved to be a guessing game. Its scale was too small, the individual plots tiny, and the owners' names, scribbled and overlapping, made it a palimpsest requiring an archaeologist's expertise to decipher. Worse, two names had been recorded for most properties straddling the valley: Greek names that seemed to come from everywhere—Kritikos, Rodinos, Gianniakos—followed by bracketed names suggesting that, at one time, the Efendi family owned much of the land. Mehmed Emin Efendi. Yusuf Ozturk Efendi. Omar Aga Efendi. The Turkish landowners before the Exchange, or so he concluded.

Could that be the connection? The arsonist selected his sites because they once belonged to the Efendi family? Why would that be? A feud, or revenge for some ancient wrong? Was the answer in the file drawers surrounding him? He was wondering where to start his search when Mayor Elefteros appeared on the precarious spiral stairs carrying a tray.

"I made coffee," he said. "Greek coffee."

Nick took the tray and set it on the table. "As long as it has caffeine, I'll drink it."

They picked up the demitasses and sipped from them.

"Who were the Efendis?"

"The Efendis?"

"It looks like they owned almost everything in the valley at one time. Here," Nick indicated, and ran through the names he had been able to make out.

The mayor chuckled.

"What is it?"

"Efendi is not a name."

"It's not?"

"It means 'sir' only they put it at the end of their names."

"They put 'sir' on land maps?"

"Do you think that Sir Thomas More's property was recorded under the name of Tommy More?"

Nick chuckled. "So much for my brilliant Turkish connection." In an instant, his first hopeful clue to the arsonist had been eliminated. The family to whom he wanted to link the fires was no family at all.

Memories.

That's what the mayor told him that he would find. Obviously, memories of some sort motivated the arsonist. Would he find them buried in the memory drawers? Would he recognize them? He hoped he had those answers before it was too late.

• • •

Father Alexis had grown up in foul circumstances: the lower end of working class in a neighborhood on the outskirts of Athens that reeked of petroleum from the refinery next door. It was the reason they lived there—his father worked the lines off-loading crude from tankers—and it was also why his mother couldn't leave. His father had been killed in an explosion, leaving her too destitute to move. She was literally stuck, and Father Alexis—back then still a boy called Manolis—would have been, too, if not for the Church. Priests recruited boys who, like him, had only two other options: the military or the refinery. Young Manolis didn't leave it to chance. He approached the local priest, seducing him with his good looks, sucking up to earn a ticket to somewhere else. That ticket took him away but didn't make him rich, and as much as Father Alexis thought chiefly of himself, he wanted to buy an apartment for his mother where she wouldn't have to smell her husband's oily death every day.

The priest carried his easel from the vestry and set it next to the altar. On it, he placed his copy of the church's renowned Crowned Madonna. The original icon hung overhead. He had only a few touch-ups before his copy would be indistinguishable from it. The painting depicted Mary swathed in a soft teal robe, idly leaning back, disdainful of baby Jesus nursing at her breast, her expression bored and sulky at the same time. It was one of the church's smaller icons, but the Madonna's dazzling crown—a gem-studded two-tiered affair with double tiaras joined together by rounded posts—made it the most exceptional.

The humble church boasted a number of notable icons, which Father Alexis had already capitalized on, as he had in his other parishes. Each village had been more miserable than the last—one reeked of pigs, another of an abattoir, and now Vourvoulos with its sardines—but they had a wealth of icons that Father Alexis painstakingly reproduced. At the seminary he had been required to master art restoration, the notion being that every priest should know how to repair aging icons or restore them if damaged in the country's many earthquakes. He discovered he had a knack for precisely matching colors and recreating textures, and taught himself how to brighten icons by dabbing away years of soot, while using ash from incense to smudge his copies—rendering both the same dull sheen. By the time he crossed the line between reproductions and forgeries, his images could have fooled the original artists themselves.

The priest moved a stand of votive oil lamps to the side and folded back the ancient cloth on the stone altar to not risk damaging it with paint. Before he started, he opened the church door for air circulation; he didn't like the buildup of fumes from paint and turpentine. The priest didn't worry if someone caught him at work making his copies. He had a reputation for painting the most authentic fake icons. It was how he managed to steal the original ones.

He unrolled the rags in which he kept his brushes and picked up his palette, and looked the Crowned Madonna in the eye. Turning back to his easel, his copy stared back at him, too. Though disconcerting to have two Madonnas giving him a disapproving look, at least he had succeeded in capturing their roving eyes.

Engrossed in his task, Father Alexis didn't notice anyone enter the open church door, and jumped with fright when he heard, "She is *awesomely* perfect!"

He whirled around.

It was Athina. Like the Virgin he was copying, she had draped a teal blue cloth loosely over her shoulders; and though not cradling a suckling infant, her clinging T-shirt left no doubt where a baby would press its hungry lips. The young priest, confronted by those demanding nipples, stepped back and bumped into his easel, smearing paint on his hand.

"Oh, look what I made you do!"

"It's nothing." Father Alexis rummaged in his voluminous pockets and pulled out a tissue. Stuck to it was Lydia's gooey green mint from the night before. Disgusted, he stuffed the offensive tissue back into his pocket and from another fished out his reliable flask of Sporell. Rubbing the clear gel on his hands, he asked, "Do you want some?"

Father Alexis believed that if the world had more Sporell users, it would be healthier, and certainly less contagious. But at that moment, it wasn't about disease he was thinking, it was about the nymph in front of him. Unlike his Roman Catholic counterparts, Orthodox priests were permitted to marry (which reduced but didn't eliminate their penchant for altar boys), so by extension it wasn't a sin to fantasize about sex; and about Athina, the priest was definitely entertaining unholy thoughts.

Athina sniffed it. "It doesn't smell like anything."

"It's not supposed to."

"Does it feel icky to touch it?"

"It's like hand lotion."

"It's not creamy."

"Do you want me to rub it in for you?"

She held out her hands, palms up, and he took them. He split the glop of Sporell between them and began to rub it in. He hadn't intended to give her a hand massage, but found himself pressing his thumbs into her palms and slipping his fingers between hers. He was reminded of when he was a little boy, his mother rubbed sunscreen all over him, taking extra care to work it in between his fingers and toes. He had tingled then, and he was tingling again, his desire for the girl barely concealed by his robe. To try to think of something else, he glanced up at the icon of the Madonna. "You look like her!" he blurted.

"Who?"

"You even have the Virgin's hands!"

Athina wasn't sure how to take that, especially since her own thoughts were anything but virginal. He might be a dubious priest, but his good looks were indisputable: a strong nose that women whispered guaranteed an eager lover, and a stubbly beard that every girl fantasized scratching her in places indecent to think about in church.

"There," he said, giving her hands a last good squeeze. "That should keep you until you have a chance to wash them."

"Thank you, Father."

"What brings you to church this morning? I don't suppose you have come for confession?"

Athina blushed. Could he know what she had been thinking about his fingers and scratchy beard? "Do people still do that?"

"Do what?"

"Confess. I mean, do people really tell you everything they've done?"

"Not everything is a sin. Besides, people have many reasons for confessing. Though I hope you are still young enough that your sins are only in your thoughts."

Oh, my God! He *had* read her mind!

Wanting to change the subject, Athina pulled her phone from her bag. "Can I take her picture?" Without waiting for an answer, she started clicking away.

Startled, it took Father Alexis a few seconds to step between her and the forgery. "Wouldn't you prefer pictures of the original?"

Athina already had enough photos and scrolled back through them. "These will definitely help Ridi make me a crown."

"Ridi?"

"My boyfriend. Well, not yet. He wants to be my boyfriend. I want him to make me a crown. For the contest."

"The contest?"

"The Miss Icon Contest, silly—I mean, Father. It's *your* contest. Anyway, I'm going as Mary, and Grandma said I should have a crown so people will know who I am instantly without having to be told. I'm not going to be dressed exactly traditionally and I don't want them to be confused."

"Ah, yes, the procession," Father Alexis replied, a little confused himself. "Mary has worn many crowns. You could have picked a simpler design."

"It has to be *this* crown because most of the people here are such cows that they've never left the island—or hardly ever—so this is the only version of Mary they really know. Anyway, Ridi won't mind. He'll do anything for me."

"You are lucky to have such an admirer."

"I know. Do you think my idea to portray Mary as a modern woman is stupid? My mom, of course, thinks my whole idea for Mary is stupid. Everything I do is stupid. She hates me."

"I'm sure she doesn't hate you."

"Okay, she doesn't hate me. She only hates how I look, what I do, and what I think. I get calls on my mobile sometimes at night and my mom acts like I'm breaking one of the Ten Commandments."

"Moses was not a modern man," Father Alexis said.

"That's funny," Athina replied, making a mental note to Google "Moses" later.

"It sounds like you need someone understanding to talk to."

"Do you mean *you*? My mom would freak if she knew I was talking to you. To start with, you're a priest, if you want to know why."

"God will forgive her."

"She would scream if she heard you say that!"

"Screaming moms. Now we don't need more of those, do we?"

Athina, realizing the priest was flirting with her, thought it was weird but liked it. She tilted her head to imitate Mary in the painting. "Do you think I'll make a good Mary?"

Before his eyes, she transformed herself into the Crowned Madonna. Her lifted chin and angled head conveying disdain for all things secular—including the infant at her breast. For the first time, Father Alexis realized that the Madonna was truly frowning at the child at her nipple, as if he were just the hungry Son of Somebody and not the Son of God. "You will be perfect," he assured Athina.

"You better wait to see my costume before you say that."

"I am certain it will be good."

"A second ago, you said I would be perfect!"

Father Alexis smiled. Now she was flirting with him.

• • •

IT SEEMED TO RIDI THAT all he did was fold blue tablecloths. Or more precisely, fold, unfold, and refold them. He was forever setting tables for meals not served. Lydia was struggling financially; that was evident from how many tablecloths he returned to the clean cupboard every night.

That evening, only a couple of tables were occupied, though admittedly it was on the early side of dinner hour. The tourists had abandoned Greece sooner in the season than usual, or so the locals complained. Ridi couldn't say with any authority. He'd arrived about that time last year when their numbers would be diminishing anyway. Still, tourists had been scared off by news coverage of the grim refugee situation on the island, when in fact the vast majority never passed through the village. Those who did never caused a problem except to slow down the line at the grocery store. Reality would have been more truthfully portrayed by filming the half dozen men hanging out on the dock and smoking. Syrians that evening, Ridi guessed; he heard them chatting in Arabic, their quiet voices carrying over the flat water as the first traces of sunset appeared in the sky.

At least setting up tables let him keep his back to Vassoula's Bar. She was always flirting and going so far as to blow lewd kisses his way. He wasn't blind. She was the stuff of fantasies. The only woman the village men, as well as himself, could imagine performing certain salacious acts. Ridi had abused himself with notions of her—which always included peeling off her patterned stockings—but that morning, he wasn't daydreaming about crude sex. Instead he daydreamed about kissing Athina's pouty lips. Closing his eyes, he whispered aloud, "*Toso omorfi eisais!*" How beautiful you are!

"Ridi," he heard, and whirled around.

As if his thoughts had conjured her up, she stood there. "Did I startle you?"

"I was only thinking," he replied.

"I do that, too, sometimes. Who were you talking to?"

Ridi blushed when he answered, "You."

"I heard what you said."

"It's true!"

"I know. Father Alexis thinks I am beautiful, too."

"Whose father?"

"Father of no one, silly. He's the priest. We call priests 'father' to subjugate women, though it's so weird, I can't explain it."

"I don't understand."

"Don't worry. All that's important is that he says I'll be a perfect Mary."

"A perfect marry, I agree!" the lovestruck waiter exclaimed.

"And he's the judge."

"The judge?" Ridi couldn't believe his ears. Had Athina arranged for a priest to marry them?

"For the Miss Icon Contest. Have you forgotten?"

"Of course I am not forgotten. I tell everyone to vote for you."

"But you haven't seen my costume yet."

"You will be most the beautiful. Another girl is not possible!"

"I know, and you are so sweet to say so. But people are supposed to vote for my costume, not me, if you understand the difference."

"I still vote for you."

"Even if I am the most beautiful girl, I might not win. That's why Grandma says I need a crown."

"A crown?"

"Yes, like the Virgin Mother's."

The young waiter thought his Greek had improved, but he had no idea what Athina was talking about. "How can a mother be a virgin?"

"That's my question, too, and my whole point in the contest. I'm trying to say Mary probably wasn't a virgin but claimed she *was* because, well, she was only *engaged* to Joseph, not really married to him. Like that was going to change what they would eventually do. Do you understand?"

"Who is Joseph?"

"Okay, it doesn't matter if you don't understand. Only I need a crown like the Virgin Mother wears. At least in our church she wears one."

"A crown?"

The girl circled her hands over her head. "A hat for a queen? Do you understand?"

"Yes!"

"Can you make a crown for my costume?"

"Sure I make you a crown. You will be a queen!"

Athina scrolled through the photos on her telephone. "Can you make one like this?"

"You want a crown so tall?" Ridi worried.

"I know, it's like two crowns in one."

"It needs an elevator." He had just learned that word, though without a single elevator in the village, it was unlikely to come in handy.

"You're not going to disappoint me, are you? Because I'm sure someone can make it."

"I don't disappoint you. Please, I can look again?" He took her phone to do his own scrolling through the pictures, which reinforced his worry about the crown's challenging design. Then up popped selfies of Athina standing next to the icon on the easel, imitating the Madonna's inclined pose, in one shot looking cross-eyed to mock her roving eyes; though Ridi, never having seen the Crowned Madonna's eyes, only thought she was acting goofy. In the last few shots, she'd pulled the priest into view, and the pictures rolled by in a silent movie of her flirting with the collared man. Awkward at first, he soon grew friendlier with the camera, and certainly with the girl. In the last photo, Athina leaned back mimicking the Madonna's disdainful expression, while the priest, hands prayerfully clasped, looked on adoringly. Ridi's mood darkened. He had competition for her heart.

He pointed to the phone. "Is this Father—"

"Yes," Athina said, taking back her phone. "He thinks I'm as beautiful as the Madonna."

"No, he is wrong," Ridi said, shaking his head.

"That's not exactly nice to say."

"You are not *as* beautiful. You are *more* beautiful."

"No one is ever more beautiful than the Madonna. I think it's a rule."

"Then you break the rule."

The girl's eyes sparkled. "Oh, Ridi, you're so sweet," she said, and kissed him, her lips lingering longer on his cheek than a friendly peck.

"Kissing our only waiter might make *him* happy, but not necessarily our customers," Lydia said, coming up behind them. "Especially when they appear to want service."

"I go make service," Ridi said, and scurried away.

"I wasn't kissing him," Athina protested. "I was thanking him for offering to make me a crown."

"It looked like a kiss to me."

"Well, it wasn't."

"It wasn't serving our customers either. Attentive service brings back repeaters, slow service—"

"—brings one-timers," Athina finished her mother's sentence. "Do you ever think about anything else?"

"Than how to support my family? No. Why are you flirting with that boy?"

"I wasn't flirting. I told you, I was thanking him."

"By calling him sweet? Boys assume things when you say things like that to them."

"I'm sure he didn't understand me. You never do!"

Athina went inside. Lydia followed her, and their argument continued.

Ridi collected the dishes from the impatient couple's table. "Do you want something more?"

"Two coffees," the woman ordered.

"Decaffeinated," the man added.

Ridi walked off wondering what was *dekafeneion* coffee.

• • •

FATHER ALEXIS MAY HAVE BEEN God's servant, but he was a man, too, and as he finished touching up his copy of the Crowned Madonna, his thoughts inevitably drifted back to Athina. She did, in fact, remind him of the Virgin he was painting, and of his mother, too. Both associations felt sinfully tainted. As hard as he tried to steer his thoughts elsewhere, they always returned to the girl. Even prayer, his usual escape from lust, eluded him. The priest was in the grip of man's oldest irritation: he was horny.

Adding a last dab of paint, he took a moment to admire his creation. It was his best forgery yet. Indeed, his copy felt as inspired as the original. He had one last thing to do: add dust. He took a wide, dry brush, dipped it into a can where for weeks he'd collected the dirt off the church's floor, and spread the combination of dust and incense ash on the back of the canvas. He took extra care to work it into the corners, wanting it to look like centuries-old buildup.

He glanced out the church's door. No one was approaching and he locked it. This was the moment—the switch—when he was most likely to be caught in his duplicitous business, so he did it in full daylight to establish an atmosphere of non-deception should anyone walk in on him. The locked door could be easily explained away by his forgetfulness to open it that morning.

He went into the vestry and returned with a stepladder, and used it to lift the Crowned Madonna off its hook. Days earlier, he had reset the original icon in its frame, making it easy to remove by twisting four bent nails. In seconds, he traded the two images. Then he hung his forgery over the altar in the ancient icon's frame, and carried the unframed original image into the vestry. Without a moment's pause he inserted it into a gaudy gold frame—another ruse to pass the original off as the copy—and returned to the church to unlock the door.

Forgery wasn't a second career that Father Alexis had chosen. It was a necessity of circumstances. In hard times, God's bill was the first people neglected to pay, and the extra generosity his handsome looks inspired didn't make up for the dwindling collections. Even his take of fresh eggs and garden vegetables had withered as people tightened their belts. On the other hand, tourists—always willing to plunder another country's patrimony—constantly asked to buy a church's icons, prepared to take them right off the wall, and two parishes ago it occurred to Father Alexis to sell copies of them. He started with fast knockoffs, but soon the combination of his talent and inherent perfectionism had him rendering them in identical detail. He gained a deserved reputation for their quality, his prices went up, and then came the unexpected visitor who offered a deal he couldn't refuse.

It was a bargain with the devil that would make it possible to buy an apartment for his distressed mother in half the time. The Crowned Madonna would secure its purchase.

Finished with his first deceit of the day, the priest went on to his second one: the crack in the bell tower. The village men, returning home from their fields or jobs, fired up chainsaws that tore through the late afternoon, cutting up what they'd taken of Lukas's beauties. The noise was a perfect cover for his treacherous business. He climbed the tower's steep steps, breathing hard by the time he reached the top where a great bronze bell filled the square cupola. Each side had a long rectangular window framed in marble, miraculously undamaged in the last strong earthquake when the ancient tower itself had crumbled.

Father Alexis squeezed around the bell to poke his head out the window to examine his handiwork. He had managed to create a jagged crack running from the window's corner, but any close examination would reveal it was more cosmetic than structural. To definitively sway the public's fickle opinion in his favor, he needed to make the damage appear even more extensive. Grasping a short hammer leaning in the corner, every time a chainsaw wailed through another log, he flung his arm out the window and pounded the wall below him, noting with satisfaction how much plaster fell away. He might actually defeat the anti-church sympathizers and be reassigned somewhere other than another miserable village! Inspired, he swung his hammer all the more fiercely and a large chunk fell off. He stuck his head out the window to look, and smiled when he saw it was no flake as Lydia had derided his other evidence. Brushing dust off his robe, he went down to retrieve it.

CHAPTER FIVE

THE FRIGID WIND HOWLING DOWN from the distant Black Sea blew tears from the corners of Nick's eyes as he walked sideways so as not to slip on the steep cobblestones that pitched him onto the wharf. A yellowish light spilling from Vassoula's Bar was the only illumination anywhere. As Nick drew closer, he heard the familiar rumble of a generator. *Afghan Lullaby* his troop mates had named it because they all went to sleep hearing it day and night.

He struggled to pull open the bar's door against the fierce wind, and once he did, it slammed shut so hard that it propelled him into the room. Everybody glanced up. Vassoula, on a barstool, cell phone to her ear, hitched her skirt to show more leg. A paunchy guy at the bar, a younger guy at the pinball machine, and a couple holding hands across a table, all took him in before the pinballer went back to pounding the machine's flippers. Takis, behind the bar, flicked black worry beads while selecting music videos. "*Kali spera*," he greeted him.

"*Kali spera*." Nick indicated the beads. "You worried about something?"

"Yeah. Smoking a cigarette."

"Did you ever try the patch?"

"I could never get one to light. I'm sorry you missed nightcap hour last night."

"What time was that?"

"Any hour—or two or three—that you wanted. Is that an ouzo, one ice no water?"

"Sounds like I'm already a regular."

"It's easy to remember. So are you. Sit where you want and I'll bring it to you."

"Is your WiFi working?"

"Until it crashes, and it will in this weather. The network is 'Vassoula' and the password is 'Greece.'"

"No special symbols or at least one capital letter?"

"I've tried to tell her."

Despite the chilly draft, Nick chose a table with corner windows; he wanted a view of the rolling boats in the harbor. He also had a view into Lydia's Kitchen and saw her long face, mournful in candlelight, assessing the weather and the night's prospects. He opened his phone and logged on, and skimmed his news feeds. No breaking news seemed likely to recall him to Athens, though that could change the moment another refugee raft capsizing attached to an especially poignant story.

Takis brought his ouzo. "Here you go, mate."

"Mate?"

The young man smiled sheepishly. "I guess I must be homesick."

They both jumped when the pinballer slammed the sides of his game machine.

"Knock it off!" the paunchy guy barked in Russian.

The kid did it again, and the Russian jerked him away by his collar. "I said knock it off!"

"Hey! Keep it friendly!" Under his breath, Takis added, "Fucking Russian mafia."

Nick asked, "How do you know he's mafia?"

"What other kind of Russian sails around in a private yacht with a Monaco registration? Let me know when you want something."

Takis went back to the bar.

Nick was left to muse over how big a role the Russian mafia played in almost everything illicit coming into Europe. He logged in to encryption mode and messaged headquarters:

SUBJ: Birch Runner, yacht, Monaco reg. Request info on captain.

He pressed 'send' and *whoosh!* it was gone.

• • •

THE RAIN PUMMELED THE WHARF. Lydia's candles flickered near the drafty windows. Odysseus's unpredictable sea had certainly been that, she mused, though another disastrous evening had not been amusing.

No sooner had the first wave of customers settled in than the wind kicked up, driving most next door to Vassoula's for an inside table. Though licensed as a bar, she got away with serving fried anchovies and chips—and bad wine, Lydia always added gratuitously, if anyone wanted her opinion. One young couple stiffed her for an expensive fish half-cooked on the grill for an indoor spot at Vassoula's. She thought to chase after them, but it would have been too humiliating. Instead she shared their abandoned meal with Athina and Ridi.

When the rain turned torrential, out her window Lydia watched Stavros abandon the small cabin on his boat and burst into Vassoula's where he snatched a tablecloth off a pile and dried off, muttering a tirade against God and the weather that she could hear next door. The whole place was laughing by the time he finished. From a long plastic bag he pulled out his bouzouki and wiped off the raindrops that had splattered it. He plucked its strings to tune it, and even that had the crowd enthralled, anticipating the melodies to come. Takis brought him an ouzo, which the fisherman raised to the crowd. "*Styn eyeia mas!*" he cried.

To our health! they cried back.

He drained his glass, which prompted some laughs, before launching into a lively repertoire. Soon he had the crowd on its feet stumbling in a line dance. From where she stood, Lydia watched the woman who stiffed her grab the handkerchief from the lead dancer and take her turn snaking the line between the cramped tables.

A strong gust rattled the window and Lydia stepped back. "Such a big storm and it's still only October. It's because of global warming."

"It's almost November," Athina said, wiping down the grill. "Besides, whenever there's a storm, you say it's global warming."

"Well, then I must be right."

Ridi stuffed the last of the soiled tablecloths into a laundry bag. "How is warming possible when I am colder this year?"

Lydia shrugged and asked, "Because butterflies flap their wings in Mexico? How should I know? But I do know it's impossible to keep the restaurant open when three dinners are spoiling for every one I serve."

"Then quit buying so much food," her daughter suggested.

"I buy the minimum I need to sell to break even. How much less would you like me to buy?"

"It's not fair to Ridi, just to announce that you're closing, like tomorrow."

"I didn't say tomorrow. I said after the contest."

"That's still not the two more weeks you promised him."

"She never promised me," Ridi spoke up, unhappily calculating his lost wages, and worrying how to woo Athina when totally penniless.

"What's he supposed to do?" the girl persisted.

"I suppose whatever he planned to do, except ten days earlier."

"How can you be so mean? Especially when he's making me a crown like Grandma suggested."

"I can't control what I can't control. January weather in October is something I can't control. Nor can I fix the economic crisis. Or the refugee crisis. Or my own business crisis because of them."

Another blow to the windows made Athina cry out.

Ridi suggested, "Maybe I sleep here tonight?"

He had slept there on other stormy nights, rolling up soiled tablecloths for a pillow and pulling others over him for warmth. He lived out a rough dirt road that wasn't safe on such rain-lashed nights, where he shared a house with other young Albanian men who'd come to Greece for work, only to find themselves as unemployed as the locals. In his first group flat, sometimes he had to wait for a mattress on the floor; but once he got a job, he found a place where he had his own room.

Lydia wasn't especially pleased with the idea that the presumed-love-smitten duo would be sleeping under the same roof, albeit a floor apart with no adjoining door. The windows rattled again. "Remember to blow out the candles before you go to sleep," she relented.

Athina said, "I'll stay and help Ridi finish cleaning up."

"Everything is done."

"Maybe he wants some company."

"I'm sure he does, but you're not it tonight. Now upstairs, and turn off your phone. Your father is already asleep."

"What if someone tries to call me?" The girl, pouting, glanced at Ridi before letting the door slam behind her.

Lydia caught the glance, and that cinched it for her: the young waiter was her daughter's new secret admirer. He had sent the mysterious message with the beating heart. "Don't let her break your heart," she cautioned him.

"Why she break my heart?"

"She breaks the hearts of all her admirers."

"All her what?"

"All her boyfriends."

"She has boyfriends?"

"Sometimes two at the same time."

"Where she hide them?"

"You don't see all the boys who come around?"

Lydia left him, following her daughter up the side of the building, regretting causing the boy such a crestfallen face, yet knowing she had to do it. She couldn't let her daughter's puppy love end with making a bad choice forever. Cute—no, handsome—hardworking, yes, and clever: things she'd want in any son-in-law. But Athina was far too young, too inexperienced to settle for the first decent guy she met. It wouldn't be giving herself a chance, and besides, it was true: the last thing they needed was another waiter. Albanian or not.

• • •

AFTER THE LIGHTS DIMMED A second time, Takis lit candles in case the generator went out altogether. Back at his makeshift DJ booth, he switched playlists, trying to keep the place jumping after Stavros had left to sleep on his boat. All evening people had drifted in and out. At some point, Vassoula came in the back door wearing the sexiest widow's weeds Nick had ever seen: a low-cut, silky tight dress worn short over patterned stockings. She was a repeat visitor to a table of Brits who swore to a man that he'd had his last whiskey for the night, until Vassoula reappeared and everyone ordered another round.

Finally it *was* the last whiskey and the Brits stumbled into the night. The young couple, earlier holding hands, took a spin on the private dance floor they had carved out between the bar and some tables. Tipsy, they made it their last dance, and left clutching each other in a united front against the wind. Other than Nick, the only customers left were the pinballer, who had played his game nonstop, and his Russian sugar daddy. Nick had no doubt that was their relationship. The boy was too young, his exchanges with the Russian too familiar, their body language easily translated.

Vassoula came to his table carrying a generous shot of brandy. Everything about her swayed to the music's seductive beat. "Hello, Superman," she said.

"I'm Nick."

"You don't want to be Superman?"

"It's not my line of work."

"Should I call you Writer?"

"That rumor traveled fast."

"Not fast for our small village. Where are you from?"

"Krypton."

"I don't know Krypton. Where is it on the map?"

"Krypton exploded."

"So has my country. What do you write about? This village?"

"I don't know yet. I'm still deciding."

"You sound like a writer."

"I do? How?"

"Someone who is always trying to decide what to write. Do you like brandy?"

"I shouldn't mix it with ouzo."

"Not Seven Stars?"

Nick pushed his ouzo glass aside. "Now you're talking."

Vassoula pressed her lips to the brandy glass, leaving a lipsticked impression of a kiss. She set it in front of Nick. "Vassoula does more than talk. You write about Vassoula, and everyone will read your book."

Walking away, her whole body wanted his attention.

"Who's Vassoula?" he called after her.

She threw her head back with a throaty laugh.

Careful not to smudge the lipstick, Nick sipped the brandy—it was the best produced in Greece—and made a final check of his messages before the lights dimmed fatally. The generator was running out of gas. Takis announced he was closing and the young pinballer grumbled that he hadn't finished his game. The power notched down again, and the machine finished it for him by sounding its tilt alarm. Takis unplugged it. "Closing time," he said. "Generator's dying."

The Russian, leaving a wad of money on the bar, grabbed his bottle of vodka and told the pinballer to follow him. Takis locked up the money and came over to Nick's table. "Do you want a bath?" he asked.

"A bath?"

"I know one big enough to share."

"You mean, you and me?"

"That would be the idea."

Nick's stomach knotted. Usually he liked to build toward intimacy, something akin to a first date, or at least a conversation that let him mention the burn scars on his back. "I didn't bring a towel," he said.

"You won't need one."

Nick shrugged. "Why not?" Knocking back his brandy, he said to Vassoula, "Thanks for the Seven Stars. It was definitely better than the ouzo."

She stubbed out her cigarette. "I'll stay open, if you want something more."

Takis opened the door, bringing rain in with the wind. Nick followed him outside.

"Be careful when he offers to wash your back!" Vassoula called after him.

Her contemptuous laughter trailed them into the squally night.

• • •

RIDI MOPPED THE FLOOR A second time when it hadn't needed it the first. They had cooked little that night, and nothing spilled. He kept mulling over what Lydia had said about Athina's many boyfriends. How naïve he had been to think that she had none. He had seen the boys, stupefied by hormones, come around to talk her up, never seeming to get anywhere. But her mother was right, girls had secrets, so maybe a lot was going on that Ridi hadn't seen. He wasn't immune to his own urges, and, when not conjuring fantasies of peeling off Vassoula's stockings, he dreamed of kissing Athina's soft, glossy lips. He wondered how many boyfriends had kissed them already, or maybe gone further.

Wringing out the sour-smelling mop, he worried that he smelled sour, too. And why wouldn't he? What else should a lousy waiter swabbing floors smell like other than a mop? Suddenly he saw himself as others must have seen him: wretched. How could he possibly convince Athina to marry him? Yet convince her he must. He loved her too much to fail. He would make her a crown so glorious that she would instantly see how his love truly came from his heart, not from stupefying hormones.

How to make the complicated crown Athina wanted? When she first mentioned it, Ridi imagined the cardboard hoop that his sister had worn to a costume party; certainly nothing as elaborate as the double-decker contraption in her pictures. He couldn't imagine what he would use to create such a thing. Pots and pans because they were silver? Too heavy. Aluminum foil wrapped around cardboard? Too fragile. Then his eyes landed on a piece of Styrofoam sticking out of the trash can, and it gave him an idea.

• • •

NEXT DOOR, VASSOULA WATCHED RIDI put the mop in a closet, and poured herself another brandy. She was in no rush to go home where only cats waited for her. The ubiquitous cats that infected Greece. She fed them because Omar had. Ultimately, only they had continued to look at him with the same devotion as before his mutilation. They actually became affectionate—the mangier the cat, the sweeter—as if they could empathize with his outcast appearance. Vassoula had cast him out, too, though she'd tried hard not to. Some villagers shunned him, and shopkeepers went so far as to ask him not to come inside because he frightened customers. Omar stopped coming to their own restaurant for the same reason: he couldn't afford to scare off customers.

Vassoula simply couldn't look at him. His gaping cheeks revealed his teeth, and when he ate—she shuddered remembering how he ate. It was obscene, like watching the functions of an internal organ with a seepage problem.

Omar had stepped off the bus one day in the village, and not long after, they became lovers. Eventually the village grew to despise him: the men whom Vassoula had spurned; the women, envious of her passionate love, stuck as they were with Greek husbands only concerned with their own quick pleasure; and especially Vassoula's mother, who threw her out of the house for their sinful relationship, made all the more disreputable because he was a Turk. When the economy crashed and jobs became even scarcer, his detractors made sure that Omar was detained by convincing the authorities in the island's capital that he was there illegally. They arrived one morning demanding that Apostolis detain him in the village's one jail cell pending clarification of his residency status. The next morning Vassoula did her own dragging, forcing the then-priest out of bed, making it clear that she'd have his balls if he refused to marry them on the spot. Suddenly Omar was destined to be a citizen and Apostolis felt obliged to free him.

Freed to be mutilated.

Vassoula poured herself another brandy.

After Omar disappeared, she was immediately deemed a widow even though it would take years for him to be officially declared dead. Still, she was used goods, especially sullied by her consort with a Turk. She'd never marry again—who would want her?—but that didn't stop the village guys from coming around almost demanding that she service them. Despite her own hounding desires, she refused to spread her legs for local germs. The Coast Guard captain didn't count as local—he had been stationed there "temporarily" for three years—and besides, he kept her generator running with free fuel. Vassoula needed a man, and it was convenient to have a decent one next door.

She sipped her brandy and thought how she hated the fucking cats meowing and rubbing her legs, pretending they loved her when they only wanted food, their humorless eyes barely concealing their willingness to scratch her for a taste of blood. She didn't want to go home, but what else to do on a stormy night when her Coast Guardsman wasn't there to relieve her essential emptiness; instead, he was cruising the channel on a rescue mission for refugees desperate enough to attempt their crossing that night. And crossing for what? Vassoula wondered. Xenophobia was a Greek word. A loathing of strangers. Hadn't Omar proven that?

Outside, she noticed Ridi rummaging through the communal trash bin. She liked to tease him; it embarrassed him, which made him seem a decent guy, and he wasn't a local. He closed the bin, and went back inside carrying pieces of Styrofoam. Vassoula wondered what he could be doing. She decided to find out and blew out the candles scattered around the bar.

◆ ◆ ◆

RIDI COMPARED THE PIECES OF Styrofoam spread on the counter to the close-ups of the crown in the photographs Athina had sent him. No simple tiara for her but an architectural masterpiece. He wouldn't let it daunt him. He was determined to make as exact a copy as possible. That's how he would win her heart. He started by cutting a circle out of the thickest square of Styrofoam and tested how it fit on his head. It was snug, which was good—he could always make it bigger. He glanced at his reflection in the window to see his square white crown in the same instant that Vassoula peered inside. He cried out and jumped back.

She let herself in. "I'm sorry if I frightened you."

Ridi's heart was pounding. "Is something wrong?"

"I saw a candle burning and wanted to make sure it hadn't been forgotten. It looks like I managed to blow it out." Vassoula produced a lighter, and flicked it. "I'll relight it."

"Don't bother," he replied, and took the square of plastic off his head. "I am finished for tonight."

She touched the pieces of Styrofoam on the counter. "What are you doing?"

"I have a project to make."

"You 'have a project to make.' You have such a quaint way of speaking Greek."

"Quaint?"

"Cute. You're cute, too."

Ridi blushed.

"I embarrass you, don't I?"

"No!"

"What kind of project are you making?"

"A crown."

"A crown?"

"For Athina."

"Is she a queen?"

"She will be!"

"Why, is she marrying a king?"

"No! In the contest for icons."

"Well, it's appropriate that she wants a crown. She's been a little princess all her life." Vassoula, bending over his phone to look at the picture of the Crowned Madonna, revealed breasts barely concealed by her silky dress. "You're copying this crown?"

"Yes."

"That's another ironic choice for her."

"What is 'ironic'?" Ridi asked.

"For Athina to portray a virgin. At this point, that would be harder than her marrying a king. She's beautiful enough, but no king would want her. She has had too many princes already."

"Princes?"

"Boyfriends."

"Too many boyfriends?" Ridi cringed. So it *was* true.

"She is almost never without one."

Lydia hadn't exaggerated!

"Why? Don't tell me that you have fallen in love with her, too?"

"Maybe."

"Stop now, because there's not a heart she won't break. And if you can't stop yourself, you need to be ready for tough competition."

"Competition?"

"Lots of boyfriends. You have been with women before, yes?"

"So many times," Ridi lied. He'd been with one.

"So you know how to make love to a woman?"

"I make it natural."

"Natural is one thing, but special is something else. Women like it special."

"Special?"

"Not like an animal. Like a lover. It's what every woman wants. I will give you one lesson."

"One lesson?"

Clutching his belt, she pulled him closer. "I bet you have never kissed before."

"Of course I kiss before!"

"Not if you have never kissed Vassoula."

Her lips closed on his, and it was true: he never had kissed like that. It had never been such an exchange, as deep and satisfying as sex itself, which he couldn't help but want at that moment. She knew it and touched him. "You come with Vassoula. I give you another lesson." She led him behind a counter.

"Here?" he asked, letting himself be pulled to the floor.

"Yes, here."

"No people can see us?"

"No people can see us."

"Are you sure?"

"It's a short lesson," she answered, already opening his belt.

• • •

ATHINA LAY IN BED WIDE awake. She wasn't sure what was needling her the most. Fantasies about Father Alexis's stubbly beard? Concerns that Ridi was cold with only tablecloths for blankets? Or her parents contented snoring: Papa Bear in the bedroom and Mama Bear on the couch in front of the telly? She vowed for the millionth time never to end up like them, snoring instead of making love like couples really in love would never stop doing. If marriage meant giving up passion, she was never getting married. Admittedly she didn't have much experience in the lovemaking department, having gone all the way only with herself, which she was trying to do again at that moment to help put herself to sleep, but even that wasn't working. Bored and unsatisfied, she got out of bed and pulled on her jeans.

Then Athina wasn't sure what to do. She couldn't watch television with her mother collapsed on the couch in front of it, and a gust of wind against the window reminded her of how cold it was outside. Ridi, she worried for the umpteenth time, must be freezing! Her parents snorted in stereo, which made her almost crazy. She decided to take Ridi a blanket and rolled up the one on her bed still warm from her body.

She slipped into the hall. The lights in the living room seemed as bright as searchlights. Athina wrapped the blanket around her shoulders to pretend to be cold herself in case Lydia woke up; otherwise, her mother would instantly suspect what she was doing. Why should she have to sneak off in the first place when all she wanted to do was something nice for someone? Her mother didn't like Ridi because he was Albanian, as if that wasn't a stupid reason not to like someone.

Lydia snorted and woke herself up. "Where are you going?" she asked.

"It's cold. I thought you might want a blanket."

"Brrrr. It *is* cold."

"Here." Athina tucked the blanket around her.

"Why are you suddenly so nice?"

"I'm always nice. You just don't notice. Do you want me to turn the telly off since you're not watching it?"

"No, it's like white noise."

"You're weird."

Athina locked herself in the WC. She leaned against the door, and counted, "One hundred, ninety-nine, ninety-eight . . ." At fifty, she flushed the toilet, and continued counting. "Forty-nine, forty-eight, forty-seven . . ." until she reached zero and opened the door.

Her mother, nestled in the blanket, murmured contentedly, the light from the television flickering across her sleeping face. The girl took another blanket from the hall closet and tiptoed out the front door.

Moonlight haunted the deserted port. The power was still out and so were Ridi's candles. He must have gone to sleep. She couldn't really expect him to work on her crown all night. She was touched that he would make it at all. He really loved her, she could tell; all his mooning wasn't only show to get into her panties. No other guys had ever made anything for her except rude noises when trying to be funny.

She tiptoed up to the restaurant's kitchen door. Peering in, she saw Ridi's feet poking out behind the counter, and felt sorry for him stretched out on the cold tiles. He would be grateful to find the blanket spread over him. Soundlessly, she slipped inside and stepped closer to the counter. His shoes, pointed up, were jiggling, and he was making weird sleeping sounds. Athina had to stop herself from laughing before she rounded the counter and saw what was happening. Vassoula was astride Ridi, his pants bunched at his ankles. Athina's body twisted in anguished disbelief as a pained bleating sound escaped her.

Vassoula glanced around and shot her a venomous smile.

Ridi tried to push her off him. "Athina?"

She was already out the door, running down the wharf, hearing Vassoula's laughter all the way to the end of it, where she tripped and scraped her hands. She picked herself up, pounding up the path to get as far away from that vile scene as possible. Only the exertion quenched her sobs. Panting hard, she reached the lofty church, its walls and bell tower milky with moonlight. It was a sanctuary in the churning night, and if there was ever a time that Athina needed a sanctuary, this was it. For the first time in her life, she wanted to pray.

Inside the church, oil lamps cast a dim smoky light that softened the Madonna's roving eyes, making them sympathetic, a mother's eyes—and Athina needed a mother's comforting. Clenching her fists, standing akimbo in front of the icon, she cried inconsolable tears.

In the vestry, Father Alexis heard noises coming from the church and frowned. He assumed it was Koufos back to steal more mints and went out to chase the deaf boy away.

Instead he discovered Athina.

Watching from the shadows, her tormented body transfixed him. The source of her suffering he couldn't know, though her abundant tears were proof of her faith that the Holy Mother could ease her distress. Surely he could help, too. "My child," he said, holding out his hands. "Let me comfort you."

"Oh, Father!" Athina cried, and threw herself into his arms.

Briefly he worried about the germs her tears might be leaking down his neck, but her heaving chest against his thin cassock distracted him from an impulse to dig for his flask of sanitizer. Instead he used the embrace he'd perfected for lonely dowagers, giving consolation at elbow distance to forestall their evident desire for more intimacy, which only encouraged the girl to cling to him tighter. No one he had ever consoled needed to be hugged more than the despairing girl, yet where to put his hands, especially given his attraction to her—which at that moment was far from subsiding. "There there," he cooed with a pat on her back; or rather, on her silky hair which fell to her waist. As her breathing calmed, she snuggled a little deeper into his shoulder, and he felt her breath on his neck—the sweet breath of youth, not sour dentures. "What has happened?" he asked.

"It was the most horrible thing," she told him, each word a puff on his skin, which sent tingles through him.

"I am here, if you want to talk about it."

Athina reared back, causing her blouse to slip off her shoulder. "I never want to talk about it! I want to forget it!" she cried, and threw herself back into his arms.

Now he was staring at a patch of her bare flesh and became more aroused. He tried to turn away so that she wouldn't feel his erection; but the girl, whose own cravings abetted her distress, had noticed. She froze. He gripped her wrists and forced her away from him. It was then that he saw that her hands were badly scuffed. "You're hurt."

"I fell down."

He couldn't resist the impulse—the girl needed his attention—and he retrieved his sanitizer from his pocket. "This might sting," he said. For the second time that day, he massaged her hands, and as he did, she looked at him adoringly, occasionally wincing. His eyes strayed to the icon over the girl's shoulder. If he had noticed her resemblance to the Madonna that morning, it was even more striking in the night's murky light. By the expressions on their faces, no two women had ever suffered more, except perhaps his mother. The resemblance to his mother, too, was amplified, especially in the girl's rapt expression. It reminded him of a photograph of his mother at her first communion. His chest heaved at the instant recognition. Overwhelmed with emotion, he knelt before her.

"Father Alexis?" asked Athina, alarmed.

"Let me clean your wounds." He lifted the hem of his robe to dab at the caked blood.

"What are you doing?"

The priest tilted his head to look into her face.

In his dark eyes, she saw a mirror of her own sorrow, and slowly knelt beside him. "You need love, too, don't you?"

He barely nodded.

Sympathetic tears welled up in Athina's eyes as she pulled him to her bare shoulder.

• • •

A HEADWIND BUFFETED TAKIS'S CAR as he wound down a narrow valley with the speed of a local's familiarity. "Do you swim every day?" he asked Nick.

"I try to."

"That's why you're in good shape."

"You are, too."

"Not from exercise. I don't get enough of it here. I just don't eat."

"How can you work in a restaurant and not eat?"

"Technically, it's a bar not a restaurant, and I'm never really sure if my sister has recycled something or not. Things left on one plate get reheated and dumped onto the next one. Round two on soup? I'm not that hungry."

"She really does that?"

"She's a whore, too. She uses that kiss-the-brandy-glass trick on every man she wants to fuck. She thinks it's sexy."

"For the right guy, it would be."

"I'm sure some guys wake up in the morning wondering where *that* ring around the rosy came from."

"I wouldn't be one of those guys."

"I didn't think so." Takis downshifted, and used it as an excuse to touch Nick's knee.

"You never said why you moved to Australia."

"I put a gun to Greece and shot a hole through the globe, and that's where it came out."

"I take it you wanted to get away."

"I wish the earth were bigger. I hate this fucking place."

"Why'd you come back?"

"Omar—he was my sister's husband—didn't deserve what happened to him. Neither did my sister. And the short answer to your next question: he committed suicide." Takis pulled off the road and cut the engine. "We're here."

Nick looked out. Black hills rose to one side, an inky sea stretched into oblivion on the other. Moonlit whitecaps rolled onto shore. "We are?"

Takis got out and stood in the open door. "We should undress here."

"Here?"

"Otherwise, everything will get wet."

"Where are we going?"

"You'll see. Hurry, because it's bloody cold!" Takis opened a couple of buttons and pulled his shirt over his head. His chest was more muscular than Nick had expected, with a patch of black hair between his nipples.

Nick, self-conscious of his scarred back, reluctantly unbuttoned his shirt. When he could, he avoided undressing in front of others. Of course he'd had no choice about stripping down in Army showers—though his scars sometimes earned him undeserved admiration when mistaken for war wounds. He was especially self-conscious when it came to sex, and that was where, hopefully, the night was headed.

Takis tossed his shoes and socks back into the car, worked off his pants, and waited for Nick to catch up. When both were down to their underwear, he said, "Take off everything, unless you want to ride home with wet balls."

They stripped, and Nick followed the naked young man onto the beach. Moonlight fell across his shoulders and showed his buttocks flexing as he picked his way across the pebbles. In a short distance, they came to the whitewashed walls of an ancient hammam. Oblong, it had a vaulted roof and a rounded snout that jutted into the sea. The wind-driven waves crashed against it. Takis planted his hands on its side and stepped into the cold rough water.

"Where are we going?"

"Just follow me!"

Immediately drenched, and quickly waist deep in the churning sea, they had to struggle to stay upright. The water knocked them one way while the undertow dragged them the other. When they'd worked their way around to the other side, they crawled onto a stone landing and collapsed, wracked with shivers, elbows tucked under them for warmth. "You call this a hot bath?" Nick finally managed to say.

Takis blindly dropped a hand on his back. "Just wait."

Nick shook his hand off, and Takis, wondering why, saw his scars. "You were in a fire?" he asked.

"I should've warned you. It's why I usually don't get naked on a first date."

"Your scars won't bother me."

"They bother me."

"Maybe a hot bath will change that." Takis stood up. The hammam's short door was unlocked and he stooped to step through it.

Nick followed him.

Warm dank air instantly enveloped them.

"Don't move until your eyes adjust to the light," Takis cautioned as he closed the door behind him. "You don't want to fall into it."

"Fall into what?"

Moonlight streaming through round vents in the curved ceiling revealed the black pool. Rectangular, it stretched the length of the hammam, and the steam rising from it smelled faintly of minerals.

"I promised you a hot bath," Takis said. "I also promise, you'll never take a hotter one."

He sat on its edge, stuck his legs out and bobbed his heels in the water.

Nick sat next to him. The flagstones felt cool on his bare skin. He copied Takis and stuck out his legs, but the first time he bobbed his heels, he retracted them. "Holy shit that's hot!"

Takis laughed.

"You actually put your body into this?"

"The trick is to go in slowly. Very, very slowly."

"The trick is not to go in at all!"

"That's the problem with very very slowly."

"What's that?"

"You'll end up not going in at all."

In the next instant, Takis slipped into the pool up to his neck. His chest heaved from the shock.

"How did you do that?"

"You have to come in, too."

"No way."

"If you want to have sex tonight, you will."

"What? Are you blackmailing me?"

"I won't sleep with a man who hasn't had a bath."

"I have a shower back in my room."

"We're not going back to your room."

Again Nick tested a heel in the water. "I can't believe this doesn't melt flesh."

Without warning, Takis grabbed his foot and pulled him into the water.

Nick flailed, and yelped.

"Are you okay?"

"No! I feel like the meat in cannibal soup!"

"Sit very still. The more you move, the hotter it feels."

"I'm surprised I can move at all. You're used to this?"

"I know what to expect."

"And you're crazy enough to still do it?"

"Afterwards, you feel great."

"Afterwards, I'm not sure I'll be able to feel anything."

"Run your fingers over the water. You'll see how it feels even hotter."

"Who wants it hotter?"

"Just try it."

Nick did, and it did feel hotter, but he was getting used to it.

Takis, too, drifted his fingers on the water's surface, and their hands touched. Fingers entwined, they pulled each other into a tentative kiss that became a long one. With lips trying to stay together, they crawled onto the cool flagstones, hands venturing where their mouths would later explore.

CHAPTER SIX

LYDIA STOOD OUTSIDE HER DAUGHTER'S door staring at the knob. Athina was forever setting new boundaries, frequently revoking rights her mother thought inalienable, the right to bedroom entry being among them. When she'd started to lock her door, Lydia worried. That had to mean some serious things were happening to her baby girl. Gradually she learned the reasons had never been more than teenage pangs: broken allegiances, broken promises, broken hearts—nothing that growing up wouldn't heal.

This time, Lydia sensed, was profoundly different.

The night before, she woke up when Athina returned. It was the constipated click of the latch that alerted her that something was wrong. Her daughter was sneaking in. She switched off the telly to ask, "Where have you been?"

"It's so cold, I thought Ridi might need a blanket, too. Is that a crime?"

Lydia hadn't articulated a rule against delivering a blanket to Ridi on a cold night, so she had to agree. "No, it's not a crime. I do like to know where you are in case something happens."

"Nothing ever happens. Besides, how would you know if something *did* happen? You were asleep. May I go back to bed, please?"

"Did Ridi appreciate the blanket?"

"I don't know. He was asleep."

"He'll appreciate it when he wakes up."

The girl didn't respond and disappeared into her room.

Lydia went to the loo, and by the time she emerged, the light under her daughter's door was already out. She went to bed, snuggling into her husband's warmth, and murmuring *good night* as she always did before rolling onto the cool sheets on her side. It never bothered Lefteris that he had to wake up before dawn; he slept well, snoring heavily, and then with a loud snort waking himself precisely on time. He had fish to catch; and some mornings, he caught Lydia, too, before he went to sea. It was when he was his liveliest. But not that morning. She'd slept fitfully, not truly falling asleep until he left—only to awaken with a start. Her subconscious screamed at her: *Your movie on TV was over before your daughter returned. How long was she really gone?*

Something had happened.

Lydia made a pot of tea and carried a cup outside. Stavros was heaving a tub of his night's catch onto the wharf, but she was in no mood to think about him or any man that morning. She worried what the man who'd slept in her restaurant downstairs might have done to her daughter. She'd been secretive, and Lydia wanted to know why.

She left the balcony, and went down the hall and tapped on her daughter's door. She didn't wait for the predictable "Go away I'm sleeping!" and grasped the doorknob to turn it.

• • •

WHEN THE DEED WAS DONE, Father Alexis had rolled onto his knees to pray to the Virgin—the icon, not Athina, who no longer was one. He grossed her out when he pulled out his Sporell and smeared himself with it under his robe. It was weird, and a disappointing denouement to her long-anticipated first going-all-the-way experience, despite going almost all the way with a lot of horny guys who, as a pack, couldn't think about anything other than doing it. Until the priest mounted her in his hirsute robe, she had never fully grasped the sex act's essential primevalness: its groping and painful intrusion, and the urgent coupling. Athina's fantasy had always been a totally naked boy in bed, their silky flesh entangled for unhurried hours in a candle-lit room where, in a long mirror, she would glimpse his bum in the starched white sheets during repeated bouts of lovemaking.

Except for the candles flickering in the church, her first time had been nothing like that. No naked bodies. No unhurried hours. No kissing, or nuzzling, or suggestion of a second go; and the first time, shouldn't there be *at least* a second go? She couldn't believe the injustice of it. She couldn't believe what had happened in an insane moment. Of course, if it hadn't been for Ridi's own insane moment, she'd still be intact; but she knew, too, that she couldn't blame the young waiter. She had fended off enough other guys more earnest than the priest. Her own primeval urges had driven her to help the beastly Father consummate his awkward embrace. If she thought she was hurting Ridi by doing it, she had awakened from her sorry night realizing she had hurt herself far more.

She heard her mother's faint tapping on her door.

Shit! Had she locked it? Athina jumped out of bed to punch in the lock. She didn't want her mother's questions when she had so many herself.

She reached it too late.

The door swung open. "You're not locking me out this time," her mother said. "You snuck out last night."

"I didn't sneak out. I took Ridi a blanket."

Lydia's expression turned to stone.

"What's wrong?" the girl asked.

"You're bleeding."

She was. There was a trickle of dried blood on her leg. "I think it's stopped," she said, worried, appealing to her mother.

"He raped you, didn't he?"

"Yes!" Athina cried, and fell into Lydia's arms.

Her daughter's distress was loudest in the words she left unsaid. Nothing about tenderness; no satisfaction in the rite of passage; no pleasure in the pain. "We weren't even naked!" she wailed. Lydia didn't pry for more details. It was enough that her daughter had been forcibly taken, or forcibly enough that it left her sad and shaken. No doubt Athina had flirted and offered a coaxing kiss, but it hadn't ended where the girl wanted. Had she actually said *No!*? It didn't matter. She was still only a child, not eighteen for another week. Any self-respecting man would have restrained himself; but, she supposed, not a horny young one, especially when a beautiful girl suddenly visits him in the night.

"He was like a horrible hairy animal!" the girl cried.

"I'm calling the doctor."

"Please don't! He didn't hurt me. Not really. I mean, the blood is natural, isn't it?"

It was, Lydia reassured her, yet no girl should be describing her first lover as a horrible hairy animal! *That* was not natural.

He had raped her.

She handed Athina her teddy bear, which had fallen to the floor. "Take a shower and have some breakfast. You'll feel better."

"Where are you going?"

"I won't be long," Lydia replied, and left the house.

Around the front of the building, she paused, debating if she should go into the restaurant and visit the scene of the crime. What would be revealed? All that she would find would be her own sad heart over her daughter's distress.

"Pompano?" Stavros shouted at her from down the wharf. "They won't be running much longer!"

"*Oxi symera*," she called back. Not today. "Lefteris is out fishing!"

"Why? I've already caught his fish! Instead he should be trying to catch you this morning!"

Lydia wasn't in a smiling mood. She didn't need a man flirting with her, certainly not the man with whom she'd had her one secret affair. It had been before she was married, but not by much; and it had been her first time, too. Sometimes she puzzled over why it had happened at all, but one thing was for sure, no woman would ever disparage Stavros as a horrible, hairy animal. She felt sorry for her daughter. Every girl dreamed romantically of her first lover, and she should: there is only one first time.

Unknowingly, she followed the trail that Athina had taken into the village the night before. Apostolis had a part-time job at a restaurant, occasionally drove a taxi, and wore the village policeman's badge when he wasn't wearing the fire chief's hat. He could be almost anywhere. Lydia decided to try to find him at home and knocked on his door.

When he answered, she told him outright, "Athina has been raped."

• • •

NICK ENTERED THE GATE. A stone wall, chest high and spotted with orange lichen, encircled the churchyard's irregular shape. A corner jutted out to embrace the controversial bell tower. Was its repair a Church or village responsibility? Giving it a good look, Nick was glad it wasn't his headache to maintain: an uneven stack of bricks so poorly laid that even glopped-on stucco couldn't camouflage the bad job. Incongruously, perched atop it was an astounding bronze bell suspended in vaulted marble windows. Using the telephoto on his phone, Nick examined the crack that sprang from a window's bottom corner and zigzagged down, he guessed a little over two feet. It was an important load-bearing point and looked seriously compromised.

Click!

Midway along the fissure, he could see where a large chunk had fallen off; recently, it appeared, from the whiter cavity left behind in the weathered stucco.

Click! Click!

Other pit marks and chips straggled the crack, but many were free-standing, clearly not caused by movement or stress. They had been made by impact, most likely someone using a hammer. Nick was snapping more photos when he heard, "*Boro se voidiso?*" Can I help you?

He turned to Father Alexis. "I hope you speak English."

"I don't have much practice to use it."

"It has to be better than my Greek, which is only good enough to order food and talk about the weather." Nick frequently downplayed how well he spoke Greek as a ploy to steer important conversations into English; it gave him more control of them, and he definitely wanted to have an important conversation with Father Alexis. He had come to the church intending to ask him about the arsonist case. Now he wanted to know why the man had manufactured a crisis over a bogus crack in the bell tower; or rather, what had likely started as a bogus crack, but now, because of the damage to it, appeared significant enough to matter.

The priest smiled ingratiatingly. "That should suffice for this village, since most people talk only about the weather. But yes, I do speak English. It is necessary to reach the higher levels of—" He stopped, unable to recall a word.

"Heaven?" Nick suggested.

The priest shook his head. "Hierarchy," he remembered.

"Hierarchy?"

"Yes, in the Church."

"Ah yes, I understand." Nick turned his attention back to the bell tower. "A minute ago, you asked if you could help me. I don't need help, but that tower sure does. I've seen minarets in better shape come crashing down."

"Minarets?"

"In Afghanistan, and they were only holding up a loudspeaker, not a big bell. That thing must weigh a ton."

"Three tons," the priest proudly informed him.

"*Metric* tons? That *is* heavy."

"You sound like an expert."

"Nick Damigos," he said, and stuck out his hand. "I only know what I've witnessed. Do you mind if I go up and take a closer look? I might be able to give you some ideas about how to keep it from getting worse."

The priest didn't want to stop the crack from getting worse. That was apparent by how his expression froze. "I wish I could accept your offer, but you must ask the mayor for permission. He has declared the tower off-limits."

"He's not here. We don't have to tell him."

"I couldn't take the responsibility. What if it fell down while you are up there?"

"I don't blame you. It's a big responsibility. In America, we'd call that tower an accident waiting for a lawyer."

"In America, who would be responsible for repairing it?"

Nick grinned. "I'm not taking sides in local politics. But I'll miss hearing the bell if you can't ring it again before I leave. Though I suppose I will hear others. There is never a shortage of churches on a Greek island. The church isn't off-limits, too, is it?"

"Not until the mayor appoints himself God and locks up His own house. Until then, you are welcome inside."

"Could I ask you to show me your famous icon?"

The priest paled. "Our famous icon? Do you mean the Crowned Madonna?"

"Her roving eyes are mentioned in all the guidebooks."

"Certainly," Father Alexis replied, feigning an easy hospitality. He didn't like the idea of a stranger sniffing around his forgeries.

"Is now okay?" Nick asked.

They entered the church. At that hour, through small openings in the dome, a half dozen pencil-thin shafts of sunlight landed on the famous icon, suspending her in a cloud of light that rendered her jeweled crown bedazzling. "She's incredible!" Nick exclaimed.

Father Alexis beamed proudly. "She is glorious, isn't she?"

Nick approached the icon for a closer look. He stopped midway, took a step to the left, a couple to the right—and laughed. "Her eyes *do* follow you!" He closed in on the image, watching her watch him, until he stopped right below her, forcing the Madonna to look cross-eyed down at him. "She's mesmerizing," he said. With his nose almost pressed to the iconostasis, Nick smelled fresh paint, and noticed a shiny patch on the icon's frame. The image, too, was shinier than he would have expected for a centuries-old painting. Perhaps Father Alexis had recently cleaned it, touching up the frame at the same time. He sidestepped the votive rack of oil lamps to get a better look, and trounced on Koufos's foot, which had slipped out of the cubbyhole where the deaf boy had fallen asleep.

The boy, lurching up, cracked his head hard as he scrambled into view. He touched his forehead and saw that he was bleeding. Making strangled yelping sounds, he turned every which way looking for an escape.

The priest blocked the entrance.

Nick stood between him and a side door.

Koufos's only way out was through the vestry. He ran into it and out its other door.

Nick sprinted after him, but stopped at the outside door; the kid was too quick. Turning around, he was face to face with a second Crowned Madonna. It was such a good copy that he glanced back into the church to make sure that the original icon hadn't somehow miraculously transported itself to the easel.

Father Alexis swooped in, all aflutter, putting himself between Nick and the icon. "You shouldn't bother with that child. He's a terrible boy."

"Is that a copy?"

"Is what a copy?"

"The painting you're standing in front of."

"Oh." The priest stepped aside.

"Did you paint it?"

"Yes."

"It's good."

"Do you think so?" Father Alexis couldn't help but beam a little.

"It's as good as the original. You've even managed to make it look old."

"We are trained how to do that at the seminary."

"To copy icons?"

"To age their repairs."

"Painting a new icon to look old, that's definitely a skill. You should sell them."

"I do."

"Really?"

"It pays better than selling postcards."

"So how much for this beauty?"

"I'm afraid it is already sold."

"For how much?"

"The good copies are very expensive."

"For work as good as this, they should be expensive. So how much?"

Nick waited expectantly, putting the priest on the spot. When he finally quoted a price, he said, "Really? Is that all? You should be getting three times that."

"You think so?"

"I don't think so, I know so." Nick pulled out his wallet. "In fact, you're getting three times that now."

"I can't sell you—"

"Sure you can. Paint your other buyer another one. Here, this seals the deal." Nick piled all the bills in his wallet on the vestry table. "I'll have more for you tomorrow."

"Truly, I cannot sell it to you."

Nick smiled. "Truly, you can, because you just did."

• • •

RIDI FLOSSED HIS TEETH. IT was something he'd learned to do in Greece. Growing up, he had never heard about it; the first time he did was when a customer at the restaurant suggested he might want to do it to save his teeth. He had asked the American woman—it turned out, she was a dentist—to write down "floss" and later watched a YouTube video to learn how to use it. The last time he went to the pharmacy to buy it, he'd thrown in a packet of Trojans as well, since they were hanging next to the register and he could do it as nonchalantly as buying gum.

The floss was being used, but not yet the Trojans. He had only one girl in mind when he bought them, and he still did: Athina. Now his chances with her were nil. What was he thinking when he allowed Vassoula to seduce him? Not counting the woman his father had bought him for an hour on his eighteenth birthday, Ridi had only been with one girl before, a sweet girl from his village. They had a short fling right before he left, which awakened him to the pleasures of sex, and now he couldn't stop daydreaming about making love with Athina. How could he have been so foolish with Vassoula!

He reread his list of that day's vocabulary words stuck on the mirror: shameful, aberration, forgiveness, faithful, and forever. He'd come up with them the night before while fleeing the scene of his offense, bouncing on his scooter along the rough road home and constructing what he'd say to Athina the next day. His lists of vocabulary words from prior days surrounded the mirror. Unlike his countrymen who reminisced about a fairytale life back home, Ridi never planned to go back home where the only true opportunity was to leave.

"Aberration," he practiced saying. "I make a shameful aberration."

Would Athina ever forgive him? She wouldn't, Ridi fretted, and lathered up his cheeks. Scraping a dull razor across them, he vowed to win her back, and was ready with a short speech when he showed up at the restaurant an hour later. No one was around, and despite the salacious acts that had taken place the night before, nothing was different except how he felt about being there. He was ashamed of himself, at every moment expecting accusations—even stones—to be hurled at him. Instead, it was only a normal, muted morning, with a clique of old men at Vassoula's flipping worry beads while discussing politics, and down the wharf Stavros clutched fish in both hands doing one of his invented dances.

The young waiter unlocked the linen cupboard and was spreading out tablecloths when Athina came around the corner. Ignoring him, she headed straight for the steps to the kitchen.

"Athina," he said.

She stopped with her back to him. "Never say my name again. It sounds vulgar coming from your mouth."

"Athina, please—"

She whipped around. "Do you understand 'never'? Or haven't you learned that word yet?"

"I did something I never supposed it to happen."

"You 'never supposed it to happen'? I didn't supposed it to happen either. None of it. Not any of it."

She stepped onto the porch.

"Athina."

She paused, keeping her back to him. "I said never say my name again."

"Your name will be on my last breath," he said.

The girl's legs trembled so much she could barely unlock the door. Ridi had spoken poetry to her when she felt so unworthy, so dirty. In truth, neither of them had done anything more reproachable than the other, but only she knew what she had done. She wondered if Ridi would be so poetic if *he* knew; and suddenly, she realized that she might have lost more than her virginity. She might have lost him when she had been losing herself to the same lustful urges. Athina was on the verge of forgiving him when she stepped into the kitchen. The memory came rushing back of his feet sticking out from behind the counter with Vassoula straddling him. It reinforced her determination. He deserved no forgiveness. He had set into motion her actions with his one misdeed.

She took a flat of eggs from the cooler and poured oil into a frying pan. Everything was so normal except inside herself. Only she could know how different she felt. How hollow. She couldn't claim her virginity to be stolen when she had given it away, but she felt cheated nevertheless.

By the time the oil was sizzling, Athina was crying and didn't hear Ridi come inside. He coughed and she whirled around. "I don't want to speak to you. I only came to make myself breakfast."

"Then only listen," he said. "Last night I make a shameful aberration. I never, after we marry, touch another woman. I promise."

"Are you crazy?" He was so earnest, so sweet, so unaware of the shame that churned inside her—shame Athina blamed him for, but was hers nevertheless. "Who said I would marry you?"

"It's my impossible dream."

"It's impossible now, that's for sure. Why did you do it? Why?"

She threw an egg and hit him in the chest.

"Is she so sexy that you had to do it with her?"

She hit him with another egg.

"You couldn't resist her?"

Another egg.

"Like some horrible animal?"

Sobbing, Athina threw eggs until they were all gone and Ridi was dipping with goop. "*I hate you!*" she screamed.

At that moment, Apostolis stepped into the tiny kitchen.

Lydia was right behind him. "He's not going to get away with it," she assured Athina.

"With what?"

Apostolis, pulling out handcuffs, asked Ridi, "What is your family name?"

"Aslani," he replied, baffled and alarmed.

"Ridi Aslani, you are under arrest for rape."

"Oh my God!" Athina cried. "I never said it was Ridi!" In fact, she had never said who it was. Between crying fits, she had only spoken of a "he" who had done it to her.

"Then who was it?" Lydia demanded.

Suddenly Athina realized what she had set into motion. Her mother had put the word "rape" into her mouth, and she appropriated it, wanting maximum sympathy for her own regretful choice. She had meant it in the abstract. Of course there was the reality of the sex act, but in that she had been a willing participant, even a greedy one until remorse caught up with her. If the priest had been a more satisfactory lover, she would have a very different take on what had transpired; she admitted that to herself. Her romantic notions had been raped, not her body, and she couldn't let Ridi go to jail for that. Nor could she bring undeserved shame to Father Alexis. It may have been ultimately a loathsome undertaking, but she had run to him, and in her heart, she knew for more than succor. Wanting to hurt Ridi, she had seduced the priest, and for that she was guilty.

"If it wasn't Ridi, who raped you?" Lydia demanded again.

Everyone stared at her waiting for her answer.

"I wasn't raped!" Athina finally cried and bolted outside. She ran around the building to their apartment's front door. So many times she had been an actress in her own drama, sobbing and flinging herself melodramatically across the bed; but that day, by the time she reached her bedroom door, Athina was no longer a little girl imitating soap operas. Sobbing she might have been, but for a woman's shame, not a child's hurt; shame, like Mary's, too humiliating to confess what she had really done. Nor could she recklessly blame the priest when the blame was shared; and if she did blame him, it would be too embarrassing that everyone would learn that her first time had been with Father Alexis. Village priests were the fantasy of thickening middle-aged women, not pretty young virgins. Athina wanted to howl over her lost status.

CHAPTER SEVEN

"IF HE DOESN'T GET HERE soon, he'll miss the sunset altogether," Shirley said, watching the sun inch toward the horizon.

"There's another sunset tomorrow," Lukas grumbled, slumped at the table. He'd spent a second day sawing up his beauties and hauling away debris.

"I know there will be another sunset tomorrow, but we invited him to watch tonight's sunset." Shirley searched a cupboard. "Now where did I put those special ouzo glasses?"

"He's a *writer*, not the prime minister. Just use the regular ones."

"He's the man who saved Dingo's life, that's who he is. I want to treat him a little special."

"He won't even notice."

"There they are." Shirley retrieved two of the slender glasses and set them on a tray, alongside a glass for her wine, and put some olives in a bowl.

A car pulled up outside and cut its motor.

"Why don't you go meet him?" she suggested. "And take Dingo with you. He probably needs to squirt."

"If he'll leave your side." Lukas pushed his chair back. "Come on, Dingo."

The dog stayed put, trembling.

"Go on," Shirley urged. "Get!"

Reluctantly the dog followed Lukas to the door. He hadn't eaten since the fire and his skinny ribs were showing more than usual. She had cut up steak for him that still sat untouched in his bowl. She was worried about Lukas, too. He was weary. Bone weary and soul weary. She'd caught him once, thinking he was alone, standing between the stumps where his beauties had once soared, letting tears run down his face as pickups carted them away in pieces.

Dingo bounded back into the kitchen, scampering ahead of the men, his hindquarters wagging as he ran between Shirley and Nick. "I think he likes you," she said. "That's the most energetic he's been since the fire. Now if he would only eat. He won't touch anything, not even fresh steak." They all glanced at the dog's bowl and watched a fly trot across the raw meat.

Nick picked the bowl up and held it out to the dog. "Come here, Dingo. Come on, boy. Eat your food."

The dog lifted his snout, nose quivering. He would have nothing to do with it.

"I know a trick," Nick said, and went back outside. He returned seconds later pinching ashes between his fingers. He sprinkled them over the meat, sparingly, as if lightly salting it. "Come here, boy. Come on, Dingo. Eat your food."

"Go on," Shirley urged the dog.

Dingo approached his bowl suspiciously.

"Go on."

The dog sniffed the food. Tested it. Took an exploratory bite. Another followed, and another, until the hungry animal had bolted it all down and skid the bowl across the floor as he licked it clean.

"Goodness! Let me give him some more." Shirley opened the refrigerator. "How did you know to do that?"

"It's how I got my dog to eat."

"After a fire?"

"Yeah. After a fire."

"Can you fix his sense of smell, too?" Shirley wanted to know. "He won't have anything to do with truffles, and he's a truffle dog. He's been trained to find them."

Exasperated, Lukas picked up the drink tray. "Enough about the damn dog! As I recall, the man has come to see the sunset, not fix Dingo's sense of smell. Let's have an ouzo on the terrace before it's sun*rise* we're waiting for!"

"Sounds good to me," Nick said, and followed him outside.

• • •

Lydia sighed outside her daughter's door. She hesitated knocking. She had checked on the girl a couple of times during the day and tried to get her to talk. "I need to think, Mom," was all she would reply. Lydia wasn't so sure. She had read somewhere that adolescents, after experiencing a traumatic event, were capable of thinking too much and hurting themselves. She worried that Athina might be that despondent.

She sighed again, debating if she should knock or not, when from inside the room Athina shouted, "You can come in."

"Are you sure?"

"I said so, didn't I?"

Lydia went into the room, and shuddered, seeing her daughter on the bed in a nightgown, hands crossed on her chest as if waiting for last rites. "I didn't want to wake you up."

"Then quit sighing so loud outside my door."

"I'm your mother. I'm allowed to sigh when I'm worried about you. May I sit down?" Lydia scooted onto the edge of the mattress. "I'm not going to ask again what happened, but it's over. You need to put it behind you and go on from here, and not dwell on it."

"Don't make it sound like I'm going to kill myself."

"Sometimes people do foolish things for all sorts of reasons."

"There'd be no point in killing myself. I've already done something worse."

"I don't know if hearing that is a relief or not."

"Mom, I wasn't raped. I had sex, but I wasn't raped."

"Why are you protecting that boy?"

"I am not protecting Ridi. He didn't touch me. How many times do I have to tell you that it wasn't him?"

"Until you tell me who it was."

"I can't. I just can't. But it wasn't very nice."

Lydia caressed her daughter's forehead. "I'm sorry, sweetie."

"You shouldn't touch me. He made me feel so dirty afterward."

"You are not dirty. Not at all. You've learned a lesson the hard way." Lydia was relieved the girl wasn't crying, though perhaps she was simply empty of tears. "Are you going to be okay here alone?"

Athina sort of nodded.

"You sure?"

"I'm sure."

"Okay."

Lydia stood up.

"Are there a lot of people tonight?" the girl asked.

"Your grandmother has organized a crowd."

"What did you tell her?"

"Nothing, which is all you've told me."

"You don't have to be mean. What did you tell Ridi?"

"That it was all a big misunderstanding."

"Then he doesn't know that anything happened?"

"He won't unless you tell him." Lydia stopped in the doorway. "You don't have to work tonight, but we could use your help if you feel like being around people."

"Mom?"

"What?"

"What if I'm pregnant?"

Her daughter looked so stranded on the bed, a face too anxious for a young girl. Lydia thought her heart might break. "If you are, we'll deal with it."

She closed the door behind her.

• • •

ON THE TERRACE, LUKAS POURED Nick another shot of ouzo while Shirley dropped an ice cube into her wine. All that remained of the sunset was a thin red line. As it faded, the instant coolness of a Mediterranean evening enveloped them.

"You live in a beautiful spot," Nick remarked.

Shirley complained, "It's not very convenient to the village."

"She means she can't drink as much wine as she would like, because she has to drive home," her husband groused.

"Who just poured his third ouzo?"

Lukas ignored her, and told Nick, "It's the land my grandparents were allocated."

"Allocated?"

"During the Exchange. The government distributed what had been Turkish land to the Greeks who were returning."

"Rubbish!" Shirley spoke up. "You make it sound organized."

"It was organized."

"It was organized chaos! People grabbed what they could and declared it was theirs."

"My grandparents did not grab this land!"

"They didn't need to. No one else wanted it."

"Why not?" Nick asked.

"The well was contaminated," Lukas answered.

"Because the Turkish owner had thrown himself into it!" Shirley exclaimed.

"Why?"

"To ruin it for the new Greek owners."

"We don't know if that's true," Lukas disagreed.

"There are lots of ways he could have killed himself if he didn't want to move to Turkey. He didn't have to ruin the well."

"It was a confusing time and people assumed he had left," Lukas explained. "His body wasn't found for weeks and so it did ruin the well. But like him, almost nobody wanted to be exchanged. It's natural for people to like where they live. For the Greeks in Turkey, that's where they wanted to be, the Turks living here wanted to stay here, and in both places, the people were all friends. I mean Greeks and Turkish people. It was the two governments that didn't get along, not the people."

"Oh, you communists are always revising history!" Shirley responded. "It's like a disease with you. If they were all friends, why did he ruin the well for your grandparents?"

"He didn't know my grandparents."

"You know what I mean. Whoever got the property was going to be Greek. That's why he did it."

"What did they do for water?" Nick asked.

"They dug a new well," Lukas said.

"He makes it sound like it happened overnight. For two years, before they could afford a well, they carried water from almost three kilometers away."

"It's my story!"

"Well then, tell it right! Shall we go to dinner?"

"Dinner?" Nick asked.

Shirley touched his arm. "You never come for only a drink."

• • •

It was a short commute between the apartment and restaurant. Out the door, around the building, a few steps to the wharf. When she had to, Athina could make it in under an Olympic minute. That night, she wasn't trying to set any records, and paused before coming around the corner to listen to the clatter and clink of cutlery on dishes. She didn't entirely trust her mother that no one knew anything; it was the village, after all, and Lydia had dragged Apostolis down the hill in public view, which would have attracted its own gossipy attention. She half expected the restaurant to be filled with women pointing judgmental—or jealous—fingers at her the instant she appeared. Preparing herself, she took a deep breath, stepped around the corner, and ran smack into Ridi carrying an overloaded tray.

"Oh, I am so sorry!" she cried.

Ridi managed not to drop anything. "It's okay. Nothing broke, and look how much could broke. It's an aberration."

"Let me guess. 'Aberration' is one of your vocabulary words today?"

"It is not a good word?"

"It's a very smart word. *That's* the aberration. Are you still talking to me?"

"I always talk to you!"

"Why haven't you sent me another heart?"

"You want that I send it now?"

"No, not now! I shouldn't even be talking to you. My mother probably has spies watching us. Ridi?"

"What?"

"You never said what you will do when the restaurant closes. Will you stay for the winter?"

"I stay where you stay."

"My mom wants me to go to Australia."

"Australia?"

"Or Germany. I have relatives in both places. I haven't said if I will go or not. Uh oh, she's watching us. She claims she can read lips."

"She can't read my lips."

"Why not?"

"Because I speak with an accent."

"You're funny, Ridi, but I don't think it matters if you have an accent. I actually think she can read a person's mind. She's spooky that way. I better go inside."

"Wait."

"What?"

"I rape you."

"You rape me?"

"If you need a father, I rape you."

It took Athina a moment to realize what he meant. "You mean, if I'm pregnant? You will be the father? I can't believe you said that. That is the most incredibly beautiful thing anyone has ever offered to do for me."

"I don't know what he's offered to do," Lydia said, approaching them, "but at least three tables haven't been served, and—"

"I brought Superman!"

Shirley's shout interrupted her.

"And Mum needs her wine," Lydia added, watching her mother, with Nick in tow, join a table where a small party was already underway. The bright chatter paused as Shirley bussed checks. "Everybody introduce themselves. Nick is a writer."

"Published?" someone asked.

"Not yet."

"Another one," a man grumped.

Lydia went up to their table. "I've already told Ridi to bring your wine, Mum, so you don't have to shout at him." She turned to Nick. "What will you have?"

"An ouzo."

"Ice and water?"

"One ice, no water."

"Ridi," she said when he appeared with Shirley's wine, "an ouzo for Superman. And bring some ice."

He told her, "My name is Nick."

"Not Superman?"

"Definitely Nick."

"Got it. Are you going to eat something, Definitely Nick?"

"Of course he's going to eat something," said Shirley, "but he needs his ouzo first."

"It's on its way. Are you ready to order?"

"You haven't given me a chance to look at the menu," her mother complained.

"It hasn't changed in two years, Mum."

"Well, maybe I have!"

Lydia sighed. "I'll be back to take your order."

The others at the table—all expatriates who had recast themselves as artists, photographers, authors, whatever they weren't before—returned to their lively conversation while carafes of wine and platters of food were passed around for everyone to share. From her end of the table, Shirley recounted in larger-than-life details the fire that nearly destroyed their house, and received mumbled condolences for the lost trees. "Oh, well, there's no use crying over them!" she said, though everyone knew that she had shed ample tears.

On his boat, Stavros finished tuning his bouzouki, and lifted a glass. "*Styn eyeia mas!*" he toasted everyone in earshot. To our health! He knocked back his ouzo and set his glass aside.

Along the wharf, the crowd grew attentive. Two of Lydia's customers scooted over to Vassoula's to be closer to the music. Stavros launched into familiar crowd pleasers—*Zorba's Dance* and *Never on Sunday*—which always inspired a few tourists to leap up, form a line, and snake their way through the tables, aspiring to an unfamiliar sensuality. Stavros knew that he had to satisfy that expectation before playing his preferred songs with their discordant riffs and irregular rhythms that traveled with such clarity over the water that they might have been heard on the close shores of Turkey. Certainly some of the music had originated there. Most conversations fell silent under his spell, and those that didn't sounded like squawking seagulls—an appropriate chorus for the fisherman's plaintive ballads. During an especially romantic song, Nick glanced next door into Vassoula's Bar, and saw Takis looking back at him. They would definitely hook up that night.

Shirley's table lowered its collective voice but it hardly fell silent. Political, traveled, and confident, their conversation hummed with the adventures—and the self-satisfaction—of their far-flung lives. All were repeat visitors to Vourvoulos. Some had discovered it decades earlier and happily continued eons-old rants. Nick, largely ignored, observed the port's goings-on. Anyone coming for dinner had to pass a gauntlet of touts boasting their restaurant's specialties before reaching Lydia's, if they made it that far. She fumed every time Vassoula suckered couples, saying in her throaty voice, "I have a romantic spot for you" while pulling out chairs in a welcoming move that was really a trap. If looks could kill, Lydia would have been a serial killer with one repeat victim. Meanwhile the young waiter who didn't know caffeine from café couldn't stop mooning over Athina, yet she couldn't decide if she wanted to be near him or keep her distance.

Eventually Lukas, who had preferred eating with his fishermen friends over his wife's international collection, came to peel Shirley away. He apologized that he was tired and looked it. He had lost what he had been certain would outlive him. That lesson in mortality's fickleness weighed on him as heavy as Sisyphus's stone. As they retreated along the port, Shirley pulled his arm over her shoulders, encouraging him to let her share the stone's heft.

They had been lucky, it was agreed, while someone muttered it wasn't much luck to lose their prized trees—he had been there to witness the first one planted over forty years ago. Had they been a target or was the fire happenstance? Or was their property simply on the path to the fuel tank? The inevitable questions mulled over earlier still couldn't be answered. "Well, talking about fires, it makes me nervous to be so close to that damn fuel tank!" one man remarked, and that was the cue for everyone to leave.

Diners all along the wharf had already started bidding their *kali niktas* and *efharistos*, wandering off to find their rooms in the maze of relentlessly uphill streets. Only Vassoula's Bar had customers who stayed on. It was clear that Takis wouldn't get away any time soon. Not keen on a smoky bar scene, Nick decided to stay put and finish his wine. He opened his phone, logged on, and went into encryption mode. He had wanted to ask more about Father Alexis at some point in the evening, but it would have been awkward. So he wrote:

SUBJ: ALEXIS, first name unknown. Vourvoulos village priest. Request any background info.

Lydia stepped onto the porch and surveyed her empty tables. There was only Nick sending a message on his phone. The moon, perched behind the fuel tank, stretched its shadow almost across the harbor. She sighed at the impotency of her situation. Captain Tsounis's assessment of the tank's state of repair made it risky on its own, and only made things easier for an arsonist to succeed; yet with the collapsed economy, the solution—a new tank—was a non-starter until the old tank failed catastrophically. She wouldn't give up the fight but had to reassess the battlefield.

Athina stuck her head out the door. "Why don't you go to bed, Mom?"

"Someone might still come."

"I know that hope springs eternal, but I don't think so tonight."

"Then I'll help you finish up."

"You look more tired than I feel. Go to bed."

Lydia was tired, and bed sounded so nice. She wanted to call it quits: quits to that distressing day, and quits to the restaurant, too. The returns had never been worth the exhausting effort. "Do you promise to come directly home when you're finished?" she asked.

"I think I *am* home. I still live upstairs, right?"

"I don't think it's a good idea for you to go out tonight."

"I'm planning on washing dishes, Mom, not going out."

Washing dishes has never stopped you before, Lydia wanted to say, but restrained herself, realizing that her daughter wasn't being her usual rebellious self. "I don't want him spending the night here again," she said about Ridi, who had started collecting the tablecloths.

"He only stayed last night because of the storm. Now go to bed. And please don't leave my light on. It's a waste of money and I'm not a little girl anymore."

"You're my little girl."

"Can we please stop arguing?"

"We're not arguing. If I stay up, it won't be to wait for you. I'm tired but not sleepy."

"Put your head on the pillow and see what happens."

Lydia laughed softly. "How many times have I said that to you?"

"At least a zillion."

"You're right. I should try the pillow trick. Goodnight."

Lydia, pecking her daughter's cheek, noticed Nick waving his glass to get someone's attention. "I'll be right there!" she called to him.

She went into the kitchen, and reemerged with a bottle of wine and a second glass.

Athina frowned at her. "I thought you were going to bed."

"A glass of wine will help me fall asleep faster than a pillow."

"You never give *me* that advice."

"I wouldn't be a very good mother if I did."

Lydia slipped into a chair at Nick's table. "Do you mind if I join you?"

"Of course not."

She filled their glasses. "Cheers."

"Cheers."

They clinked glasses.

"How is your book coming along?"

"I'm still getting ideas."

"I'm sure you heard some colorful stories tonight."

"It was a lively crowd, that's for sure."

"Mum's been collecting her friends for years. I couldn't have stayed open without them. Not with the crisis, and not after she moved in next door." Lydia nodded in Vassoula's direction, who was laughing it up at her bar with a group of rowdy drinkers.

"What do you mean?"

"Usually she stands out front and no one can get past her. It's like she drags them in with a big fish net."

"Or fishnet stockings."

"So you've noticed?"

"She's hard to miss."

"If I were sexy in her way, maybe I'd flaunt it, too, especially if it made the difference between staying in business or not, but I'm not."

"Everybody is sexy in their own way."

"Thanks if that was a compliment, but I meant I'm not staying in business. I'm closing the restaurant."

"Permanently?"

"Yes, permanently. Some weeks, if I add up all my customers, I barely have a full house."

"You barely have a house at all," Nick remarked. "At least no tables inside. Could you expand the porch to create a real room?"

"You can't build anything new in the port," she answered. "You can renovate but you can't construct."

A burst of Vassoula's throaty laughter came from next door.

"If I had her place, I could make it really something," Lydia said. "Not just a bar with a deep fryer."

Nick's expression froze. It had been a deep fryer that scarred his back, and the mention of one was unexpected.

"Did I say something?" Lydia asked.

Nick shook off his thoughts. "No. I was thinking about something. Why isn't she as worried about a fire as you are? She'll be burned out, too."

"Maybe for the same reason I sometimes wish this place *would* burn down. Insurance money. Who buys used kitchen equipment in this economy?"

"Sounds like you have a motive to start a fire yourself."

"A lot of people are in the same bad situation. Except her. When the weather knocks the power out, she can rely on her generator to stay open. With free fuel, she can afford to."

"I can guess why it's free," Nick said, recalling the bare-chested captain closing the door behind Vassoula two nights earlier.

"If your guess is tall, dark, and handsome, you're right, and you should put *that* in your book. Meanwhile, I'm putting myself in bed. Goodnight."

"Goodnight."

Lydia disappeared around the back of the building. Moments later a light came on upstairs. Next door, the crowd had thinned, but not enough to suit Nick's mood. He decided to stay put and check the news on his phone.

• • •

RIDI STACKED THE LAST TABLECLOTHS in the cupboard and locked it. Nothing else needed to be done outside. Wiping down the stove, Athina had her back to the door when he came into the kitchen. "Can I help?"

"*Ah!*" she cried out, startled.

"I'm sorry to scare you."

"I didn't hear you. I was listening to Stavros's music. He plays so beautifully."

"Did you see how everybody goes to Vassoula's when he starts his music?" Ridi asked.

"Not everybody. Two tables."

"Tomorrow, they go first to Vassoula and not come here. Why not make his music come here?"

"We can't make his music come here. He plays on his boat."

"He can move his boat, yes?"

"He always docks at that spot."

"Then make him free dinner if he plays first."

"First?"

"Before dinner. He brings more people who stay for dinner. I already make a name for the program."

"The program?"

"If you name a program, more people come, and then more people stay for dinner. Maybe twenty percent more. I make the calculations. You want to know my name for it?"

"Of course!"

"Cocktail Serenade."

"Serenade? That's a funny word to use."

"Funny?"

"Not everybody learns a word like serenade."

"It is almost the same in Albanian. *Serenate.* It is only for the romantic songs."

"I know what it means."

"Cocktail Serenade. I make the name for you."

"You are so sweet, Ridi, when I don't deserve it."

"Why you don't deserve it?"

"I just don't."

"You don't like my idea?"

"I think it's a wonderful idea. You should tell my mother."

"She won't listen to me. I am Albanian. She stupid think I am!"

Athina laughed. "She stupid think you are?"

"Me Albanian stupid I!"

"You're making a joke, I hope."

"No kidding! You too stupid too!"

Then Athina was sure of his joke, and laughed so hard she had to wipe tears from her eyes. "Stop it!" she pleaded, though in fact, after a day of real tears, it felt good to be laughing again. "You always have good ideas, don't you, Ridi? Cocktail Serenade. It's such a great idea."

"I have so many ideas. More than I can describe because I don't know enough Greek words. I practice words." He pulled from his pocket that day's vocabulary list, only intending to display it, not expecting Athina to snatch it from his fingers.

"What words are you practicing today?"

Shameful, she read.

Aberration.

Forgiveness.

Faithful.

Forever.

If she had to choose words for that day, those would be hers, too; and she realized, Ridi had his own guilt, his own remorse, his own need for forgiveness. Their self-recrimination was equally shared. Both had done something unwonted, driven by passions stirred up by the other. "You're not stupid at all," she said. "Not with all your practice words."

"Maybe stupid only about you."

"Stupid about me?"

"Stupid in love. I am stupid in love with you."

"Me too," Athina said. "I'm stupid in love with you."

Stavros's music, every note a serenade, swelled romantically as they kissed.

◆ ◆ ◆

LYDIA FRETTED UPSTAIRS. SHE HAD been listening to the sounds coming from the restaurant's kitchen—clanging pots, running water, a muttered conversation—but suddenly all that stopped. It made her suspicious of what was happening. She wasn't feeling especially trustful of anyone on any account; certainly not her daughter, who had proven herself capable of poor judgment; nor Ridi, only that morning a rape suspect, now simply another lustful guy. He might not have been part of whatever took place the night before, but Lydia didn't doubt that he shared the same culpable desires. She tread heavily across the living room floor, wanting to convey her uneasy wakefulness to her daughter, even though she knew that the headstrong girl would ignore her. Athina would do what she wanted, despite how doing what she wanted the night before had ended in an experience so disappointing that it would haunt her forever.

Lydia stopped in the middle of the room and looked around. She had new eyes for it, though nothing had changed—the same clutter on the coffee table, dishes in the drying rack, an ironing board that hadn't been put away for weeks. Yet the last twenty-four hours had changed the lives of everyone who lived there. Her daughter had crossed a line. It was melodramatic to think that overnight Athina had become a woman because she lost her virginity. Womanhood was a lot more complicated than that. Still, Lydia couldn't reconcile herself to the notion that her little girl had grown up, or almost—and went back down the hall to turn on her daughter's bedside lamp.

Restless, she wandered onto the balcony. From down the wharf came Stavros's longing notes. She wasn't alone listening to his village serenade. His trebling fingers stoked many a woman's desire—those who'd had him and those who wished they had—and all listened to him, pressing a clandestine ear to a window, muting a favorite soap opera, straining to hear over a husband's snore. Lydia remembered when he had actually sung that particular song to her, its lyrics the poetry of life, and his voice, like his bronzed skin, was rough, textured, and tender, too.

Suddenly, he *was* singing the song—her song and her lyrics. She could hear the village grow still quieter. Every woman listening claimed that song to be hers, but Lydia needed no convincing that Stavros had sensed her tough day and played it for her. She needed that song. She needed to feel the generosity of love. For the only time that day, Lydia didn't fight back tears, instead letting them roll down her cheeks and drip onto her blouse.

Stavros's song ended. Across the village, shutters squeaked as they were closed. Lydia dried her eyes and went inside, glad no one was there to see that she'd been crying. On her way to bed, she stopped in Athina's bedroom and turned off her little girl's light.

• • •

THE KISS TAKING PLACE INSIDE the kitchen reminded Nick of his own amorous notions. Next door, Takis was serving drinks to a handful of hangers-on, and he decided to try to spring him for the night. Predictably, Vassoula had perched herself at the door to lure the last stragglers inside for a nightcap.

"You have decided the party is here?" she asked as Nick came up.

"I wasn't invited to the one next door."

As if sensing their stares, Ridi switched off the kitchen light.

"He is a beautiful boy," Vassoula remarked. "I think you notice such things."

"I do."

"Do you notice that she is beautiful, too?"

"I notice everybody."

"Including Vassoula?"

"Definitely including Vassoula."

He slipped past her and went inside.

The air was stale. The room, crowded all evening, still had traces of sweat and cigarette breath. The paunchy Russian, pouring from a bottle at his elbow, smacked the stubby glass on the bar for his pinballer friend, who stayed at the machine playing his game. Takis was hanging glasses over the bar by their stems when Nick slipped onto the stool in front of him. "I wondered when you were going to come over."

"Is it still nightcap hour?"

"It sure is. What do you want?"

"You. On the rocks, or anywhere you suggest. When can you leave tonight?"

"As soon as you finish your drink."

"Then pour it short."

Takis did, and handed it to him. "What did my sister want?"

"Me. But she didn't say on the rocks. I don't think it mattered where."

"I told you, she's a whore."

"And I was beginning to feel special."

"Don't let her bother you."

"She doesn't bother me. She doesn't strike me as your sister, either."

"We're not brother and sister by birth. We were both adopted."

Nick drained his glass. "I'm finished. Let's go find those rocks."

"Okay, folks," Takis addressed everyone in the room. "Drink up, pay up, and be on your merry way!"

Vassoula appeared in the doorway. Looking at Nick, she said, "I'll stay open, if anyone wants another round."

"That's our cue to leave," Takis said.

Vassoula stood sideways in the door.

They had to squeeze past her to get out. She put a hand on Nick's chest to stop him. "You prefer my brother's asshole to me?"

"Let him go," Takis told her.

She dropped her hand.

Nick stepped around her.

"*Pousti!*" she said, and spat on the ground. Faggots!

• • •

NICK POURED THE LAST OF the wine into Takis's glass. On his terrace in patio chairs, with a hint of honeysuckle from an overhead arbor, they listened to every warbling note that Stavros plucked on his bouzouki down in the port. The moon had disappeared, leaving the Milky Way to scatter its stars across the inky sky.

"So, that's not much detail about Afghanistan," Takis said, continuing a conversation. "What did you do most of the time?"

"Duck."

"Duck?"

"Not the quacking type. Duck, as in run and hide. And set fires."

"Set fires?"

"Sometimes we set them to force the bad guys out of buildings and into the open. Eventually, it made them mix more with the civilians, so we were smoking them out, too. I saw kids get shot. I couldn't do that again, not voluntarily, and it would have been voluntary if I reenlisted knowing that's what I'd be doing. That's the second reason I didn't reenlist."

"What was the first?"

"I wanted to live long enough to meet someone like you." He pulled Takis into a kiss.

"For an old guy, you're a romantic," Takis murmured.

"Old guy? What's old about thirty-four?"

"Twelve years on me. Don't worry, I like older guys."

Stavros finished his song. "That was really beautiful," Nick said. "I'm surprised the whole village doesn't break into applause."

"His music is the only thing that I miss from here."

"You don't miss this?" Nick opened his arms to the red-tiled roofs spilling down the hill. "Most people would love to live in such a charming place."

"Which is full of not-so-charming gossips."

"What about the stars at night?"

"We have stars in Melbourne."

"And the sea?"

"We have a huge bay."

"It's not the same as the Mediterranean. Besides, it's in a city."

"You don't like cities?"

"I don't like city beaches. I swim at them when I'm forced to, but for me, this place is special." He pulled Takis to him, and while they kissed, Stavros started playing bouzouki again. "Do you want to go inside or have a splash more wine?" Nick asked.

"Let's stay out a few more minutes. It's never this romantic in Melbourne."

"I'll get the wine."

Nick retrieved a bottle from the refrigerator and uncorked it. On his way back out, he looked in a mirror to check the scars concealed by his beard. The burning oil that ruined his back had splashed his face, too, and he wished he hadn't trimmed his beard so short that morning. The scars had turned bright pink despite sunblock. His back, too, had sunburned while swimming. The scars were bad enough without the sun to exaggerating them. Not for the first time, Nick contemplated the gods' eternal unfairness as he stepped onto the terrace.

Coming outside, he refilled their glasses and said, "Even if you hate this place, I'm glad you came back."

They touched glasses.

"Your sister must be glad you came back, too, and to help her for a year. That's a long time."

"The truth is, most of the time I don't really like her. Sometimes I even hate her. Still, what could I do after Omar disappeared?"

"I thought he committed suicide."

"He drowned himself. His boat was found but not his body."

"That's tough on everybody, not to have real closure," Nick said, thinking: a missing body is more than a little suspicious in suicide cases.

"Vassoula could have handled tough. She'd always been tough. She watched out for me in the orphanage. Here, too. Kids picked on us because we were adopted. If you can't have kids, something is wrong with you, probably morally. Something is wrong with the kids, too, or why would they be up for adoption?"

"Why were you?"

"Why are most kids? Teenage pregnancy. My mother wasn't allowed to keep me. It was too shameful to have a bastard."

"At least you weren't abandoned."

"Vassoula was. They guessed she was two years old when someone left her outside the orphanage."

"How old were when you were adopted?"

"I was eight. Vassoula fourteen."

"That's old, isn't it? Especially fourteen."

"We'd been farmed out on our own a couple of times, but never really adopted. Only experimented with for a few months, then brought back."

"Experimented with?"

"People who thought they wanted to be parents, and then realized they didn't really like kids, or more than once having the ulterior motive of hoping to have sex with us eventually. When eventually came—and it did for both of us—we both fought it off and got sent back to the orphanage. When the staff started doing the same stuff in the orphanage, Vassoula protected me better than she managed for herself. We were already calling ourselves brother and sister when our parents showed up looking for a son and picked me. The staff convinced them to take Vassoula as well. They wanted to be rid of her and told them we were inseparable.

"It worked. Our parents took us both. We used to joke that they got two slaves for the price of one, because that's all they wanted: workers. They were getting older and had no kids to take care of them, which is how it's supposed to happen in a village. Our mother was injured in a car accident that made it impossible for her to have children, which made her undesirable as a wife, and our father had been caught playing around with someone on the beach. They were forced into an arranged marriage."

Nick chuckled. "Playing around on the beach? I didn't know good Greek girls did that."

"It wasn't a girl. It was a guy, and his parents married him off to stop the obvious rumors. Since Zeeta—that's our mother—couldn't have children, there would always be a plausible excuse for their childless marriage. Any excuse to cover up his homosexuality."

"So your father is gay, too? Is that nice, or weird, or don't you talk about it?"

"He's dead."

"Dead?"

"There was a fire at the house. Both our parents were killed."

"A fire?" Nick was suddenly very interested.

"There was a leak from a gas bottle for cooking. My father walked in smoking a cigarette and the whole place blew up."

"That's terrible. When did that happen?"

"Three years ago."

"Did you both know the other was gay?"

"He never would have used that word for himself."

"But you knew?"

"I'd grown up hearing snide remarks about him, and more than once had to go out with girls to prove to my friends that I wasn't like him. I always knew I was gay, even if I didn't know the word, and doing it with girls didn't change that. But I didn't know what guys really did. So I followed him, four times, always on a Sunday when my mother was at church, and I'm sure they were praying for different things. It was no mystery where guys went for sex, only supposedly a secret who did. Out past Poustis Point."

"Queer Point?" Nick translated.

"It's what people call it. I stayed up in the hills where he wouldn't see me, and followed him as he walked way down the beach. With binoculars, it was easy to watch him. Each time, he stood by the same rock, or if the waves weren't splashing too high, he sat on it. It was his spot. I could see a couple of other guys had their spots, too, but I didn't recognize them. They came from other villages. He waited for guys to come by, and when one stopped, they'd duck behind the rocks. They never took long to do it. Afterward, usually my father smoked a cigarette while the other guy went away, sometimes running because he was so ashamed of what they had just done. He never talked to me about it, even when he must have known that I was gay, too. He never stopped my mother from washing out my mouth with soap when, too young to know what I was saying, I came home repeating what someone said my father had been seen doing.

"That fourth Sunday, after his trick ran off, I decided to confront him. As soon as he finished his cigarette and started for home, I ran as hard as I could through the hills, and dropped into a cove just as he came around the rocks. We stood so close I smelled his cigarette breath. He noticed the binoculars hanging around my neck and knew instantly the situation. He laughed a little and asked me, 'Isn't it late in the season for bird watching?' I told him I wasn't watching birds, and he said he could imagine what I *was* watching. He wanted to know why. I told him he had never been honest with me, and *I* wanted to know why. He said he didn't want to encourage me. He wanted me to be happier than him and hoped I'd outgrow it. He had never gotten over being gay, so I asked why he thought it would be different for me. He said no one had prayed for him, and he prayed for me every time he left the beach. He prayed I wouldn't end up doing the same thing. Then he told me that my mother blamed him for my being gay."

"She knew?" Nick asked. "Or had guessed?"

"I think people always know, especially parents, they just deny it. She thought my father corrupted me."

"She thought he had sex with you?"

"She couldn't imagine that something so unnatural could come naturally. I told him, 'She must hate you.' 'Your mother never loved me,' he admitted, and kept on walking. I watched until he disappeared around the headland. Then I went and sat on his rock."

"That's quite a coming out story," Nick said.

"Yeah. Poor guy. He got stuck forever on a tiny homophobic island. At least I had the chance to escape to Melbourne."

A gull cried overhead, a sheep bell tinkled, a distant ferry blew its deep horn. Nick set his wine glass on the ground and pulled the young man into an embrace. They kissed, working at unbuttoning each other's shirt without letting their lips come apart, and felt the cool night air on their shoulders when they pressed their bare chests together.

"Let's go inside," Nick murmured.

They did, stumbling to the bed where they kicked off their shoes before sinking onto the mattress. Grappling with belt buckles, they pulled of the other's clothes, until Takis only had on his socks. Nick put his legs over his shoulders to peel them off, and then teasing with his tongue, closed his lips on his cock. Takis moaned with pleasure, but pulled Nick off him. "Let's make it last" he said.

They did, kissing and touching everywhere except Nick's back, which he kept turned away. "I want to see your back," Takis finally said.

"Nobody sees my back."

"I did last night."

"Not in its full glory."

"Do you think a few scars are going to put me off?"

"They might."

"I've already felt them. Turn over."

Reluctantly, he let Takis nudge him onto his belly.

"What happened to you?"

"Burning oil."

"Burning oil?"

"Like what they used to pour over castle walls on invaders. Seen enough?"

"No. Were you in a fire?"

"I told you, I was an invader."

"Is that why you have a thing about fires?"

"I didn't know I had a thing about fires." Nick tried to roll back over.

Takis stopped him by straddling him.

"What are you doing?"

He gripped Nick's hands to stretch out his arms and hold him down, and bent to kiss his shoulders. Nick tried to buck him off, but Takis rode him, and dragged his tongue down the slick trails left by the burning oil. Never had Nick imagined his ruined back to be erotic, yet he had never been so aroused. He fumbled in the bedside table, and with a backhanded flip, tossed Takis a condom.

CHAPTER EIGHT

A GLOOMY DAWN BROKE OVER the channel. Dense blue fog obscured Turkey's close hills. High waves, pushed by north winds, crashed on the shore; and the water, retreating through the pebbles, sounded like thousands of glass bottles shattering all at once. It was deafening, and brisker than Ridi expected; he wished he owned a heavier coat as he made his way down the beach, working the tips of his shoes into the pebbles to kick aside the larger ones. He was in search of jewels for Athina's crown, and the smallest pebbles naturally worked their way the deepest. The colorful array, spewed from the island's volcano millions of years ago, surprised him. He uncovered green, orange, and red pebbles—and even a couple blue enough to pass for lapis. To make sure they would shine up nicely when he oiled them, he wetted each one in his mouth, tasting the salty sea that had worn them smooth over many thousands of years.

So preoccupied was he with his search that he didn't see the rubber raft emerge from the fog riding the swells until its passengers started screaming as it sank. The captain had slashed one side, making their craft unseaworthy to guarantee that they would not be turned back, but he cut it too soon. The heavy surf flipped the raft over, tossing into the sea its load of five men and a woman.

Ridi didn't think about the fact that he was a poor swimmer and ran into the water to help them. He paddled furiously, struggling to stay atop the incoming waves that swamped him. By the time he reached the flailing woman, he needed rescuing as much as she; and they both nearly drowned when she clung to his neck and inadvertently pushed him underwater. He pried himself loose and kicked to the surface. Gulping air, he heard a loud, booming voice. At first he thought it might be one of the men who had gone overboard with the woman, but then the Coast Guard cutter emerged from the fog.

The crew tossed them life preservers. Ridi grabbed one and shoved it at the woman, who, reaching for it, took a wave in the face and went under. When she didn't reappear, he let go the preserver and dove underwater, throwing out his arms and legs hoping to find her by touching her, before he was forced to surface for air. The life preserver had floated away and he was swimming for it when something bumped his leg. He reached down and pulled the unconscious woman to the surface. She was dead weight, and as drained as he was, he could barely keep her face above water.

Aboard the cutter, a guardswoman, assessing Ridi's distress, stripped off her boots and jacket and dove overboard. With a few strong strokes she made it to them, and slipped an arm around the woman to keep her head out of the water. Another life preserver landed within reach, and she made sure Ridi had a firm hold on it while she propped the woman's head on it. She signaled to be hauled in and slowly they were drawn to the cutter. A harness dropped over the side, and the guardsman slipped it around the unconscious woman. She was dangling over their heads when a second harness splashed next to them. Seconds later Ridi was hoisted onto the deck.

Without bothering to remove the harness, a guardsman started pumping on the unconscious woman's chest. When she didn't respond, he pinched her nose and blew hard into her mouth. Still no response, so he pressed all his weight on her chest, forcing out seawater. Finally she choked and spewed out seawater. The guardsman rolled her on her side to drain her of more.

Ridi, leaning against the deckhouse, finally managed to stop coughing up his own share of the Mediterranean, and stepped over to look at the woman for whom he'd almost lost his life. She's young, he was thinking, when her eyes fluttered open. It took them a moment to focus, but when they did, they widened in astonishment just as she was lifted onto a stretcher and an oxygen mask slipped over her face. She tried to say something, and repeated it more urgently when the guardsmen picked up the stretcher.

"Wait," Ridi said. "She wants to say something."

They paused and lifted her mask.

"Ridi?" she asked, her voice weak.

Had she said his name?

He stepped closer to peer at her. Astonished, he said, "Jura?"

"It's me, Ridi."

A guardsman replaced her mask before they carried her below.

• • •

NICK WOKE IN THE SAME state he had fallen asleep: in love with the beautiful young man in bed next to him; or if too soon to call it love, he was certainly enamored with him. They had played much of the night before finally nodding off. Now it was mid-morning, judging by the sunlight sneaking through the shutters. Takis stirred.

Nick draped an arm over him, prodding him to wake up.

"Again?"

"Why not?"

"Wait."

Takis slipped into the bathroom and peed. He came back, his breath smelling like mint toothpaste, and Nick made his own bathroom run before returning to bed for a morning romp. They had just collapsed into each other's arms when a key rattled in the door and swung open.

"What the fuck!" Nick blurted, and pulled the sheet over them.

Athina took in the situation. "Oh cool!" she said. "You're still here and you're doing it!"

Takis told her, "Get out of here."

"Oh shut up, Takis. Everybody knows you're queer."

"What are you doing here?" Nick asked.

"Cleaning your room, and I hope your toilet isn't too yucky."

"I thought you worked at your mom's restaurant."

"I have to have one job that pays in real money and not food, and yes, you can tip the maid. It's encouraged." Athina pulled her phone out of her bag and instantly started taking pictures. "But this is so cool! I've been posting a whole photo thing on what I find in hotel rooms."

"No!" the men cried in unison, and jumping out of bed, pulled the sheet over the girl's head.

Athina screamed with laughter. Inadvertently they knocked over a bedside table. Nick's travel wallet fell out of its drawer, spilling out his FBI badge.

Takis picked it up and gave Nick a curious look. "You work for the FBI?"

Nick laughed it off. "It's from the souvenir shop. You give them a picture and they make a fake ID. It's fun to show at parties."

Athina pulled the sheet off her head. "What are you talking about?"

"Nothing," Nick said, and snatched her phone.

"Hey, that's mine!"

"Trade you." He swapped it with Takis for his ID.

Takis started pressing keys on the phone.

Athina grabbed for it. "Wait! What are you doing? Don't mess it up, please!"

He handed it back. "I reset it to factory settings."

"You *what*? You deleted *everything*? All my *everything*?" On the verge of tears, she checked her phone, and glared at him. "You said that just to be mean."

"I deleted the pictures you took of us. If I missed one, I better not see it posted anywhere."

"Can you come back later to clean the room?" Nick asked.

"If you don't walk off with the outside key. Some people do, and then they blame me when their room's not cleaned."

"I didn't know there was an outside key."

"Everybody leaves one outside, usually over the door so little kids can't reach it. Goodbye, creep!" she aimed at Takis. "If you erased anything else, I'll post it that you're queer."

"According to you, everybody already knows."

"I'm the first eyewitness."

"*Figa apo etho!*" he said. Get out of here!

• • •

KOUFOS WAS NAKED, BATHING IN the sea, when the body floated up to him. He had never seen a dead man before. He had seen dead animals—birds in a field, a stinking goat carcass on the beach, cats run over on the road—so he instinctively knew that anything living could be killed; but he had no sense of death's certainty: not the many ways it could happen, nor the fatal sentence of longevity. He had no concept of years—or for that matter, old age—so for all he knew, people he recognized as old people could have been eons old, from the beginning of time old, not only seventy or eighty years old. What reason did he have to think that people didn't live forever unless an accident befell them, like a bird breaking its neck on a window or a bug crushed underfoot?

He dragged the dead man onto the pebbly beach and examined his face: colorless, eyes half open, jaw slackened. Always hungry, Koufos checked his pants pockets for food, and pulled out a sesame bar. He devoured it, ever attentive that the man, though dead, didn't somehow try to snatch it from him. The man's hands were already waterlogged, so Koufos had a hard time twisting off his ring, which he wanted to trade for a special dinner. Two of the pearly buttons on the man's silky red shirt were hanging only by threads, and he carefully removed it before pulling off the man's mustard-colored pants. He spread the wet clothes on wild rosemary bushes to dry.

He was curious about the man, especially the naked parts (the man wore no underwear) that he had never seen before except bending over trying to look at himself. Something primal made him want to touch him and something primal stopped him from doing it. So he didn't, and instead, sitting cross-legged on the pebbles, he pulled the man's head onto his lap. He put his hands on the man's shoulders—they were clammy from the sea—and kneaded them, pressing his fingers into their flesh. Looking at the body stretched out before him, Koufos had a new sense of himself. For the first time he saw a man naked from head to toe, and realized that this was every man's end—that death would be his end, too. Tears sprang from his eyes spontaneously, as did a soulful cry from his throat, mourning inevitable mortality. As his tears landed on the man's chest, he spread them across his shoulders and far down his belly, howling until his throat was raw.

The man had come from the sea. He had been a gift. Koufos's enlightenment was also a gift, though a sad one. He pulled the body back into the water, its joints already stiffened, and swam from shore tugging it along until he felt the swift, cold currents and let the man go.

Then Koufos swam back to collect his new clothes.

• • •

FATHER ALEXIS HAD A FITFUL night that was enduring well into the morning. He had a tough decision to make. Nick's wad of money sitting on the vestry's table tempted him as much as the Russian's Faustian promise; more, considering what it would let him do. Nick's offer for the Crowned Madonna—and he thought he was buying the forged one at that—would make it possible for the priest to buy his mother an apartment immediately. Otherwise it would be another year or two of his mother living in that oil-drenched graveyard longer than absolutely necessary.

Accepting Nick's offer would also mean crossing Vladimir Azarov, captain of the *Birch Runner* and indefatigable looter of Greek icons. When they met three years earlier in the village that reeked of pigs, the priest had assumed that Vladimir was merely another member of Russia's ruling criminal class who wanted to bequeath a splashy collection of art to the Hermitage Museum to atone for his earthly sins. He trolled through the Greek islands, collecting icons while leaving forgeries in his wake, not to build a memorial to himself but to his mother. His father, a director at a state-owned oil company, had met her on holiday in Greece, and lured her back to Saint Petersburg, promising it was the Paris of Russia. "Only if you squint," she said once she got there, and by the time she grew tired of squinting, she'd already given birth to young Vlad.

His father, a member of the Party, had grown accustomed to carousing and womanizing; habits which became all the more debauched when he became an owner of his newly privatized oil company. His parent's relationship turned hateful. His mother, trapped unless willing to abandon her son to return to Greece, sought solace in the religion she had been all-but-forced to abandon when she moved to godless Russia. She requisitioned a room in their palatial apartment where she created a private chapel filled with Greek icons, none of special value, and some made simply from photos she had glued to wood. As the walls filled up, her depression deepened and she rarely left it, often missing meals, and eventually absenting herself from her husband's obligatory business functions. It was in the chapel that Vladimir was sure to find his mother when he came home from school.

Then one day, she was gone.

She wasn't in her chapel. She wasn't anywhere, and from what they could determine, she had taken nothing with her. She simply vanished. Suicide was suggested, perhaps she had jumped from a bridge and been swept away, but Vladimir, only ten, was convinced his father had killed her. He went through the motions of reporting a missing person and contacting her relatives in Greece, but he never demonstrated a glimmer of hope that she might be found. On the first anniversary of her disappearance, he had carpenters dismantle her chapel. Vladimir never learned what happened to her many icons.

That much Father Alexis had learned about the Russian's motivations over the years, and likewise, the Russian had learned about the priest's ambition to buy his mother an apartment. They found it amusing that they both entered into their Faustian contract wanting to do something for their mothers. Unhappily, Vladimir's mother disappeared before her mark on his character had become wholly indelible. It was his brutish father's influence that saw him into manhood. Since he first appeared in Father Alexis's church, negotiating for a copy of Saint George slaying the dragon, the priest glimpsed something dark in his soul. He was wary of the Russian and didn't want to double-cross him. Yet how could he resist Nick's extravagant offer?

When the Russian had shown up looking for the icon of Saint George, he hadn't expected to find a priest already knocking off copies so exquisitely rendered that, with little extra effort, they would be indistinguishable from the originals. On the spot, he commissioned Father Alexis to make a perfect copy, including a convincing accumulation of dust. For that, Vladimir offered a handsome price and the priest embraced the challenge, perfecting skills he had never considered as a copy artist—front and center, mimicking dust buildup—and in three months he excelled in every respect. With mortars, he extracted tinctures from plants; used only brushes made from natural bristle; and scavenged old wood and rusty nails to stretch his canvases.

Eventually he challenged Vladimir to distinguish the original from his copy and placed them side by side on easels. Arms crossed over his belly, the Russian examined both paintings, stepping closer then back again, looking with his head tilted at assorted angles—and grunted. He circled them, examining their wood frames for any signs of recent tooling, and found none. He picked them up, angling them to catch the light. Each had the same sheen beneath a thin veneer of dust.

"Papoose! You are a masterpiece!" he exclaimed, and clapped the priest on his back, who cringed at the man's bastardization of his title, *Pappas*. "It is so perfect that now I take the original."

"The original?" Father Alexis feigned surprise, though he had always guessed Vladimir's true intention.

"Why not?"

"Not for the price you have offered."

That brought short the Russian's good humor. "We have a deal."

"For the copy."

"A painting is a painting."

"Then take the copy."

"I will ask you to paint many more icons. You will make so much money from Vladimir!"

"Not for what you are offering. I can sell enough cheap knockoffs and make twice as much money in half the time. And with no risk."

"Papoose! We will make a deal! No risk!"

When their negotiation concluded, each had a good deal; notwithstanding, of course, that the transaction was thievery, which bothered neither of them. A Russian borne of a miscreant culture and a priest in the Church: they were perfect comrades for a dishonorable venture. The possibility that what they were doing might land them in jail was never discussed.

And so their venture began.

Over the next three years, Father Alexis produced a dozen forgeries for the Russian. In that time, he was rotated two more times on the Church's rural circuit—where most young priests endured purgatory before ascending to a respectable parish—which had the unanticipated advantage of putting at his disposal new troves of icons to plunder. He made no effort to conceal that he copied them. On the contrary, he painted them in public view. Sometimes he had several underway of the same subject, all but his true forgery hastily finished for quick sales, which he used to repair irksome problems: broken steps, squeaky seats, drafty windows. He wanted no one grousing that he was making a profit for himself using Church resources, so he kept people happy with small gestures, retaining for himself only what the Russian paid for his true forgeries.

In Vourvoulos, the priest had another concern. The small church had few icons that interested the Russian, the Crowned Madonna being the most interesting, which is why Father Alexis delayed painting it as long as he could on the excuse it was the most difficult technically. Once Vladimir had the Madonna, the priest wondered how many more commissions he could expect while stuck on that miserable rock in a sardine-laden sea. No, he had to accept Nick's offer, there was no doubt about it. Somehow he would delay the Russian. Maybe he would simply be honest. The irony was that Vladimir wanted the original painting while Nick thought he was buying a copy, so in theory, Father Alexis could give each man what he expected to buy, except for the troublesome detail that the island's most renowned icon would be missing. He considered if any of his other Virgin Mary knockoffs-in-progress could be upgraded to a full-fledged forgery, but they were obvious copies: too facilely executed rather than attuned to every detail. He didn't have time to make another masterpiece. He briefly contemplated a to-hell-with-it strategy of selling them both and claiming that the original had been stolen—could he blame it on the deaf boy?—but that sounded like a Pandora's box he did not want to open.

An equally urgent question was how to keep the Russian from taking the Crowned Madonna that very day, when that was what Father Alexis had arranged for him to do? Vladimir could be coming up the hill that very minute! He panicked, until his eyes lit upon his painter's palette. Wet paint! He could put Vladimir off using it as an excuse and gain a couple of days to sort out a solution.

Hurriedly he swabbed more gold paint on the already gaudy frame. The icon deserved to be displayed far more beautifully, but the priest's notion was that the cheesier the frame, the more likely the trafficked painting would be overlooked by customs officials, dismissed as a copy, albeit a good one.

The Russian flung open the vestry door. "Papoose!" he cried, and pushed past him to stand in awe before the Crowned Madonna. "She *must* be the original," he finally murmured.

"She is," Father Alexis admitted.

"She will be the queen of my collection. From the first time I see this Mother of God, I see my mother. She is exactly my mother!"

"She must have been a beautiful woman," Father Alexis replied, as he did every time the Russian repeated himself; and not for the first time wondering how they each saw their own mother in the Crowned Madonna, when they themselves bore no resemblance whatsoever.

Unexpectedly, Vladimir burst into tears. He grabbed the icon off the easel and pressed his lips to it, not realizing the frame had wet paint.

Horrified, the priest wrestled it from him. "Let go! You'll ruin it! You have paint on your hands!"

The Russian looked at his hands. "It is not ready today?"

"I touched up the frame for you."

"You know I destroy your frames."

Father Alexis passed him a rag. "That's not the point. They get you through customs. Now I need to repaint the whole thing."

"I come later to take it."

"This paint needs two days to dry."

"Now that she is finished, I must have her."

"And risk ruining her? Besides, you have to put it in something—you can't just walk out of here carrying it—and for that, it needs to be completely dry."

Vladimir grunted. "Two days," he said, making it sound like a threat. He turned to leave, and that's when he noticed Nick's pile of banknotes on the table. "What is this?"

"Someone bought one of my copies," the priest replied, chagrined that he hadn't put the money out of sight. It would have been tantamount to accepting Nick's offer, so he left the money on the table, wishing the whole foul situation would simply go away.

The Russian looked at him suspiciously. "It's a big price for a copy."

"He's an American. He doesn't know what prices should be."

"You are lying. You sell *my* Mother of God!"

"He wants the copy, not the original. He offered a lot of money."

"And you give me what?"

"You get the original as soon as I paint another copy."

"Not in two days!" the Russian bellowed, and swept Nick's money onto the floor. From his own pocket, he pulled out a wad of bills secured by a rubber band and plopped it down. "I have paid for my painting. In two days, I take what is mine!"

Vladimir stormed out.

The priest's hand was shaking when he closed the door behind him.

• • •

NICK SET A TRAY WITH a coffeepot and mugs on the small table. The honeysuckle arbor was especially fragrant in the warming sun. Down in the port, a tour boat tooted its horn signaling its departure, while out to sea a small regatta raced past Bird Island.

"You must love waking up to this view," Takis said. His hair was still wet from the shower.

"I could get used to it." Nick chuckled while pouring coffee.

"What is it?" Takis asked.

"That was a pretty funny wake-up call this morning."

"Athina? She doesn't matter. I'm probably the only guy in the village who hasn't tried to fuck her, so she's okay with me."

"Who are you when you're not here?" Nick asked.

"I'm a techie. I wanted to do something in Australia other than work in a restaurant. If that's all I was going to do, why leave? Forgetting for the moment that I hate the place, and if I was leaving to meet guys, I could probably meet guys in Athens. But I wanted a real job, not a restaurant job, and I wanted to meet a guy who wasn't totally fucked up about sex—and that man probably doesn't exist in Greece, that's how fucked up this country is for gay men. If I wanted a job, I knew I needed a skill, and learned how to code. At least enough to get a job, and I did."

"That's great."

"If what happened to Omar hadn't happened, I would never have come back. It was just too terrible for Vassoula, and I knew nobody was helping her. Ironically, what happened to him sums up why I hate this place."

"Tell me."

"You have to remember that Omar was as handsome as Omar Sharif."

"Omar Sharif was Egyptian, not Turkish."

"It didn't matter. That's what the girls called him, and he did look like him."

Nick poured more coffee. "Now I'm really intrigued."

• • •

VASSOULA WOKE UP IN A lonely bed. It had been lonely since Omar disappeared. She couldn't bring herself to say died or killed himself because she hoped that, despite how gruesomely the skinheads had cut him, he would miraculously come back to her whole again. In that fantasy she envisioned handsome and dancing the *syrtaki* better than any Greek, a black stubble generously shadowing his cheeks—his cheeks that went missing.

Omar. He had given her a life when he came into hers. Unless she married, she was destined to remain her wretched mother's handmaiden; and Vassoula would have nothing to do with the local boys, certainly not enough to marry one. She was darker complected than the Vourvouliani, and the boys, starting in their teens, called her Gypsy bitch for not putting out. She was adopted, so they freely assigned to her any origin that they wanted, but Vassoula knew she wasn't Gypsy. She was Turkish. A nun at the orphanage disliked her for it, and wanted to be rid of her enough not to mention it to prospective parents. Secretly, Vassoula reveled in her Turkishness. She nurtured it because it nurtured her to know she was different from the people who treated her so harshly, abusing her verbally—and otherwise, as some did eventually, before she was liberated from the orphanage's form of incarceration to become a servant in another.

Ten years of mopping floors later, Omar arrived in Vourvoulos. Movie star handsome with dark moody eyes, clever, and Turkish;

she had conjured him many times, dreaming only of men like him when she gave pleasure to herself. Beyond that pleasure, she dreamt of a man to free her from servitude, not trade one enslaved situation for another. Instinctively, Omar understood that. His family, too, had suffered from discrimination for being Turkish, or certainly the consequences of it. Only after she moved in with him did he confess that his family had once lived on the island; an extended family, and prosperous when you added up all their land; land too rocky and scrubby for the Greeks to bother with, though their ancient ancestors had been the first to terrace it. It was those stony plots—sometimes no bigger than four strides long and two deep—that Omar's peasant ancestors had worked, finding them sufficiently fecund to sustain their families.

All that ended with the Exchange, when the diaspora Turks and Greeks were forced to trade places, overnight becoming refugees in their own countries. Omar's great grandparents left Vourvoulos with little more than their crying fifteen-year-old son—his grandfather—unable to understand why he had to lose all his friends, Greek and Turkish. Once back in Turkey, everyone knew, they knew they'd never recreate their village no matter how much they would miss it, but instead would flee to relatives if they knew their whereabouts, or be shuffled off to temporary camps—as was Omar's family—while a useless bureaucracy scrambled to do what little it could for the many tens of thousands like them. Omar's grandfather, having just wished his boyhood Greek friends a forever farewell, had to do the same to his Turkish mates only a few hours later when their boat made its landing in what still stood of Smyrna.

Though the fires that destroyed the legendary city had been put out, a charred smell hung heavily in the air. On the docks, hucksters and shysters descended on the refugees even as government agents shunted them into buses to take them to a camp—equally rife with hucksters and shysters. Thus began decades of poverty inflicted on Omar's family, starting before he was born. All his growing-up years, he heard reminisces of their lost island: its fresh air, azure sea, and wild lavender roses—a sharp contrast to their stuffy apartment in a shanty neighborhood of sprawling Istanbul.

Omar had simply appeared in Vourvoulos one day, not ten Greek words in his head, and soon became the curiosity of the village. Turks rarely visited the tiny village, and still fewer stayed for more than a night or two, but Omar rented a room for a month, letting his landlady know that he would likely keep it longer. He only did the usual things tourists do—hike in the hills, swim in the sea, learn the four-syllable Greek word for thanks—but that didn't stop rumors from spreading that he was trafficking drugs or might be a white slaver. Certainly, he was up to no good; no Turk ever had been. Omar, though, was undaunted. At once, he was enamored with the mythical lost island of his storied childhood, and equally glad to escape the grinding conditions back home. He had no intention of leaving.

Omar kept it a secret that his family had lived there for generations. If it were known, he worried it would only stir up fears that he had returned to reclaim property or seek revenge, when he wanted neither. He wanted the idyllic life described from afar, not hardscrabble Istanbul, which was becoming more unbearable under the growing power of intolerant imams. By age twenty-five, he'd made the decision not to spend the rest of his life kowtowing to men who dressed their women in sacks, forbade everyone simple pleasures, and governed through fear. Fending off his mother's relentless efforts to get him married, he waited tables in two restaurants, earning excellent tips because of his extraordinary good looks. By the time he was thirty, he had saved enough money that he wouldn't arrive in Greece a penniless refugee, but an immigrant able to sustain himself until he found a way to make a living. He'd gambled and he'd won.

The risks Omar could not have anticipated were the threats posed by Greece's internal turmoil, especially its Depression-era economy giving rise to a fascist insurgency. Or so Vassoula was mulling over that morning, after rousing herself from her lonely bed to sip coffee on the terrace, perched high over the village with a clear shot of the long beach stretching into the distance until it melded with the coastline. That view had once brought her such joy, not only for its beauty but for what it represented: her second escape, and the first into an unexpected freedom. Her first escape had been from the orphanage, the second from her adoptive servitude. She had escaped into

Omar's liberating arms, holding her on that terrace through long talks she had never imagined possible; and when they felt like making love outdoors, they did.

She could almost see him again, walking down that long beach, becoming a speck before turning back. He worked hard, he partied hard, he loved hard—and he needed time alone. He needed a time not to talk to anybody, though he talked to himself, gesticulating and working out whatever needed working out. He did that most mornings while other village men gathered in the *kafeneios* for their first coffee. Initially Vassoula was suspicious of Omar's need to be alone, and spied on him through the binoculars, watching him approach Poustis Point because it was there that her father loitered; and sometimes it was there where Omar turned back, but not always, not if he was having a particularly troubling conversation with himself. But never once did he disappear out of sight too long to be accused of her father's sort of sordid absence.

The morning when it happened, their lovemaking had been especially tender. Only the night before, they had decided to have a baby, and made love then, too. When Omar left for his walk, she felt a special longing—a worried hollowness—and took the binoculars from the cupboard. She knew his body language better than her own and easily spotted him.

Omar, distracted by the conversation with himself, approached Poustis Point. She saw the skinheads before he did. Three of them hovering in the rocks, conferring and planning their attack. *Turn back!* she wanted to shout. *Stop talking to yourself and look up!* But her voice would never carry that far.

She saw everything that happened.

She even knew what was said because Omar survived to repeat it.

"Do you have a cigarette?" a skinhead asked.

"I am sorry. I do not smoke."

"Maybe the problem is, your cigarettes are wet."

Vassoula saw Omar tip his head questioningly.

"I am sorry. I do not understand."

"Maybe you help your friends swim across."

"I do not swim here. I walk here."

"Did you hear that, guys? He walked here."

"Then he must've walked on water," a second skinhead scoffed. "With his accent, he wasn't born here."

The third added, "He's probably a Turkish cocksucker."

"Is that why you're out here? Hoping to get your cock sucked?"

"Probably by a refugee."

"Or do you suck theirs?"

The skinheads laughed.

Omar sensed he was in trouble. "I don't understand."

"Hear that guys? He doesn't understand. What can we do to make him understand?"

"I go home," he said, and pointed to the village. "My wife waits for me."

Vassoula saw him point. *Come back!* she was screaming inside.

"You should never have left home," sneered the first skinhead. "None of your filth should've."

"I go back now."

Omar turned and took a couple of steps.

"Not so fast," the first skinhead said. When Omar didn't stop, he barked, "Hey!"

Omar paused.

Just keep walking! Vassoula begged.

"I'm not finished with you."

Omar faced the skinhead. "My wife waits for me."

He turned away again.

The skinhead signaled, and his two pals ran up and grabbed him. Omar struggled to defend himself, but together they managed to wrench his arms behind him.

The first skinhead approached him, menacing him with a knife.

Vassoula, seeing it flash in the morning sun, was going mad. *Please God, no! No!*

He kicked at the skinhead, who laughed, and stepped around him and put the blade to his throat. "Please don't," Omar begged.

"Fucking. Faggot. Filth. Feeding the refugees then fucking them. There's probably some Arab greasing up his asshole waiting for you behind the rocks."

"My wife is waiting for me."

"Fucking bitch is going to wish you never came home."

Vassoula, through the binoculars, couldn't make out what happened next. She saw the skinhead flick his knife twice, each time tossing something to the seagulls on the beach. Then they released Omar and his hands instinctively covered his face. For a moment, she thought they had cut out his eyes; and later remembering that first thought, she would wonder if it might not have been more merciful than letting him see his own ruined face.

At that moment, though, she wasn't thinking of anything except saving Omar, and flew out of the house. "HELP! HELP! Omar's been stabbed! Help!" she never stopped crying as she flung herself down the village path. A dozen people trailed after her, looking past her wild hair to Omar stumbling toward them. For Vassoula, the blood seeping through his fingers glistened so bright red that the rest of the world turned gray.

They stopped, only feet apart. Vassoula could see they hadn't cut out his eyes, but what the skinheads had done would forever haunt them. Omar would never see anything the same again. He certainly would never be looked at in the same admiring way.

His eyes pleaded for help as he lowered his hands.

Hers expressed horror when he did.

His knees buckled and he collapsed.

Four men ran up and grabbed his arms and legs to haul him cumbersomely back to the village. Another two trotted alongside, stripped of their shirts that they pressed to his slain cheeks to stem the blood. Vassoula stumbled after them, too shocked by what she had seen to believe it possible; and yet there was Omar, being toted in front of her, the tagalong women ululating their distress as if he had already died. He wouldn't, not then. He would survive to live a freak's hell.

That morning, longing for Omar, anguish overwhelmed her. Only thirty years old and doomed to be in mourning for the rest of her life. She couldn't imagine anyone after Omar. When the skinheads cut away his cheeks, they cut out her heart, and when Omar committed suicide, he killed her, too. She sobbed, wanting the life that had been stolen from them, preferring to join him in death than endure a life without him.

The cats, risking her swift kicks, rubbed against Vassoula's legs to remind her that they wanted to be fed. She stomped her foot to scatter them and went back inside. Opening the kibble bag sent them into a zigzagging frenzy between her feet, and that time she did kick at them. "Go away!" she cried, and hurled kibble at them, which they dodged before darting around to scarf it down. "I hate you! God, I hate you!" she screamed while throwing more handfuls at them. Her laughter was seeded with madness as the animals cowered under the furniture to eat the pellets that rolled there.

Takis walked in and saw the kibble on the floor. "I see you fed the cats."

"They were hungry."

"They're always hungry in the morning."

"What did you eat for breakfast? Cock?"

"Don't start."

"You should never have gone to Australia. Look what it turned you into."

"I was always like this."

"You're going to end up just like father, hiding behind rocks to have sex."

"No I'm not. I'm going back to Australia where I don't have to hide behind rocks to have sex. Why did you hate him so much? Didn't you feel sorry for him at all?"

"He was pathetic. He settled for Zeeta because he'd been caught doing something with another man one time. He didn't try to explain it away as a youthful experiment or some drunken mistake. Or that he'd been seduced against his will. Over one incident, he settled for her, for a nothing life. What kind of man is that?"

"A gay man in Greece," Takis answered. "Most of them end up unhappily married. Sometimes you forget that he rescued us from the orphanage. They both did."

"I don't forget. I only wish they had been different parents."

He poured kibble into a bowl, which brought the cats running. "They were who they were."

"Neither one of them had a life, especially him, because of your kind of love."

"You're as bad as the rest," Takis said. "What kind of life could he have had? He was never going to have a *relationship* with a man."

"Is Superman the right man for you?"

"Yeah, Nick's my type, only he doesn't live in Melbourne."

"I didn't know there were types, only faggots."

"Okay, he *is* a faggot, if that's the word you want to use. He's also an FBI agent," Takis boasted.

"FBI?"

"The American police."

"I know what FBI is."

"So he's not a faggot in the way you think."

"He must be investigating the fires," Vassoula suggested. "Why else would he be here?"

"He says he's writing a book."

"Be careful what you say to him."

"What are you talking about?"

"He might try to make a connection to you. In fact, he might have come looking for you."

"Why?"

"Why do you think?"

• • •

By the time Nick ordered his breakfast at Lydia's, it was already brunch. While waiting for his food, he sipped coffee and eavesdropped on the conversation a couple of tables away between Apostolis, the village's part-time Everyman, and the Coast Guard captain. Occasionally a few words drifted his way: *drowned*, *saved her*, and *Albanian boy* chief among them. When Athina, not Ridi, brought his plate of runny beans and sausage, he realized that Ridi was probably the Albanian boy they were talking about.

"More coffee?" she asked.

"Never ask, just pour." He tipped his head in the direction of the two men. "It sounds like something happened."

"It's so horrible!"

"What is?"

"Five men drowned."

Athina told him how Ridi, on the beach to collect jewels for her crown, had witnessed a small raft scuttled too far from shore, and without a single thought for his own safety dove into the rough sea, managing to rescue the only woman, but apparently all the men drowned. "He's kind of a hero, isn't he?" she asked.

"He risked his life to save someone, and that definitely makes him a hero," Nick assured her. "Is he okay?"

"I think so."

The girl didn't sound confident. The young waiter had been shaken when he telephoned to say he couldn't come to work that morning. He was still shivering from the cold sea and shocked by the experience. "Isn't it horrible that people are so desperate?" Athina lamented. "Sometimes they even try to swim from Turkey and drown when they're almost here!"

She broke into tears and fled. Nick ate quickly, hoping for an opportunity to speak to the Coast Guard captain. It came when Apostolis's phone beeped. After checking his message, he said a hasty goodbye.

Nick leaned over to say, "*Yeia sas, Kyrios.*"

The man glanced up. "*Yeia sas.*"

"You are the captain of the Coast Guard here, is that right?"

"That's right."

"I saw you at the church a couple of nights ago."

"I recall you, too. Are you visiting for a few days?"

"I'm writing a novel."

"Set here in Vourvoulos?"

"It could be. I'm still working on my story. In fact, you might be able to help. Do you mind if I join you for a minute?"

Before the man could say anything, Nick was on his feet sticking out his hand. "Nick Damigos," he introduced himself.

"Captain Tsounis. Are you Greek?"

Nick slipped into a seat. "Greek American."

"You speak good Greek."

"My mother insisted that we speak it at home. Athina told me about the raft capsizing this morning."

The captain's expression turned grim. "It was a rough sea but we had it on the radar and thought it was going to be okay. Whoever was steering it knew what he was doing. We were more worried about a second raft and were headed for it when the first guy slashed his raft too soon. They do that so we can't send them back."

"Are they from the second raft?" Nick asked, pointing to the dock where young men smoked, kids ran up and down, and women spread clothing on the wall to dry.

Captain Tsounis shook his head. "No, the second raft made it to shore. We picked those people out of the water yesterday. If they get tossed overboard and don't drown, they don't have to walk to town. They get a bus."

"Lucky them."

"There's nothing lucky about them, and when they get to the camps, some are going to wish they had died. All you smell is shit. Shit everywhere."

"Can I ask you something about the fires?"

"Sure."

"I know that Lydia's map shows the fires coming closer, but why's it assumed the whole village is the target? Why not something more specific?"

"Like what?"

"The Coast Guard station," Nick suggested.

"We haven't had any direct threats."

"You rescue refugees. Some people would prefer that you let them drown."

"Why would they make a game of it?"

"What's your theory why someone would want to burn down the village?"

"No one has listened to my theories in the past," Captain Tsounis answered, clearly bitter.

"About the eleven fires?" Nick probed.

"No. The Takis Fire."

"The Takis Fire?"

"Named for the kid who works next door. Takis Vatis. Both his parents were killed in it."

"That sounds like it might be a good story for a book," Nick said.

"If you write murder mysteries, it'd be one hell of a story," the captain agreed. "The day it happened, Takis took home a spare bottle of cooking gas. It leaked, and when his father walked in smoking a cigarette, it caused an explosion."

"Was it suspicious?"

"Takis closed up the kitchen when he left the gas."

"Closed it up?"

"It was usually his job to close the kitchen shutters at sunset. Zeeta, his mother, had some peculiar habits and that was one of them. He claimed he did it early because he wasn't sure he'd be back by sunset. It trapped the gas."

"It could still be an accident."

"There was an investigation. Nobody could prove it wasn't accidental, but nobody believed it was, either. Everybody knew how much Takis hated his mother. She was bedridden from a fall and couldn't have stopped the gas in the kitchen even if she smelled it."

"So you're saying it was murder? Of his father, too?"

"Nobody can say if he intended to kill Markos or not, but there was no love lost in that family."

"It's a good mystery all right," Nick said.

"The real mystery is why the boy's not in jail. He left that gas bottle leaking. Intentionally or not, he should be in jail for manslaughter. I lost a man in the fire when the first bottle, still hooked to the stove, exploded. We thought that was the bottle that had already exploded. We didn't know about the second one or we wouldn't have gone so close." Captain Tsounis finished his coffee. "If you'll excuse me, I have an unhappy report to make."

The men stood and shook hands.

"Thanks for your time," Nick said, "and your story ideas."

"You never said, what's your book about?"

"After you told me about the Takis Fire, I'm thinking it might be a book about heroes."

"Heroes?"

"Stories of men and women who risk their lives—or lose them—saving other people. You know, people who die fighting fires to save a village, or risk drowning to save a young woman tossed overboard in a storm."

For the first time, the taciturn captain smiled. "It sounds like a book I'd like to read," he said, before disappearing into the Coast Guard station.

Nick, his mind reeling from what he had learned, realized he needed to know a lot more about the Takis Fire, and Takis himself. He pulled out his phone, went into encryption mode, and typed:

> *SUBJ: VATIS Takis, male, 22. Req background check. Adopted by VATIS Markos. Implicated in "Takis Fire" 3 yrs ago. Both parents and one Coast Guardsman killed. Can you locate official report?*

He reread it, and *whoosh!* it was gone.

• • •

RIDI TRUDGED UP THE PATH to the medical clinic with trepidation. Growing up in Albania, he learned that the last place you wanted to go was a hospital because the likelihood was that it would be the last place you ever went. Hospitals were only for the extremely ill, which was ironic, because the doctors had little to dispense except advice, and usually for nothing more exotic than the flu. When he arrived at the small clinic's door, a handwritten note taped to it read *Closed today except for emergency*. He knew the reason was Jura and felt like fleeing. She had been unconscious and so sallow when they loaded her stretcher into Apostolis's pickup, he worried what bad news might await him inside.

He tried the door handle.

It turned.

He stepped into the waiting room. A half dozen straight-backed chairs were pushed against a wall decorated with cheerful paintings by schoolchildren. Two doors led off the room, both closed. "Hello?" he said. "*Yeia sas*?"

A moment later, a door opened and the doctor stepped out. A mass of red curly hair fell to the shoulders of her spotless white coat. "The clinic is closed today," she said. "Do you have an emergency?"

"Is Jura here?"

"Are you Ridi?"

"Yes."

"She asked for you."

"She comes from my village."

"She's very weak."

"Will she be okay?"

"I think so. But she lost her child."

"Her child?"

"She was pregnant. Around six months."

Ridi paled. "Six months?"

"Under other circumstances, I might have been able to save him."

"Him?"

"Yes, a little boy. He had suffered too much trauma. Jura was hemorrhaging. It was all I could do to keep her from bleeding to death."

Thunderstruck by the implications of what the doctor had said, Ridi asked, "Can I see her?"

She took him into the second room. Light sneaked through the shuttered windows to spill across the bed's rumpled sheets. Ridi stepped up to the bed, still in shock that Jura was the person in it, and he had saved her from drowning only that morning.

"She's asleep. Do you want to stay?" the doctor asked.

"I think I should."

She put a sympathetic hand on his shoulder. "Are you the father?"

"I don't know."

"She'll be glad to see you when she wakes up."

The doctor left, closing the door behind her.

As soon as she did, Ridi leaned closer to the girl's face, drifts of her fair hair on her forehead and pillow. He couldn't believe it was she: he couldn't reckon the chain of events that put her in that clinic's bed. How many coincidences did that involve? Though not so coincidental if she had come looking for him, which he feared she probably had. He'd last seen her in a bed, with her hair similarly splayed on a pillow, though it hadn't been limp and dulled by residue from the sea, but the beautiful lush hair of the prettiest girl in the village. If he had stayed, they would likely have married. He could have had his choice of the village girls, being the brightest, most ambitious boy his age; yet because of those same qualities, he wanted none of them—he didn't want to be trapped in a life as predictable as the sunrise, barely scraping by, his chances of getting ahead forever confounded by a system fueled by corruption, not hard work. Ridi didn't dream of seeing the big world, but settling someplace where he would have a chance to make an honest living. So he set his goals, saving toward the day he could emigrate legally to Greece, and finally announced a date for his departure—much to the dismay of the village girls, not only because he was the most desirable among the lot of current bachelors, but he was also their best hope, too, of escaping their mean lives.

Jura had been the most distraught, convinced if he stayed he would marry her. She'd have the best life a village woman could expect, because her husband would be kinder and gentler than the others; but if he got away, he would be gone forever. As the day of his departure approached, she finally relented on the notion of marriage, confessing that she had resigned herself to a future of enduring other men she might sleep with, though Ridi would be the only man she ever truly desired. She had to have him before he left. Ultimately, he succumbed to her seduction, meeting secretly his last week, freely pleasing each other; but if her intent had been to change Ridi's mind, she had underestimated his determination. However compatible their lovemaking proved to be, it wasn't enough to snare a life of bigger dreams.

How different she looked that last afternoon in their village, flush from sex, not so pale that death could have already snatched her were it not for her shallow breathing. From bed, she had watched him pull on his pants, tears spilling from her eyes. He had bent down to brush her lips with a farewell kiss, brushing back strands of hair stuck to her forehead; and now the sadness he felt at that moment six months earlier returned to him in that clinic room. Tears welled in his eyes, sorry for her miserable condition, and feeling unaccountably responsible for it. As he had before, he brushed back the hair on her forehead.

Jura's eyes fluttered open. "Ridi?"

"It's me."

"I found you." She smiled weakly.

"You came looking for me?"

"Your father told me where you were."

"I wasn't hiding."

"I never heard from you."

"I am never sure what to write."

"That you still love me?"

"We said goodbye, Jura. I couldn't write more than that."

"But you did. I saw you, bent over a table, writing each word to me."

"I never did."

"I memorized all the ways you had said you loved me."

"I never said it."

"I brought you our baby. I want us to be together when our baby is born."

"Our baby?"

"It's our baby. I'm sure. He's always kicking. He's restless like you. Here." She tugged at his hand and pressed it to her belly. "Do you feel him kicking?"

Ridi pretended to feel for it. "He must be asleep. You should sleep, too. You've been through a lot."

"You won't leave me again, will you?"

"I won't leave you."

"You promise?"

"I promise. Now go to sleep."

When he was sure she had drifted off, he left the room.

• • •

AN ARSONIST INTENT ON BURNING down the village is likely motivated by a slight to him or his family profound enough to have the weight of history behind it. Only eternal guilt demanded such fierce justice, or so Nick conjectured as he descended the spiral steps into the City Hall's archives. Otherwise, why not just slash someone's tires for revenge, or poison his dog? No, in the arsonist's mind, the whole village was guilty of something.

The mayor had said that the Greeks adopted worry beads from the Turks. For two days, Nick mulled that over, wondering if there was a connection between the ornate beads in a file drawer and the cheap ones coming in the mail. He sensed, if the old beads could talk, he'd know the who and why of his case. Opening the drawer, he picked up a string of them, one by one slipping the smooth red beads down the short chain, musing on how many worries had been counted on them. Unlike the cheap plastic ones arriving in the mail, the old beads had heft, and he flipped them around his hand, remembering his father instructing him how to use the *komboloi* in the same conversation that he taught him about the birds and the bees. Only years later did he understand how stressful that conversation must have been for his father.

He shut the drawer on the old beads and rummaged through other drawers, making his way around the circle of cabinets, skimming letters and diaries that were mostly indecipherable except for the commonplace reports about school attendance, crops, and weather. Amongst them were records of sardine catches going back decades that still smelled faintly fishy. Yellowing photographs of the church's ancient bell tower proved that its destruction was indeed an unfortunate loss when compared to the present-day eyesore.

One drawer held a trove of photos and newspaper clippings about the village's most heralded celebration, the Miss Icon Contest, originally an ancient fertility festival that early Christians had subverted to celebrate Mary's virginity. Over the centuries, it had evolved into a quasi-beauty contest. In it, young women, portraying saints depicted in familiar icons, paraded on boats past the sea side of the harbor's long dock, along which the villagers crowded to choose the winner with their applause; who in turn was supposed to toss a copy of her icon into the sea for the village boys to compete to retrieve. Only unmarried young women and eligible bachelors participated. Notionally, with the blessing of the saint, the winning boy and girl might marry. Nick knew how competitive—indeed, even murderous—beauty contests could be in the States, and wondered if the arsonist's hatred of the village had somehow been fueled by it. Had a winning boy been scorned? Had a winning girl been pressured into a bad marriage? Had someone blamed his or her ruined life on the popular procession and, by extension, the village itself?

For the moment, Nick had no clue, and closed the contest's file drawer when the mayor came down the spiral stairs carrying coffees on a tray. He relieved the older man of the tray and immediately noticed the string of black beads looped around a spoon. "Did they come from Melbourne?" he asked.

"No. Someone left them hanging on the front doorknob."

"Did you touch them?"

"Again, no." The mayor lifted them with the spoon. "I have learned many tricks from your American movies."

"I'm glad you're working on our side. Tell me," Nick said, and pulled open the drawer filled with the old ornate beads. "Why are these here?"

"Those are *tesbih*. Turkish worry beads. I'll show you."

It was the mayor's turn to rummage in the drawers and hand Nick a couple of photographs, grainy and yellowed with age. One showed families in a line to board a boat, wearing fine clothes if they had them, the others garbed in loose peasant pants, robes, and headscarves. The scene was somber—no smiles or hearty farewells—and the men dangled worry beads from their fingers. As they stepped onto the gangplank, apparently they had dropped them on a pile, which the second photograph captured in a close-up.

"The Turks wanted to leave their worries behind," the mayor explained, "or maybe give them to the Greeks who'd be replacing them on the island. Of course, when they reached Turkey, they had new worries, and I suppose they bought new beads."

Nick also used the spoon to dangle the black beads between them. "These are the first black ones, right?"

"Yes."

"It's a message. The game is over. No more orange or pink beads. The arsonist plans to strike, and sooner rather than later. That's why he left them on the doorknob. There isn't enough time for a letter to arrive from Australia." Nick dropped the beads into an evidence bag. "Do you see how the fuse just got shorter?"

◆ ◆ ◆

Ridi had acted weird all morning. Of course Athina understood that he was upset—who wouldn't be?—by the boat capsizing and five men drowning. When she suggested he should focus on the fact that he was a hero for saving the girl, his expression darkened. "I'm no hero," he said.

"To her you are."

"Especially not to her." He abruptly walked away.

Athina couldn't know what bothered him. She had guesses. Maybe the girl's husband had been one of the drowned men, and Ridi blamed himself, as if he could have been the second Superman to show up in a week and save them all. What did it really matter? He was sad to his soul when instead he should be so proud of himself. He *was* a hero. More and more she realized he was a man worth loving.

She paused at the churchyard gate and plopped her shoulder bag on the short wall. She had to catch her breath, not only for the steep trek up the hill, but because she was soon to come face-to-face with Father Alexis for the first time since the incident. The incident. How else to describe it? Mutual seduction is what she finally told herself had happened, though that wasn't entirely accurate either. They never vied for who would make the first move. She had. She had brought his hungry lips to her bare shoulder.

Three girls arrived at the gate at the same time. "Hi Athina!" they all said.

"Hi."

"Are you going inside?"

"I'm waiting for Viki, but Sofia and Vangelia are already here."

Father Alexis had called a meeting of the Miss Icon contestants to go over last-minute details for tomorrow's procession. Athina didn't want to attend. She never wanted to see the priest again, and had to hold off panic attacks every time she thought of him. What was there to go over? Everyone had seen the procession a zillion times. She didn't want to be disqualified, though, for not showing up at the official planning meeting, and Father Alexis might be looking for any reason to disqualify her. He was weird enough to do something like that. Her confusion over how much responsibility for their mutual seduction to assign to the priest—or for that matter, how much blame Ridi should share, since his own seduction sent her running to Father Alexis in the first place—left her debating whether her expression should be contrite or combative when she entered the church. Her only definite sentiment was disgust at all of them, herself included, for what they had each done.

Viki, her best friend, came up the path. Pert, with violet eyes, and a mass of black ringlets that Medusa would have envied, she asked, "Are you going in?"

"I didn't want to go in alone."

"Why, do you think Father Alexis will bite you?"

Athina paled. "Why would you say that?"

"It's just an expression." Viki peered at her curiously. "Are you okay? You look a little strange."

"I wish we didn't have to go. It's such a waste of time."

"I know. I haven't finished my costume yet."

"Me either," Athina admitted.

"Who are you going to be?"

"I can't tell you!"

"What's the difference now? It's too late to copy someone else's costume."

"It's more fun when it's a secret."

"What's more fun?" asked their friend Irini, arriving for the meeting.

"Keeping secrets," Viki told her.

"I love keeping secrets!"

Athina rolled her eyes. "Sure. Just what you do all the time."

"And I have a new one!"

"Like I said."

"Let her talk," Viki said, and asked Irini, "Who are you in love with now?"

"Father Alexis!"

"What?" cried Athina.

"I know he's a priest, but he's so cute!"

"*Cute?*"

"God, you should hear my mother go on about him!"

"Your mother is like thirty-something."

"Forty-two, but who's counting?"

"That's so icky."

"Why not? He's just a regular guy underneath his robe." Viki giggled. "I didn't mean it quite like that sounded."

Athina thought she might burst into tears, though her friends' remarks reminded her that she had once thought Father Alexis cute enough to flirt with him; innocently, of course, never consciously intending to take it as far as it went; or maybe she had, in the way that the subconscious works, creating incidents and reconciling them before they happen. Maybe the priest hadn't been so bad. Maybe all first times have an element of disappointment. "Maybe sometimes he's cute," she halfheartedly admitted.

"Well, I've decided he is *all* the time," Irini declared.

They followed her into the church. The streaming light, passing through the stained glass windows, colorfully played across the iconostasis, where Father Alexis stood surrounded by a dazzling pantheon of holy figures. "Well, our malingerers have finally decided to come inside," he said, and made a quick count. "Eight, so that's everyone. Here, sit together." He waved the girls into the wooden seats attached to the wall.

Athina avoided looking at the Crowned Madonna hanging over the priest, certain that her roving eyes would be filled with reproach. The more she made herself not look, the more she was tempted, and finally did. Sure enough, Mary was staring at her, but not in rebuke. Her eyes were tender and sympathetic, urging the girl not to be so hard on herself. She almost imagined the Madonna's lips curling at the priest, which made Athina glance at him as well. She caught him watching her, and realized that he dreaded their encounter as much as she did, worried what she might reveal. Athina didn't know how yet, but she was going to use his uneasiness to her advantage.

The wooden seats squeaked as they sat down. It was no surprise who was competing in the procession. Only their costumes remained a secret, and even those were less relevant than their fundamental popularity in the village; and, of course, their beauty. In that regard,

Irini was Athina's only serious competitor. Viki was the cutest of them, but she couldn't really be called beautiful, though people were shallow enough to vote for cuteness over beauty, especially if she had a really knockout costume. But she wouldn't. It wasn't Viki's style, and none of the other girls stood a chance. Certainly not Sofia, competing for her third year, who spent her days pushing an empty baby carriage through the village hoping for a husband to help her fill it; nor Elefteria with a hooked nose and hairy mole on her cheek, so witchy-looking that the local boys let it be known at last year's procession that they wouldn't retrieve her icon if she won, fearing they might be coerced into marrying her; nor Vangelia, sadly cross-eyed, and such an inept cook that she managed to burn spaghetti noodles for the only potential suitor her father had ever tempted to their house. None of those was likely to pull off a surprise win despite coming from big, noisy families who always screamed their lungs out as their floats passed.

When all the girls were seated, Father Alexis clasped his hands and asked, "Shall we start with a short prayer?"

No one responded.

"Well, I am not surprised. Praying is not very popular among teenagers."

"Sofia's not a teenager," Irini reminded him. "She's already twenty."

"That's a good point," Viki piped up. "Isn't there some kind of age limit for being in the contest?"

"There's not exactly an age limit," the priest replied. "Contestants must be unmarried women, that's the only requirement."

"And virgins. Isn't that required, too?" asked Sofia.

"Well, I suppose that's implied by not being married."

"Probably one or two of us should be tested," Sofia went on, "and that doesn't include me."

"That must be sad at your age," Irini said.

"Now girls, I know this is a competition, but that does not justify being unpleasant," Father Alexis chided them. "We simply must have faith that everybody obeys the few rules that there are. So, about the procession tomorrow. Who has a question?"

No one stirred.

"Somebody must have a question. Or two?"

"I have two questions," Athina announced.

"Good! And for going first, I'll let you ask both."

"Okay, only the first one has two parts. Why are we at this meeting if we don't have any questions, and who would rather be home working on her costume instead?"

Every girl's arm shot up except Irini's.

"And my second question is—"

"That was already two questions," Irini interrupted her. "Now it's my turn to ask a question."

"I explained that my first question had two parts."

"You can call it 'two parts' if you want, but it was still two questions."

"Let Irini ask her question," Father Alexis said.

"Can I go last in the procession?" Irini asked.

"No, you can't," Athina answered for the priest.

"Why not?"

"Because that was my next question."

The girls turned to the priest for justice. He was still trying to understand why they were vying for last place in the parade, but they had it all worked out: whoever went last had the best shot at the wow factor if her costume was truly special. Everything else that came before would suddenly pale by comparison, and the crowd liked being blown away at the end. Irini, racing to be last in the lineup, must have something very special planned. That unnerved Athina, who up to that minute was confident her costume would be the best, and certainly the most provocative. Obviously her friend was equally confident. "I think Irini should be in first place," she suggested.

"I didn't ask to go first!"

"You're the most beautiful, everybody knows it, and for sure people will stay to see you again when sometimes they go home after the first pass."

Irini looked at her as if she were crazy. "Nobody goes home early! You're such a phony liar!"

Athina met the priest's eye. "I was raised to always tell the truth. To. Any. Question. About anything."

Father Alexis didn't miss her subtle blackmail. "Do you swear that your second question was to ask to go last?"

"I swear."

"Then I must honor it."

"Are you kidding?" Irini protested. "She gets to go last?"

"Isn't going first better?" the priest wanted to know.

"*No!*" Irini cried.

"Then where do you want to be? Second? Third? Next to last?"

"First, of course!"

"I thought you said you didn't want to be first?"

"Only if I can't be last," Irini said, and let out a disbelieving breath. How clueless could he be? "Otherwise, you're just in the middle."

"Jesus was in the middle at the last supper, and who do you always see first?" Viki said teasingly. "And you haven't seen my costume yet!"

"Well, I'm glad that's settled," the priest said, with a withering smile in Athina's direction. "Any more questions? No? Then be ready to launch just before sunset."

Irini stormed out followed by the others. Only Viki held back waiting for Athina. "Are you coming?"

"You go ahead. I want to talk to Father Alexis about something."

"About what?"

"It's church stuff, so it's private."

"Church stuff? *You?*"

"Yes, *me*."

"You're weird." Viki left to catch up with the others.

Father Alexis, suddenly alone with Athina, looked uneasy. She was becoming a troublesome girl. "Well, I thought that went pretty well," he said. "You got the place in the procession that you wanted. That should make you happy."

"Don't you think that we should talk about what happened?"

"About what happened?"

"Yes. About what happened. Isn't it a little not okay that we did it in the church?" Again Athina saw no reproach in Mary's eyes; instead, they seemed to have grown bigger, clearer, cautioning.

Father Alexis said, "Often confession can bring peace of mind. I will hear yours, if you want."

"Confession?"

"God always forgives you. You only need to ask."

"I wasn't exactly thinking what happened was a sin. It was something natural, too, but if it *was* a sin, shouldn't we confess together?"

"Together?"

"We both did what we did. It's not like you didn't participate."

Neither did Father Alexis feel especially sinful for what he had done. He had allowed himself to be seduced by a number of parishioners in each of his lousy villages, always older women wanting something closer to a religious experience than their husbands were providing, and all wanting to keep their rendezvous as secret as he did. Never had he had such a nubile girl, indeed a virgin he realized after the deed. She had been his first virgin, and if he had known, he might have tried to make it more special; but he reminded himself, she had chosen the spot, drawing him atop her on the floor. He felt no remorse for the deed itself but only for defiling the church with their unsanctioned lust, and forcing the Crowned Madonna to witness them from her perch over the altar. Though frankly, the more he'd thought about it, the more he didn't feel especially responsible. "I think you came to the church that night with an intention," he said.

"With an intention?"

"You came looking for me."

Athina stared blankly at him, until it dawned on her what he meant. "You mean, to have sex with you?"

"You wouldn't be the first woman to think of her priest in those terms."

"Is that *your* confession?"

"Confession is a private matter. I have cleared my conscience through prayer."

"Well, for the confessional record, I did not come to church that night to seduce you. I had just seen something horrible and upsetting and I wanted to pray that it wasn't true. I prayed for time to go backward. Or maybe I just needed a place where I could cry. I don't know exactly what I wanted, or needed, but it wasn't sex with you."

Or was it, she had to wonder, as payback for what she had just witnessed between Ridi and Vassoula? Did she want to hurt Ridi, or was it an excuse to indulge her own lusts? She'd been giving the priest some benefit of the doubt, until he had the nerve to blame her alone for what ultimately took place. As if she had forced him!

"Your husband was just like him," she told Mary, looking her straight in her roving eyes.

"Like who?" the priest asked.

"Like you! For not taking responsibility for what you do. For having sex, and then making the woman come up with excuses if there are consequences."

Athina sank to her knees, plopping her shoulder bag on the floor next to her.

Father Alexis looked alarmed. "What are you doing?"

"I want to make my confession."

"Here?"

"We did it here, didn't we? And you have to promise not to interrupt me."

Father Alexis knelt beside her. For a moment, he wondered if it might not be a ploy to seduce him again. Though the whole affair had been hasty and ended rather miserably, perhaps Athina had, despite all, enjoyed herself. In fact, he assumed she had; he'd been told by more than one housewife that he bested their husbands in bed.

"I will be talking to the Panayia, not to you," Athina emphasized.

"Her forgiveness is the same as God's."

"That's good, because I think I'm going to need it."

Athina took a moment to sort out what she wanted to say. Initially she had heaped guilt on herself for making the first move; though when she really analyzed it, Father Alexis had made the first move by kneeling and embracing her legs. How sexy had *that* been? How seductive his mournful eyes? Yet now he accused her of plotting the whole affair! It was the same double standard that she wanted to portray in the Miss Icon procession. Treat women as sexual objects then blame them for the sex. Force them to come up with all the excuses why it occurred and bear whatever consequences. Mary blamed her pregnancy on God. Father Alexis wanted to blame their encounter on Athina. God may have given Joseph a pass, but Athina was determined the priest wasn't going to have it so easy.

"Two nights ago, I had sex with a man for the first time," Athina told the Madonna. "I'm not exactly ashamed that I did. It was going to happen sometime, and not everybody gets married first. You can certainly understand that. Some people think what I did is a sin, so I am asking for forgiveness, even though I am not convinced that what I did qualifies as a sin. I do know it was definitely not the right thing to do in the church, and I am sorry for that."

Athina paused, and when the priest didn't reply, she asked, "Aren't you going to forgive me?"

Father Alexis said, "You are not sufficiently penitent."

"You said I only had to *ask* for forgiveness. You didn't say I had to actually want it."

"At least you need to be sorry for what you did."

"You're not. Besides, I am sorry for what I did, but I am more sorry for my second sin."

"What is your second sin?"

"I need forgiveness for my first sin first."

The priest rolled his eyes, exasperated by being caught up in a charade he helped create. "All right. You are forgiven."

"Thank you. Are you ready for my second sin?"

"I am ready."

"Technically it's probably not a sin either, but it definitely should be." Athina looked again at the Crowned Madonna, and told her, "I did it for the first time with the totally wrong man."

The priest bristled next to her.

"You already know how icky it was because you were watching the whole time"—she heard his sharp intake of breath—"but that's not what made it bad. It's because I don't even like him."

"Confession is not a joke!" Father Alexis snapped.

"Today, when he had a chance to say something nice, instead he accused me of planning the whole thing—like I had taken advantage of him, when he actually started it all."

"You will not continue!"

Athina surprised herself with the courage to add, "Men never take responsibility. Joseph didn't, and look at the crazy story you had to come up with."

The priest leapt to his feet. "This is blasphemy! You will not say these things in a church!"

"So, does God forgive me?"

"Get out of this church!"

Athina scrambled to her feet. "You said I only had to ask!"

"Get out!"

The girl stepped out of his reach. "She's a symbol for the repression of women by men like you! She's *your* saint, not ours! That's going to be my message in the procession."

"I shouldn't even allow you to be in the procession," he hissed.

"Why, because I'm no longer a virgin? If you kick me out, I'll tell people whose fault that is!"

"You wouldn't dare."

"You don't think so?"

Trembling with rage, Father Alexis snatched her bag off the floor and hurled it toward the entrance, its contents scattering in every direction. "*Get out!*" he thundered.

Athina fled for the door grabbing what she could off the floor. Father Alexis, arms outstretched, swooped down on her like a huge bird of prey ready to pounce on his kill. "*Get out!*" he cried. "*Get out!*"

The girl screamed and ran outside. If God existed, surely He would strike her with a bolt of lightening for her sacrilegious confession, and a second one to finish her off for insulting the priest. Neither was forthcoming, and the farther she ran from the church, the more justified she felt for having done both. It was sad enough that her first time had to be blamed on anyone, let alone blaming it on her entirely. It made Athina more determined than ever to portray Mary as Everywoman too repressed to express her essential self.

• • •

"My guess is that the arsonist is somebody from the village," Nick told the mayor. They were still in the archives room discussing the case. "A stranger would be noticed in the village. My second guess is that he or she was at the meeting in the church. Arsonists like to see their crimes."

Who had been in that crowd? both men pondered. Nick remembered a half dozen people he had since seen around the village, but he knew nothing about any of them. The mayor, on the other hand, knew everyone; if not intimately, at least by lineage and general disposition. For his whole life, they had been his friends, neighbors, and now constituents. He couldn't imagine any of them contemplating such a hateful act. He shook his head, muttering, "It's impossible that he is from Vourvoulos. Who would do such a thing?"

"Someone with a motive," Nick replied. "We just don't know what it is. Tell me about the Takis Fire."

"That was over three years ago."

"Wasn't Takis gone for two years, and when he returned, the fires started?" Nick asked, hating himself for casting suspicion on the young man.

"You think Takis is the arsonist?"

"Tsounis thinks he set one fire purposefully."

"Because Takis had closed the kitchen shutters."

"He told me that."

"Captain Tsounis makes it sound menacing, when it had been Takis's chore since he was a boy. Sometimes it seemed that she made the kids do things just to make them work. She was hard on them."

"Hard enough for Takis to want to kill her?"

"I never believed it," the mayor replied. "Both children were adopted, so they didn't grow up loved by the whole village in the same way as other children. Vassoula was a little older and more mature, so it may not have mattered so much to her, but for Takis, everything was more difficult. He was quiet, and different in a way you couldn't say. People explained it by his being adopted, but he never outgrew it, and he never had many friends. He was always a little lonely."

You don't outgrow being gay, Nick thought, certain that Takis's homosexuality explained much of what made him different. For that alone, in any Greek village, he would have grown up lonely.

"The boy made it no secret that he wanted to leave for Australia," the mayor continued. "He was always doing something to make a little money. Carrying groceries for people. Feeding a pet. Cleaning or fixing something. It wasn't much, certainly not enough to buy a ticket, so when people heard about the insurance money, the rumor started that he killed his parents for it. Then when he bought a one-way ticket to Melbourne, people were convinced that he was guilty and running away. In reality, he could only buy a one-way ticket because he didn't plan to come back in a year, but people twisted things like that and used them against him. The same with the insurance."

"How is that?"

"He didn't even know about the insurance until his parents were dead."

"Then how could it have been his motive to kill them?"

"People didn't believe him. They said he must have known. Otherwise, why would he contact the orphanage?"

"The orphanage?"

"Markos and Zeeta purchased life insurance when they adopted the kids. The orphanage required it to protect the children until they were eighteen in case something happened to the parents."

"So why did he contact the orphanage?"

"He says he didn't. He claims the investigators contacted it for information on their adoption, and the orphanage contacted him."

"He wasn't already eighteen?"

"Not for another couple of weeks."

"How lucky was that?" Nick asked.

The mayor shrugged. "People said the same thing you're suggesting. I couldn't believe Takis was a murderer."

"Maybe an arsonist?"

"I can't say. In America, quiet boys do bad things. It's never happened here."

"How much was the insurance money?"

"Not enough to murder two people."

"You would be surprised how little people kill for."

"I hope not for a one-way ticket to Melbourne. He didn't get much more than that."

"He got a chance at a new life. That's worth more than money to a lot of people."

"It sounds like you think Takis is guilty."

"I'm not convinced that he's not," Nick admitted. "He's a nice guy, hopefully too nice to do something really terrible." He started to load things into his daypack. "Well, I'm off chasing fires."

They climbed the spiral stairs and crossed the grand reception room. At the front door, he said, "Now that the arsonist has made the threat very clear, he's going to expect you to do something. He's going to want to know that you are taking him seriously."

"What should I do?" the mayor asked.

"Call another meeting."

"Tonight?"

"No, not tonight. The arsonist wants to see us nervous, not panicked. If we panic, he might panic. Tomorrow would be better."

"Tomorrow is the procession. Everybody will be busy with that."

"Then the day after," Nick said. "That might buy us some time. The arsonist will be curious about what's going to be said."

• • •

NORMALLY RIDI RODE HIS SCOOTER home for a short afternoon siesta, but he couldn't stop thinking about Jura. She had come looking for him, bearing his child, bearing him new responsibilities—certainly new if the child had survived. He didn't deny his role in his own undoing, nor did he want to discount their lifelong friendship, ending in a startlingly passionate though brief affair; and yet, he felt ambushed. It left him with a sinking feeling in his stomach. All his hard work, the future he had planned, his love for Athina: all were threatened. How could it have happened? He had resisted temptation so many times; why did he succumb to Jura only days before he departed? And how was it possible that she got pregnant? He had been so careful. He went to a pharmacy in Tirana where he could anonymously finger through the packets of condoms, never imagining so many choices—extra thin, pre-lubed, flavored—and ultimately settling on extra thick: they sounded the safest.

Safe! He wanted to weep, he felt so vulnerable.

The note, saying the clinic was closed, was still taped to the door. How could it have been only that morning that he saved the girl from drowning, or first saw that note? In half a day, he had endured an age of worries. That very morning he had learned, in the same breath, that he was a father and then not. He might have had a son if the clinic had been better equipped to save a preemie after the heavy, pounding sea beat him from his mother's belly. The notion of having lost his first son deepened Takis's gloom as he went inside.

The doctor's door was ajar.

"Doctor?" he said softly.

He heard a chair scoot back. A moment later, the doctor stood in her open door. "Hello, Ridi," she said, and gave him a warm smile.

"Jura is okay?"

"I told her she lost the baby."

"She will not die, will she?"

"No, she will not die. She is weak and very sad. She needs time to heal."

"It is okay if I see her?"

"Of course. She would like that. Her door is open." The doctor smiled and went back into her office.

Ridi tapped on Jura's door, heard nothing and went inside. The little light squeaking past the shutters plunged the rest of the room into darkness. Approaching the lumpy bed, at first he couldn't see the girl. "Jura?" She didn't stir, and he stepped closer. "Jura?"

She rolled onto her back; her face the same gray as her sheets. "Are you here, Ridi?"

"I'm here."

"It scared me when I woke up and you were gone."

"I had to go to work."

"I thought you had left me."

"I'm here now. Don't be scared."

"Sit here, Ridi, next to me where I can see you."

He scooted onto the edge of the bed. "The doctor says that you are going to be okay."

"How can I be okay again? I lost our baby."

He touched her arm. "She told me."

She clutched his hand, and whimpered, "It was a boy."

"I know."

"He might have been your son."

"Might have been?" For a fleeting second, Ridi wondered if his paternity was in doubt.

"If he had lived. I know you don't want to believe me, but I have only been with you."

"Then I have truly lost a son."

"Are you angry with me, Ridi?"

"Why would I be angry with you?"

"For coming to find you."

"Of course I'm not angry, but why did you come through Turkey? Didn't you have a passport? Albanians can come to Greece. You know that."

"It was stolen at the border. There was a crowd and people were pushing and I was pickpocketed. I was frantic. You can't imagine! I knew I didn't have time to get a new passport before the baby came, and then I would need a passport for the baby. I had to come now and a man said he could help me. He said he could bring me to your island."

"He probably stole your passport so you'd need his help. That's how the smugglers operate. It was dangerous for you."

"I wouldn't have come without Ruben."

"Ruben? Your brother?"

"He took me to the border, and when my passport was stolen, he said the same thing, it was dangerous for me to go alone with that man. So he said he'd come with me to find you. Did he drown?"

"They're searching for all the men."

"The other four were brothers. Ruben didn't know how to swim. None of us did."

"Which makes what you did even crazier."

"We pretended to be husband and wife so the other men wouldn't try to touch me."

"You should've turned back. You should've gone home."

"After a week, it was so hard we almost did, but then we heard borders were closing everywhere and I was afraid I might not be let back into Albania. If I didn't have a passport, how would they know

I wasn't a refugee? I didn't want our baby born in a camp, and every day we were one day closer to you. I wanted you to feel him kick. He was so strong, and now I've lost him. I'm so sorry that I lost him!"

Ridi touched her arm. "It's okay. At least you're alive."

"A baby was my only chance. I knew you would never abandon your child. I thought, if only I could get pregnant!"

"You thought what?"

"I wanted it to be a boy. I was sure you would never abandon a boy."

"You *tried* to get pregnant?"

"And now he's dead!"

Ridi pulled away from her. "What did you do?"

The girl brushed away the hairs stuck to her cheeks. "I know what I did was wrong."

"Tell me what you did."

"I poked holes in your things."

"My things?"

"Your rubber things. With a needle so you wouldn't notice."

"You poked holes in my condoms?"

"At least two or three holes. They were very thick."

"I know. I chose them to protect us. Both of us."

"I'm sorry, Ridi. I am truly sorry."

"You're sorry? You did all this to trap me? To make me stay with you?"

"To let me escape with you."

"By getting pregnant? That's not usually an escape."

"It was my only chance."

"Damn you, Jura. Damn you! Those weren't my condoms, those were our condoms, to protect both of us from something we didn't want."

"He was your son, Ridi, however it happened."

"You stole him from me. The last thing I wanted to give you was a child. You cheated me, and you cheated him!"

"He's why I came to find you."

"It wasn't the way to make me love you."

"You won't abandon me, will you, Ridi? Not after all I've been through for you. Not now that I'm here."

Ridi couldn't answer her. There were too many things to think about, and he couldn't think, not in that suffocating room. He fled, and before he was out the clinic's front door, the girl's mournful cry erupted. He heard the doctor scrape back her chair to go and comfort her.

• • •

LYDIA HAD MAPPED THE LATER fires describing physical markers, much as old maps had, placing a property line as so many meters from a rock outcropping or corner of another terraced plot. It wasn't exactly GPS, but Nick usually found the scorched patch within minutes. For the tenth fire, there were no markers, only an X approximating where the fire had been. He poked along the valley's steep hillside trying to reconcile curves on the map with bends in the road. Deciding he had arrived, he pulled over.

Look straight up. Those were Lydia's only instructions.

Nick used the binoculars to scan the ancient terraces that ascended like a giant's staircase for any sign of the fire, or a building. That had been the only consistent thing about the fires: they were always near ruins. A village, a settlement, a house. Sometimes only a broken wall remained to attest that someone had once lived there. It could have been happenstance, but Nick thought not. At the top, he spotted the corner of an old house. Whatever path to it that likely existed was no longer evident. No doubt that's why Lydia hadn't given more precise bearings for that particular fire; she hadn't climbed the giant's steep steps.

The terraced plots were still farmed. Rolled-up black nets had been placed under the olive trees in readiness for the approaching harvest. Stones stacked in the corners to make it possible to climb from one level to the next, though often they were at opposite ends of the terraces. Nick zigzagged his way up the hill, which grew steeper, and the terraces eventually narrowed to four or five trees in a single line.

About halfway up, it was obvious he'd missed an easier approach to the old house but pushed on. The physical effort helped keep his mind off Takis and his possible culpability for the fires. The mayor had said that everyone seemed ready to damn him, which always made Nick as suspicious of the finger pointers as he was their target. Though he had to admit, he could more easily build a case against Takis than anyone else. Timing, opportunity, motive: on circumstantial evidence, Takis could be found guilty on all counts.

Nick clambered over the last wall of stones and found himself facing a small house, missing its roof and windows, but the walls, cracked and stained, were largely intact. The island's ubiquitous wild lavender roses had wrapped themselves around a stone well outside the front door. He could imagine the family life in the yard. Chickens underfoot, laundry on a line, wife forever sweeping their patch of hard dirt while the farmer, from his perch, admired his olive trees planted all the way down to the road. Or had there been a road back when the last family lived there? More likely a donkey trail.

He peered through the broken door at the leaves littering the floor. He entered, stomping his feet to reveal any snakes hiding under them but none showed themselves. Only patches of the original stucco remained on the walls. A broken sink suggested where the kitchen had been. Through a doorway into a second room, he saw out the window where in the distance, valley, framed by headlands, fell into the azure sea. The farmer and his wife had woken up to that view every morning.

In a couple of steps, Nick crossed the second room to stand at the window. He heard a rustle behind him and wheeled around to see a fleeting glimpse of someone running away. A male, that's all he could tell, as he chased him to the front door and watched him disappear in the trees. "Wait! Wait!" he cried after him, but the man didn't come back. Returning to the second room, Nick noticed the bedding of rags on the floor and a plastic bag stuffed with leaves to make a pillow. Curiously, next to it, a set of decent clothes had been neatly spread on the floor: a red shirt with pearly white buttons tucked into mustard pants, and socks sticking out of the cuffs. It was peculiar, but what interested Nick more was what he saw in the corner.

A Styrofoam detonator.

He bent over to look at it. Nothing distinguished it from the others in design, but it hadn't melted. It had been a dud. There were smudge marks where a couple of cigarettes had burned down, but apparently not burning hot enough to ignite it. Or maybe some unexpected rain doused it. Touching it as little as possible, Nick slipped the detonator into a plastic bag that he tucked into his daypack. He took photos of the clothes and the ragged bedding. Next to them was a neat stack of flattened squares of aluminum foil. He examined a couple, and sniffing them smelled traces of food.

Wondering if he'd discovered the arsonist's hideout, he followed the path the mysterious man had taken through the trees and soon came to a clearing. Meadow-like, it was wet and green, and in the middle was a clump of burnt shrubbery. Nick could imagine why a first detonator might not have caught on fire, which would be the one in his daypack, but apparently a second one had. The fact that the arsonist targeted that spot twice supported Nick's speculation that none of the sites was random. They'd been selected, but why?

In a couple of minutes he reached the road and walked back to his car. Had he stopped in the next bend, Lydia's instruction to *Look straight up* would have been all that he needed to see the burned trees. He hadn't needed to climb the steep zigzag ladder of terraces. That was the other consistent thing about the fires: they had all been set only a couple of minutes' hike off the road. The arsonist wanted to get away quickly; or perhaps he was more wanting to get back somewhere before being noticed absent, creating the illusion of an alibi.

Nick pulled his car onto the road and gunned it, wanting to see how fast he could get back to the village.

• • •

ATHINA CLOSED HER SHOULDER BAG with a defeated sigh. No matter how many times she searched it, her phone was not there. It had fallen out when the priest threw her stuff at the door. She couldn't believe she had left it behind. It was the only thing she owned that was truly important. Her whole life was on it. Without it, she wouldn't know how to telephone anyone—the only number she had memorized was her own.

Retracing her steps up the hill, she dreaded the prospect of running into Father Alexis. In hindsight, she was embarrassed by what she had said. Maybe she had gone too far with a priest, though at the end, he really did terrify her, swooping toward her and ready to pounce. Athina shuddered, recalling how suffocating his robe had been when it fell across her face the moment he *had* pounced on her for his quick satisfaction.

She eased open the gate so it wouldn't squeak and hurried to the church door. Peeking in, she didn't see the priest and went inside. She heard sounds in the vestry. It creeped her out, knowing that Father Alexis's copy of the Crowned Madonna was in there with him, with the same roving eyes watching everything that he did, just like the Madonna over the altar was watching her at that moment. It dawned on her that the priest was almost never out of her sight, and she wondered if he carried her around his apartment with him. She had to stop herself from giggling when she imagined the Madonna propped on the back of the toilet while he took a piss. Where would her roving eyes be focused then?

She didn't see her phone anywhere. Other stuff was still scattered around, and she grabbed her makeup brush, mints, and tissues—but no phone. With no furniture except for the seats fixed to the walls, there weren't many places it could be hiding. She checked under the seats and for the first time noticed the cubbyhole. Her phone had landed way back in it. She started to crawl in, but there was a funky smell like some animal lived there. Scaring herself thinking about it, she bumped her head scrambling back out. She held her breath, hoping Father Alexis hadn't heard the loud thump.

When he didn't come charging out of the vestry, Athina returned her attention to her phone, and had to suppress a laugh imagining it ringing under some old lady's ass during services. But how to retrieve it? There wasn't even a long candle to extend her reach. Then she hit on an idea. Maybe she wouldn't be so afraid if she crawled backward into the cubbyhole. Squatting on all fours, she aimed for the opening, and managed to get far enough in to reach her phone, but the space was too cramped for her to turn and grab it. Instead, she shuttled it between her feet until she successfully hooked it and punted it forward. Phone in hand, she was ready to crawl out when the vestry door opened. She stayed hidden.

Father Alexis, carrying a stepladder, brushed past her and set it up behind the altar. Then he did the very unusual thing of locking the church door. He disappeared back into the vestry and reemerged a moment later with his copy of the Crowned Madonna. Or so Athina assumed it was the copy, though to her, the icon the priest leaned against the ladder and the one over the altar looked identical.

Something was clearly fishy. Athina switched on her phone in time to videotape the priest switching the icons. When he finished, he carried the ladder—and what she incorrectly assumed to be the original icon—back to the vestry. She prayed he wouldn't forget to unlock the church door. He didn't. A moment later he returned with the key and then shut himself in the vestry.

Athina ran out of the church. She wasn't sure exactly what she had witnessed. It might be something as innocent as the priest taking away the original icon to repair it, and putting up one of his copies to hold its place; but then, why all the secrecy? She was already devising a plan to have some fun at the priest's expense.

• • •

IT TOOK NICK SEVENTEEN MINUTES driving fast but not too recklessly to reach the edge of the village. Another two minutes dodging tourists before the road dipped to the port.

Call it twenty minutes total.

Forty round trip.

Another twenty to futz with the detonator, lighting its dozen or so cigarettes.

An hour for the arsonist's whole operation.

A lot of people could disappear for an hour without being missed.

By the looks of it, the Coast Guard captain had been missing most of the day. He had been out searching for the five drowned men when Nick came by after leaving the mayor at midday; and he still was out, judging by the fact that the gray patrol boat wasn't back in port.

Nick retraced his route through the village before cutting over the hill on the road to the hammam. Could that first time with Takis have been only two nights ago? Was it possible that only last night the young waiter had licked the scars on his back? Easily two of his most erotic experiences, and yet the memories of both had tarnished as soon as Nick heard about the Takis Fire. Any fire remotely associated with an arsonist case was something to follow up, though he never expected Captain Tsounis's undisguised accusation that Takis had started the fire and was a double murderer. Of course, Nick knew he had to rein in his infatuation for him. He should be pragmatic and use their relationship to get any information relevant to his case. He hated that notion.

Nick pulled off the road. Way down the pebbly beach, he saw the hammam's dome. He guessed it was along that stretch of deserted beach where the raft had capsized that morning. The sea, violent only hours earlier, was skillet flat.

He got out of the car, stripped, and tossed his clothes back onto the seat. He reached for his swimming trunks and changed his mind; the opportunity to swim nude was too rare to pass up. He locked the door, and was headed for the water in his untied shoes when he heard his phone beep back in the car. He looked at the rapidly falling sun, and in his order of priorities, a swim was higher on his list than a message that would still be there in an hour. He decided to ignore it and kept walking.

It beeped again.

He had to check it. His joke with the mayor about the arsonist's fuse getting shorter was no laughing matter. They *were* only hours away from the start of a new month.

Hobbling back to the car, he took his phone from the glove compartment. An SMS alerted him that he had been sent an encrypted message. He logged on and read:

SUBJ: ALEXIS Manolis, priest. 32. Greek national from Refinio, oil refinery town on road from Athens to Korinth. Subj has no criminal record. Father killed in refinery fire when Subj was 17 y.o. Mother still lives there. Cause of fire never determined. Subj entered seminary two months later. Standard rotation through parishes on islands Skyros and Patmos. Church on Patmos destroyed by fire one month prior to reassignment to Vourvoulos. Determined to be an accident. Fourteen months in current post.

"In other words, a firebug," Nick said to himself as he stuck his phone back in the glove compartment.

He picked his way over the pebbles and lined up his shoes at the water's edge. Burying the car key between them, he arranged some reddish stones to mark the spot in case his shoes were stolen. He waded into the water and dove in, pulling himself deeper as ticklish bubbles escaped from his beard. When he surfaced, with strong strokes he aimed for Turkey's chalky hills, feeling winter's tenacious approach in the cold currents trickling over him.

Nick was glad for the message from headquarters. It gave him an opportunity to suspect someone other than Takis for the fires. Already he knew Father Alexis to be an unsavory character—indeed, a criminal—but being an art forger didn't automatically nominate him for the arsonist, though his father dying in a refinery fire might have planted the seed for something he would do later in his life. Or perhaps he had started the refinery fire? Did he kill his father purposefully? Young Manolis had been seventeen at the time, an age when boys are becoming men, and conflicts naturally erupt between fathers and sons. Had theirs gotten out of hand? Had Manolis been a religious boy, fervent, driven by demons that pushed him too far? Was it a calling that motivated him to enter the seminary a few weeks after his father's death, or guilt?

Fire can be addictive. It can also be a handy tool. If the priest had been forging icons on Patmos, he might have decided burning down the church was the perfect way to cover his tracks. If it worked once, why not again? Though to have a second church burn down on his watch might bring suspicion on him. Instead, if the fuel tank was blown, and the church destroyed in the resulting fire, Father Alexis couldn't be blamed. But why an elaborate year-long buildup? Was it some game the priest had concocted, dispensing fear and death like God, which he was playing out on unsuspecting Vourvoulos? Or was it simply to create the myth of an arsonist to keep fingers from pointing at him?

Nick, still swimming away from shore, mulled over the same questions for Takis. Why burn down the village when he could simply return to Australia and never come back? Did he need to punish it? If so, why not take it out in one blow? Why start eleven fires before the big one and risk getting caught? Why alert people at all? Nick didn't know the priest's secrets, but he could imagine Takis—a lonely child, adopted and not loved—ultimately blaming the village for an unhappy childhood.

The young waiter and the priest were Nick's only suspects by default. No cloud of suspicion had gathered over anyone else. Except for insurance money that Lydia mentioned herself, he couldn't imagine what her motive might be, and she hardly seemed maniacal enough to burn down the village to recoup the cost of kitchen equipment. Someone else, though, might have a lot to gain, and he made a mental note to find out who were the largest property owners in the village. But Nick didn't sense that the case was mercenary. Something visceral drove the arsonist. Someone hated the village enough to want to create panic before destroying it. What could drive a person to want to do that?

Then a thought occurred to him.

Omar.

Could he still be alive? Was his suicide a ruse in an elaborate plot to seek revenge for what the skinheads had done to him? The fact that his body had never been found left room for deceit. Had it been Omar running from the ruined house that afternoon? His clothes so neatly spread out on the floor? Nick was brought up short by that thought, and stopped swimming to tread water; mulling over who might recognize Omar's clothes, particularly a distinguishable red shirt with pearly buttons?

A whitecap broke in his face, a reminder that the winds were picking up. He headed back to land, swimming hard against a current that wanted to pull him away from where he had parked the car. When he finally made it to shore, he crawled out of the water, not caring that the pebbles painfully dug into his knees, and collapsed. He stayed sprawled out, absorbing the sun's warmth retained in the stones beneath him.

When he was ready to move, he easily spotted his shoes. They were the only things on the beach for a hundred yards in either direction. As he got closer, they looked different. Were they darker? Had a wave splashed over them? He didn't think so, because they were lined up exactly as he left them. Then he realized, they weren't his shoes at all, and picked one up. It was soggy; they had been in the water a long time.

He dug in the pebbles for the car key.

It wasn't there.

"Shit!" he said aloud, and straightened up to assess his predicament: naked in a cold wind, locked out of his car, and nearly an hour's walk to the village, not to mention the likelihood that people would see his ravaged back. He had no choice but to break a window to retrieve his clothes. Then he worried perhaps they had been stolen, too. Why would someone take the key and not the car, unless it was to take the stuff inside it?

As he approached his car, he could see the key in the door, and his clothes were on the seat where he left them. He patted down his pants for his wallet and checked for his phone. Everything appeared to be there, though as he started to dress, he couldn't find his boxers. He searched through everything and looked under the seat in case they had somehow migrated there, but they hadn't. Whoever found his key had taken them along with his shoes. A little bewildered, Nick pulled on his pants, feeling that a joke was being played on him that he didn't get. He scanned the hills for any movement to find the prankster. He saw no one, and drove barefoot back to the village.

CHAPTER NINE

ATHINA FELT GIDDY ONCE SAFELY away from the church with her video of the priest exchanging the icons. Her own good mood made her think of Ridi and what a nice guy he really was. He certainly had been that day. Saving a girl from drowning, risking his life to do it, learning only later that she was from his village. He hardly knew her, he said, seemingly to downplay what he had done, but in Athina's eyes that made him all the more a hero.

The sun, cutting the horizon, would soon disappear in a flash. Her mother was expecting her to set up for the dinner shift, but Athina, passing right by the clinic, decided she wanted to visit the girl from Ridi's village, really more for his sake than the girl's, as a way to demonstrate how proud she was of his bravery that morning. The girl could probably use some company, too, no doubt scared to be in a hospital—well, a small clinic but still smelling of antiseptics—in a foreign country.

The *Closed* note posted outside the clinic didn't stop Athina from entering. The doctor's door was ajar. She heard soft snoring and peeked to see her napping on a couch. Athina quietly retreated and tested the second door. It opened.

Jura, facing away, rolled onto her back. "Ridi?"

"It's not Ridi," Athina said and approached the bed.

Jura said something.

"I'm sorry, I don't speak Albanian. Do you speak Greek? Or maybe English?"

"Only English I take from school."

"That's more than I know in Albanian. Do you want me to turn on a light?"

"What?"

Athina touched the bedside lamp. "Do you want some light?"

"It's okay."

Athina took that to mean yes and switched it on. Despite her ordeal at sea, Athina could see the girl was pretty; and she wasn't so much a girl as a young woman, like herself around eighteen.

Jura asked, "Where is Ridi?"

"At work. I am his friend."

"His friend?"

"He works at my mother's restaurant. He will come again tomorrow."

"Not tonight?"

"It will be too late tonight. You will already be asleep."

"I not sleep!"

"Don't be silly. You must sleep."

Tears welled in Jura's eyes. "Ridi not come again."

"Of course he will! He's worried about you."

"He never come again," the girl moaned.

Athina pulled over a chair to sit next to the bed. "Of course he will. He told me that you are friends."

"He hate me now!"

"Hate you? He saved your life this morning!"

"He not know it is me."

"That makes him even more of a hero, doesn't it?"

The girl started to weep. "I lose my baby!"

"You had a baby? Oh, how horrible!" In all the talk around the village about the incident, no one had mentioned a baby.

"Six months. My baby was six months."

"I'm so sorry." Athina sympathetically touched the girl's arm.

"I want to be dead!"

"No, you don't. You were meant to live, don't you see? It's like a miracle. You come from Ridi's village, and there he was on the beach to rescue you."

"I not make a miracle. I come for finding Ridi."

"You came looking for Ridi?"

"To bring him his baby."

Athina was totally mystified. "His baby?"

"He is my husband."

"You are married to Ridi?"

"When he makes his baby inside me, he must be my husband."

"Your baby?"

"I lose my baby. He was a boy."

"You mean you were six months *pregnant*?"

Nodding, Jura broke down, barely able to choke out, "He was son of Ridi."

"Did Ridi know you were pregnant?"

"Today I tell him. Today."

So Ridi hadn't known he was going to be a father when he left Albania. Still, that didn't exonerate him from all responsibility, and he should have stayed in contact to make sure he hadn't gotten the girl pregnant. And what was this girl to him? A girlfriend? A wife he'd abandoned? Athina was crestfallen. The guy she had told she loved, whom she thought she could count on to be more responsible than most men, was just another feckless dickhead.

Jura took her hand. "Please, I am scared."

"Don't be scared."

"I wanted Ridi to come home for his baby. Now I have no baby. No husband. Only sad heart!"

"Shh... shh... I'm your friend now."

"I'm scared! If Ridi not come see me, what I do?"

"He will come see you."

"He won't!"

"I'll make him help you."

"Tell him I am sorry. So sorry."

"I will."

"I am so sorry."

"I will tell him."

"Thank you. Thank you."

The girl squeezed Athina's hand before rolling onto her side, her whole body crying. Athina stayed next to the bed, waiting for the girl to calm down, and only when she appeared to fall asleep did she turn off the light.

"Goodnight," she whispered, and slipped out of the room.

◆ ◆ ◆

Nick stopped at his room for a quick shower and a change of footwear, glad he had packed extra shoes. He was still puzzled why someone would take his shoes, and especially his boxers, when the thief could have had his wallet and cell phone. He slung his daypack over his shoulder and headed for the port. The mysterious man whom he barely glimpsed fleeing the ruined house—could he be sure it was a man?—and the black worry beads contributed to his sense of an imminent menace. He'd already decided to bring Captain Tsounis into his confidence when he walked into the Coast Guard station.

It was a cramped space with two desks in a front room where guardsmen filled out paperwork for boat captains wanting to overnight in the port. That evening, all five members of the local crew sat around the desks, resolutely passing a bottle of ouzo between them and knocking back shots. They were definitely off duty after a hard day.

"Come back in the morning to get your permit," one of them told him.

"I'd like to speak with Captain Tsounis." Through the cracked door to his office, Nick saw him talking on the telephone.

"It's too late today."

"I have an appointment," he lied.

Kyra, the only female among them, consulted her watch. "Was that a table for one at nineteen hundred hours?"

Nick smiled. "I'm not late, am I?"

Everyone chuckled. Their gloom briefly lifted.

"Your name?" she asked.

"Damigos. Nick."

She leaned back from her perch on a desk to call to the captain, "Nick Damigos is here to see you."

"Who?"

"Superman!" a guardsman shouted.

Everyone laughed.

"The writer," Nick spoke up.

The captain came to his door. "If you are looking for heroes for your book, you're in the right place."

"Are you going to be in a book, Captain?" Kyra asked.

"No, you are, and Yiorgos, too."

"All in the line of duty, sir," the young guardsman replied.

"You didn't see me jumping into that water, did you?"

"You have some years on us."

"And rank!"

"Why go in the water?" Nick asked.

"Kyra rescued the girl this morning," Captain Tsounis answered, "and Yiorgos jumped in to retrieve a body this afternoon. It was a tricky current with too many swells. Our equipment would have torn the body up. He was naked so there was nothing to protect his skin."

"Naked?"

"Stripped clean without a mark on him. We can't figure it out either. Come on in."

Nick went into his office.

The captain shut the door behind them. "Take a seat."

Nick quickly took in the room. It was a man's office: spare and to the point. Nothing especially decorative. A couple of photographs of the captain standing with dignitaries he must have admired, but Nick didn't recognize them. Pressed into a corner was a single bed, its blanket squarely tucked in. Noting the back door he'd seen Vassoula enter two nights earlier, he could imagine the tryst that had transpired.

"Do you live here?" Nick asked.

"Sometimes somebody has to be here. It's for emergencies and it's usually me. What is this about?"

Nick showed his ID. "I'm not a writer."

"The FBI?"

"Federal Bureau of Investigation."

"Yes, I know what it is."

Nick brought the captain up to speed on his investigation. He described the mayor's letter to the embassy that prompted his arrival, and how the worry beads—especially the black ones left on City Hall's doorknob—had convinced them that burning down the village was the goal and the threat was imminent. "Fortunately the mayor sent his letter to the embassy. We weren't aware of the threat, and like I said, you operate an important humanitarian asset here. It's fair to suspect the arsonist will strike in the next calendar month, and it might be tomorrow to coincide with the pageant. Your fuel tank needs to be secured, Captain. Guarded round the clock."

"I'll volunteer for tomorrow, and then work out a regular schedule with my crew."

"Good."

There was a knock on the door.

Yiorgos poked his head inside. "Everybody's gone home. Do you need anything, Captain?"

"Yeah, whatever is left in your bottle and two glasses."

"You got it."

The man returned with two short glasses and a bottle, and set them on the desk.

The captain, pouring shots, commented, "This looks like a fresh bottle."

"You'd be drinking air if you drank what's left in ours. Anything else, Captain?"

"Not tonight, Yiorgos. You can leave my door open."

The man left and the captain pushed an ouzo in Nick's direction.

They tapped glasses, said "*Styn eyeia mas*" and knocked them back.

Nick shivered as the fiery alcohol burned its way to his stomach.

"Another?"

"Sure."

The captain refilled their glasses. "Ten minutes earlier, we could have stopped them from trying to land. Instead, five men are drowned."

"Presumed drowned."

"They're drowned. It was rough and the currents are too strong."

"How's the girl?"

"The doctor says that she's badly beat up. She lost her child. I thought I'd give her a day to recover before questioning her."

"There was a kid?"

"She was six months pregnant."

"Maybe the father drowned."

"It's possible. *Styn eyeia.*" The captain killed his second ouzo.

Nick knocked his back, too, but when offered more, he waved the bottle away. "I'm good for now. So tell me about the case of Omar the Turk who went missing about a year ago."

"The suicide?"

"Presumed suicide," Nick countered. "His body was never found."

"In the channel, they almost never are."

"Have you ever considered the possibility that Omar didn't commit suicide? Maybe he just wanted people to think that he did?"

"If he's not a ghost, where is he?"

"Hiding in the mountains and setting fires," Nick suggested. "Playing out his revenge."

Captain Tsounis shook his head. "That's a crazy idea."

"It's crazy, but what happened to him is enough to make somebody crazy. Did they catch the skinheads?"

"That was easy. They were from the main town."

"What happened to them?"

"They didn't kill him, so they couldn't be charged with murder."

"They got off with assault?"

"The one who cut him got five years. The others, three."

"And Omar got a life sentence," Nick remarked. "Did you see him after he was cut?"

"Too many times. And if your next question is, would I want revenge, of course I would. But Omar is a ghost."

At that moment, the public announcement system crackled to life. At City Hall, the mayor blew into the microphone to test it, sending the sound of gale-force winds whipping through the village from the many speakers mounted on electric poles. Then with a phlegmy cough he cleared his throat to say:

> *Kali spera, kyries kai kyrioi. In two days, there will be a meeting to decide which project to start: repairing the church's bell tower or moving the Coast Guard's petrol tank. We have new information—let me repeat, we have new information—so everyone please attend for the final vote. That is two days from now at eleven in the morning in the church. And remember, the Miss Icon procession begins tomorrow at sunset.*

More crackling, and the PA system went silent.

Nick stood. "Thanks for your help. By the way, what was Omar's last name?"

"Ozturk. I helped search for his body."

"Ozturk," Nick repeated it. "That name is on the map." He took Lydia's fire map from his daypack and unfolded it. In cross-checking the fires' locations with the records in City Hall, when he felt confident he could identify the landowners, past or present, he had jotted down the names. "Here," he said, pointing to where he had written it. "The Ozturks owned this land."

"That doesn't surprise me."

"Why not?"

"'Ozturk' is about as common as 'Smith' is in America. You probably can't find land around here that didn't at one time belong to an Ozturk."

"So no connection with Omar Ozturk?"

"None was ever mentioned, and at some point, I think it would have been. But that's not the name you need," Captain Tsounis reminded him.

"What is?"

"I already told you, Takis Vatis, and he's no ghost. You can find him two doors away."

"I haven't forgotten," Nick said, and walked out.

• • •

THE MAYOR'S PUBLIC ANNOUNCEMENT SENT Father Alexis into a tither. His fate was unexpectedly arriving with less than forty-eight hours' notice. The mention of new information sounded ominous, and no doubt was to the opposition's advantage. Father Alexis, as hard as he was waging a campaign to repair the bell tower, in fact more adamantly had decided that he did not want the fuel tank moved for his own venal reasons. He wanted it blown up and the resulting fire to sweep through the village, collecting the church in its path and incinerating the evidence of his forgeries. That had become his plan. It worked in his last village when he manufactured an electrical short that sparked and caught the hay in the Christmas crèche on fire. The flames, fueled by his paints and cleaning fluid, gutted the church, destroying a dozen of his better forgeries, but no icon of real value was lost because the originals were already safely—albeit dishonestly—in the Russian's collection. Villagers had begun to wonder about Vladimir's frequent visits, and on a couple of occasions, Father Alexis had caught people sniffing around his paintings a little too diligently. Once he was gone, those icons could easily have been shipped off for carbon dating that would have exposed even his most perfect forgery. He was beginning to feel similarly overexposed in Vourvoulos. That's why he wanted the fuel tank to remain where it was. Blowing it up would be the simplest solution for him. The steady breeze off the water would blow the flames straight up to the church; and if that failed, Father Alexis was ready to sabotage the church to make it appear that they had.

So determined was the priest that the fuel tank not be moved, he considered closing the church to the public meeting, but realized that would do no good. It might forestall a decision for a few chaotic minutes, but it would still be made, and it was that vote to repair the bell tower—and thus deplete the resources that might otherwise be used to relocate the fuel tank—that Father Alexis was determined to win. Far too much depended on it. Losing the vote would reveal how bogus his reports had been about successfully bringing the leftist villagers back into the Church's fold. He could forget leapfrogging over his fellow brethren for a plum position in a civilized town. He'd likely be banished for the rest of his priestly life to hovels like those he had endured with their pigs, slaughterhouses, and sardines—and old sagging women drooling on his ring. He shivered at the tortured prospect, and grew even more determined to prevail in the vote. By good fortune, only the day before he had stumbled across the tool he needed to ensure his success: a full-sized sledgehammer.

Father Alexis found it propped up in a corner of the dank and web-infested garden shed. Not a man of nature, he spent as little time as he could in places where insects lurked, so it wasn't surprising that he hadn't noticed it before. He instantly recognized its usefulness and lugged it up the tower's steep steps where he leaned it in the corner to wait for his first chance to use it. He had come to regret choosing the side of the tower most visible to the village to manufacture his crack. His intention had been for the villagers to live with a real sense of a growing threat, but the longer the crack became, the more difficult for the priest to take discreet swipes at it with his short hammer.

He had to hang out the window too far, and strike the wall too many times, to make any significant change. The same effort would require only one or two good blows with the heftier sledgehammer.

He needed the right moment when he could inflict more damage unnoticed. The mayor's broadcast alerted him that his chance was coming up soon. Every announcement the tiresome old man made, he repeated precisely ten minutes later, so anyone not catching it the first time would have another chance to hear it. His droning over the crackling PA system would provide sufficient cover for a few hammer blows.

He hiked up his robe to climb the tower. He thought of its uneven steps as the links in a chain that held an albatross around his neck. He was gambling his future on first saving the tower before ensuring that fire destroyed it. He sensed in that a paradox of biblical proportions.

Fire and brimstone. Had they not driven him to his calling?

The crèche fire had not been his first. The refinery fire was.

His father, always a mean, temperamental man, had grown angrier after being diagnosed with lung cancer. Only in his forties, he felt life had been stolen from him, and when he wasn't pitying himself with booze, he had brutal words—and sometimes a brutal fist—for everyone else. Father and son had never had a good relationship, and their fights over any subject grew so angry that they verged on spinning out of control. That fatal afternoon, the boy—Manolis at seventeen—returned home from school. His mother told him that his father wanted him to come to the refinery. She didn't know why. "And don't let your father smell cigarettes on your breath," she said, which was almost a joke, since he'd offered his young son a first cigarette at fourteen. It was the only paternal act Manolis could recall.

He hated everything about the refinery: its stinking petroleum, its ruinous hulk on the beach, its thuggish workers—his father among them—with grit under their nails and blackheads on their necks. It was a life he couldn't wait to escape, which is exactly what he was thinking when he flashed his pass at the guard and walked past the trashcan with the reminder *Keep your butts out of here!*

He headed for the noisy dock thick with fumes where his father hooked up and unhooked oil tankers. He'd worn the same orange outfit and hardhat for as long as the boy could remember. Seeing him approach, his father hollered for someone to take over what he was doing, and motioned for the boy to join him in the glass booth that served as his boss's office.

In it, the outside noises of equipment were muffled. Manolis shook the boss's hand. His father got straight to the point, reminding them that he was dying, with six months to live at best—and he looked it, his eyes already sunken, his cheeks sallow. His biggest worry was not having provided well enough for the family, which would have been a different matter if he had twenty more years; but he didn't, and that meant everybody had to sacrifice something. He knew what he had to say didn't fit into Manolis's hopes for going to the university, but the boy was just going to have to forget those plans. They were impractical anyway. Who had money for the university? His boss had agreed to hire Manolis. They'd be working side-by-side, father and son, and eventually when he became too sick to work, Manolis would take his job. That way he could provide for his mother. Maybe they'd even learn to like each other, his father added with a cocky grin, as if all the spiteful words they'd exchanged could be forgotten with one smile.

The two men had worked it out. They would make it easy for him and themselves. His father would get off the hook for checking out early and not providing better. His mother would be taken care of. Manolis would be guaranteed a job and the boss would inherit a trained worker. It was a good deal all the way around, but what did the boy think? His father knew exactly the sacrifices being asked of him and worried that his son's response would jeopardize his careful construct for providing for his family once he was gone.

"When do I start?" Manolis inquired, and watched relief settle on his old man's face.

The boss answered, "We've got a man out sick. You might as well come in with your dad tomorrow morning."

"Thanks."

Young Manolis walked out of the hut without saying a word. Seething inside, he wanted to throw a tantrum equal to any his father had ever thrown. He hated the man for laying on him a dying wish that he could only fulfill by abandoning his own ambitions: wanting a job that didn't make him smell like an exhaust pipe, and an education that, if his parents couldn't afford, he would make happen himself. It was a selfish last request by a working-class brute who never believed in his son. The boy's dreams and plans were dismissible.

Fuck him. Fuck the rules. Fuck everything. He wanted a cigarette and lit up, took a puff, took a second one and coughed. It tasted like an ashtray: like lung cancer, like their living room with its permanent cloud of tobacco smoke. Disgusted with himself for taking up his father's filthy habit, he tossed what he vowed to be his last cigarette into a trashcan, and plodded on past equipment sheds and holding tanks. He had reached the refinery's exit before the siren went off. He looked back, and seconds later, he heard an explosion powerful enough to rumble the earth and send flames high into the sky.

Manolis didn't stop running until he reached home. His mother was in the yard watching the roiling acrid smoke rise over the refinery. She grabbed him, and held him so tight it hurt, her own body heaving in relief that he was alive, and also heaving for what she feared to be a dead husband with only poverty as her inheritance. Investigators never determined the cause of the fire, surmising a random spark had ignited a buildup of fumes; and Manolis could attest that the fumes had been strong on the dock that day. He also knew with certainty that his last cigarette had set the trashcan on fire, sending windborne sparks back along the dock where the explosion occurred.

Had he intended to kill his father? He never thought so, not consciously. Subconsciously, anger plotted its own way. He had been reckless to toss aside a lit cigarette. He was a young, impressionable boy, sensitive and passionate, and ultimately to his father, nothing that distinguished him mattered. He had bequeathed his son a sense of expendability without living long enough to retract it.

It angered Father Alexis every time he thought about how a kid could be so dismissed; and, before that, so ignored. By the time he reached the top of the bell tower, he was furious again with his father. He picked up the sledgehammer ready to hit anything. Moments later, he heard the PA system crackle to life a second time, and braced himself in the window. As soon as the mayor started to repeat his message, the priest swung at the wall below him until some stucco gave way. With another couple of heavy blows overhead, he dislodged a large chunk that whizzed past his head filling his mouth with dust.

The priest ran down the steps to collect his booty.

• • •

ATHINA DECIDED THAT SHE WOULD deliver the sad girl's plea for Ridi's help and then never speak to him again. She felt deceived; he'd lied when he claimed not to know the girl well. All this time, he'd had a girlfriend back home, and now she happened to be up the road in the clinic's bed recovering from the miscarriage of his son! That couldn't have been a coincidence. They must have had a plan. He was waiting on the beach for her. No wonder he had acted so weird all day, trying to keep that secret inside.

Coming up the wharf, she could see there were no early customers at her mother's restaurant. In anticipation of a busy evening (the eve of the Miss Icon Contest always was), Ridi had spread fresh blue cloths on all the tables, and in the center of each, placed small bouquets of flowers in pickling jars. Proudly surveying them, as might a real proprietor, he smiled as the girl walked up.

"I am not talking to you," Athina said, brushing past him.

His smile evaporated. "What did I do?"

"I said that I am not talking to you."

"But what did I do?"

Athina stopped in her tracks, sighed heavenward, and faced him. "I suppose I need to speak to you one last time, and then I never will again."

"Then I hope it is a long conversation."

"How can you make jokes at a time like this?"

"It's my nervous way."

"When were you going to tell me that you have a girlfriend?"

"What girlfriend?"

"The girl in the clinic."

"You went to see Jura?"

"So you admit it. She's your girlfriend."

"She's not."

"She says you're married."

"We are not married!"

"Then why does she call you her husband?"

"She is crazy!"

"Was she pregnant with your child?"

"She says yes because she trick me!"

"You don't believe her?"

"Maybe I believe her."

"And you left her when she was pregnant in Albania?"

"I didn't know. I only learn about the baby today."

"But you knew it was possible?"

He shook his head emphatically. "No! I thought it is impossible!"

"It's never impossible," Athina told him, disappointed that he was trying to wiggle out of his responsibility.

"I make my best to make impossible," he said, and told her about the extra-thick condoms that unfortunately had been easily pricked by Jura's needle.

"She really tricked you?"

"Yes."

"This morning, you weren't waiting for her on the beach?"

"No! I was finding stones for you."

"Stones for me?"

"For your crown." He dug into his pocket to show her a palm full of smooth pebbles. He fingered them, pointing out, "This is a ruby. An emerald. These are diamonds. I have so many diamonds!"

"They even look like diamonds."

"Diamonds are easy to find, but not lapis. Look." Ridi reached into another pocket for two chips colored deep blue.

"They're beautiful," Athina said. "They even look real. But I'm sorry, I can't wear your crown."

"Why you can't wear my crown?"

"Not until you help Jura. You can't abandon her."

"I don't bring her here."

"It was still your stuff that got her pregnant."

"Because she tricked me!"

The young man had heartbreak written all over his face. She felt so badly for him, and even sadder for herself. "I take back not talking to you, but I can't take it back about not wearing the crown. Not yet. Not until you help Jura."

"Help her how?"

"I don't know yet."

"It sounds like another trick."

"I'm not trying to trick you. Now I better go to work." Athina took a couple of steps before adding, "The flowers on the tables are pretty."

"Thank you."

"Though my mom won't like the fact that you used her pickling jars."

"She will like the more business."

"You're right," she replied, and touched his arm. "I'm sorry about the baby. I'm sure that's sad news, even if you didn't know about it."

"It's been a sad day," he replied.

◆ ◆ ◆

THAT SETTLES THAT, LYDIA THOUGHT, stepping back from the balcony's rail. The young lovebirds' relationship was over before it started. He already had a girlfriend, and he'd already gotten her pregnant. Even her daughter wouldn't see a future in that history.

Lydia was not an habitual eavesdropper. She had been watching for her daughter, continuing to worry about the consequences—psychological or otherwise—of her mysterious seduction. She was still determined to identify the male culprit, though now she was confident that it had not been Ridi. Theirs had not been a conversation between a horrible, hairy despoiler and his victim, but between two young people faltering in their efforts to fall in love. It was sad for them, but better in the long run. She was proud of Athina for handling it so maturely by reminding the boy of his responsibility toward the recovering girl.

From down the wharf she heard a hoot. Stavros, with a flower behind an ear, was dancing again, rocking his boat and brandishing a fish in each hand. "*Pa-la-MEE-da!*" he sang, the black bonitos glistening in the sun. "*Pa-la-MEE-da!* The last of the season!" Seeing Lydia on her balcony, he called, "You want my *palamida* today?"

Yes, she did, and shouted back, "Ten kilos!"

"I save you my best! *Pa-la-MEE-da!*" he sang again. "Swimming in my hands! *Pa-la-MEE-da!*"

Already the women in earshot of Stavros's song were showing up—the older ones hitching up knee-high stockings, the younger exposing less-wrinkled bosoms, each wanting her daily dose of the errant fisherman. As he picked out fish, he tossed some aside, and caught Lydia's eye letting her know they were for her. He still knew how to seduce. He had caught her eye eighteen years earlier, which launched their mad affair. Soon to be betrothed to Lefteris, she wanted her taste of the fisherman before he was off-limits. It lasted a short while, not even a month; she couldn't have kept it secret much longer. She had used every ruse she could to find short hours with him, and one whole glorious afternoon on Bird Island with only seagulls to witness their frolicking in the open air. She never seriously considered leaving Lefteris for him—Stavros's ways were already too wayward for a husband—but for those brief weeks, the fisherman made her heart sing.

Waywardness was not her worry with Ridi, regardless of whoever the girl in the clinic turned out to be. In all the important ways, he seemed as steady as Lefteris, and she could wish for nothing more in a man for her daughter. It was their hardscrabble life that she wanted to keep Athina from repeating; the meager days when the fish weren't running or the tourists weren't coming or the weather forced her to close early. One economic crisis atop another had left them struggling. She wanted her daughter to have more security and didn't believe a poor Albanian boy could provide it.

She didn't have to fret so much about that now. It turned out that the young waiter had a female preoccupation other than Athina, and by the time that all got sorted out, her daughter would be on to a new boy, hopefully less seriously inclined than Ridi. She wanted Athina to get away from the island, not marry too quickly—get at least a lick of life if not a full taste. Ridi wasn't a bad boy. In fact, the opposite: he was a nice young man who took initiative. Lydia hoped it worked out for him and his eventual other girlfriend. She liked his ideas, too. The flowers on the tables were a nice touch, and he had made an effort to clasp the tablecloths extra tight so they looked especially crisp. He was right, she'd be glad for "the more business" if her filched pickling jars drew in extra customers. Hopefully the stiff winds on the other side of the island would cooperate and stay over there.

A couple of customers had shown up at the restaurant while Lydia was loitering upstairs. She decided to go down, and gave Stavros a last glance before she did. He seemed to have been waiting for her to look, and plucked the flower from behind his ear to offer it to her. He definitely still knew how to seduce. Smiling for the first time that day, she left the balcony.

• • •

KOUFOS HAD NEVER WORN UNDERWEAR.

He had seen it. On mannequins. Riding high on a man's waist. Poking out, sometimes, when a man missed zipping up all the way.

Meticulously, he inserted the boxers into the mustard pants spread on the ruined house's floor, leaving a half inch of its elastic waistband showing. He got goose bumps from the satisfaction of having collected a man's complete outfit. Stripping off his threadbare rags, he retrieved the boxers and slipped on that day's trophy. He admired the puckered elastic clinging to his flat belly and snapped it a couple of times.

Slowly he donned everything else.

Pants.

Undershirt.

Shirt.

Socks.

All with a trace scent of the rosemary plants he had spread them on to dry.

Then he put on his other trophy for the day: dry shoes.

When Koufos finished, he had no way to see himself. There was no piece of mirror or anything shiny enough for a reflection. He stuck out his arms to see his wrists encircled by the shirtsleeves and stared at his feet to see his cuffs dangling almost to his ankles—and smiled.

He had never worn such fine clothes before. Slipping on the dead man's ring, he left the ruined house dressed for dinner.

• • •

After his meeting with the Coast Guard captain, Nick took a table at Lydia's Kitchen close to the water's edge. The chilly winds from the other side of the island had yet to shift around the point, though the bright fishing boats bobbed and creaked in the impinging sea. It was a lively crowd strolling along the wharf, excited with anticipation of tomorrow's procession. Next door, he watched Takis tend bar. Nick didn't want to admit that Captain Tsounis was right: the young waiter was a far likelier suspect than some farfetched ghost story about Omar. For that matter, so was Father Alexis, but it was Takis who most interested Nick. Prime suspect or not, his attraction was real. He wanted to be Takis's lover, not accuser.

Lydia brought him a glass, a bottle of house white, and a plate of anchovies. "It's on me and say thanks, not that I shouldn't have."

"Thanks."

"That's better. Are you working on your novel?"

"I'm working on the backstory of one of my characters."

"Is she based on me?"

"It's a guy, but maybe I can make him partly you. A piece of you here, another piece there, pretty soon there's a lot of Lydia in Louie."

"Is that how writers make up their characters?"

"All the time."

"Thanks, but I think I'd rather keep all my pieces intact."

She walked off, and he poured himself a glass of wine before reaching into his daypack for his phone. He smelled cigarette ashes, and looked around to move an offending ashtray, when he realized the smell was coming from the dud detonator that he had forgotten to take out and leave in his room. He zipped his pack closed and encrypted a new message:

SUBJ: OZTURK Omar. Turkish national. Married Vassoula VATIS. Mutilated by skinheads approx two years ago. Presumed suicide. Body never found. Request any information.

He sent the message, and settled back to sip his wine when Shirley arrived with Dingo prancing ahead of her. She had a new international entourage in tow. They settled at a table, and when Shirley spied Nick sitting by himself, she sent the dog over to lick his hand to convince him to join them. He did, contributing his anchovies and wine to the table. Their glasses never stayed empty as Shirley presided over her chatty friends.

Then one by one, the crowd began to grow very quiet.

"You can't *imagine* what I was thinking!" Shirley exclaimed, wrapping up a story, and stopped as she heard herself over the spreading silence. She looked around. "Is that the deaf boy?" she asked.

Koufos had practiced that moment. If he had known the word debut, he would have owned it that evening. He had grown up an observer—and mimicker—and rehearsed how every footstep, tip of his head, or turn of his wrist should be made. Though to Koufos, as playacted as it might be, the moment was not theatre to him. That night was a rite of passage he had chosen for himself.

Ridi waved him into a seat. When Koufos realized people were staring at him, he flashed everyone a goofy grin. For tourists, that was enough entertainment and their conversations sputtered back to life. The locals, though, knew how extraordinary it was for Koufos to be all dressed up and at a table. They couldn't stop staring at him.

Neither could Nick. He recognized the red shirt and mustard pants from the ruined house, and his own purloined shoes were on the boy's feet. He was the kid who Nick accidentally stepped on in the church. The boy couldn't have been more than thirteen or fourteen, with a downy black moustache auditioning on his lip, and clearly he was going to be tall; his arms and legs comically stuck out of his clothes. Nick had almost convinced himself that it was Omar living in the ruined house. What he wore made it clear that it was this strange boy instead.

Ridi brought a menu which Koufos made a point of studying before pointing to several items. The waiter took the menu from him, turned it right-side up and handed it back, evoking snickers from nearby tables. The boy, unable to hear the remarks but only seeing their smiles, laughed back making a chirpy, high-pitched sound. When he scooted back his chair and stood up, disappointment palpably passed through the crowd. No one wanted him to fail in his effort to order dinner.

The boy, though, wasn't leaving, and signaled for Ridi to follow him. He wound through the tables, and when he saw something he wanted, he pointed to the person eating it; and then, like a caricature artist, exaggerated something about that person. It was his way of naming the dish: the meat the man scratching his head ordered, or the vegetables for the woman touching up her lips. Over years of scavenging food scraps, he'd come to recognize the regulars, and lampooned them beautifully: the peevish birders' perpetual something-smells-bad wiggling of their noses, someone else's haughty posture, Shirley's flamboyant toss of a scarf over her shoulders. It was all good-natured, and everyone, even those less kindly portrayed, appreciated the humor in what was unexpectedly turning into a dinner show about a deaf kid ordering his first meal in a restaurant.

Next, zeroing in on Nick's anchovies, the guileless boy recognized him from the beach, and gave a guilty glance at Nick's shoes on his own feet. Nick shrugged, which encouraged the boy to lift his arms and imitate Nick walking barefoot over the beach pebbles, even reenacting a couple of small stumbles. The crowd thought he was dancing, and loved it when Stavros picked up his bouzouki and played a riff from *Zorba's Dance*. A few people took up clapping rhythmically, but the deaf boy, never in synch with them, stopped on his own beat.

The harbor lights dancing on the water, the gently rocking boats, the easy chatter along the wharf all belied the threat only steps from where they sat. Nick conjured an image of the stalwart tank perched on concrete footings suddenly exploding. He knew it could happen because someone was determined to make it happen, and he guessed that Koufos might have had two chances to see the arsonist: when he lit the dud detonator that never caught fire, and when he returned with a second detonator that did catch fire. The boy had found the dud, but had he seen the arsonist? Nick needed to know even if it meant blowing his own cover. The threat to the village was too imminent.

He unzipped his daypack and removed the dud. He put it on the table and reset a couple of cigarettes that had come loose. Koufos's eyes widened when he recognized it and was ready to bolt. Nick motioned that everything was okay. The boy didn't need to be afraid. Never breaking eye contact with him, he asked the people around him, "Who has a lighter? I need a lighter, please!"

Someone slipped him one. He flicked it and touched the flame to a cigarette butt stuck in the glob of white plastic. Then he pretended to light the others, moving from one to the next as if lighting candles on a birthday cake while the boy watched him intently. *Who did it?* Nick silently asked with a shrug and waved the lighter at the crowd.

He pretended to light another and pointed to a man. *Did he?*

Another cigarette. *Did she?*

Another cigarette. *Who?*

He cupped his hands for breasts. *Was it a woman?*

He stroked his beard. *Or a man?*

Koufos finally shook his head. *No.*

No what? No man? No woman? No what?

Koufos plucked all the cigarettes from the Styrofoam and set them aside. Then picking one up, he put it between his lips, lit and stuck it upright in the plastic.

He looked at Nick. *Do you understand?*

Nick shook his head. He wasn't sure.

Koufos brought a second butt to his lips, lit it, and reset it in the Styrofoam. *Now do you understand?* his expression asked.

Nick did. The cigarettes hadn't been lit like birthday candles. The arsonist had lit each one like the cigarette it was before sticking it into the detonator. He motioned for Koufos to light more of them. He did, and the boy's proclivity to mimic began to change his body language. He was morphing into the arsonist, and getting to the point of revealing who it was, when Jura stepped out of the shadow behind him.

"Ruben?" she asked hesitantly.

Koufos was oblivious to her and lit another cigarette.

"Ruben?"

He inhaled.

"Ruben!"

Exhaled.

She dropped a hand on his shoulder.

Startled, he whirled around.

She staggered back, shrieking.

He fell back, too, making a pitiful cry. He had never seen such a madwoman. Sunken eyes, her mouth a round black cavity, arms twitching and hair flecked with phlegm. Blood spreading between her legs on a hospital gown. Koufos's only instinct was to run. He dashed past her and sprinted down the wharf, unable to hear her screams that followed him until she crumpled in a faint. Ridi dashed to her, lifted her in his arms, and carried her off.

The buzz in the port was instant. Electrified. Some people thought it had been a stunt, especially when Ridi ran off holding the overcome girl. A few people even applauded before they realized that the locals weren't laughing. A couple of boys chased after him and came back to report that the doctor, fortunately, stayed at the clinic when she realized the girl had disappeared, imagining she might need her help again; and she had, she was hemorrhaging. Ridi told them that he knew the girl from his village, and Ruben, the name she'd called out, was her brother. She must have mistaken Koufos for him.

"Oh, that poor deaf boy," Shirley said. "When you think that he's been left to grow up on his own."

"Not entirely on his own, Mum," Lydia, standing nearby, corrected her. "We put food out for him."

"The cats eat better!"

"The cats eat what he doesn't take. They never eat better."

"That doesn't mean he should be abandoned to grow up wild. There ought to be a law!"

"There *is* a law," someone replied, "and if they enforced it, he would be living in some horrible institution being sexually abused. He's probably better off on his own."

"We don't even know where he lives," Shirley complained. "He moves around one season to the next. Oh it's terrible!"

"I know where he's living," Nick spoke up. "I went for a hike today and came across a ruined house. Inside I saw the clothes that he had on tonight. What's his name?"

"Koufos."

"Deaf?"

Lydia shrugged. "It's what people call him."

Nick touched the detonator. "I found this in the house. Who is he?"

"A kid the Gypsies left behind."

"More like threw away," Shirley griped.

"How long ago?"

"Four or five years ago."

"It's been almost six years, Mum."

Nick said, "That's pretty young to be living on your own."

"A couple of families tried to take him in, or at least give him a place to sleep. He wouldn't stay. The best we could do was to give him food when he came around."

"He might stay now. I don't know where he got all the clothes, but he's been working on assembling them." Nick described how they had been displayed in the ruined house, laid out as if being worn, the shirttail tucked into the pants and socks coming out of the cuffs. When he found them, Nick had no reason to think in terms of what was missing from it, but now he knew it had been underwear. Shoes the boy already had, albeit the soggy ones that he traded for Nick's, but only lacking underwear explained why that was all he took from the car. When he dressed for dinner that night, his outfit was finally complete. "I'm not a psychologist, but it wouldn't take a very smart one to sort out that he wants to join society. Tonight he was testing it," Nick concluded.

Shirley snorted. "I guess that didn't work out too well for him, did it?"

"Do you think he started the fires?" Lydia asked. "Why else would he have a detonator?"

"More likely, he found it," Nick answered. "It was probably a dud."

"Where's the house that's he's living?"

Nick described its location the best he could without outright identifying it as the site of the tenth fire on Lydia's map. That would be a surefire giveaway that he was more than a floundering writer out on a hike.

"That's the Turks' house," she remarked.

"Where?" Shirley asked.

"The Turks' house, Mum. Above the next cove from you. Fire number ten."

"Koufos is living *there*?"

"It looked that way to me," Nick said. "You must leave food for him in aluminum foil."

"How do you know?"

"He saves all the pieces folded up in a little pile in his room."

"Why would he do that?"

"By now he probably worships aluminum foil. It's manna from heaven. It means food."

"*Mom!*" they all heard Athina shout from the porch, a plate in each hand and an exasperated expression on her face. She locked eyes with her mother. "There's more to running a restaurant than talking to your customers. These plates need to be served to number three."

"She's right, back to work. Busy night and suddenly no Ridi." Lydia drained her wine. "I'll rejoin you when I can."

Nick used her departure to leave as well. He only went next door, but stepping inside was moving from the innocent to the profane: from the wharf's fresh air and romantic music to loud rock and a room thick with cigarette smoke. He slipped onto the only free barstool.

"It's on the house, whatever you want," Takis told him.

"You?"

"I thought you wanted me on the rocks."

"There, too. It's a busy night. Where's your sister?"

"Banging the Coast Guard."

"The whole fleet?"

"She's a whore, but I give her credit, she's selective." Takis poured him an ouzo. "Is ouzo okay, or do you want my sister to do her brandy thing again?"

"I'll pass on the brandy," Nick said, and sipped his ouzo.

Takis said, "It's weird that kid showed up tonight. He's never done anything like that before."

"He's good at charades, that's clear. Has he really grown up wild?"

"Nobody even knows how old he is."

"He has peach fuzz on his lip," Nick commented, "so maybe twelve or thirteen years old, which means he's been on his own since he was six or seven."

"Poor kid," Takis remarked. "Shall I top that off?"

Nick had a sudden change of heart. He wanted Takis but not more ouzo. The all-nighter he wanted wasn't a boozy one. "I just came to make sure you're coming to my place when you get off."

"You're not going to stay?"

"You'll be working until dawn, so wake me up."

"Any special way?"

"Surprise me."

Nick didn't know how many hills he had climbed that day, he just knew it was a lot, and the one to his room was about the steepest. He paused at the top to catch his breath. The sea stretched milky white to the horizon, as if the drowning moon had spilt cream over it. A whiff of honeysuckle, wafting over his garden wall, made the moment deliriously romantic. He desired Takis and wished their situation hadn't become so unpredictably complicated.

He pushed through the squeaking gate and crossed the perfumed garden to enter his room. Moments later, he reemerged with a last glass of wine and stood where the terrace jutted out over the sloped yard. Laughter drifted up from the port. At one point, he heard Takis, and recalled the flash of his smile following him out the door. He knew he'd be another couple of hours. The only "last call" Nick had ever heard in Greece was sunrise. He went inside to shower.

He dried off, and on his way to bed, turned off the lights to look at himself in the mirror. He had a good build, with a swimmer's strong shoulders and muscled legs. He twisted around to see his back and stood on his tiptoes to glimpse his buttocks. He hated his scars on his ass the most, and in the moonlight, he could almost convince himself that they were going away. Of course they weren't. It was the wishful thinking of infatuation. In a crueler light his scars would still be there. But that pale light would illuminate their lovemaking that night, and in it, Nick could almost convince himself that he was sexy.

He slipped on his boxers, considered a last nightcap, and decided he was woozy enough. There was no way he could wait up for Takis. He would have to wake Nick if he wanted to have a good time, and he was sure Takis would. He pulled back the bed covers, or tried to; they were tucked in tight. Athina must have returned to remake the bed sometime during the day. He yanked a corner loose enough to get between the sheets and jabbed his legs down to make room for his feet.

He was asleep before his head hit the pillow. Dreaming of nothing, and then suddenly he was in the sea, diving down, bubbles caught in the hair on his legs tickling him as they rose to the surface, drifting up his belly and chest. Then, a sting on his thigh, another on his shoulder; inconsequential pricks that his dreamer's mind dismissed as jellyfish larvae in the warm water. They were annoying, not painful. Nevertheless, he kicked his feet to swim faster, and the stinging became more intense.

He woke up with a start. Something *was* stinging him! Biting him and crawling all over him! He scrambled from bed and turned on the lamp, and flicked a spider off his arm. He saw its red belly. A black widow! He felt more tramping through the hair on his chest and brushed those off, and then knocked off the ones dangling by their fangs from his ankles. He ripped back the bed covers and saw the nests that his feet had disturbed.

Nick bolted for the bathroom, accidentally sending the bedside lamp crashing to the floor. He fished a pocketknife from his dopp kit and sat on the toilet slitting open the bites, pinching out blood and venom. He sucked on the ones he could reach and spat the foul mixture into the sink. By contorting himself in the mirror, he tried to open the bites on his back; but he couldn't, not successfully before tremors set in. A nauseating dizziness swept over him. He slumped to the floor, closing the bathroom door with his body.

• • •

ATHINA SAT ON THE BED staring at her cell phone as she might a crystal ball anticipating predictions for the future. Almost the totality of her information came over the device in her hand. Yet while she relied on it for so much of her life's content, at that moment it felt especially lifeless. Certainly not something that could express the emotions churning through her. In her mind's eye, she had replayed the scene with the priest in the harsh light of honest memory, and realized that what had happened ultimately mattered very little; it wasn't something that would scar her for life or change her prospects. It had happened. It wasn't rape. She would never laugh about it but she would get over it. And when she finally gave the priest his comeuppance, it would not be for his part in their encounter, but for his backpedaling on taking equal responsibility for it.

Initially she had accused Ridi of a similar misdeed, lumping him together with every man who shirked responsibility for getting a woman pregnant. If Athina didn't believe in the first Immaculate Conception, she wasn't likely to be convinced about a second one; and Ridi, to his credit, had not denied his affair with Jura. The girl had tricked him, manufacturing her pregnancy against his will; though giving in to his animal needs had put him in the position where he could be tricked. But then, she herself might be pregnant by the priest, and without the excuse of someone having poked pinholes in a sheath of protective rubber. Who was she to criticize anyone for what they had done? Even Jura's deceit had been an act of love, however hateful the consequences.

All evening, Athina had ridden her emotional roller coaster. By helping in the kitchen more than usual, she had kept her distance from the young waiter, but it didn't keep her from fretting over him. It didn't seem possible that they had been flirting with each other—*seriously* flirting with each other—for fewer days than counted in a week. He had texted her a heart, and now hers was broken; and his was, too, if his heavy steps and solemnness were reliable proof. By her insistence that he help the girl, Athina knew she had compounded the weight of his troubles, and yet she was loath to retract it. Though as the evening wore on, she started to wonder if she was blaming him unfairly. Shouldn't the girl in the clinic bear the heavier responsibility for her duplicity? It mirrored the dilemma she had in assigning blame for what happened between herself and the priest; the difference being, Ridi had taken precautions. He'd worn a condom. The priest had not. Ridi was now taking responsibility, helping the girl. When he swept her up in his arms and without breaking stride carried her up the dark hill to the clinic, Athina knew that she loved him, and in the same instant realized that she had lost him. She had pushed Ridi back to the other girl. She alone was responsible for the lonely miserable life she would suffer without him.

Ridi had come back late from the clinic, terse, only saying that the doctor thought Jura would be okay. By then, the last diners were leaving, seduced by the promise of a livelier nightcap at Vassoula's next door. In silence, they set about closing down the restaurant in their usual way. Sending Athina's mother upstairs was always their first task; they were much more efficient without her telling them to do what they already knew to do. Besides, that night they wanted to be alone. They had for a long time, the girl realized; but it was not to be that evening. Lydia lingered on until they were all finished. She reminded Ridi to lock up and chaperoned her daughter upstairs.

That's what it had felt like—being chaperoned—leaving Athina stranded in her bedroom while Ridi, banished downstairs, glued the beach pebbles-cum-gemstones onto her Styrofoam crown. She had threatened not to wear it until he helped Jura, and certainly rescuing her twice on the same day qualified as helping her. She would wear the crown, which was hardly a relief in a day overcrowded with disappointments.

It dawned on her that Ridi's pockets must have been filled with the small pebbles he'd collected when he dived into the sea to save the drowning girl. He could have emptied them instead of being weighed down in that wind-tossed sea, but to please Athina he hadn't; or so she wanted to believe, when it was as likely that in the emergency, he hadn't remembered the faux gems. He just ran into the water. No matter which version of the story was true, both made him heroic.

She could forgive him everything and wanted him to know it. Struggling to see her phone through blurring tears, she found the young waiter's heart message from a couple of mornings earlier and messaged it back to him. Clasping the phone to her breast, she hoped it wasn't too late.

• • •

FROM THE DECK OF HIS boat, Stavros, playing his bouzouki, might as well have been plucking Ridi's heart. The young waiter, cross-legged on the kitchen floor, crown-making materials scattered around him, assumed he was employed in a futile exercise: finishing a crown Athina would never wear. His despair made the fisherman's trebling melodies all the more poignant.

After several trials, he landed on a solution for constructing a copy of the Crowned Madonna's double-decker headpiece by running souvlaki sticks, which he sharpened at both ends, through the center of rounded Styrofoam posts, and sticking a coronet on each protruding end. He tucked and smoothed aluminum foil over the whole thing to imitate silver and reinforce its whole structure. Studiously, he compared the jewels in Athina's photographs to his supply of colorful pebbles, hoping to replicate the lineup of jewels of the original crown, but soon realized it was futile. The icon's crown was laden with diamonds while what he'd collected was mostly the red spit of ancient volcanoes worn smooth by the zillions of waves that had swept them out to sea and tumbled them back onto shore again.

As he set about gluing them to the crown, Ridi felt as if he, too, had been swept out to sea and tossed back. That morning, he literally had been, but surviving that ordeal was tame compared to the tsunami of emotions that repeatedly swamped him. He couldn't help but feel pity for the girl stranded in the clinic: a lifelong friend, a brief lover, and in the end, a trickster; but she had tricked herself if her intention had been to trap him, though it would have worked if his son had survived. Son or daughter, Jura knew that Ridi would never abandon his own child. He wasn't a man who could; he would deny himself first. Through cold treachery, she had intended to subvert him by taking advantage of his nobler instincts. Her brutal miscarriage relieved him of a paternal duty, but still, there was Jura at the edge of death because she had come searching for him. Where was his responsibility in that uncrafted conundrum?

He worked steadily, positioning each pebble, careful that the heavier ones were closer to the bottom for balance, and used the smallest fake diamonds to fill in all the empty spaces. As it took shape and became something truly worthy of a queen, he wept, imagining the crown forever abandoned on the kitchen floor, the detritus of its creation scattered like toxic waste around it.

Despair.

That would be his first vocabulary word to learn tomorrow. In his native Albanian, he knew the word well. He had lived it, internalized it, certain it would define his life if he never escaped his village.

Treachery.

He could certainly claim to be a victim of it.

Unforgivable.

Another word he needed to explain what he was feeling. He only lacked one: a bigger word for sad than sadness. Then he landed on it.

Wretched.

That was the word. That's how he felt—wretched. Heartbroken and miserable. Once he articulated it, he couldn't hold back his tears. They ran down his cheeks. He wiped them away but more kept coming. Soon his hands were wet, and when he touched the pebbles on the crown, they turned shiny. He dabbed tears on all of them, making them shimmer in the low light, but to what end?

Futility.

Another word he needed to learn. Who cared how beautiful the crown if Athina never wore it? She might not even look at it! In an instant, it changed from being a symbol of his love to a haunting reminder that he had lost her. Sobbing, he lifted his fist intent on destroying it, when his phone pinged. He stopped and reached for it.

Athina had sent him a heart.

Another sob escaped him, but that one was for joy. He sent a heart back to her, and kissed his phone wishing he could send himself, too.

• • •

VLADIMIR AND THE PINBALLER WERE having a spat. That was evident by how hard the kid punched the game machine's buttons, as if he could accelerate the pinball, when in fact the flippers always made their jerky movements at the same speed. He would've had a better chance gambling on a change in the tilt of the earth. Instead he set off the *Tilt!* alarm for the umpteenth time and Takis decided that was it for the night. "That's it, closing time," he announced.

The Russian pushed his shot glass across the bar. "One more," he ordered.

Takis poured vodka. "Make it fast."

Vladimir knocked it back and slammed the glass down. "Was that fast enough?" He left money on the bar and walked out.

The pinballer hit the game machine and followed him.

Takis loaded the last dirty glasses into the dishwasher and, with a last swipe of a sponge on the bar, checked that nothing else needed to be done. Vassoula usually left him to close up and he preferred it that way. Like most Greeks, he was a night owl, but in Melbourne at least it had a purpose other than making him hungover the next day. His whole life had opened for him there—his night life in particular—and if he had any hope of scoring in tiny Vourvoulos, it would only be at the drunken end of the night. Occasionally he had, but that night there weren't any tipsy guys to cruise; and even if there were, he'd be ignoring them knowing that Nick was waiting up the hill.

He turned off the lights and locked up the bar, and minutes later pushed open Nick's gate. The drowning moon had long disappeared, leaving the Milky Way to light the garden path. He didn't bother looking for the key over the door; he knew it would be unlocked and went inside. The bed was tossed but he couldn't quite make out Nick. A strip of light seeped under the bathroom door and he guessed him to be in there. He thought he would surprise him and be in bed when he returned, so he quickly stripped down to his briefs, then decided those should come off, too. Scurrying to the bed, he tripped over something and reached down for the bedside lamp. Nick must have knocked it over, but why hadn't he picked it up?

"Nick?" he said in the dark.

No answer.

"Nick?" he repeated a little louder.

Again no answer.

He flicked on the lamp.

It took him a moment to comprehend what he saw: rumpled sheets spotted with blood, and spiders—black widows!—crawling in them. Alarmed, he swung around to the bathroom door. "Nick! Are you all right?"

Takis tried to open it but it was blocked. He pushed harder and Nick moaned. Working the door wider, he squeezed his way into a nightmare. Nick had a dozen puncture wounds on his arms and legs and bloody drool in his beard. Nick was burning hot with a fever, and his breathing shallow and congested. He looked close to death and needed urgent help. Takis tried to rouse him but couldn't. An ambulance from the island's capital was an hour away and something had to be done sooner. The only person he could think to call was his sister. He did, describing the scene while stomping on spiders. "They're fucking everywhere!" he cried. "And Nick's barely alive!"

Vassoula said, "Make sure all the spiders are dead. Can you boil water?"

He glanced around and saw a kettle. "Yes."

"I'm coming."

Takis turned off his phone, quickly dressed, and checked the bed. Some spiders were still burrowed in the sheets. He rolled them in a big ball and left it on the terrace, then sought out any spiders still lurking in the room and smashed them with a shoe. When confident they were clear, he turned on an electric kettle in the corner that served as a kitchen, and went to rescue Nick from the floor. The bathroom was so small that he had a hard time angling him through the door. His wounds trailed blood. He managed to lift him onto the bed when Vassoula let herself in.

Without a greeting, she went to the bed to look him over. "At least he knew enough to try to get the poison out. Have you checked his back?"

"No."

"Let's turn him over."

They did it together.

"What happened to him?" she asked about his scars.

"He was in a fire when he was a kid."

"Too bad for such a handsome man." She examined Nick. "He has four bites on his back that he couldn't reach."

The kettle clicked off.

Vassoula pulled four shot glasses from her purse.

"I'll get the towels." Takis darted into the bathroom, grabbed every towel and dumped them next to the bed. Vassoula lined up four shot glasses, and unsheathed a knife that he recognized. Their mother had used it to bleed them on occasions when they had been dangerously ill. Short but elegant, its silver handle was thick to ensure a steady hand, and its stubby blade was scalpel-sharp. Takis stopped up the sink, poured the boiling water into it, and dropped in the shot glasses. He swished the knife around to sterilize it. "Do you think bleeding him will still help?"

"Nothing else will."

He wet a dishcloth for her to clean the bites on his back. Then he handed her the knife. She pressed it to one of the wounds just enough to dimple his flesh and nodded at Takis when she was ready. He plucked a shot glass from the steaming water as she pierced Nick's skin. Only a hint of blood welled along its blade. Vassoula withdrew it and instantly Takis capped it with the glass. The suction created by its heat pulled blood and venom from the wound. In quick order, they cupped the other bites. Nick moaned each time the burning hot glass touched him but remained unconscious. They watched as blood pooled inside the glasses until Vassoula said, "That's enough." When she pulled them off, Takis pounced with towels, soaking up the blood that spilled out and pressing hard to stop the cuts from bleeding more.

When the whole event was over, Takis leaned back against the wall, taking in the pile of bloodied towels and linens. "It looks like a slaughterhouse in here," he said.

"Black widows don't nest in beds. Someone tried to kill him," Vassoula replied.

"That's crazy. Why?"

"Or at least make him very sick. You said he was an FBI agent. Maybe someone else knows that and doesn't like him snooping around."

"I made that up because you were making fun of him," Takis confessed. "He's not an FBI agent. He has a souvenir badge that he bought in a store."

"Do you think they sell real-looking FBI badges in tourist shops?"

"I believed him."

"Who else knows he works for the FBI?"

"Athina, though she didn't actually see the badge. She heard me say something about it. Why would she want to kill him?"

"Maybe she's the arsonist."

"Athina?"

"Or she mentioned it to someone, who mentioned it to someone, and the arsonist finally heard."

Vassoula started rummaging through Nick's bureau.

"What are you doing?"

"I want to see his fake ID."

"You can't go through his stuff."

"He won't wake up for a long time."

"That's not the point."

Vassoula opened a second drawer. It was empty.

Pulling out the bottom one, she said, "So it's what I thought."

"What?"

Vassoula lifted a clear plastic bag containing one of the detonators. "He has three of these. That was no fake ID you saw. He's here because of the fires. He's not here looking for love either."

"What do you mean by that?"

"He's come looking for you because of the Takis Fire. He might think there's a connection."

Takis paled. "Don't call it that."

"Everybody calls it that. Everybody thinks there's a connection between you and the fires, too, because they started when you came back."

"Don't try to frame me."

"I'm trying to warn you. A lot of people have noticed the coincidence. I'm sure your FBI boyfriend has, too."

Nick's shoulders suddenly spasmed. With a second convulsion, he gagged and drooled bile onto the mattress.

Vassoula touched his forehead. "His fever broke. He's going to live." She picked up her bag. "Roll him on his side. That way, he won't drown in his own puke. And be careful what you say when he comes around."

Nick spit up again.

"Maybe you should give him a big deep kiss and make him feel better." With a derisive laugh, Vassoula was gone.

He rolled Nick onto his side, tucked a pillow under his head, and propped another one against his chest to keep him from rolling onto his stomach. Of course Vassoula would cast aspersions on the nicest guy he'd ever met. Handsome, too, though at the moment it was hard to see past the blood and sputum. His sister had almost thrown herself on him. That's what made it all so crazy: they could each desire exactly the same flesh, and yet for Takis to do so was somehow wrong.

He gathered up the bloodied towels and dumped them on the bathroom floor. From the closet he took an extra blanket and draped it over Nick. He took off his shoes and crawled into bed, and spooned with him for warmth. Maybe Nick had come looking for him, but even if their encounter was less than happenstance, their attraction was honest and mutual. Besides, the last thing Takis worried about was unintentionally incriminating himself. Some lies he'd told so often that they'd become real to him. He'd be willing to take a lie detector test on the Takis Fire, so he wasn't worried about an FBI agent, in some unguarded moment, cajoling the truth from him.

The truth about Takis was that he wanted to go home. He'd paid his dues by helping his sister. He could be on an airplane to Melbourne in a couple of days, or in Athens spending more time with Nick. Both possibilities cheered him as he reached to switch off the lamp and realized it wasn't on. The sun had already crept high enough to light the room.

CHAPTER TEN

VASSOULA HAD NEVER LOST ANYONE she mourned until Omar's disappearance. Carrying a large basket of lavender roses, clipped from the overhead arbor he planted when they opened the restaurant, she kicked off her shoes and waded into the water. The smooth stones bruised her feet as they likely had Omar's shoulders rolling on the bottom of the sea. His boat had come ashore at that spot, a point where converging currents conspired to wash up detritus. Had his boat beached itself, or had Omar beached it, abandoned it to go missing by choice? Going on a year, every day Vassoula prayed she could wake up from her nightmare, promising God that she would become an ardent believer if He made that happen. When she woke up, there would be Omar, so handsome again. She wished it so hard and knew it would never happen. Never handsome again. Omar deserved his revenge. She could almost convince herself that he was still alive and the fires were his. Certainly they belonged to him.

The wild lavender roses belonged to him, too. Omar had recalled how his grandmother waxed poetic about them—"a scent as sweet as our lives back then"—when reminiscing about the old days in Greece before the Exchange. It was a time his grandmother barely remembered, but her mother's stories—Omar's great grandmother's stories—had been told so often, they became all their memories. The roses still grew on what had been his family's property; it's how he knew for sure that he had pinpointed it. He cultivated them, sticking rooted clippings in the ground to mark the plots of other Turkish families. The lavender roses flourished, their stems seeming to grow a foot a day and always abloom with dozens of the scented flowers.

That morning, Vassoula tossed handfuls of her roses into the backwash of the waves, wanting them to float out as far as possible, hoping they reached wherever Omar had finally come to rest. Soon the water was carpeted with them. She contemplated throwing herself into the sea and letting it take her life as it had taken his. Ahead of him, he had only envisioned an outcast life. Their love would never recover from his ruined face; and she knew, he had chosen death to spare her his tormented presence. Yet the fact that she had known his passion, and now must live without it, was its own abhorrent fate.

Omar.

She whispered his name.

Omar.

And tossed the last flowers out to sea.

• • •

RIDI REVIEWED THAT DAY'S VOCABULARY words a final time before slipping the page torn from a notebook into his shirt pocket. He had practiced aloud what he wanted to say to Athina, writing down the Albanian words and looking them up in Greek. Each time he ran through them, he heard the conversation he intended to have; and with an uneasy certainty, knew it would never come off that easily. It didn't matter; he'd be crying when it finished, happy ending or not.

He revved up his scooter to shake off its morning sluggishness. Predictably it backfired before he zoomed off through the stone hills. The changing weather, with winds and rains, and now a sparkling day, had left things fresh and clean. He could hear birdsongs above the rattle of his scooter.

His heart, too, was singing, and why not? The night before, in the depths of despair, Athina had sent him a heart. It had been a message of mercy that could only mean one thing: she loved him. She loved him and she forgave him. He sent one back. He wanted to reassure her that he still loved her. Whatever she had done was forgiven, too.

Forgiveness.

That was his first word on that day's vocabulary list. He would forgive Jura, too. How could he hate her for despairing as much as he had over the notion of spending a whole life in their miserable village? Her methods were scurrilous, but her motivations were as valid as his own. She had taken a great risk. He wouldn't abandon her. Neither would he abandon himself for her.

Limits.

The word itself seemed so heavy and confrontational. At once a word of aggression and barriers. He hoped he could explain what he meant in tenderer terms that conveyed the sympathy he felt without the harshness that "limits" sounded. But he felt he needed to use that word, not to shirk his responsibilities but to remind everyone to keep his responsibilities in perspective. Already achieving more than anything he could have eked out in his village, Ridi wasn't looking for excuses to stop. Or go home. Or change courses or marry someone to whom he had already said no. There were limits to his responsibilities for Jura's folly.

Ambitious.

He was proud to be ambitious. It stood him apart. Certainly apart from his fellow countrymen, who had also found their way to that small Greek village, which he was reminded of every morning when he chugged into town on his backfiring scooter and passed the little café where they all gathered for coffee. Fairer, bluer-eyed, and less furrowed than the Greeks, they sat there blearily, rousing themselves to work another day to earn the beers they would piss away that night; while Ridi had a list of vocabulary words in his pocket, a scooter he owned transporting him to work, and bigger dreams in his head than pissing foamy liters into a urinal.

Eager to glimpse the girl whose heart he had apparently won, Ridi showed up at work especially early that morning. He also needed extra time to set things up for that night's Miss Icon Contest. Behind Lydia's Kitchen, to one side towered the fuel tank, but to the other was an abrupt hill with a couple of outbuildings, and in those he would find extra tables and chairs, and strings of lights to hang, too. He climbed narrow steps to the storage room that had once been a goat shed and still smelled gamey. It took him several trips to carry down four tables and enough chairs to go around them. Once emptied, the room was cozy. Five or six small tables could be squeezed comfortably into it; and a window, an easy thing to knock out of a stone wall, would have a view of the sea. Ridi figured it could be the kind of place where tourists would nurse coffee or wine while checking emails and sharing photos, or working on the novel almost every one of them said they wanted to write. Who cared if it was only a dozen coffees or glasses of wine or sandwiches sold a day? It was still more than nothing, which was all the unused shed was earning now.

Athina appeared at the bottom of the stairs. "I was going to help you carry down the tables," she said.

"I came very early."

"Me, too. At least early for me. I think the last time I was up this early was when my dad forced me to go fishing with him."

"He forced you to go?"

"I think he wanted me to know what a crummy life he chose, in case I had the idea of becoming a fisherman, or marry one I suppose—as if I would ever want either one. The truth is, I hate the smell of fish. Can I help you carry stuff?"

Ridi shook his head. "This is the last chair."

"Then I need coffee. Do you want some?"

He did, and they went into the kitchen. Athina tucked a filter into a coffeemaker. "Is *not* Greek coffee okay?" she asked.

"It's okay."

"Good, because I don't like the way it sticks to my teeth." She poured water into the machine and flicked on its switch. Instantly it made little popping noises. "My mom is worried about the wind coming up tonight. She's not worried of course that we might capsize in the procession because of the wind but because she might lose money."

"Today is exactly the same as yesterday. No wind."

"God could tell her that and she would still worry. She's weird that way."

"The wind is easy to fix."

"If it is, she's never figured it out."

Ridi explained how her mother could attach clear plastic sailcloth between posts buried in heavy pots at the corners of her property. "That way, the wind is stopped when people still see the sunset. With no wind, it takes only a minute to roll again the plastic."

The coffeemaker sputtered, signaling it was ready. Athina filled two cups and handed one to him. "Tell me about your calculations."

Ridi had run the numbers, keeping track of how many people left when the wind kicked up, how many drifted next door to Vassoula's for a nightcap or three, or simply moved on; and estimating how many might have stayed instead at Lydia's for dessert or another pitcher of wine, if it weren't for a little too much breeze. Even under the worst-case scenario, the small investment would be profitable in a short time, not to mention encouraging repeat customers. "Your mother needs music, too," he said. "Stavros's music."

"People can hear him from his boat."

"It's not so close enough. In the night, when he plays music from his boat, people can listen from anywhere. But when they eat, people want to sit close to the music."

Again the young waiter ran through some numbers, but Athina wasn't listening very hard. The mention of Stavros's music reminded her of how romantically the fisherman had played the night before, bringing tears to her eyes for the earnest young man now explaining his calculations. She had texted him a heart, and with hardly a beat missed, he sent one back. She went to bed, in love, content that they could put behind them whatever had happened; and woke up remembering Jura. She wasn't just a worry or memory, but a real person who couldn't be so easily relegated to his past. What if Ridi *had* loved her? Could he be tempted again? She interrupted him to ask, "Did you see Jura this morning?"

"I will go after I finish here."

"And I should start," Athina said. "I have to finish the prep for the whole night before I put on my costume."

"I will help you later."

"You are so sweet, Ridi. Thank you."

He set down his coffee. "You don't have to worry about Jura."

"Well, someone needs to. What is she going to do?"

"I mean, you don't have to worry that I love her."

"Oh."

"I don't love her."

"She must think you do, or why would she risk coming here? Is it really so bad in your country?"

"Half she loves me and half it is so bad in my country. Half and half."

It wasn't exactly a reassuring answer, until Ridi added, "But with you I am one hundred percent. Not even one percent with Jura."

"I guess that's a sweet thing to say."

"I am faithful," he emphasized, and left the kitchen.

Faithful.

He smiled to himself. He had managed to work another vocabulary word into their conversation. He only had one word left on his list and knew the moment he hoped to use it.

• • •

Nick's eyes fluttered open.

He saw a pile of bloody towels a few feet away. Outside, croaking birds sounded like the vultures of Kabul. Someone slept pressed against his back. He felt wounded with stabbing pains all over. He could taste his sickness and smelled his own foul breath, but his mind was too muddled to sort out what had happened or where he was. His bladder insisted on relief and he started to get out of bed.

"Are you awake?"

It was Takis.

"I'm not dead?"

"You almost were."

"I need to take a piss."

Nick took a couple of wobbly steps.

"Do you need a hand?"

"Where are you suggesting?"

"It sounds like you'll survive."

Nick looked at his arms and legs. "What the fuck happened to me?"

"You don't remember the spiders?"

"They were real?"

"Go take your piss. And brush your teeth. I'll make coffee."

Nick, toothbrush buzzing in his mouth, checked his wounds in the mirror. "What the fuck are those red circles on my back?"

"My sister bled you."

He came back into the room. "She bled me?"

"We wanted to get as much poison out as we could. You had already done a pretty good job on the bites you could reach."

"You actually bled me?"

"Don't worry, and it won't leave scars."

"I already have scars."

"I meant more scars. Coffee?"

"I'll meet you on the terrace."

Nick slipped on shorts and a T-shirt, and joined Takis outside. The sun was high and the day warm. "Is it already afternoon?"

"You needed to sleep. I guess we both did."

Suddenly dizzy, Nick dropped into a chair.

"Are you okay?" Takis asked.

"Just a little woozy. It comes in waves. Tell me what happened."

As Takis described finding him on the bathroom floor, Nick slowly recalled the evening. A late night with a little too much wine, almost asleep before he got into bed, and waking up with spiders biting him. He recalled the spider nests in the cemetery. "Are they really common here?" he asked.

"They don't nest in beds. My sister thinks someone tried to kill you."

"That takes a lot of bites, doesn't it?"

"You had enough bites. You might have died if she hadn't bled you, and for sure if you hadn't bled yourself first. That took a lot of guts to do that to yourself."

"When I was a kid, a friend of mine survived a rattlesnake bite by doing that. I never forgot it."

"You really work for the FBI, don't you?"

"How did you figure that out?"

"You have three of those Styrofoam things in your bottom drawer."

"You went through my stuff?"

"My sister did. I couldn't stop her."

"What was she looking for?"

"Anything interesting. So am I a suspect?"

"Maybe. Tell me about the Takis Fire."

"I hate that name for it."

"I bet you do."

"Not for the reasons you might think."

"Tell me."

"It happened the day that I confronted my father on the beach."

"About being gay?"

"About both of us being gay."

"You mean, right after that, he went home and was killed?"

"I think he committed suicide."

"Why?"

"They found pieces of the house that showed the shutters had been closed. That was usually my job and I didn't do it that day. I brought home a new gas bottle and left for the beach. I knew I'd be back before sunset to shut them."

"I heard a different version of the story."

"The version where I closed the shutters early because I'd be back after sunset?"

"That's what I heard."

Takis told him, "That's *my* version. I made it up."

"Why?"

"The investigators would have eventually come to the same conclusion that my father had killed himself. No one else closed up the kitchen. Zeeta fell a couple of days earlier and couldn't get out of bed so she couldn't have done it."

"What about your sister?"

"Vassoula hadn't come back to the house in a year. Not since she moved in with Omar. It had to be my father. I know how unhappy he was. He went home, and you're right, he saw the gas bottle and decided to end it."

"And kill your mother, too?"

"I'm sure he wanted to kill her many times." Takis shook his head, remembering the man. "Poor guy. Can you imagine what his life was really like? Gay and stuck in this village? The only thing he knew to do was grow olives. He couldn't take his trees to Athens or Thessaloniki, and where else can you live in this country if you're gay? Then he ends up getting caught taking care of a simple urge with a guy on the beach and he's forced to marry Zeeta. She didn't have a good heart, she had a cold one, and adopting kids didn't change that. We were constant reminders that she couldn't have her own. She never loved us. She felt she had done us a favor, and that was the most she could feel for us."

"Sounds like a miserable situation."

"It was, especially for Markos. Probably she gave him a hand job on their wedding night and that was the last sex they had. What kind of cure for homosexuality was that supposed to be? Of course it wasn't, and every once in a while there would be another snide remark made about him. For a while, at school I was kidded about losing my virginity, which confused me because I thought only girls could be virgins. Somebody explained what they were talking about, and I realized that people imagined all sorts of things could be going on between Markos and me. Nothing was, except at some point, I knew that I was gay, too, and I didn't want to be gay. I didn't want his unhappy life. Shame, and secrecy, and his olive trees: that's all he had. So for a long time I tried to deny it. I went all the way with a couple of girls because I could, but afterwards, I felt as unhappy as he was. It didn't seem fair that I had to live with being adopted and then live with being gay, too. It wasn't until I moved to Australia that it clicked up here"—Takis tapped his head—"that it wasn't being gay itself that made my father unhappy, but the people who made him feel so ashamed that he was gay."

"And *they* drove him to suicide, not your conversation with him," Nick interjected.

"It was the day I outted him. That had to contribute to it."

"You outted him to you and nobody else. It had to be a conversation he'd anticipated many times. He couldn't predict the binoculars, but when it finally happened, he already knew what was going to be said."

"He wouldn't have killed himself that day without our conversation."

"You're wrong. He wouldn't have killed himself that day without the gas bottle being there. Otherwise, he would have done it another day. He came home and saw the opportunity he'd been waiting for. You know I'm right," Nick concluded.

Takis teared up when he replied, "He wasn't a bad man. That's why I lied for him. He died ashamed of himself. The ridicule had never really stopped. He'd lived with the shame of being gay all his life, he didn't need the shame of suicide for all eternity. So I lied, saying I had closed the shutters, and why not? It made no difference to me."

"Except to make you a murder suspect," Nick reminded him.

"It could never be proved. What evidence would there be?"

"So you're saying, it might be true?"

"And you're saying, I *am* a suspect?"

Nick answered: "Tell me about the insurance money."

"Five hundred sixty-seven euros and sixty-eight centimes."

"You got to Melbourne on that?"

"I had some savings, too."

"What did your sister do with her money?"

"She didn't get insurance money. It was only good until we were eighteen. I had two weeks to go. That makes me suspicious, doesn't it?"

Nick's phone beeped inside his room.

"Can we still be friends?" Takis asked.

"Let's see how things go."

The phone beeped again.

"I better check that," Nick said, and went inside.

He had a message—*SUBJ: VATIS Takis*—and attached to it was the official report on the Takis Fire. He left the phone on the counter and went back to the terrace.

Takis was gone. Nick had hoped learning more about Takis would allay his suspicions. But, in fact, he'd now leapfrogged into being Nick's prime suspect when his motive became so much clearer. He had many reasons to hate the village in his own right. He'd been ridiculed, and blamed for a fatal fire he didn't start.

Nick retrieved his phone to read about the Takis Fire.

• • •

ATHINA WEDGED THE LAST TRAY of chopped vegetables into the refrigerator. "I'm so nervous!" she said to Ridi, sponge in hand, wiping down the counter.

"Nervous? Why nervous?"

"Because of the contest, silly! Why do you think?"

"I'm not nervous, only I hope your mother has her biggest night of all the nights tonight. She bought extra food."

"Don't get your hopes up. She could sell a million sardines and she'd still close the restaurant in a few days."

"Do you think there are still a million sardines in the sea?"

"There won't be tomorrow, if my mother sells them today." The girl dried off a couple of knives and put them away. "You never said, Ridi, what you'll do when my mother closes the restaurant. Will you look for another job?"

"What another job? There's no another job. Maybe I try to make my own job."

"Doing what?"

He replied with his own question: "Why your mother want to close everything?"

"She can't serve food in winter without tables inside."

"The storage room is big enough for five tables."

"It's a smelly old stables!"

"I can clean it. Four coffees pay for the heat on a cold day. Everything else is profit. I make the calculations."

"You and your calculations! I hope you calculated my crown correctly."

Ridi gulped. It was show time. "We try it now?"

"We better, because I need to get ready."

Ridi retrieved the crown from a cupboard. He had fit the Styrofoam skeleton to her head, but she had not yet seen it covered with stones, which added to his mounting anxiety over the end of the conversation he'd been practicing all day. What if she didn't like it?

He didn't have to worry. As soon as he held it out for her to examine, the light hit it and the faux gems sparkled brighter than real ones.

"Oh my God!" Athina exclaimed. "It's more than beautiful! It's more gorgeous than the original! Oh. My. God."

"Do you like it?"

"Do I *like* it? I *love* it! I hope it fits! I'll shrink my head if it doesn't!"

Ridi pulled in a chair off the porch. "Sit here and let me test it on you."

Athina sat, and he set the crown on her head.

"How does it look? Oh, I know it's beautiful!"

He moved it around, rocking it to test it with the weight of the stones. "It is too big," he announced.

"Too big? It doesn't feel too big."

"On the boat, it will fall off."

"I can hold onto it."

"Don't move. I can fix it."

Returning to the cupboard, he proudly displayed some Styrofoam wedges he had prepared to solve that exact problem. "I fix in five minutes."

He took the crown from the girl and started to glue the wedges inside the rim. "What will you make all winter?" he asked.

"You mean, what will I do? My mother wants me to 'go see the world' as she says, but all that means is going to see my cousins in Australia or my aunts in Germany. That's not exactly seeing the world, especially since I've already been to both places. It's all because she wants me to live the life that she wants, when I'm happy with my own life. I don't need *her* dreams. Besides, I see enough of the world on the news to think that I don't want to see much more of it."

"What if your mother closes the restaurant forever?"

"Forever? Why would she do that?"

"She makes no money."

"She says that, but I never know if I should take her seriously or not. She complains about a lot of stuff."

"I think she makes no money."

"Because you've made your calculations?" Athina teased him.

"I have still more ideas for a restaurant."

"More than Cocktail Serenade? Or turning the storage room into a mini-restaurant?"

"More."

"What good are your ideas if she closes?"

"Ideas are good, if only to have them. If I have a restaurant, I make Jura the waitress. And Koufos, I make him be out front. Like an actor not a clown, but still people will laugh. I make that idea after I see him last night."

"You're always thinking, aren't you, Ridi? And you're right. He'd be perfect. People would come because he's an actor not a clown, and that would be so nice for him. That's so sweet of you to think of both of them. It really is. What about me?"

"I make you the boss!"

"The boss?"

"You make a good boss. Okay, I am finished."

Again he placed the crown on her head. It fit snugly and he stepped back to look at her. He could not imagine a more beautiful woman and the crown was worthy of her! To think how close he had come to smashing it.

"I need to see it." Athina gasped when she peered into a small mirror next to the door. "It's so incredibly beautiful. After all the sad things that have happened, for you to make something so beautiful, it's like a miracle!"

Tears sprang to Ridi's eyes, not only because of what she said, but for what he wanted to say, yet he hadn't been sure how he was going to get there. She had given him the word miracle, so he used it saying, "I hope for a miracle, too."

"What miracle?"

Too emotional to speak, Ridi pulled out his list of vocabulary words and tore off the last one. "This is my miracle," he said, handing it to her.

She read it. "Marry?"

Ridi nodded.

"You?"

He nodded harder.

"Me marry you?"

He couldn't hold back his tears any longer.

"I love you, too," she said, and they fell into each other's arms.

• • •

THE SEA COULD NOT HAVE been more azure, the clouds billowier, or the air fresher. It was a perfect day, not a day to be thinking about death and suicide, but that's what Nick had on his mind as he wound along the narrow coastal road. The report had filled in details about the Takis Fire, but nothing that would suggest a link between it and the arsonist. The conclusion was accidental death. From where the bodies were found, the assumption was that Markos Vatis had opened the kitchen door smoking a cigarette and set off the explosion. The whole house was immediately engulfed with flames. A gas leak from a spare bottle was blamed. The bottle itself had not exploded; thus, presumably, it had emptied itself but the gas had not dissipated because the shutters had been latched. Takis Vatis admitted to delivering the spare gas that afternoon and closing the shutters before he left for a walk. A second gas bottle, connected to the stove, exploded once the fire became melting hot, killing a Coast Guardsman and wounding two others fighting to contain it.

Nick knew, of course, that Takis had not closed the shutters; instead his father had upon returning to the house. The two stories differed only on that one point—who closed the shutters—but something didn't feel right. Mulling it over, he turned into the narrow valley, and soon found the correct turnout for the ruined house. He hoped Koufos was home. He was certain the deaf kid had seen the arsonist. He knew how the detonators had been lit—not like a birthday cake, but puffing on each cigarette to light it—and his body language, too, had started to change as he reenacted what he witnessed. He bet the kid could sign the arsonist's arrest warrant with his imitation. Nick simply needed him to perform it.

He got out of the car, taking with him a lunch he asked Lydia to prepare. She had cooked up a couple of the boy's favorite things; he seemed to scarf down anything with cheese the fastest, so she included fried feta, along with some of the island's ubiquitous sardines. Nick had asked her to arrange it nicely on a plate and cover it with plastic wrap so he could leave it for the boy. He also brought cutlery and a cloth napkin. Nick wanted to send a message: the boy's own message had been received. He could stop being a hermit and join other people; if indeed that had been his message, conscious or not, of taking himself out to dinner the night before.

Nick climbed the hill along a relatively easy path compared to the strenuous zigzag he'd climbed up the terraces the first time to reach the ruined house. In the hard-packed yard, he stopped to catch his breath. He was about to shout *Hello!* until he reminded himself that Koufos couldn't hear him. He thought about picking up a stick and tapping the ground. Maybe, like a snake, the boy would feel the vibration.

He looked inside the ruined house. The boy wasn't there though his special clothes were: the pearly buttoned red shirt, mustard pants, socks—and Nick's boxers—all neatly arranged on the floor. Nick put the lunch plate on the floor beside them. He laid out the folded napkin, then slipped the handle of the fork into one shirt cuff and the knife into the other.

He went back outside. Certain the boy was watching him from somewhere, he wanted to communicate with him, but how? Were gestures innately understood or did they require language first to make them comprehensible? Were outstretched arms always regarded as an embrace? Was a roll of the shoulders a question or signal of disinterest? All he could do was try.

Cocking his head, Nick spread his upright palms as if asking a question.

He curled his fingers to reel the boy in.

And tapped his heart.

He repeated the gestures.

What do you want?

Come to us.

We will love you.

He did it in all four directions. If the deaf boy was watching, even if he didn't understand, at least he would realize that Nick was trying to communicate.

He walked down the hill to his car. His phone beeped as he was getting in. He had two messages from headquarters.

> *SUBJ: AZAROV Vladimir. Owner of yacht Birch Runner. Former CEO of RussOil. Retired. No known criminal connections. Frequents Greece. Art collector and major donor to Hermitage Museum.*

Vladimir Azarov might not have known criminal connections, but Nick suspected that he was a crook himself. It was too coincidental that an art collector who frequents Greece happened to be in Vourvoulos just as Father Alexis was finishing his forgery of the Crowned Madonna. Nick shot back a message asking to check with the harbormasters in Patmos and Skyros if the Russian had frequently docked there. If he had, it would suggest he and the priest had been in cahoots for a long time.

Then he checked his second message.

> *SUBJ: OZTURK Omar. Turkish national, confirmed. Married VATIS Vassoula, Greek national. No more information available.*

Nick started his car.

No more information available.

That pretty well summed up what clues he had to go on.

And it was the first day of a new month.

D Day.

He was certain of it.

• • •

ATHINA COULD BARELY CONTAIN HERSELF. Inside she was churning with emotions. She had told Ridi that she loved him, but did she? She assumed what she felt was true love. It certainly felt more profound than anything she had ever felt for another boy—or man, she supposed she should call him, if he was going to be her husband. Boy or man, she had never fallen for such a decent guy, which was partly how she would justify herself to her mother, who was going to have a fit! "Oh God, he's *Albanian*!" the girl worried aloud. She was only beginning to sort out the full impact of what she had done.

She didn't have time to think about that now. Her mother had refused to help with her costume, saying she still didn't approve of portraying Mary as a pregnant hooker, missing her point entirely about reinterpreting Mary as a metaphor for male fecklessness. She should have stuck it to Joseph instead of blaming the inconvenient result of their premarital sex on God; and worse, forever being worshipped for letting the guy off the hook! If Joseph had been forced to admit his responsibility, it would have changed the course of history. Women would be more respected and sex less sullied. She knew her message was obscure, and was counting on shock value to win the contest so she would have an opportunity to explain herself.

She pulled on her patterned stockings and donned the stomach pouch made plump with a pillow to appear unmistakenly pregnant. Over everything, she draped bed sheets dyed teal blue. Originally, she had planned to wear a nun's habit to conceal her secret costume, but when her grandmother suggested the crown, it became obvious that she should portray the Crowned Madonna in the village's church. Her teal robe was as much a signature of the icon as was her jeweled headdress. Athina had no doubt that she would be instantly recognized.

Tilting her head in the mirror, she adopted Mary's bored expression, and pressed her teddy bear to a breast. She wished she had the crown to wear, too, but Ridi planned to take it directly to the launch site. She had one last matter to attend to before she joined him. On her way out the door, she retrieved from a printer an especially incriminating photo of the priest switching the icons earlier that day.

She left the apartment and climbed the steep deserted paths to reach the church. She needed a copy of the Crowned Madonna to throw into the sea if she won and the priest's forgery would be perfect. The crowd, believing it to be the original, would be further amazed by her audacity, and even more amazed when they leaned about his deceitfulness.

The gate squeaked when she opened it. She froze in place expecting Father Alexis to appear. When he didn't, she slipped inside the church.

An old woman stood before the altar praying to the Crowned Madonna. Obviously Athina couldn't snatch what she presumed to be the copy of the icon until the woman left, and her inconsolable weeping suggested that wouldn't be any time soon. Athina, risking being late for the procession, had no choice but to opt for the icon in the vestry. She slipped back outside and ran around the church to the vestry door. She listened, heard nothing and tapped lightly on it.

No response.

She knocked a little louder. Again no response.

She tested the door. It opened, and she peered inside.

Father Alexis was not there.

"Hello?" Athina said anyway and stepped into the room. "Hello?"

The room smelled sour from the many thick robes tinged with incense and sweat that hung on a long open rack. She heard water running, and moaning, and concluded it must be the priest singing a weird chant in the shower. It creeped her out that there was a maze of rooms off the vestry where he lived; she imagined them musty, smelling like his robes, and grimy without much light.

Propped on an easel was the Crowned Madonna. Her roving eyes watched Athina approach. The girl couldn't make out the Holy Mother's mood; her eyes seemed suspicious, as if wondering what Athina might be up to next. But when she stopped, she thought she saw a smile in the Madonna's conspiratorial eyes. *Do it!* they urged her. *Grab me!*

Athina did.

She picked up the icon by its sticky gold frame.

"Ick," she said, looking at her smeared palms, and wiped them on one of the priest's robes.

The shower stopped running and she needed to act fast. Recalling that it hadn't taken the priest very long to switch the icons, she checked the back of the frame, and saw it was easy. Turning four bent nails, the painting fell right out. She propped the frame back on its stand.

Now she had a new problem. She couldn't run all the way to the port with the icon in one hand and her teddy bear in the other, especially with a bouncing pillow at her waist. She decided to leave the bear behind and situated it in the gold frame. Under its arms, she snuggled the picture of the priest switching icons, and had to stifle a laugh imagining Father Alexis's face when he saw it. Then tucking the icon under her costume of teal robes, she flung open the door and fled.

• • •

IT WAS HIS THIRD SHOWER that day and Father Alexis still did not feel clean. Following Athina's humiliating confession the day before, the guilt that he had successfully repressed about their misconduct in the church returned to consume him. It wasn't about the sex itself that he felt sinful. He had certainly counseled enough women that it was a natural act, and personally proved the point on enough occasions. No, his guilt lay in the fact that they had done it in front of the Holy Mother. He had given her no choice but to watch the whole base act, and because she so resembled his mother, he felt especially dirty.

The priest groaned a last time before turning off the shower and snatching his flask of Sporell off the counter. In a self-loathing rage, he smeared his body with it, stopping only when he heard a loud bang. Had someone slammed the vestry door? He tiptoed down the short hall to peek into it. No one was there but the outside door was open. In a couple of steps, he closed it. Turning around, he instantly noticed that the icon was missing. In its frame was a teddy bear holding a note! He assumed the Russian had stolen the painting and seethed at the man's duplicity. What miserable excuse had he penned in a note? But when Father Alexis stepped closer, he saw it was no note at all, but a photograph of himself switching the icons!

In that single image, he saw the undoing of all his careful plans. He'd be revealed to the world as a forger, likely excommunicated and jailed, and never a hope of rescuing his mother from her hellish situation—all because he had offended the Crowned Madonna with his indiscretion. She was punishing him! Heedless of being naked, he burst into the church, startling the weeping old woman, who screamed when she saw him running toward her and fled as fast as her rickety legs allowed. Oblivious to her, the priest dropped to his knees, repeatedly crossing himself and begging for the Madonna's forgiveness.

• • •

As Nick came down the hill, he could see that the Russian's yacht wasn't docked at its usual spot along the dock. Once he reached the wharf, he saw that it had only been repositioned to that side of the harbor. Immediately he was suspicious that the Russian was going to take the Crowned Madonna while everyone was distracted by the procession, and having his boat on that side of the harbor would facilitate his getaway. He headed for the Coast Guard station to alert

Captain Tsounis of the probable heist. Before going inside, he peeked around back and was relieved to see a guardsman dozing on a chair, ostensibly guarding the fuel tank.

Captain Tsounis agreed to keep an eye on the *Birch Runner* and give chase if she left the harbor. He also assured Nick that he would personally be guarding the fuel tank during the procession so his crew could enjoy the festivities. "I'll still be able to see some of it from here," he said. "You shouldn't miss it. The costumes are always good."

In a short time, the wharf had become busy with people promenading up and down, or having their first ouzos, in what was certain to be a festive night. The wind was still, and the sun's long, golden rays lingered on the red tile roofs climbing to the ancient castle. It was a magical late afternoon, and Nick walked to the dock's end where he watched the sun first touch the sea.

He took it as a cue for walking back. Everyone on the wharf took it as their cue for rushing onto the dock. Before he knew it, Nick was having to push through people to make his way. Across the harbor, the wharf was empty except for a few restaurant owners prepared to miss the procession in case they had some customers. He glimpsed Lydia in her kitchen. Vassoula was perched on her stool smoking a cigarette.

Takis was nowhere to be seen and that made Nick more than a little nervous. There was no way to verify which version of the Takis Fire was true: the one in which Takis's father committed suicide, or Captain Tsounis's assertion that Takis had killed his parents for the insurance money? Whichever was true didn't diminish two facts: Takis hated the village, and the fires had started when chilling circumstances brought him back from Australia.

Again he looked for Takis and didn't see him.

Nick squirmed through the crowd, barely advancing a foot with each step. A couple of times he felt dizzy, no doubt from the spider venom still lingering in his body, and paused to catch his balance while keeping watch across the harbor.

Still no Takis.

Then a huge roar went up when the lead float came into view.

• • •

THE CONTESTANTS HAD GATHERED AT a small launching platform away from the harbor so their costumes could be kept secret from the public as long as possible. All the other girls were already on their boats by the time Athina arrived and checked out the others' costumes. Their uninspired efforts boosted her confidence. Even her friend Viki's effort was too simple: a soft purple gown, chosen to highlight her violet eyes, with a battery-powered halo over her head. Cute, but not a winner. The bow of the lead boat, where Irini should be, was entirely hidden behind a screen of bed sheets. Beneath them, Athina could make out movements but that was all.

"You're late," Mayor Elefteros scolded her.

"I'm sorry. I had something to do."

She rushed over to Stavros's boat, where Ridi waited with her crown. The fisherman held out a hand to help her aboard. "Okay. I'm ready," she said. "Let me put it on."

"Sit down first," Stavros told her. "The crown is heavy enough to make you wobbly."

Athina arranged herself on a taverna chair on the bow. "Okay."

As Ridi fit the crown on her head, she asked, "What's Irini's costume?"

"I don't know."

"You didn't see it?"

"It is a big secret."

"A big secret?"

The girl's anxiety level shot up when she heard that, but it temporarily abated when she saw how, in the long rays of the setting sun, her crown's faux gems flashed every color in the spectrum. She didn't have to look in a mirror to see it was dazzling. That was clear in everyone's awed expressions.

Ridi asked, "How does it feel?"

"Awesome. How do I look?"

"More beautiful than the Madonna."

"You shouldn't say that. It might be bad luck."

"You want me to lie?"

"Not to me."

"It's not a lie that I love you." Ridi wanted to kiss her, but didn't feel comfortable doing it in public; their romance was still unannounced.

"Are we missing anyone else?" the mayor called out.

"Father Alexis," Stavros reminded him.

"Well, the sun sets on God's time, not at our beckoning nor the priest's. We will start when Athina is ready."

"I'm ready!"

"*Pame!*" the mayor shouted. Let's go!

There was a last-minute frenzy on Irini's boat. Her brothers brought down the hoisted sheets. Athina could only see the back of a huge cross, until Irini's boat made its U-turn to head for the dock and passed her.

Athina's mouth fell open in astonishment. Her friend appeared to hang on the cross by ropes around her wrists, though her feet were planted on the deck. She had cut her straw blonde hair, dyed it brown, and curled it to appear like the flouncy hair in every flattering portrait of Jesus. She'd pasted short brown hairs on her face to pass for a stubbly beard, and glued more to the chest of her flesh-colored body sock that flattened her breasts. Though there was no rule against portraying a male saint, traditionally the Miss Icon Contest had been an event for young women to announce their readiness for marriage, and what young woman would want to show herself with chest hair? Obviously Irini flat-out wanted to win, and planned to do it on shock value alone.

Athina heard the crowd's first roar when the floats came into view. It was the second roar, when they had their first real view of Irini on the cross, that made her heart sink. She knew she had lost the contest. "I will never win!" she wailed.

"Who thinks it is beautiful for a woman to have chesty hair?" Ridi asked, trying to reassure her.

Athina could not be consoled. "I keep telling you, it's not a beauty contest!"

• • •

"WHY IS EVERY FUCKING CHURCH built on top of a fucking mountain?" Pinballer grumbled.

"To give you something else to complain about," Vladimir answered, and opened the church gate. He had decided simply to take the Crowned Madonna. Father Alexis be damned for trying to double-cross him. He brought the kid along in case he needed extra muscle if the priest tried to stop him. That created another predicament: what to do with the kid later? He was a pain-in-the-ass travel companion. Vladimir had planned to complain to the escort service, but now the problem was: the kid was about to witness his theft. Who knew what he might say to retaliate?

Vladimir knocked on the vestry door. No answer. Another knock, another no answer, and he tried the handle.

It was unlocked.

They let themselves in, and Vladimir immediately saw the teddy bear perched in the gold frame where the icon should have been. Something was tucked under its furry little arms. He approached it, and saw the photograph of the priest switching icons. Vladimir, enraged, couldn't make sense of why it was there. Was it a way to mock him, or confuse him about which icon was which? With a blow he sent the teddy bear flying and stormed into the church.

Father Alexis, on his knees in a blubbering trance, didn't notice the intrusion.

The Russian snorted derisively at the priest's bare ass and went behind the altar to reach for the Crowned Madonna. He tried several times without being able to unhook it. "Come here," he said to the pinballer, and cupped his hands to hoist him up by his foot. The kid managed to grab the icon, but Vladimir shifted and he fell onto the rack of votive lamps. Oil splashed across the ancient iconostasis which instantly burst into flames.

The Russian stuck the Crowned Madonna into a garbage bag he'd brought to conceal it. "Let's go!"

From the church door, he glanced back.

The priest had not stopped praying.

"Hey, Papoose! *Papoose!*"

He still didn't move.

"Fucking crazy priest," the Russian mumbled, and hurried back to the harbor.

• • •

ATHINA WAS NOT GOING TO let herself be upset. On the first pass, the response to her costume had been lukewarm compared to Irini's, but now her friend's shock value was over and hers was yet to come. Her crown alone had elicited swoons of appreciation and waves of applause, but she had saved her radical Madonna outfit for the second passing of the floats. The first was to show the people the costumes; the second was for their vote. She was still confident that her pregnant Mary would shock them every bit as much as Irini's chest hair.

As the boats approached the dock for a second time, another roar greeted Irini, but decidedly less enthusiastically than before. Athina, her hope of winning revived, stood up as she came into view. No more an idle Madonna, she was a fierce Amazon—an Everywoman for all women. When her moment came, she flung off her teal sheets, and turned sideways so no one could miss the outline of her very pregnant belly.

She hadn't expected the complete silence.

She had misread everything! No one got it. No one wanted to get it. Not one but all her worst fears came true.

Until the crowd roared.

It was spontaneous and grand. Filled with laughter and shock. A noise so uninhibited that everyone—whether they loved, hated, or didn't get her costume—still recognized her as the winner. In unison they began chanting, "*A-thin-a! A-thin-a! A-thin-a!*"

She had won! She couldn't believe it!

It was the moment she was supposed to throw a copy of her icon into the sea. Not knowing the priest had switched the icons a second time, Athina assumed she had grabbed the original one from the vestry. She hesitated, worried about the repercussions of destroying the venerated image, but the chanting crowd was too insistent for her not to do it. Lifting it over her head, she plunged it into the water while young men were already diving off the dock hoping to retrieve it and win her hand.

As she watched it sink out of sight, the church bell started ringing wildly. Everyone looked up the hill and saw the flames shooting from the church. Athina, assuming she had caused the fire with her blasphemous act, couldn't stop screaming.

• • •

SOMEWHERE IN FATHER ALEXIS'S GUILT-RIDDEN mind he had wormed his way to Hell. He could smell its fire if not its brimstone; the flames around him a holy vision until they came too close, too burning hot, and he wakened from his trance to the spreading fire. He ran outside and rang the bell, not minding that the bits of the tower sprinkling him soon became a heavy dusting. He heard a crunching noise, but masked by the bell, he didn't take it for the serious warning that it was; and when he heard it a second time, it was too late. The wound he had inflicted on the tower gave way and brought the whole structure crashing down with a final, muffled toll of the bell.

It fell right on top of him.

• • •

NICK'S FIRST THOUGHT WAS THAT the arsonist's target must have been the church, never the fuel tank. His second was to wonder if Takis had set the fire, but at that moment the young man came running out of his sister's bar. He appeared to be confused, unsure why there was such an uproar as people pushed and shoved to get off the dock. From where he was, the buildings along the wharf block his view of the church up the hill, and he shouted at people running past asking what was happening.

Why wasn't Vassoula there to tell him? Nick wondered.

She had disappeared. He searched the crowd swamping the wharf, some aiming for the church, most just wanting to get away. It was twilight and hard to discern their faces. Then he saw Vassoula come back outside, pausing to smell a lavender rose dangling from the overhead arbor before starting to walk against the crowd. She swung a jerry-can in her hand. It was an odd time to collect her petrol, but maybe an afternoon romp with Vassoula was another reason that Captain Tsounis had stayed back to guard the fuel tank.

Then it dawned on Nick.

She was the arsonist!

Vassoula had more reason than her brother to hate the village after what happened to Omar. Destroying it would be her revenge. How had he not seen it?

The fires hadn't been random but specifically sited. All had been set on land once owned by Turks. Land Omar had marked by planting the lavender roses of his family's lore. He was Turkish, and Nick bet his family *was* the Ozturk family named on the land map. That would explain why he came to that particular island, and why Vassoula held the whole village responsible for the brutal attack on him. Had his family never been expelled, there would have been no homecoming decades later. Omar would have already been there, and that alone would have changed his fate. In a circle of upright dominos, one knocked over the next, until the full circle had fallen, returning Omar to his ancestral home—only to be brutally cast out again. Vassoula wanted revenge going back as far as that first domino. That's why the whole village was her target; they were all to blame for their history—a history that ultimately destroyed Omar, destroying her. Nick was certain that was her convoluted thinking.

Around him, everyone pushed and jostled for their chance down the dock's narrow steps. Nick, penned in, watched Vassoula vanish behind the Coast Guard station. He prayed that the jerrycan was empty. If she had to fill it, he'd have an extra minute to stop her. If she ignited it full, the explosion would be enough to set the leaky fuel tank ablaze.

• • •

For a last time, she sniffed the arbor's lavender roses that Omar planted the day they opened the restaurant. People were rushing past her talking excitedly about the church on fire. Had the bell tower really come crashing down, too? That news had the older women wailing in distress, and if Vassoula were successful, they would soon be grieving over a cataclysmic fire as well. She had worried that when the day came, she wouldn't have the courage to go through with it, but the destruction of the church urged her on. She wanted it all to burn down, and reminded herself that her own searing pain would be over quickly. Those moments she would have to endure her flesh melting, she would dedicate to Omar.

Omar.

Slain not by his own hand. The skinheads had ended his life when they mutilated him. He would survive his indecent wounds but not his indecent appearance. Their trial had lasted longer than his living torture, but under the law, it couldn't be called murder. They had murdered him, but not in the chronological order of the law.

Omar.

He came on a quest for lavender roses. He wanted to find his family's Paradise Lost, to see the places that had been mythologized when recalled from the distance of scrappy Istanbul. As awful as his attack was, people didn't feel compelled to come to his defense when rumors started about why he had been out at Poustis Point, insinuating that maybe he deserved what happened. Vassoula knew why he was out there. They all did. They all knew everybody's business, only pretending not to when it suited them to tell an altered truth. They all knew Omar walked that long beach almost every day, well past Poustis Point, talking to himself until he talked himself out and turned around; the whole time oblivious to the ragtag queers of the village, her father among them, who stumbled out there for hand jobs. Omar was so much more a man than any man in the village. Than in Vourvoulos: its name luscious, suggestive, yet its women, ruined by God, and then by husbands who ignored them like discarded chrysalises after bearing their children. Except Vassoula, and that's why every man had wanted her. Still wanted her. They resented Omar when he showed up and he was the first man she took.

Omar.

Their adoptive mother had never had a man she fervently desired. If she had, she wouldn't have thrown Vassoula out of the house for having an affair with Omar; she would have borne the shame if she had experienced such illicit passion. She wouldn't have set out to have him deported, nor would she have continued her campaign after they married, declaring he had been illegally in Greece when they wed, and denouncing their marriage as a ploy to allow him to stay—in itself, a criminal offense. Twice officials came to the village to interview them and determined Omar was there legally, but that didn't stop her bigoted mother from trying to change their minds. Given the rising anti-immigrant sentiments in the country, Vassoula feared she might succeed. Zeeta made the mistake of telling her that she was going to cancel the life insurance policy they'd been required to buy when they adopted her. That was the first time she'd heard about the insurance. She didn't know what it was worth, but it was definitely more than the nothing she had earned all those years working as Zeeta's scullery maid. Vassoula had shut the shutters (why Takis claimed he did, she couldn't ask without revealing herself) and opened the gas bottle. She had anticipated a refrigerator spark igniting it, killing only her mother, but Markos returned home earlier than usual that Sunday, smoking a cigarette and causing an explosion. Her double murders hadn't paid off exactly as planned. She didn't get the insurance money because she was older than eighteen; something Zeeta must have known about, and so her threats were only to taunt Vassoula, which made her hate the old hag even more. She was still glad she had done it. It gave her and Omar a future. A future until Omar's had been cut away. Fed to the seagulls. Bleeding him even after the blood had been staunched.

Omar.

He'd always had a plan. A plan to come to Vourvoulos, a plan to open a restaurant, a plan to have a baby with her. A plan for a long life amidst his grandmother's lavender roses, only to be foiled by some skinheads' vile hatred. Vassoula made a plan, too, for revenge; a plan as carefully constructed as all of his had been. She made it worthy of Omar's intricate thinking. She hoped to witness the villagers' mounting fear, though the mayor disappointed her by never revealing the worry beads. The fire, so devastating, would be repeatedly scrutinized, her motives endlessly analyzed, until one clever investigator would realize that all the fires had been on Turkish properties. She had used them to point a finger at the village guilty for Omar's destruction. The penultimate fire had been on his great grandparents' land where Shirley and Lukas now lived. It was Omar's great uncle who tossed himself headfirst into the well to contaminate the water for its new Greek owners.

Her plan would conclude that day. It had an end, and with jerrycan in hand, Vassoula walked to the back of the Coast Guard station. In the middle of the yard, Captain Tsounis watched the flames from the church lick the darkening sky. "Where's your brother?" he asked.

"Napping in the restaurant."

"You sure he wasn't playing with matches in the church?"

"Why aren't you up there helping?"

"Someone has to guard the tank."

"You guard it now?"

"For the time being."

"Why?"

"Hunches, mostly."

Slipping a finger under the top button of his shirt, Vassoula pulled him closer. "Do your hunches let you take a ten-minute break?"

"What do you have in mind?"

Her lips brushed his. "You know what I want."

"You brought your can. It looks like you want petrol."

"I want to pay for it first."

"I have to wait for one of the crew to relieve me."

"I'll relieve you," she purred suggestively, and slipped a hand down to touch him.

He pulled it away. "Come back after the procession."

"I will. But I'll fill this now, since I have the can."

He carried the can to the hose. Opening the padlock, he unwound the reel a few spins, and stuck the nozzle into it. With another key, he turned on the pump.

Vassoula gripped the nozzle's handle.

"What are you doing?" he asked.

"Sometimes it jerks and I don't want it to fall out." The hose spurted just then, and she added, "You see?"

"It's only air caught in the hose."

The jerrycan quickly filled up. When it had, she pulled out the nozzle and turned it on the Coast Guardsman, dousing him with fuel. "Get back!" she barked, chasing him away from the pump's switch.

"Are you crazy?"

With her free hand, Vassoula flicked a cigarette lighter. "Get back!"

"Okay. Okay. I'm getting back."

With the captain at a safe distance, she pointed the nozzle to the ground to pool petrol at her feet.

Nick ran into the yard and took in what was happening. "Don't do it."

Vassoula laughed. "Superman to the rescue!"

He took a step toward her.

She flicked her lighter and splashed petrol in his direction. "Don't come any closer!"

Takis appeared. He had seen Nick racing behind the station and knew something was up. "Vassoula? What the fuck are you doing?"

"Omar wouldn't want you to do this," Nick told her.

"What do you know about Omar?"

"That he wanted you to have a life. He knew you'd never leave him, and he'd be a freak forever. That's why he took his own life. To free you."

"He drowned us both when he drowned himself."

She turned the nozzle on her neck, letting the petrol run down her body.

"No!" Takis cried, and ran toward her.

She splashed him and he backed off.

"You haven't done anything serious yet," Nick tried to reason with her. "You haven't hurt anyone, but if you do this, you're going to kill a lot of people."

"I wish I could shut the shutters on the whole village and kill everyone!"

"Shut the shutters?" Takis asked. "*You* shut the shutters?"

"Who do you think did? That bitch wouldn't have gotten out of bed. She's the one I wanted to kill. Always trying to get Omar deported. Father walking in with a cigarette was a bonus."

"I thought he shut them."

"To kill her?"

"To kill himself. I only said that I closed them so people wouldn't think he had committed suicide."

"Suicide? He didn't have the courage."

Vassoula flicked the lighter and touched it to her blouse. Flames shot up from her waist.

Nick had braced himself for that moment. It didn't matter if she dropped the lighter; it would go out the instant she let go of it. He expected her to set herself afire, and knew he had only seconds before she collapsed into the gasoline soaking her feet, igniting the jerrycan as well. It would be enough to blow up the tank.

He charged her, knocking her clear of the pooled gasoline, and rolled with her on the ground. When the flames were out, he ended up on top of her. She was unconscious but alive. He looked over his shoulder at the looming fuel tank and bowed his head with a relieved sigh.

CHAPTER ELEVEN

SHIRLEY DIDN'T HAVE TO RECALL the sound of blue plastic bags twirling in the wind for a bit of erotic pleasure that morning. It had been Lukas's turn to awaken with such notions, though not frisky enough that the earth should have moved when it did. It didn't stop shaking, and her husband, moving rather vigorously himself, didn't notice. Finally she whispered, "Lukas."

"What?"

"I think we're having an earthquake."

He stopped. "An earthquake? Why are you telling me that now?"

"Because it's happening now."

"What do you want me to do?"

"Well, I suppose finish unless the roof caves in."

Lukas rolled onto his back. "Good God, woman! How can you expect a man to finish after interrupting him like that!"

The ground continued to tremble.

"That's a long earthquake," he said.

Shirley suggested, "Maybe we should crawl under the bed."

They heard grinding engines and people shouting.

"What the dickens is going on?"

Lukas slipped out of bed. "I'll go see."

She balled up his briefs and tossed them at his back. "You better wear something more than your bare ass."

He pulled on his pants and went outside.

Shirley could hear him talking, but couldn't make out what was being said because of the noisy engines. What in the dickens *was* going on? Wrapping herself in a bathrobe, she went to look out the window. A dozen men, driving tractors and a backhoe, had made their way up the short hill to their house.

Lukas appeared in the doorway, smiling for the first time in days. "It will make you very happy."

The men set about digging out the stumps of the four beauties. They attacked the first one with axes and the backhoe, chained it to the tractors, and inch by inch urged its roots to let go. Shirley made pot after pot of coffee and toasted up all the bread she had. She sent Lukas off to get more of everything, and he was back in five minutes, tagging after a caravan of cars with Lydia in the lead. The village women arrived provisioned to make the day a celebration. Ridi set up tables for their casseroles and salads before stripping off his shirt to join the men.

Shirley set about unpacking a case of wine.

"That's not all for you," Lydia reminded her mother.

Shirley glared at her. "It's too early for me to drink."

"By how many minutes?"

A cheer went up as the first stump gave up with an agonizing groan with Nick, the mayor, and Captain Tsounis looking on coast guards.

"In the end, we're lucky that Azarov stole the painting," the captain remarked. "Otherwise, it would have burned in the fire."

"Unless the priest had already made the switch, and so the Russian saved the forgery," Nick pointed out.

"Fortunately, whichever one Athina threw into the water was retrieved almost immediately," the mayor told them. "It wasn't in the water long enough to harm it, only give it a good bath."

"Probably can't say the same for the Russian's friend," Captain Tsounis said. "He has to be fish food by now."

Once Vassoula had been whisked off in an ambulance, Nick realized that the *Birch Runner* had weighed anchor and disappeared into the night. He alerted the Coast Guardsman, who sent his crew in hot pursuit. The Russian protested his arrest in international waters, when in fact the channel between Greece and Turkey was too narrow for there to be an international inch. The pinballer wasn't onboard but the Crowned Madonna was.

"They both left on the same boat and there was no place where the kid could have disembarked," Captain Tsounis explained. "We'll press murder charges with or without a body assuming we can ID the victim."

"We can help on that," Nick said, meaning the FBI. "We have lots of connections in Russia. But what I'm wondering, are the icons that supposedly burned in Father Alexis's last church actually in Azarov's collection in Saint Petersburg?"

"The priest burned down another church?" Mayor Elefteros asked.

"We don't know that he burned down *this* one," Nick replied. "We only know that it burned down. His last church as well. It was declared an accident, but now, I'll request that the investigation be reopened. I'm stationed in Athens, so it's largely my call."

"How badly is she burned?" the captain wanted to know.

"I understand, badly. Especially her face."

"She'll want to die. I guess I really missed it on that Takis kid. It wasn't him, it was his sister."

"It's easy to miss something when somebody confesses to what they didn't do."

"Why'd she want to do all this? Because of Omar?"

"I haven't talked to her, and you know her better than me, but my guess is, she blames the village for what happened to Omar, but not just Omar. His family, too, going all the way back. They were cast out of here and he was an outcast coming back. What happened to him wouldn't have happened if he were Greek."

"It might have," the mayor spoke up, "if they suspected he was a homosexual."

"From what I've been told, some things were said about that, but it was his accent that bothered them. They knew he was Turkish."

"When Takis left for Melbourne, to me it felt like he was running away.

"He was, only not from what you thought."

"Then the fires started when he came back," Captain Tsounis continued. "I misled you on the Turk's name, too, didn't I? Omar Ozturk's name, that is, when I told you Ozturk was like Smith."

"You didn't mislead me. It is like Smith. I misled myself by not following up, because I had already misled myself thinking Efendi was a name. Besides, what relevance could names really have from a hundred years ago?" Nicked shrugged. "It was my mistake, too, because I dismissed a clue."

"Now I have a new problem," the mayor spoke up. "I have a budget and nothing to spend it on. The bell tower does not need to be repaired, it needs to be entirely rebuilt, which shall be the Church's problem, and I'll make sure this time it's built on its own damn property. And the fuel tank is no longer threatened, so there's no reason to move it. Suddenly, we have a surplus!"

"Don't say that too loudly," the captain warned him. "Athens will make sure that it doesn't happen twice."

Another cheer went up.

With a wrenching sound, the second stump let go.

"And you said yes?" Lydia asked her daughter.

"I sort of did. He asked me to marry him in such a sweet way that I told him I loved him, too. We've been sending hearts back and forth."

"I thought so."

"Why do you ask me when you already know?"

"Because what if I don't know? Anyway, you never said yes. Saying you love somebody doesn't mean you have to marry him."

"But I want to marry Ridi."

"Honey, you're too young."

"Why? Because he's more decent than any boy in this village? And smarter and harder working?"

"And outside the village?"

"Can you promise I'll find someone better?"

"I want more for you."

"What? And where? In Athens? What can I do in Athens except be a waitress? So why leave here in the first place? If you think I need something more, that's for your satisfaction, not mine."

Lydia sighed; it was a losing battle. "You said he wants to take over my restaurant?"

"I said he has ideas for it, but that was before everything else happened. Now he's eyeing Vassoula's place. It has indoor space."

"So he's off my place?"

"It's an option. Maybe for expansion in the summer."

"And the goat shed?"

A cry went up.

The third beauty had let go its hold on the earth.

Nick and Takis, glad to see the third stump dragged away, found a bit of shade. For an early November day, it was warm, and they'd built up a sweat. Takis wiped his brow with a bandana and handed it to Nick.

"Thanks," he said, using it, and gave it back.

"So how do you figure Koufos having a detonator?" Takis asked. "Was he helping Vassoula?"

"I think he found a dud or maybe extinguished one. Doing his charades, he imitated someone lighting cigarettes—now we know it was your sister—and I'd sensed it was a woman. A little bit; I won't say definitely. He'd probably watched her and put it out as soon as she left. She went back a second time and that's why eventually there was a fire on that property. She had her spots mapped out. You never suspected her?"

"Whenever she wasn't around, I assumed she was screwing the Coast Guard guy, and the fires never amounted to much. Sometimes they got reported a couple of days later. Somebody would come into the station asking if we knew about a fire someplace we never knew about. They had never spread. But I have an important question."

"What's that?" Nick asked.

"Are you sure you can't stay longer? Not even one extra day?"

He shook his head. "Two boats capsized off Libya yesterday. That's two hundred dead before they start counting. The EU's called an emergency summit."

"It sounds like you're important."

"Not me, but this week two hundred dead refugees are."

"Before they start counting."

"This time they can't be ignored. So, are you still headed Down Under in sixteen days?"

"Now *you're* counting!"

"In minutes until we have to say goodbye. I'll drive you to the airport if you come to Athens a few days early."

"Would a week be too long?"

"You could squeeze two weeks into sixteen days."

"You can't imagine the complications I'm going to have here. I'll be lucky to have two days."

"Do you want me to call the airlines to extend your ticket by a month?"

"Can you do that?"

"I'd be willing to try. You're a witness in a case."

"I might end up wanting to stay longer."

"I won't let you."

"Why not?"

"You belong in Melbourne."

"Maybe I've changed my mind."

"I know you haven't changed your mind about living in Athens, and I don't want you to change your mind because of me."

"Why not?"

"I'm an older guy."

"You only have twelve years on me."

"*Only?* That's a change of tune. Sorry, but you're stuck with Melbourne. I assume you're closing your sister's bar."

"I told Ridi he can have it for the rent. He's keen on a place of his own, and it's not worth anything to me. What's going to happen to my sister?"

"It's a long list. Murder. Attempted murder. Arson and attempted arson."

Takis's expression was pained. "I never expected Vassoula to be happy, and then, there was Omar. He was the miracle man who came true, even down to being Turkish. I suppose she would have eventually gone with a Greek—I guess she has, with the captain—but she had this thing for Turkish men."

"A bit like you with not wanting anything Greek," Nick reminded him.

"I'd compromise for a Greek American."

"Like I said, you're stuck with Melbourne. Did you ever guess that Vassoula had done it?"

"I wondered about it, especially because it could have been me who walked into the kitchen first."

"You wouldn't have been smoking," Nick reminded him.

"I could have done something to create a spark."

"Opening a door wouldn't do that, and you would have smelled the gas before you did anything else. No, she counted on a spark, or probably your father's cigarette. Personally, I never believed he committed suicide. If he opened up the gas bottle, then went out for a smoke and came back inside with his cigarette, the bottle wouldn't have had time to completely empty itself, and it was empty because it didn't explode."

"Who told you that?"

"I read the official report."

"So you have been investigating me?"

"You were my main suspect."

"Is that why you slept with me?"

"Are you kidding? Besides, you were only a suspect for a few hours. Did you ever suspect your sister was the arsonist?"

"Never. I never thought about it. She was always back before the fires were noticed, and whenever she was gone, I assumed she was next door screwing the Coast Guard guy. It was never longer than that."

"You told her that you saw my badge, didn't you?"

"She called you a faggot. I wanted to impress her. I wanted her to know that faggots are sometimes FBI agents."

"Well, you impressed her enough to put a lot of spiders in my bed. She wanted me very sick, or dead."

Takis replied, "I'm glad that's one murder trial I won't be testifying at."

"Me, too."

"It's weird to think, she might have saved your life by bleeding you."

"I suppose she had to, if that's what she knew to do. It'd be suspicious if she didn't."

"She had it all planned, didn't she? Even trying to frame me by somehow sending the beads from Melbourne."

"Not in a serious way. You were a distraction for anyone sniffing around. She never expected to survive. Ultimately she wouldn't need a fall guy."

"I don't know if that makes me feel any better. Any idea how she actually managed to send the beads?"

"She's not been questioned yet."

"How bad is she?"

"Second degree burns on her face."

"She won't like that. She'll want to die, like Omar wanted to die. They both always got by on their looks. They can't make me come back for her trial, can they?"

"You can probably testify by video. If not, you always have a place to camp in Athens."

A rousing cheer went up. The final stump had been pulled out. No sooner had the last beauty divested her roots and been hauled away than a flatbed truck rolled up carrying four mature red eucalyptuses. It took five men to carry each tree up the hill and set it upright in one of the holes left behind by the dug-out beauties.

"Where did they find those trees?" Shirley wondered aloud.

Lukas didn't know. Overwhelmed, he had to fight back tears. They weren't as tall as his beauties all grown up; it was more like they were teenagers, and he would have a chance to see them grow some more. He had a passing sense of how it would feel to have all of his girls home again.

"I think my grandfather is going to cry," Athina said, brushing dirt off Ridi's shoulders.

"He must be very happy."

"Not as happy as me," she added, "but I talked to my mom."

"She is unhappy?"

"She'll get over it. Do you think Takis was serious about the restaurant?"

"He made the offer. I never asked for anything."

"My mom wants you to take over her place. Isn't that crazy? Overnight, from having nothing to having two restaurants and a goat shed! I can't believe so much has happened since I threw that stupid icon into the water. At first I thought that's what started the fire."

"It was lucky for us."

"The fire?"

"The icon. It was my good luck to make you a crown. I am the most lucky man today. More lucky than all your boyfriends all together!"

"All my boyfriends? What has my mother been telling you?"

"I want to make it official."

"Make what official?"

Ridi reached into his pocket for an envelope folded into a small packet. Opening it, he removed a ring made from aluminum foil with one of his faux diamonds glued to it. A little smushed, he reshaped it before offering it with a trembling hand. "Please, you marry me?"

Suddenly Athina realized the gravity of her answer. Her mother was right: saying you love somebody is different than committing to marriage. Love was the frivolity of a relationship: the fun romantic moments, the gay times, the ups with few downs. Marriage needed something else. Ridi had used the word faithful. Responsible was another one. Her final message in the procession, though lost on everybody once the church caught fire, was about men taking responsibility in a relationship. Faithful and responsible: sturdy words to nourish a relationship. Ridi had proven he was both. But were they too sturdy for her young age? Too confining? Was her mother right that she needed to see the world before settling down? What made her decision so difficult was that she knew that she would eventually demand those exact qualities in a man, and to say no to Ridi risked never finding another truly decent guy. What made her decision easy was that she knew she loved him. "Yes, Ridi, I will marry you," she said.

"Will you wear my temporary ring?"

"I'll never take it off."

She held out her hand.

He slipped it on her finger.

"Temporary. Was that on your vocabulary list this morning?"

"How do you guess?"

"It's a long word. There's a more important word I hope you learned, too."

"What is that?"

"Forever."

"It's on my list!"

Their long kiss announced their romance to the world.

A truck rumbled up the scrubby hill and stopped at each of the holes, unloading piles of topsoil to fill in around the new trees. Takis, taking off his shirt, said, "Let's help."

Nick worked alongside him, slinging dirt into a hole, when they saw Koufos approaching. They paused, and everybody soon stopped to see what the wild deaf kid wanted. He was dressed in his pearly buttoned shirt and mustard pants, and carried the lunch plate and napkin that Nick had left for him the day before.

"Maybe he's hungry," Takis speculated.

Nick stuck his shovel into the mound of dirt. "I don't think so."

He faced the boy, and when they were looking only at each other, he made the same series of gestures he had outside the ruined house. He spread his hands, curled his fingers, and tapped his heart. He dropped his hands to his sides waiting for the boy to respond.

Koufos only stared at him.

People whispered, "What's happening?"

Nick repeated the series of gestures.

What do you want?

Come to us.

We will love you.

The deaf boy set the plate on the ground and made the same gestures back.

People murmured, "What's that mean?"

"What are they saying to each other?"

"Crazy kid!"

"What's he doing?" Takis asked.

Nick smiled. "Coming in from the cold," he said, and lifted a shovel offering it to the boy. *Do you want to join us?*

Koufos did, but first he removed his red shirt with its pearly buttons and set it safely aside. Then taking the shovel, he set about using it. Nick grabbed another.

They were all shoveling dirt when Takis asked, "What did you say to him?"

"I don't know. I made it up."

"Well, he's got the right idea."

"What's that?"

"Taking off your shirt. Why sweat it out?

"I look like a war zone. Several war zones, and your sister contributed a few more scars yesterday. That's why."

"Do you think anybody is going to care? You're a hero. You saved the village. You've earned your scars."

Not entirely convinced, Nick peeled off his shirt. No one took any notice, and soon he forgot about being shirtless, too, as the three men worked together shoveling dirt around the new trees.

The sun was setting by the time they were all planted. The tractors and backhoes rumbled off. Koufos slipped away. Nick and Takis left for a bittersweet night together, knowing it was their last on the island, and one of their last forever. Once Takis returned to Melbourne, they would stay in touch, but possibly never see each other again. Their lives had crossed but their fates hadn't changed.

Weary from a full day of people, Dingo wandered off to find a place to sleep. The rich earth under the new trees was soft and full of good smells. Circling a spot, he plopped down. Sniffing something interesting, he nudged over a clump of earth with his snout.

Out rolled a white truffle. The woman would be pleased. She always was when he found one.

With a satisfied snort, Dingo rested his head on his paws.

About the Author

Timothy Jay Smith has traveled the world collecting stories and characters for his novels and screenplays which have received high praise. *Fire on the Island* won the Gold Medal in the 2017 Faulkner-Wisdom Competition for the Novel. He won the Paris Prize for Fiction for his first book, *A Vision of Angels*. *Kirkus Reviews* called *Cooper's Promise* "literary dynamite" and selected it as one of the Best Books of 2012. Smith was nominated for the 2018 Pushcart Prize for his short fiction, "Stolen Memories." His recent novel, *The Fourth Courier,* received tremendous reviews. His screenplays have won numerous international competitions. He is the founder of the Smith Prize for Political Theater. Smith lives in Nice, France.

Also by Timothy Jay Smith

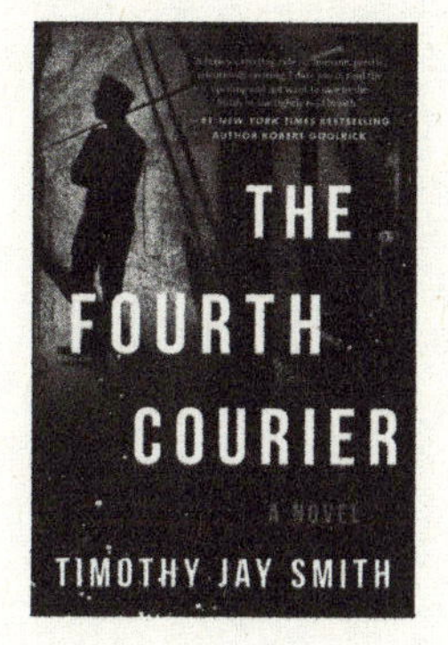

The Fourth Courier
A Novel
Hardcover / $24.99 US/ $33.99 CAN (available now)
978-1-948924-10-8

For International Espionage Fans of Alan Furst and Daniel Silva, a new thriller set in post–Soviet era Poland.

**** "Smith skillfully bridges police procedural and espionage fiction, crafting a show-stealing sense of place and realistically pairing the threats of underworld crime and destabilized regimes." –*Booklist* ****

It is 1992 in Warsaw, Poland, and the communist era has just ended. A series of grisly murders suddenly becomes an international case when it's feared that the victims may have been couriers smuggling nuclear material out of the defunct Soviet Union. When a Russian physicist who designed a portable atomic bomb disappears, the race is on to find him—and the bomb—before it ends up in the wrong hands. Suspenseful, thrilling, and smart, *The Fourth Courier* brings together a straight white FBI agent and gay black CIA officer as they team up to uncover a gruesome plot involving murder, radioactive contraband, narcissistic government leaders, and unconscionable greed.